GHOSTS
OF
ALBION
ACCURSED

GHOSTS
OF
ALBION
ACCURSED

AMBER BENSON

AND

CHRISTOPHER GOLDEN

BALLANTINE BOOKS · NEW YORK

A Del Rey Trade Paperback Original

Copyright © 2005 by Benson Entertainment, Inc., and the Daring Greatly Corporation

Published in the United States by Del Rey Books, an imprint of
The Random House Publishing Group, a division of Random House, Inc., New York.

DEL REY is a registered trademark and the Del Rey colophon
is a trademark of Random House, Inc.

Library of Congress Cataloging-in-Publication Data
Benson, Amber.
Ghosts of Albion : accursed / Amber Benson & Christopher Golden.
p.   cm.
ISBN 0-345-47130-X (pbk.)
1. Plague—Fiction.   2. Supernatural—Fiction.   3. London (England)—Fiction.
I. Golden, Christopher.   II. Title.
PS3602.E685G47 2005
813'.6—dc22
2005048407

Printed in the United States of America

www.delreybooks.com

9 8 7 6 5 4 3 2

Book design by Mary A. Wirth

To my family—without you I wouldn't be the person that I am.
I love you all unconditionally.

And to mbl—don't be tired and I won't be sad.
—A.B.

To Rob Francis, one of the good guys.
—C.G.

Also by Amber Benson and Christopher Golden

WITCHERY: A Ghosts of Albion Novel

Available from Del Rey

ACKNOWLEDGMENTS

The authors would like to thank the entire team at Del Rey, most especially Steve Saffel, Keith Clayton, and Colleen Lindsay, for their enthusiasm and support. Thanks, also, to William Schaefer at Subterranean Press; Jose Nieto and Tom Canty for their artistic contributions; Agnes Bell, James Butler, and Kim Zemek for research assistance; and Tim Brannan, Garner Johnson, and Alex Jurkat at Eden Studios.

We gratefully acknowledge the fantastic contributions of those talented individuals who worked on the BBC web serial version of Ghosts of Albion, including Rob Francis, Martin Trickey, Jelena Djordjevic, Martha Hillier, John Ainsworth, Kim Plowright, Emma Ko, James Goss, Ann Kelly, Roger Danes, Rebecca Kirby, Marc Wilcox, Keith Graham, Alex Mackintosh, Claudine Toutoungi, Maria Ogundele, Mario Dubois, Steve Maher and all of the animators at Cosgrove Hall, animator Nick Hilditch, Jason and the crew at Big Finish, the extraordinary composer Peter Green, and, of course, the remarkable cast, Jasmine Hyde, Rory Kinnear, Anthony Daniels, Emma Samms, Joe McFadden, Paterson Joseph, Roy Skelton, Elliot Falk, Trevor Littledale, India Fisher, and Leslie Phillips. In our heads, the voices are always yours.

And, finally . . .

Thanks to my friend Kim Simerson and her teacher, design historian Eleanor Schrader Schapa—who hooked me up with some wonderful articles and websites on Victorian fashion.
—A.B.

Thanks to the real, original Tamara Swift, for the inspiration.
—C.G.

GHOSTS
OF
ALBION
ACCURSED

PROLOGUE

The young woman slipped out of the doorway into a maelstrom of men and women moving up and down the cobblestoned street. Her body was entirely covered in a bright red cotton sari and stanapatta that were far too thin to protect her from the evening's chill.

The stench of the river filled the air to the point that the ramshackle buildings and filthy, winding alleys of London's Shadwell district seemed saturated with it. Nevertheless, the night was alive. Drunken oafs stumbled out of taverns and haggard, filthy prostitutes hawked their wares. Music drifted from an open doorway, punctuated with laughter. Rough-hewn men with stony eyes and gruff humor— sailors and dockworkers all—prowled the alleys in packs, speaking the languages of a dozen nations.

The woman kept her covered head down so that no one could see her face, or notice the fear in her eyes that would clearly identify her as prey. At first, she kept her speed equal to those who jostled around her, but like a frightened animal she picked up her pace as much as she could, until she was almost running as she weaved in and out of the uncaring crowd.

Her heart hammered in ragged time against her ribs, like a tiny, frightened bird screaming for release. She wanted nothing more than to silence it, but that would mean death, and surely nineteen years on this Earth wasn't enough. She knew that the quick only danced for a few precious moments before being swallowed by their partners, that it would catch her someday—this death—this thing that struck the fear of the gods into her very soul. But why did it have to come so *soon*?

She thought of her twin daughters, Chhavvi and Chhaya, and prayed that she would live to see their beautiful faces again.

From somewhere behind her, she heard someone call out her name.

"Avani!"

Desperately she ignored it, pushing forward, colliding with a pair of young sailors who regarded her with a hungry look. Terrified that they would grab her, that they would stop her there, she veered into a dark, empty alleyway to get away from the crowd and shake off her pursuers.

Immediately, she realized her mistake. She should have stayed hidden in the crowd. They would not murder her with so many witnesses around. But in the filth of the vacant alley . . .

She reached a new intersection, took another turn, and plowed deeper into the maze of the slums of Shadwell.

This new alley was as desolate as the last. Ordinarily she would have been terrified to encounter a stranger in these hidden passages, where life was worth nothing and people took what they wanted. But now she prayed for the intervention of a stranger. Even an open door, some sanctuary where she might find protection for herself and for . . . the other.

The thing she was carrying inside her.

It had happened against her will. The man had been possessed, had forced her onto the ground behind the marketplace, and had defiled her. She hadn't told her husband, or her family, because she knew what they would do. But the very next morning, when she awoke, she found herself heavy with child, and knew that her life had reached its end.

Now as she ran, she reached down and cupped her bloated belly. She had loved carrying the twins, cherished the pleasant feeling of new life growing inside her. But this experience was nothing like that. This time she felt misshapen and ugly, full of something poisonous that fought wildly within her, weighing her down and depleting her energy, so that even the effort to draw breath exhausted her.

Behind her she heard the clamor of feet on cobblestones and knew they were still on her trail. She tried to run faster, but her back and stomach were aching more than ever. When her foot caught on an up-raised piece of stone and she tripped, falling and scraping her hands and knees, she was almost relieved.

The inevitable had come.

Tears burned her cheeks, and she felt as if something had burst in-side her. She reached down and felt a viscous fluid issuing from be-tween her legs. There had been small droplets earlier that day, of a thick green paste, and now this. She was glad of the dark, so she could not see the color of this new humiliation.

She tried to pull herself back up, but did not have the strength. Deep, heaving sobs issued from her mouth, and though she tried to prevent them, covering her face with her hands, her body would not comply. She began to shudder, not from grief or fear, but from a hor-rid sickness that was making its way through her.

The men followed her tears to where she lay on the ground. Though she recognized their features, there was no trace of love or sorrow, or even pity in the faces of her father and her husband. Only her younger brother, Tek, did not glare angrily down upon her. In-stead his large, almond eyes held a mixture of fear and shame, and he would not hold her gaze.

"Avani, you have shamed your family," her father said as he stood over her.

Her husband, Rajeev, had dark brown eyes that had once gazed upon her as though she were a golden lotus flower. But now they held nothing but contempt. She was soiled, now, tainted forever. In his mind, she had betrayed him, and deserved nothing less than what she got.

Avani felt her heart shatter into a million tiny shards. She had never guessed that anything could hurt so much. She had loved them all so dearly, and now, when she needed them most, they had forsaken her.

"Rajeev, please—" she begged.

He spit on her.

She reached out to touch his foot, but he kicked her hand away.

"But I *didn't*—" she said, but stopped, knowing it was futile.

She watched as her father pulled an unlit torch from the cloth bag bound at his hip and lit it. He glanced around to make sure that they were alone, then he motioned for her husband and brother to lift her up. Avani fought as they grasped her roughly by the arms and stood her on her feet.

With a cry to Shiva, she closed her eyes and prayed for a quick end.

The night sang with a strange, jangling noise like discordant music, and she heard Tek scream. But the sound seemed to come from some distant place. Then the acrid smell of burning human hair filled her nostrils, and slammed her back into reality. Even as she opened her eyes, he released her arm, and she saw his singed eyebrows and eyelashes. He had been burned, somehow, and she saw the terror in his eyes as he turned and fled back down the alley the way they had come.

"Let the girl go!" came a voice from behind her. With Rajeev still gripping one arm, she managed to turn, and saw an old man leaning upon a walking stick. He was Indian. His skin was dark, his eyes were bright, and he stood in the middle of the alley, glaring at her father and husband. Everything about him indicated an air of command.

Her father gathered his wits and handed the torch to Rajeev, then walked toward the old man.

"This does not concern you," he said through clenched teeth. "It is a matter for family."

"You must let the girl go," the old man said again. "This has *nothing* to do with family. Evil has touched her, but she may still be cleansed, if you will stand aside."

Her father moved forward again and shoved the old man. Avani gasped, thinking he had hurt the poor fellow, but she was surprised to see the old man still standing.

"I have warned you," the newcomer said, before lifting his stick and pointing at his attacker's heart. Silver light flashed from the tip and enveloped her father in a halo of white flames. He shook as though in the grip of the gods, and then collapsed to the ground, unconscious.

Rajeev took a step back, pulling her with him, but the old man moved swiftly now. The same silver light leaped from his walking stick and struck Rajeev. He shuddered uncontrollably, and his grip slipped away. She watched as her husband fell to the ground, and did not stir.

Avani dropped to her knees and began to cry again.

"Please spare us, oh great one . . ."

The words were no sooner out of her mouth than a wave of pain swept over her, racking every part of her body. She wrapped both hands around her voluminous belly and screamed.

"Too late," she heard the old man whisper in the language of her homeland. "Damn her, I'm too late."

∽

𝓣HE OLD MAN could only watch and mourn as the girl dropped to the ground, her body lurching uncontrollably. The toadlike creatures began to drop from between her legs, an unholy, hideous parody of birth. Their bulbous, sickly yellow eyes gleamed preternaturally in the shadows.

But there were too many of them, and they wanted to get out.

Her belly split with a sickeningly wet tearing noise and a splash of blood and viscera, and then they came flooding out of her. The girl's wide brown eyes stared glassily at the night sky. By this time she was beyond pain. She twitched once, but she was already dead as the small creatures, their bodies covered in a sickly greenish slime, hopped away to disappear into the maze of alleys and crumbling buildings, into the deeper shadows.

The old man wept for her, his heart heavier than all creation.

One

It was a rare day in Highgate. The sky above was a brilliant blue, and the sun lured from the landscape vivid colors that were seen so infrequently as to achieve near-mythic status.

Ordinarily Ludlow House seemed to loom upon the hill, gazing balefully across the lawns that surrounded it. The gardens were vibrant and beautiful, but the façade of the house was almost monastic in its plainness, a grim visage of window and stone with a thorny crown of gables and chimneys. Yet on this day, the Swift family home managed an elegant nobility. Though the sprawling manse cast long shadows eastward, they did not engender the sense of foreboding that had so often been their companion.

There was a southwesterly view from the rear of Ludlow House. The elevation of the hill was such that High Street was visible in the distance, and on a day as clear as this, those of keen eyesight or imagination might see the spire of the chapel at Highgate Cemetery. Yet it was neither the view nor the rare brilliance of the spring day that had prompted Tamara Swift to host afternoon tea in the observatory, rather than within the house proper.

Inside the house, even in the front parlor, her guests might have heard the mad howling that came from the second floor, the screams of her father. Or, more accurately, of the thing that lived within him.

Much had changed in the months subsequent to the death of her grandfather, Sir Ludlow Swift. Tamara and her brother, William, had inherited a host of responsibilities they could never have imagined, and the loss of her beloved grandfather, combined with her father's affliction, had cast the bleakest of shadows across her heart.

Yet she felt a sense of purpose now that she never had before. No matter how frightful her current circumstances, she knew she would not have willingly erased the events of the past several months. Once her greatest concerns had been the attentions of young men and the scribblings she authored under the pseudonym T. L. Fleet, stories published in pamphlets they called penny dreadfuls on the street. Once upon a time, her taste for the macabre had been mere musing. Now her writings leaned toward those of reporter, rather than tale-weaver.

But the darkness could be suffocating. For too long in recent months, she had chosen to ignore invitations and gentle inquiries from friends. Now she had at last determined that it would be prudent to escape into the trivial from time to time.

This afternoon's tea was attended by four young ladies of North London whom she counted as her friends and, unfortunately, Miss Sophia Winchell, whom William was courting. Absent from the gathering was Marjorie Winterton, who was attending to the needs of an ailing dowager aunt. Marjorie had sent her regrets, and Tamara shared the sentiment. Sophia was a poor substitute.

This tea was meant to signify Tamara's return to society, and the throwing aside of the shroud that had cloaked her spirit so much of late. And she found now that the gathering was indeed fulfilling its purpose. The sunshine and the flowers that were blossoming so fully, ripe with color, out across the grounds, had lifted her spirits. But nothing healed her so much as the company of her friends.

A titter of naughty laughter rippled through the observatory. One of the girls had no doubt said something scandalous—no surprise in this group—but Tamara had been lost in thought, and she had missed it. She feigned amusement politely, but she couldn't entirely escape the weight of the dark truths she had learned in the wake of Sir Ludlow's savage murder.

At times she wondered if she should share her burden with one or more of her closest friends, yet she knew there was no way she would dare to do so. Ignorance of the evil that hid in England's shadows was indeed a gift, and it was one she would give them freely. No, she would keep her own counsel. In those moments when she could not bear the weight of the dreadful truth, she would seek solace in her brother's calming voice. In his reason.

Or she would rely upon the kindness of ghosts.

But she would not place the burden of knowledge upon her friends. That would be too cruel.

And the truth of it was that part of her conviction sprang from selfishness. Simply being in their presence eased her mind, let her become once again, albeit briefly, a part of the mundane world. She hadn't realized it until today, but in their ordinary concerns and their gossip and their laughter she found respite. For the first time in months she wasn't dwelling upon the certainty that night would fall once more; that they would depart and the light of whimsy would be extinguished.

No, while they were here, she would be as she had been. Just another girl—no, just another high-born *lady* of London town.

She took a sip of lukewarm tea—she didn't dare try to use magic to warm it in the presence of her friends—and turned her gaze toward the windows. Tamara had always found it peaceful here in the observatory, if a trifle chilly. The gardens of Ludlow House were renowned, arranged as they were with an almost architectural precision. Tamara's grandfather had entertained many a guest here, to exploit the glorious view of the prize tea rose garden.

Tamara still missed the grizzled old man terribly, but time had begun to scar over her tender wounds. They would never heal altogether; the thought that they would was a myth. Yet, brushing away the momentary pain, she turned her attention back to the conversation in progress.

"—I truly believe that if I were ever to find myself in the company of our Mr. T. L. Fleet, I would just expire," said Victoria Markham, her face so flushed as to make her cheeks nearly as red as her hair. "I would be just that—for lack of a better word—*stimulated.*"

Tamara almost laughed, but managed to hold herself in check by pretending to cough into her silk handkerchief. She perched on the edge of the soft red velveteen settee, blue eyes wide with curiosity. Somehow, while she was lost in reverie, the topic of conversation had come around to her own writings. How odd it was to be privy to gossip that was, however indirectly, about her.

Victoria dramatically raised a hand to cover her mouth, as though she had been scandalized by her own ribald insinuation, her mischievous, pixielike features doing little to make her pretense convincing.

Tamara so treasured the girl. In the aftermath of Sir Ludlow's death, Victoria had continued to make overtures of friendship, long after everyone else had ceased trying. She had stubbornly refused to let Tamara surrender completely to grief, and had finally called at Ludlow House—uninvited—the week before, hoping to coax Tamara back into society.

It was entirely due to her urging that Tamara had promised to sponsor a tea for their friends this afternoon.

Victoria lowered her hand and continued. "My cousin Roderick swears that T. L. spends his evenings with that bawdy actress Lucille Hammond. Can you believe that an author of his accomplishments would even *call* on someone so base?"

There was a pause and then Helena Martin looked up from her sketchpad, a dusty piece of charcoal clutched between her thumb and forefinger. "Well, I must confess that *Stained Scarlet* gave me goose bumps."

Tamara smiled, the compliment giving *her* goose bumps.

"I couldn't put it down, not until the very last word," Helena continued, a small, self-conscious smile blossoming upon her face. "I was so terrified." At that, she quickly returned to her sketching, a rather faithful rendering of a nearby vase of roses.

Helena wiped a strand of chestnut hair out of her eyes, leaving a dark smudge across her high cheekbone. Tamara had known her since they were toddlers, and didn't think she had ever seen the young woman without her sketchbook in hand.

"It was suspenseful," Victoria agreed. "He raises the penny dreadful to high art. And I'll wager he's even more handsome than his characters."

"Honestly, is there no other more suitable subject for conversation, or are you all so obsessed with this bawdy fantasy?" Suzanne Hastings muttered.

Once she had been Tamara's dearest friend, but they had found little opportunity to enjoy each other's company in recent years. The dark-eyed, Rubenesque girl had married two summers before, and spent much of her time at her husband's estate in Cornwall.

"How *absolutely* dull of you," Victoria said with a sigh. "Now that you're a married woman, I think you're simply coveting the freedom the rest of us have. You'd be thrusting out your bosom and batting your eyelashes with abandon at our T. L. if you weren't saddled with that old nanny goat of a husband."

Tamara was surprised at the intensity of Victoria's fascination with the mysterious author, though she supposed that if she were unaware of the author's true identity she, too, might find herself enamored of the "adventurous scribe." Then it struck her that the very thought was laden with devastating hubris, and she brushed it away.

The barb hit home, and Suzanne's face flushed scarlet with suppressed rage. But she took a deep breath and shot her friend a sly smile.

"Victoria, my darling, perhaps one day you will learn that simply because a thought pops into your pretty head, that doesn't mean you ought to put voice to it. For example, just because we all know that you couldn't snare a husband even with that embarrassingly large Markham fortune of yours, that doesn't mean we need to comment on the fact."

Victoria stiffened, and Tamara thought for a moment that she might throw her tea in Suzanne's face. But instead she began to laugh.

"Touché, Suzanne. You always did have a way with words. I cannot even *begin* to compete."

Suzanne took her win graciously. "My dear Vic, were I this gruesome scribbler you so fancy, I have no doubt I would find you irresistible."

The irony of it all was as frustrating as it was delicious. It was all Tamara could do not to reveal herself. *And I don't spend my time loi-*

tering outside music halls, lusting after round-heeled actresses! she would have declared.

As much as she wanted to tell her friends the truth, her brother, William, had made her swear upon pain of death never to reveal her literary identity. He was worried that public knowledge of her *career* might do irreparable harm to their good name, which she found amusing in light of what outcry might arise were the public to become aware of the *other* avocation that was increasingly drawing their attention and time.

Once again she glanced around at the friends she had gathered in the observatory and felt perfectly at ease, allowing a smile to play at the corners of her mouth.

Her pleasant musing was shattered by a tight, supercilious voice that came from outside their circle. "I cannot believe that any young lady from a proper family would dare read such trash."

Sophia Winchell stood by the windows, mouth twisted up in disapproval that tainted her otherwise beautiful face. She was one of the most stunning women Tamara had ever known. Suzanne and Victoria looked like charwomen in comparison. Tamara could see why her brother was taken with Miss Winchell, despite her personality.

Victoria rolled her eyes. She had been upset at first when she had learned that Tamara had invited Sophia to come to tea. It seemed that no one, aside from her brother, was fond of the girl. Tamara had made an earnest effort to like the young lady who was the object of William's fancy, but subsequently she had found that she would rather eat soap than spend an afternoon alone with her.

When Tamara had invited Sophia, she had felt certain the girl would find some excuse to decline, but to her surprise William announced that she was thrilled to be included. Tamara was sure that the word *thrilled* had been an embellishment on his part, as Sophia had barely spoken since her arrival.

Now she gazed at Tamara, a challenge filling her eyes. If Tamara hadn't known better, she would have thought the girl knew something.

"I'm sure a little harmless amusement won't be the death of anyone," Tamara said, forcing a pleasant smile.

Sophia pursed her lips, but did not reply.

Tamara continued, "Don't you agree, Sophia?"

Sophia shook her head. "I do not, Miss Swift. Nor do I think the author of such drivel should be complimented or admired for such hideous imagery as he foists upon the public. It is the lowest form of entertainment, not art but filth, and a base appeal to the ugliest facets of human nature."

Victoria seemed even more startled and offended than Tamara. "Miss Winchell, one should never condemn what one has not read—"

Sophia raised an eyebrow and interrupted. "Oh, but I have," she began, the sarcasm palpable in her voice. "I have had the *pleasure* of reading this trash, this *Stained Scarlet,* and find it not only offensive, but very poorly written, at that."

Tamara stood and crossed the room, striding toward Sophia. "That's enough."

At first, the other girl stood her ground, but as Tamara got closer, she stepped back against the window, placing her hand on the warm dark wood of the sill. She may have been intimidated, but she never took her eyes away from Tamara's.

Keeping her voice even, Tamara said, "Miss Winchell, if you must disdain our amusements, and our company, you might at least have the good taste not to do so when you are *in* our company. Your rudeness knows no bounds."

Sophia met her gaze evenly. "You don't frighten me, Tamara Swift. I know exactly what you are."

Tamara nodded. "And what is that, may I ask?"

Sophia bit the inside of her lip, her hazel eyes slitted as she glared at the woman who stood before her. She put a small, pale hand to her hair, unconsciously smoothing it.

"I shall tell William how wicked *all* of you are," Sophia said shrilly. She glanced quickly at the other girls, as if memorizing their faces for some subsequent vengeance. Then her features softened and Tamara almost thought she saw regret in her eyes.

But the moment passed, and Suzanne laughed harshly. "You may tell him whatever you like. I've known William Swift most of my life, and I daresay all you will elicit from him is a furious blush and a bit of an embarrassed cough. And after all, he's husband to none of us, dear. Not yet, at least."

Sophia set her teacup down on a side table and started for the door. As she did so, she turned and peered over her shoulder. "Good day, Miss Swift. I hope you realize that I only accepted this invitation because William pleaded with me to do so."

As she opened the door, Tamara called out, "And *you* should know that it was only extended under the same duress."

Sophia didn't stop to reply. The resounding slam of the door was more than answer enough.

Tamara let out a loud sigh, then plopped back down on the settee. *Whatever shall I tell William?*

∽

As the afternoon light waned, William Swift shifted in his chair so that his shadow did not fall across the papers on his desk. The wind had conspired on this day to brush aside much of the grime and chimney spew that so often stained the sky above the city. Yet he had been unable to take any pleasure in the weather, trapped, as he was, in his tomb of an office within the walls of Swift's of London. He shared little in common with Coleridge's Ancient Mariner, but nevertheless the bank had become his own albatross. His father had truly enjoyed this work, but William had never been able to force himself to take a genuine interest in it.

Yet now it was his duty. Swift's of London had been controlled by the family for generations, and he would be damned before he would allow it to crumble under his stewardship.

So he tried to focus upon his work, but found himself staring blankly at the sheet of numbers that sat on his desk. He knew he was supposed to review the documents, and then put his signature on the paper agreeing to a merger of some sort, but somehow all he could do was stare at the page.

It wasn't actually the figures themselves that interested him, but the way they were arranged on the paper. He couldn't help but compare them to the architectural structure they suggested: that of an Egyptian pyramid. It reminded him of his avocation previous to his father's incapacitation. William had been an apprentice architect, and that was still where his interests lay.

Not here.

Anywhere but here.

William blinked, clearing his mind. He ran his hands through his thick black hair and reached for his fountain pen, which he had set down near the edge of the desk. He took the dropper from a small bottle of ink that sat next to the blotter and began to fill the pen.

There was a knock on the door, and the pen slipped from William's grasp, spilling ink on the desk before it fell to the floor. He thought briefly about compelling the flood of ink back into the bottle with magic, but there was another insistent hammering on the opposite side of the door.

"*Damn it!*" He slid down off his chair to retrieve the pen and barked at the door. "Enter!"

Hinges squeaked as the door swung wide to allow entrance to his assistant, Harold Ramsey. He was only a year younger than William, but Harold's baby face and pale blond hair often led strangers to think he was still a schoolboy.

"Pardon me, Will," Harold said. Then he noticed the pool of ink on William's desk. "How in the world—" he began, but his sharp eyes instantly alighted on something they found of more interest. He nodded to himself, bemused.

"You're still having a go at those?" he said, pointing to the drafting paper covered in William's spidery scrawl. William immediately shoved the architectural sketches underneath a prospectus and glared at Harold.

"Not a word," William warned.

Harold took a step back, hands raised in mock supplication. "Wouldn't dream of it. Though I haven't any idea why you should be so concerned. It's no secret that you'd much rather return to your apprenticeship than preside over Swift's."

William laughed softly. "Dante said it is better to rule in Hell than to serve in Heaven. I'd argue the point."

He and Harold had been at Cambridge together, which accounted for the easy familiarity between them. In fact, when Henry Swift had become ill the year before, and William had taken over the family business, he had purposely sought Harold out. If he was to captain a vessel as massive as Swift's of London, he wanted someone he could trust at his side.

"You don't fool me," Harold told him. "You don't despise *every* moment you spend here."

William arched an eyebrow. "Yes, there's lunchtime." He grinned. "But as you say, old friend. I'll allow that the people who toil here at Swift's make the days bearable. And there is some pleasure to the challenge of the responsibility that's been thrust upon me. But you know I have other ambitions, and they call to me."

Harold nodded. "I know. And I hope you can return to them one day. At the moment, however, you might want to attend to Miss Winchell."

"Sophia? What of her?"

"She's downstairs."

William frowned. "Sophia's meant to be at Ludlow House today, for tea. This doesn't bode well."

"Shall I bring her up?" Harold asked.

William gestured at the spill of ink on the desk. "I'm afraid I've made a mess here."

"I don't think she'll care. She seemed rather upset, actually."

William sighed. "Oh, Tamara, what have you done?"

"What shall I tell her?" the younger man asked, straightening his jacket and stepping farther into the office. He glanced over his shoulder, and William could see past him into the main hall of the bank, with its etched-glass tellers' windows, oil lamps at each station, and the column-encircled atrium at the center with glass above to let in the daylight. It was the most elegant building on Threadneedle Street.

"Where is she now?" William asked.

"I left her at the manager's desk but her maid, Elvira, is having quite the time keeping her there. She tried to follow me, but the old woman wouldn't hear of it. Muttered something about a lady of 'breeding.'"

Harold looked as if he was amused by the memory.

Indeed, the idea of Sophia behaving improperly put a smile on William's face. So much of his time was spent worrying about propriety that he often found himself thrilled by Sophia's boldness.

Today would no doubt be an exception.

"Send her up, Harold. Putting her off would only delay the inevitable."

After Harold left, William tried as best he could to clean up the spilled ink, but only managed to smear more of it across the wooden surface. When he straightened up again, he found Sophia standing in the doorway, watching him.

She was so exquisite that it seemed as if his memory could never quite hold the fullness of her beauty for long, so that each time he saw her he experienced the realization of her anew. Her dark hair hung in ringlets that framed her face, draped across high cheekbones, and culminated in a loose chignon at the back of her neck. Her pale skin was ivory smooth and in deep contrast to the burgundy of her dress. William thrilled at her tiny waist and the way her delicate fingers peeked out from her lace cuffs.

As he studied the face beneath her burgundy bonnet, he registered the flash of anger in her hazel eyes. Then she smiled, and the anger drained away, leaving only alert intelligence in its wake.

"Hello, William." Her voice was warm, and sweet as honey.

The hair on the back of his neck stood up. He tried to swallow, but found that his throat had gone dry.

"What brings you here this afternoon, my dear?"

Sophia stepped over the threshold. Bypassing the armchair in the corner, she moved to the desk and crossed behind it. There she pressed her hands atop the desk and hoisted herself up, sliding her bottom across the wood and yet somehow managing to maintain a certain elegant decorum. She was, of course, careful to avoid the pool of spilled ink.

William felt a small tremor go through him. Sophia was sitting facing him, her right thigh resting on the desk inches from his hand. If he had wanted to, he could've reached out and rested it on her waist or her knee. Just the nearness of her flesh, even covered as it was by burgundy silk, drove William to distraction. His pulse quickened and abruptly all his hesitation began to evaporate. An almost predatory desire rose in him.

Sophia gazed at him intently, as if studying him. She had to have seen the effect her nearness and her decidedly unladylike perch had produced, and yet she only smiled thinly, one eyebrow arching again.

He stood and walked over to the door.

"I would hate for anyone to walk by and see you sitting so near and ... and mistake my assuaging your frustration with ... I mean to say, misinterpret my intentions." He closed the door and paused to take a breath before turning to face her again.

Sophia shook her head in fond humor. "And what about *my* intentions? In any case, William, I hardly think that my sitting on your desk would be any more scandalous than the fact that the two of us are behind closed doors, in your place of business."

His eyes widened. He'd been in such a hurry to afford them some privacy that he hadn't even considered—

Sophia laughed, the sound ushering from deep inside her throat. "You are so incredibly proper, William Swift. You needn't worry. My Elvira can certainly be counted upon for her discretion. And as for your employees, why, they *are* your employees, aren't they? They rely upon you for their livelihood. I shouldn't think you would have to worry overmuch that their tongues might be wagging."

She slid her own tongue out over her lips. "Mine, however ..."

William cleared his throat.

"Perhaps we ought to quit this dreary place, my dear. The Hotel Edison has a lovely tearoom. Have I taken you there? I think not. We can't stay here, really. I've spilled ink all over the place and I wouldn't want you to ruin your dress." The words escaped his mouth before he could reel them back in. He felt like such a fool, babbling on like that. And now images flashed through his mind of the sort of activities that might cause Sophia to ruin her dress due to the ink on the desk. Her dress ... spread across the desk.

Part of him was *terrified* of being alone with Sophia Winchell. She was like one of Odysseus's sirens: mesmerizing and exotic, completely foreign to his experience. Yet because she was so entrancing, he knew he wouldn't have the strength to resist her siren song. He would gladly dash himself upon the rocks to reach her.

"A little ink won't hurt anyone, darling William," she said, beckoning him toward her.

His eyes locked on hers. Warily, he returned to his desk, but did not sit down. The way she sat there on the edge of the desk, her dress had risen enough that he could see her ankles and calves, the smooth curve of muscle. His breath caught in his throat.

"Harold said that you seemed upset," he said, forcing his gaze away from her legs.

Sophia took his hand and laced her fingers with his, then drew him toward her and leaned her head upon his shoulder. "I *was* upset. Then I saw you, and everything else seemed insignificant."

"Well, I'm pleased to have such an effect upon you."

"It is far from the *only* effect you have on me."

Sophia's words echoed inside him. William could scarcely breathe now. Blood rushed through him, embers stoked into open flame. With his free hand, he began to stroke the small of her back. He could feel the hardness of her corset underneath his fingers.

"William," she said. "I do have something important to tell you."

The smell of her hair, lavender and vanilla, made him tremble with desire. He found himself having a hard time concentrating on her words.

"What is it, my love?"

"I'm concerned for Tamara. Her friends are vulgar girls of low character, and her very association with them impugns her. With your father incapacitated, I know there is a great burden on you to be master of Ludlow House, and yet you have indulged your sister with love and patience. I wonder if this has instilled in her too much independence."

"Sophia, you must understand that Tamara is . . . difficult. She has a mind of her own. She always has. I could importune her to be more thoughtful about her choice of companions, but—"

A look of irritation swept across her features. "She was unconscionably rude to me. She had the gall to tell me that the only reason I had been invited this afternoon was because you had asked her to."

William blanched. "Sophia, I . . ."

Sophia shook her head. "Your sister and I have never seen eye-to-eye, and we both know why. She is intolerably jealous of your love for me."

There was some truth to what Sophia said, but William knew it was only a half-truth. Sophia was accusing Tamara of being stubborn and willful, and less than demure. *But you are more alike than either of you cares to admit,* William thought wryly. If only they realized how much more could be accomplished if they put their differences aside.

"I shall speak to Tamara tonight, my dear. I will let her know that such rudeness will not be tolerated."

This seemed to satisfy Sophia.

"Thank you." She gave him a quick peck on the cheek. "Shall I see you tonight? At the Wintertons' dinner party?"

He nodded.

"Then, tonight, my William," she whispered as she slid from the desk and straightened her skirts.

She offered him her hand and he took it, slowly leading her to the door. As he reached for the knob Sophia reached up for him, her soft lips pressing wantonly against his own. He was so surprised that at first he kept his mouth closed, but as the kiss continued, he opened his lips to her, feeling their soft fullness, enjoying the gentle play of tongue and lip.

He wrapped his arms around her thin shoulders and she melted into him, her soft body pressing against his own. He was sure he could feel her heart beating between them. After a few moments, he broke off the kiss and stared down into her eyes.

"You are the loveliest creature I have ever seen," he rasped. She smiled shyly up at him, and then abruptly reached out and opened the door.

"Good afternoon, Mr. Swift," she murmured.

Then she was gone, across the lobby and into the shawl her maid Elvira held waiting for her. She waved at William as he stood watching her from the doorway of his office.

"She truly is a woman to be reckoned with," Harold said as he came from behind the tellers' counter to stand beside his employer.

William could only nod. Every time they parted, it was only in the wake of her departure that he would realize she had stolen another piece of his heart.

"This just arrived for you," Harold said as he handed William a sealed envelope.

"From whom?" William inquired.

Harold gave him a perplexed shrug. "That I cannot tell you. One moment my desk was clear, the next there was this envelope, addressed to you."

William ran his fingers over the textured paper. Heavy, expensive stock. *Interesting,* he thought as he split the seal with his finger and opened it.

> *The Algernon Club cordially invites you to a dinner*
> *in honor of Sir Darius Strong . . .*

William's interest was instantly piqued. the Algernon Club was a very private, very secret gentlemen's club whose members were all magicians, some of the stagecraft variety and others dabblers in actual spellcraft. His grandfather Ludlow Swift had been a member. Until recently, he had assumed that his grandfather had been a member because he enjoyed the company of other stage magicians. But then he had learned that Ludlow was the Protector of Albion, the mystical defender of England. Upon their grandfather's death, William and Tamara had inherited the magical power and the duties of the office.

And now William wondered . . . old Ludlow had been in a different class not only from the stage magicians but also from the amateur spellcasters who belonged to that club. So what did his grandfather benefit from being a member?

Could it be as simple as companionship? he wondered. *Was it merely that he had friends there?*

He frowned as a darker thought capered across his mind. *Friends, and perhaps enemies, too.* It was possible that Ludlow had participated in the activities of the Algernon Club to keep an eye on those magical dabblers. If so, it was something William and Tamara ought to be doing, as well. And if some of the stage magicians there were old friends of his grandfather's, well, it would be disrespectful of him not to accept their invitation.

He finished reading the invitation and sighed. It requested that he come alone.

This was not going to sit well with Tamara.

～

THE EARLY-EVENING sky was turning from purple to gray and a
chill was descending as the old man wound his way through the dirty
labyrinthine streets of London's East End. His path had taken him
south from Fleet Street, nearly to Blackfriars Bridge, and then east
along the Thames by Earl Street. The river was so thick with the repugnant outflow of the city's sewers and the offal that spilled from
fisheries and canneries upon its banks that the stink of it was staggering. The old man covered his mouth and nose with a scarf and
breathed through it out of necessity, and even then through thinly
parted lips, only sipping the filthy air.

If the wind was right, he had heard, the stench of the Thames
could drive a man to his knees.

Soon he turned slightly northward once more and immersed
himself in the crooked lanes making up the slums that had spilled
over from the docks, not far away. Cargo was never left behind on
those docks, but humans often were. Sailors with nowhere left to go,
unable to find a ship that would hire them. Who would *choose* to live
in this filth and stink, after all? Only those with no choice at all.

He wrapped his threadbare overcoat around gaunt shoulders,
hoping to keep the worst of the cold away from his bones. Laughter
erupted from a night-house, one of the taverns where only thieves
and water rats dared to congregate. He kept his eyes pointed forward
and walked on, his gait confident though his joints ached from too
many years of overuse. It had been a lovely day, an unusual one in this
gray, smoke-choked city, and the sun had brought warmth to the early
spring. But now that night was falling, the echo of the waning winter
only increased his pain.

He tried to imagine the warm sun of Calcutta shining on his face
and arms, scalding him with warmth. The old man narrowed his
eyes to slits; for a moment, it worked, then his foot caught on a raised
cobblestone and he fell forward, only stopping himself from injury by
catching hold of a man who had appeared suddenly beside him.

The man bent under his weight, but did not fall. When he began
to offer his thanks, he saw that his savior wore the twist of dementia
on his leathery face, and carried in his eyes such madness that he

ought to have been at Bedlam Hospital. But the stink of alcohol and rot on the man suggested that he might not live long enough for it to matter whether or not he received treatment.

This was the duality of life, this idiot who knew nothing of the help he had given. It reminded the old man of the *siva ardha-nari*— the Shiva Half Female—who was the divine representation of the interconnection between the gods and humanity. The ultimate duality.

He sighed, wishing now more than ever that he were back home, released from the terrible burden that was his alone to bear. But such was not to be. The nightmare was his alone to prevent. So he tried not to breathe, and followed the snaking path his senses guided him along, deeper into a twisted knot of alleys where the streets were coated with filth and the structures seemed only moments away from crumbling in upon themselves.

Yet when he found the small building, a two-story structure only slightly less dilapidated than the rest, he knew immediately that this was the place. Magic emanated from it with such power that he could feel it, and he could see a corona of bruised purple light limning the doorway. What magic there was inside was darker than the night and filthier than the streets. His stomach churned with nausea, and bile burned up the back of his throat as he went up to the front of the place.

He put his hand to the door and pushed it open.

Inside, the smell of fear and death was palpable, overriding even the stench of the river. As he walked down a dark, garbage-strewn hallway, tired eyes gazed at him from half-open doorways, which led into shadowy flats. Some of the faces he saw were curious, others dull, and still others cruel. The aroma of spices from his homeland drifted from one open door, but he ignored this distraction and followed the other smell, the corrupt scent of death. At the end of the hallway there was a final door.

He found it locked. Without a word, he closed his eyes and lifted his right hand. A spark of green flame flew forward and the door crashed open, nearly tearing from its hinges.

The old man stepped through the doorway and out into a large courtyard. It was open to the night sky above, but there was no fresh air to be found here, not in the bowels of London town.

The courtyard had been turned into a makeshift hospital. Under a large tarpaulin were row upon row of cots, each one occupied by a horribly suffering man or woman. In the slums of the East End, death lingered constantly in the night, keeping a constant vigil, waiting to carry away the souls of those whose flesh had surrendered.

A woman's cry cut through the moans of the afflicted, so piteous that the old man found himself inexorably drawn to her. His feet made no sound as he walked across the dirt. He found her resting on a small cot in the middle of the filthy courtyard. She had once been pretty, with aquiline features that would have rendered most men speechless. Now her face was taut with pain, her features gaunt, her lips drawn back in a grimace revealing brown, semi-rotten teeth.

When she saw the old man, she reached out toward him with one thin brown arm that was almost cadaverous. He could detect almost no flesh at all beneath the parchment skin. She moaned something, but her mouth was so dry that no true words passed between her lips.

He took the woman's hand in his and squeezed, ever so gently. She tried to speak again, but he shook his head.

"I understand, my child, there is no need to explain," he said in Hindi.

She was so weak that when she began to cry, the tears merely leaked from the corners of her eyes. The old man bent painfully over her and placed his other hand on her distended belly. She didn't flinch, allowing him to rest his palm there without complaint.

He bowed his head and began to chant. The words were soft and unintelligible. As his lips moved in time with the words, the woman's features began to soften.

She looked up at him, her brown eyes clear for the first time, and smiled. *Thank you,* she mouthed. Then her eyes closed and her breathing slowed. Finally, it stopped altogether.

The old man watched the woman's abdomen deflate, her belly shrinking until it was as it had once been.

"What are you doing?" demanded a voice from behind him.

The old man turned slowly, one hand on his back where the muscles were complaining that he had bent so low. A young Indian man stood there glaring at him, demand etched across his face. A doctor, perhaps, or a man of some medical knowledge, administering to the poor and the lost.

"I come in the glorious name of Vishnu, the creator, to give what help I can," answered the old man.

This seemed to calm the young doctor. He nodded and beckoned the old man to come with him, to the far side of the courtyard. There, the doctor turned and sighed.

"It's safer here, and there's a bit of a breeze. The air is cleaner. You can feel it when you breathe," the doctor said.

The old man nodded. The air was still filthy, stinking of the city's viscera, but the smell of fear and death was not as strong here.

"Was that woman a relative of yours?" the doctor asked.

The old man shook his head. "I came to help those who are beyond your expertise." His Hindi words punctuated with emphasis, like a chisel on stone.

The doctor cleared his throat, and he eyed the old man carefully. "You are a fakir—"

"No," the old man said strongly. "I am only a humble servant of the gods. Nothing more."

"But I saw what you did in there, with that woman—"

Once again the old man cut him off, this time laying a hand on the young doctor's shoulder. "I did nothing."

The doctor's eyelids fluttered drowsily and his flesh took on a jaundiced hue. When he focused on the old man again, his eyes were glazed with a white film, a sticky veneer that would dissipate in moments. As he spoke, he began to smile, as though he had just learned a wonderful secret.

"Of course," the doctor said. "And we are grateful for your aid."

The old man nodded gravely. "Tell me what you can of this plague, Doctor, this strange sickness."

It took the doctor a moment to register what the old man was saying, then he smiled again. "I was a doctor in India. Here I am nothing but a friend to these unfortunates. My brother was a sailor for the East India Company, but they said he was difficult, that he did not follow orders, and so they hired more crewmen here, and left him behind. He wrote our family to tell us of the squalor so many of our people are living in, some by choice and others because they have no alternative. I came to do what I could to help.

"I have never seen the like of this hideous plague before," he continued. "The women become bloated. There are boils and sores, odd chafing to the skin. And when the sickness subsides they are filled inside with foul creatures that burst forth and escape into the night. It's nothing natural, I am certain of that. This is not so much plague as curse. Many men are stricken, too, but their illness does not subside. They are either killed by it or they become . . ."

The old man frowned at this last part.

"*Become?*" he said.

"Let me show you," the doctor whispered as he led the old man past a curtained partition and into a tent.

Within the tent were many young men, all of them suffering. The old man laid a hand here and there as he walked, and gradually the din of agonized murmurings subsided. The doctor stopped at a random cot and drew back the sheet that was covering the body that rested there.

The young patient had hard features, the hands of a worker, and the scars of a fighter. These were human qualities, and yet his basic humanity was surrendering to something else. Calluses had given way to an almost reptilian skin. Sleek scales ran down the sides of his face in diamond cascade patterns that continued onto his throat and chest. His dark hair had begun to fall away, revealing a smooth, gleaming head. And all of his flesh was tinged with a dark, sickly green.

"They *become*. I cannot explain it any further than that," the doctor said sadly. "I saw the first of them two weeks past. Two more last week. Yesterday there were four. Today, seven more."

The old man looked at the patient, who began to shake.

His eyes—strange, yellow, reptile eyes—went wide, and he opened his mouth in a cry that began as a low hiss and grew in volume as he shook his head from side to side. The cry became a scream and the patient arched his back, straining at his bonds, madness in his eyes.

Then he went still, breathing raggedly. His flesh seemed darker, and the rough area of scales had spread farther across his chest and abdomen. For a moment the old man thought that he had fallen asleep, but then the patient lolled his head to one side and gazed at him. His eyes were no longer mad. Instead his gaze was full of fear, and it seemed as though he looked out from within some cage of horrid flesh.

The afflicted man wept silently.

"This is powerful *tantrika*. Your medicine is no match," said the old man.

The doctor shivered, then tore his gaze away from his patient. He scowled. "We have no medicine here. There is no money. We can only give comfort to the suffering. We have asked the Crown for help, but to no avail. We are just the poor bastard children of England's empire."

"The governor general, Eden, he is not a bad man—"

A look of hatred crossed the young doctor's face. "They are all bad, old man. The English have stolen our country. They steal our people and send them far away to help them steal other people's lands."

But the old man was not swayed.

"It is not our place to judge."

The doctor snorted derisively. "Why do you think this plague has come? It is to punish us for being cowards. It may have started with us, but it will continue until even the ignorant English themselves feel the gods' wrath."

This time the old man did not reply. He knew that no matter what he said to the young physician, it would fall on deaf ears.

Two

The lovely spring day had given way to a cool, dark evening. Each gust of wind carried a reminder that the year was still young and that winter had departed reluctantly. The warmer weather had arrived, to be certain, but hints of its less appealing past lingered, reminding Tamara of many of the more interesting men she had met.

The curtains in her bedroom danced languorously with the breeze, and the imperfections in the glass that covered her lamps warped the light that came from the flames within. Lights and shadows danced around the walls. Alone in her room, trying to decide what to wear to the Wintertons' dinner party, it all felt like a strange bit of theater to her. The setting, at least, was dramatic, even if her own activities were rather mundane.

With the gentle breeze caressing her, she stood naked before the chest in which she kept her undergarments. She was holding a beige silk chemise in her left hand, but it took her a moment to find the drawers to match. Martha had put her things away, of course, but Tamara had dismissed the aging maid for the evening. The encounter with Sophia had left her in a foul mood, and she hadn't wanted Martha to have to suffer her presence. The idea that she would have to endure the presence of Sophia Winchell at the Wintertons' this evening kept her outlook bleak.

No, she did not have the heart to summon Martha after having already left her at liberty for the night. Thus she determined to dress herself. In truth, this was the best choice. Once upon a time, Tamara had not liked to be alone, but as she grew older and found that she and William had different interests, she had come to appreciate her privacy. There was an intimacy in loneliness that was fantastically bittersweet. And a sense of discovery, as well.

She found the drawers she was looking for, and, with her undergarments in her hands, Tamara crossed the chamber to the mirror. She stood before it and regarded herself. Her auburn hair was loose and hung wild around her shoulders. In the flickering lamplight, the shadows fell across her body in a way that caused her breath to catch in her throat. The curtains rustled once more, fluttering, and the cold touch of the night wind hardened the dark nubs that tipped her pale breasts.

Tamara felt her cheeks flush with warmth and she shifted her weight deliciously from one foot to the other, slowly, relishing the feeling of her legs sliding together.

"Silly girl," she whispered. "Better get dressed, or you'll never make it to the party."

She slipped the chemise on, the silk whispering over her skin. With her drawers still clutched in one hand, she turned away from the mirror and went to the bed. Though Martha had gratefully accepted release from her duties for the evening, she had still set out a dress for Tamara to wear, along with a corset and petticoats. Putting on the corset would prove to be problematic without help, but Tamara could enlist her brother to tighten the thing. William would blush, no doubt, just as he had been doing ever since she had begun to blossom into a fitting shape for a young woman. But he would assist her.

Even before their father had become incapacitated, she had enlisted him for such tasks from time to time. That was the result of living without their mother to look after them.

Tamara shifted the petticoat and corset aside to look at the dress Martha had chosen for her. The bodice had a basque, giving it the appearance of a jacket, and was open over a chemisette of white muslin with a lace frill of *broderie anglaise.* It had a pointed waist that she liked, but it was the color that appealed to her the most, an emerald green that would set off her hair nicely. Though Tamara had shown no eye for suitors in the nearly half a year since her grandfather's death, it was always possible that there were some fit young men who would have an eye for her.

She raised the dress off the bed and returned to the mirror, still wearing only her chemise. The chill breeze felt wonderful. She draped the dress across her body and studied the effect.

The green was sumptuous, really, and though the dome of the skirt was a bit wider than she liked—the styles were beginning to change—she thought Martha had made a wise choice. Tamara turned slightly, first to the left, and then to the right, the mirror image shifting with her.

"Oh, no. Please, *anything* but that. You might as well join the convent."

It was a man's voice. Tamara spun, holding the dress in front of her in a hopeless attempt at modesty. Her first instinct was to flee from the bedchamber into her sitting room and out into the corridors of Ludlow House. But even as she turned, her heart quickening, she recognized the voice.

The room, of course, was empty.

Tamara planted her feet, the dress still pressed against her, and raised an eyebrow. Shadows danced in lamplight, but none was deep enough to hide an intruder.

"How long have you been here?" she demanded, glancing about the room.

The voice returned. "Long enough to sample the delights of your garden, my dear. Spring brings the loveliest flowers, and the breeze carries only their sweetest scents."

She narrowed her eyes. "Why spy on me? It's nothing you haven't seen before."

"I honestly hadn't intended to spy. I arrived to find you flushed with self-regard, and was so lost in my admiration that it never occurred to me to make my presence known until it became clear you intended to wear that awful, stuffy, old woman's gown to your soirée this evening."

Tamara frowned. "It's a lovely dress, and perfectly proper."

The lamplight seemed to freeze in place, the flames pausing in unnatural hesitation. Between her bed and the door that led out of her chamber there appeared suddenly the spectral form of a man, a roguish phantom with dark, curly hair and a boyish charm to his features. His eyes danced with playfulness, though he crossed his arms and gazed at her with affected disapproval. His sudden materialization was accompanied by a crackling noise, as of damp wood blazing in the hearth.

"Proper?" the specter cried in alarm. He shook his head disapprovingly. "My dear Tamara, how is it we have been acquainted so long, had so many late-night conversations in this very room, and you are still capable of uttering the word *proper* as though it were a quality to be admired? I accept that you are not yet prepared to indulge in full-fledged decadence, but surely there is *something* in your wardrobe that would be more appropriate for an evening out. Something that accentuates your loveliness, rather than hiding it away."

Tamara could not prevent the smirk that lifted one corner of her mouth. "By *loveliness,* you mean, of course, my breasts."

"Every inch of you is lovely, dear Tamara, but I hardly think I might convince you to attend the party in a state that would reveal your perfection in its entirety."

"Oh, yes, wouldn't that be a sight?"

"It is," the ghost replied. "Trust me."

"Nothing like scandal to destroy the family name completely. It isn't as if William and I aren't having trouble enough deflecting the less savory suggestions about the nature of our father's illness."

The translucence of the ghost flickered, and for a moment there was only a suggestion of a form, shimmering in the lamplight. Then the spirit solidified further, so that if she hadn't been peering directly at him, it might have seemed as if he were a being of flesh and blood. Standing there in his wide white collar and the red velvet Italian coat he always wore, the only thing about him that would have drawn undue attention was the anachronism of his fashion.

"I don't know," he said, mischief still twinkling in his eyes. "William could use a bit of scandal. And it's true, you know, that modesty retires after six o'clock."

For a long moment she gazed at the specter, at the ghost of the poet. Then she smiled. "Now that you mention it, I *do* have something new. Something with a bodice that . . . plunges a bit more."

The ghost uttered a high, childish giggle. "There's my girl. Oh, yes, we'll make a bohemian of you yet."

Tamara smiled even more broadly. Brazen, she crossed to the bed and laid the dress out neatly. "I can't wear this chemise, however," she said, fingering the neckline on the undergarment. It was too high for the bodice she had in mind.

Without bothering to acknowledge that she wasn't alone in the room, she drew the chemise over her head and tossed it on the bed beside the matching drawers. Entirely nude, she paraded back to the chest on the far side of the room and withdrew a fresh white chemise and the drawers to match it. The specter watched her all the while. He had been a scoundrel in life, she knew, his appetites as decadent as one could imagine. Yet in death he had become her friend and confidant, and though he had neither flesh nor blood, he was the only man to have seen her unclothed since her childhood.

A sad state of affairs, that.

Tamara pulled on the white chemise.

"Oh, that's *much* better," he said. "It's practically indecent."

She smiled, basking in his approval.

As she stepped into her drawers, there came a soft knock on the bedroom door. Tamara frowned and glanced at the ghost. She had dismissed Martha for the evening and the butler, Farris, would not have entered her sitting room without first knocking on that outer door.

It could only be William.

"Yes?" she called.

"Tamara? It's me. Can I come in?"

"You'll have to come back later!" the ghost replied. "She's not entirely dressed. Wouldn't want to offend your tender sensibilities."

Tamara held a hand to her mouth and laughed softly.

"Is that Byron in there?" William barked from the sitting room. "Tamara, really!"

"Oh, just a moment, William! I swear, you have the patience of a princess."

"And the sense of decorum," Byron muttered.

Tamara could not help laughing aloud at that.

"Now, see here!" William shouted.

She could imagine her brother's bluster as he protested helplessly. With a sigh, Tamara took a robe from its hook and slipped it on. She glanced at the ghost of Lord Byron, who gazed at her curiously from beneath those dark curls.

"I'm certain I know what this is all about," she whispered.

"I'll leave you to it, then," the poet said, and he began to fade away once more, his body becoming ever more transparent, seeming to flicker with the lamplight until at last he was gone.

Tamara firmly tied the sash of her robe and pulled open the door that led to her sitting room. Her brother was already dressed for the dinner party, looking smart in a dark jacket, with a red-and-gray-patterned waistcoat beneath. He stood by the window and gazed out at the night, trying as best he could to make it seem as if he hadn't been shouting at the closed door to her bedroom only moments ago.

"William," she said.

He took a long breath, then turned to face her. His expression was serious, but the gravity of it did not reach his eyes, which held a certain sadness. That was ever the way he slipped past her defenses. Much as they might argue, it was his eyes that always gave away the truth of what he was feeling, and reminded her that he was the brother she loved.

Though she knew he had come to chastise her, she saw that he hated having to do so for the sake of his affections for Sophia.

Tamara disliked the girl all the more for it. She spoke to break the silence.

"If you don't allow me to finish dressing, we shall arrive in Mayfair at an hour the Wintertons will no doubt consider unconscionably rude."

William nodded. "Well, it's helpful, I'm sure, to have a ghostly valet to help you choose your attire. Has Martha taken ill?"

"I gave her the evening's liberty. I thought you might help me with my corset."

Once more he nodded, his gaze searching the room for anything else he might study instead of her face. At last he looked upon her again.

"Sophia visited Threadneedle Street today. She tells me that you were less than polite at tea this afternoon," William said. "Had I known you would behave so churlishly, I might have suggested she spend her time at some East End tavern. At least there she would have known to expect harsh treatment and loose talk."

Tamara only stared at him as he spoke. When he finished, he waited for her response, and she let half a minute go by as they glared at each other.

"Are you through playing the lovestruck fool for a moment, then?" she asked.

William stood up straighter, his back rigid. "Excuse me?"

"I will not!" Tamara snapped. She brushed her hair out of her eyes, and then tightened her robe. "You are in love with the girl, Will. In light of that I allow for a certain amount of idiocy. It comes with the territory. But I won't have you treating me like the villain when it's your sweet Sophia whom you ought to be admonishing. She was distant at best upon her arrival for tea. I might go so far as to say petulant. She made no effort to be pleasant to my friends, then proceeded to insult each and every one of them, calling them nothing short of whores, and myself chief among them, apparently."

William raised an eyebrow, considering her words. "I've overheard a conversation or two that you've shared with Victoria and the rest of that crowd. Not very ladylike, at times."

"And that's to our credit, I'd think. We have minds of our own, and if we care to exercise them, whether with social debate or a bit of naughty humor, you should be thrilled that we do so among ourselves, behind closed doors, and not in public."

His mouth opened in a little O of surprise. "You wouldn't dare."

"Perhaps. Perhaps not."

William sighed. "You'll apologize, of course."

Tamara crossed her arms. "I'll do no such thing. Sophia is the one who owes an apology."

He frowned deeply, and when he spoke again his voice had lowered an octave. "Perhaps you ought to stay home this evening, then.

Without a chaperone, it might not be proper for you to attend, in any case. I'll make your excuses to the Wintertons."

"You'll do no such thing," she said, laughing derisively. "And how *dare* you?"

"There's a simple solution to this. Just promise that you'll apologize."

"I will *not*. And you will push this conversation no farther, or I might have to take this party as the perfect opportunity to declare the true identity of T. L. Fleet. I'm certain the Wintertons and their guests would be *thrilled* to discover that they have a celebrated man of letters in their midst."

That brought him up short. William was used to his sister's independent thinking, and even her stubbornness, but Tamara knew that the revelation of her writing career would embarrass him unendingly. Not that William himself disapproved of her authorial efforts, but there were far too many who would. If she were to write something that might be considered more appropriate for her sex, it might still send tongues wagging, but she would be thought of as merely eccentric, rather than altogether scandalous.

"Tamara, just . . . please," William said, waving one hand in the air. "Try to get along with Sophia. For *my* sake?"

For several moments she only looked at him. Finally, she nodded slowly. "All right. But you'll need to have the same chat with her, if you want my efforts to bear fruit. Now go on, and leave me to dress. You'll have Farris bring the carriage 'round?"

"Twenty minutes?" William asked.

Tamara considered her unruly hair and how quickly she could tame it. "Best make it thirty. We don't want to offend our hosts, but I'd like to look in on Father before we go."

William hesitated as though he had more to say, then seemed to think better of it.

"Thirty minutes, then."

∽

Aᴏᴛᴇʀ ʜᴇʀ ғʀᴜsᴛʀᴀᴛɪɴɢ argument with William, Tamara had been even more determined to follow Byron's suggestion. As promised, she wore her most daring dress, a deep saffron with a bodice that cut low across her bosom such that her every breath might draw the eye. It was a lovely dress. Tamara had purchased it while shopping with Victoria Markham one afternoon the previous year, but she had never had the temerity to wear it. Now that she had at last put it on, she found it a bit heavy, the domed skirt spreading broadly around her. It certainly had not been created for comfort.

Much as she loved her brother, there had always been a certain friction between them. By his very nature he was cautious, relying too much upon logic and too little on instinct. Tamara was his opposite in so many ways. Like her grandfather, she had many passions and loved to indulge her imagination. In the absence of a mother—for theirs had died quite young—William had taken it upon himself to watch over his younger sister, and she had bristled with his every attempt to subject her to his own claustrophobic sense of propriety. He was a kind and decent man and a good brother, but Tamara knew that they would never quite understand each other.

The house was disturbingly silent now as she made her way up the stairs to the third floor. There were only three rooms on this floor: the music room, the nursery, and the bedroom that had once belonged to the governess who had looked after William and Tamara when they were very young.

Until the previous fall, all three of the rooms had been empty for years. Now a constant din arose from the nursery—the one farthest from the main hall of the household. Mad screams could be heard echoing through Ludlow House at all hours of the day and evening.

Her boot heels scuffed the stairs as she trod upward, a bowl of cold soup in her hands, her reticule dangling from her left wrist. A pair of lamps were mounted in sconces on the wall at the top of the steps, but they offered only a very little light. In truth, the darkness always seemed deeper up here, as though no matter how brightly the fire might burn it could push the shadows back only so far.

Each time she strode down this hallway she felt ice form along her spine, and her throat went dry. Her eyes burned with tears she would not allow herself to shed. They would be wasted should she allow them to fall, and Tamara was stronger than that.

There would come another time for tears, of that she was certain.

For now, however, there was life to be lived and a war to be fought. A war against the darkness. And if she could not yet win the battle against the fiend that was locked in the room there at the top of the house, well, she had not surrendered hope.

Nor would she ever, as long as she drew breath.

In the gloom of the hallway she had to narrow her eyes to see the figure standing in front of the door of the nursery. Only as Tamara grew nearer could she make out the image, more like the suggestion of a presence. If she turned her head slightly the form would disappear, but from a certain angle the image of the specter was clear.

Had she still been of flesh and blood, the ghost would have been the tallest woman Tamara had ever seen, taller even than most men she had known. Her red hair was a wild tangle that fell down around her shoulders all the way to her perfectly rounded breasts. Sigils of magic and warfare were painted on her naked form, and she clutched a spear that was taller than she was. The shadows seemed to cling to her, but rather than lend her a modesty she did not possess, they instead made the sight of her all the more sensual.

Yet the sight of her was also a reminder of the pain she had endured while she lived. A fierce warrior—the queen of a savage tribe and a fearsome army—she had fought to drive the invading Roman soldiers away from the shores of Albion in a time so long ago that to most she was merely a legend. There had been sorcerers among the Roman forces, and they had allied themselves with demons. The queen's two daughters had been raped and murdered by one such creature, a demon-beast called Oblis. She had turned to magic herself, to spellcraft that required those symbols to be painted on her flesh. They had been painted in blood.

And while she was naked, in the midst of performing the ritual, the Romans had caught her off guard. She had died that way, unclothed, and so she remained in the afterlife, though by choice. Her nudity caused William to look away, but Tamara admired the ghost for her stubbornness. Queen Bodicea would never allow herself to appear vulnerable, whether covered in armor or bare to any blade that might cut her.

Though none would do so, ever again.

"Good evening, Tamara," said the spectral queen.

"And to you, Bodicea. He's been awfully quiet, hasn't he?"

The ghost shimmered, there in the half-light of the corridor. The substance of her form glowed darkly within, as though some night-black flame burned inside her. And perhaps it did, a fire of hatred. Bodicea glanced over her shoulder at the door, and then focused once more on Tamara.

"If he is quiet, it is only that he is thinking. He has interrupted his torment of the household to consider other ways in which he might cause anguish. The demon does not rest, Tamara. I know you realize that it is not your father inside this room, but it is difficult to see a human face and not ascribe to it at least some human qualities. Shed from your heart any tenderness you carry, for Oblis will recognize it, and exploit it."

Tamara nodded once. The demon had been trapped here long enough that she did not need Bodicea's warning, but she knew the specter could not resist the urge to offer it. Just as William and Tamara were haunted every moment by their father's fate, so was the ancient queen seared by the memory of the defilement and murder of her daughters. It was cruel irony that the two tragedies would be so entwined.

There was always a guard for the room at the top of Ludlow House. Some of the other ghosts would go inside, to stand sentry over Tamara's father, as would the Swifts' friend Nigel Townsend, when he took his turn. But Bodicea never entered that room, and perhaps that was for the best.

Otherwise Tamara might fear for her father's life.

The soup bowl felt suddenly heavy in her hands. She took a deep breath and met the ghost's gaze straight on, unnerved as always by the translucence of Bodicea's eyes. Tamara always felt that, if she could only catch a glimpse of those eyes without their transparency, their dark glow might provide a window onto eternal night, into the afterlife. Into eternity.

Then she glanced away. If such a sight were possible, she was far from certain she would welcome it.

"I'll be wary," she promised. "But if he *is* up to something, I want to know what it is."

The ethereal flesh of the ghost seemed to churn, and rather than stepping away from the door, she *flowed.*

Tamara balanced the cold soup bowl in one hand and with the other reached for the doorknob. Bodicea whispered her name, and she glanced back at the specter.

"You look lovely," said the queen, her voice another sort of ghost, as if the observation pained her. Her faded eyes spoke of loss.

"Thank you," Tamara replied.

But as she opened the door and stepped into the darkened room—with only the dim moonglow to light her way—she felt vaguely absurd. Coming here, dressed this way. She knew now that she ought to have looked in on Father before dressing for the party. The very idea of a party, of any kind of celebration, seemed somehow *wrong* now.

She shut the door behind her.

"Tamara, is that you?"

The voice floated on the darkness, shuddery with doubt and weakness. Henry Swift had been prone to headaches and a general malaise, not a malingerer but a gentle soul who could not abide conflict in any way. The loss of his wife had only exacerbated the fragility of his spirit, and had made Tamara quite protective of her father, despite the fact that she had little in common with him. He'd been a man of little passion and even less imagination.

He is, she corrected herself. That sort of thinking made her prey to the very voice that had just issued from the shadows.

She gestured at an elegant lamp that sat atop the chest of drawers that stood in the corner. *"Accendo,"* she commanded, and the wick ignited with flame, soaking up oil, sending a flickering light out across the room.

In a high-backed chair, next to an empty bed, Henry Swift sat with his arms chained behind his back. The bonds were attached to the legs of the chair. Where her father had once been a jovially rounded man, now his features were thin, almost cadaverous. Dark circles stained the skin that sagged beneath his eyes. The moment the room brightened he looked up at her, with an expression that seemed helpless and lost.

"Tamara?" he offered again in that same querulous voice.

It would have been tempting for her to think a miracle had happened, hearing that voice, seeing the pleading look in his eyes. But she had learned painful lessons in the past about unfounded hope.

"Oblis," she replied darkly. She preferred the bowl of soup. "I brought you something to eat. I am quite rushed, so I'm afraid I won't be able to endure your usual chatter this evening."

"You don't have to stay at all, daughter," the demon said, still in her father's voice. Yet now the trembling was gone, and a malign spark flickered clearly behind his eyes. "I'm quite capable of feeding myself."

Tamara sniffed. Next he would suggest that she unchain him. There were magical bonds in place throughout the room, as well, but she wouldn't even entertain the idea of setting his hands free. It was a game he played, and she had tired of it months ago.

"You've been terribly quiet since my guests departed," she said, bringing a spoonful of the cold soup to his lips. Tamara fed the demon so her father's body would not die, and Oblis ate for the same reason.

"It was rude of you not to bring your friends inside to see your dear father," he said. "I've known some of those young ladies their entire lives."

"My father knows them. You do not." Tamara fed him another spoonful of soup. "What are you scheming so silently up here, Oblis?"

He gazed salaciously at her, running his tongue lewdly around his mouth as though to relish the sight of her, rather than the flavor of his meal. "How I might split you in two, lovely daughter, how it will feel to fuck you till you bleed."

Tamara gaped at him in revulsion, and for a moment she was frozen with her disgust. Oblis brought his knee up beneath the bowl and the cold, clotting soup splashed up at her. With a sneer Tamara raised her right hand and instantly the air crackled with bright green light, magical energy that formed a shield, keeping the contents of the bowl from ruining her dress.

The bowl fell and shattered on the ground. Cold soup dripped from the air onto the wooden floor. With a hushed sound the magic evaporated, and Tamara lowered her hand.

"I think that's all for your dinner this evening," she said.

"You asked a question," the demon replied. "I simply answered."

Tamara pushed aside her disgust just enough to produce a taunting smirk. "You are a Vapor, Oblis, nothing more. Without my father's flesh, you're chimney smoke with a rotten child's temper. And you haven't the tumescence, I'm afraid, to live up to your imaginings."

Her father's upper lip curled back and the demon fumed.

"Enjoy the party, Tamara. You'll need me soon enough."

This was the voice of Oblis, now, like a capricious child in timbre, but with a rough, graveled edge. It brought her up short as she was about to leave the room. Already, William would have grown impatient awaiting her. But there was something in those words, that tone. This wasn't merely empty bluster.

Frowning, she turned to face him again. "Why would I ever need you?"

"You both shall, and soon," Oblis sneered in that hellish voice. "You wanted to know how I spent my afternoon, once your whorish friends departed? My throat was ragged and parched. I paused for a breath. And then, rather than making all that noise, I decided that I would *listen*."

"Listen to what?" Tamara asked.

Oblis only smiled.

~

Though it was only a few doors farther along St. James Street from White's Club, the Algernon Club had little in common with its neighbor.

From its earliest years to the days when Beau Brummel sat by the vast bow window at the front of the building, holding court and casting judgment upon passersby, White's had always been about being noticed. White's Club was conspicuous.

The very nature of the Algernon Club was to be *inconspicuous*. To the unknowing public strolling past on the street, it was simply another address along St. James. There was no bow window, nor in fact any window at all that offered outsiders a view of what lay within. The gentlemen at the Algernon had no interest in putting the duke of Argyll on display, even if they had been willing to allow such a buffoon to darken their doorstep.

Otherwise, the differences between the Algernon and other gentlemen's clubs were less evident. In the many rooms of the first floor, members gathered in small groups, some standing in darkened corners and others seated comfortably around low tables. The air was redolent with the smell of burning pipe tobacco, and the servants wore black knee breeches not unlike those worn by the employees of Boodle's. The dining room was always in use, it seemed, with the kitchen acceding to all demands. Glasses clinked as gentlemen toasted one another's health, or that of their families or fortunes.

There was a card room, but it wasn't common for games of chance to be played at the Algernon Club. Where cards were employed, it was far more likely to be in an example of prestidigitation, a new pass that the amateur magicians of the club wished to teach or to learn. The professionals were another matter entirely. They shared nothing with the other members, unwilling as they were to reveal their techniques to anyone who might one day become a competitor.

Yet from time to time—ordinarily in the rooms upstairs where only the club's directors were allowed—other sorts of magic were addressed.

Tonight, however, a more mundane task had presented itself. Each month the directors gathered in the Board Room to consider applications for membership. The room bespoke the wealth of the club's early-eighteenth-century founders. The ceiling boasted a series of hand-painted and hand-carved medallions, and the intricacy of the crown molding and the woodwork that framed the hearth was stunningly artful. A grandfather clock stood at one end of the chamber, and at the other were two separate doors, one through which the directors had entered and the other for servants.

Both were presently locked.

A tablet stained with ancient Egyptian hieroglyphics hung above the fireplace; an enormous portrait of the queen, only recently commissioned, had been placed beside the clock. Above each door was a long, horizontal seascape, showing dark silhouettes of double-masted ships riding high on storm-wrought waves. The two pieces seemed to be halves of a larger painting, though one revealed the dark heart of the storm, and the other showed a break in the clouds, with just a hint of clear sky.

Lord Blackheath loved the seascapes that hung above the doors. Since the first time he had entered this room—the day after he had been named a director of the Algernon Club—he had tried to discover their origin, but to no avail. Nowhere in the club's records was there any mention of the founders acquiring those paintings. It seemed as if they had always been there, as though they themselves were a bit of magic.

A mystery. Lord Blackheath had a fondness for mysteries, small and large.

"Now then, gentlemen," he said, "have you any further candidates for membership this evening?"

Lord Blackheath studied the faces of the men who had gathered around the table, the youngest of them perhaps forty and the eldest, Sir Horace, eighty-seven. They glanced at one another, a susurrus of low conversation ensuing, and after several moments determined that they were through. Thirty-two new members had been considered tonight, and only three had been admitted. the Algernon Club differed from other gentlemen's clubs in the criteria it utilized to judge applicants, but its members were no less discriminatory. More so, in fact.

"Very well," Lord Blackheath said. He settled into his dark leather chair and steepled his fingers beneath his graying beard. "There is one final candidate *I* would like to bring to your attention. I have taken the liberty—as director of the Algernon Club—of inviting him to attend Sir Darius's birthday gala, so that you may all have a chance to evaluate him."

Sir Horace cleared his throat. His back was so bent that he seemed always about to pitch forward onto the table, and when he turned to focus on Lord Blackheath it was painful to watch him shift his body. His flesh and bone were mutineers, unwilling to obey his commands, and so he had to force them to do so. Yet his eyes were alight with clarity and intelligence.

"You have that right, Blackheath, but it's damned unusual for you to exercise it. Who is this man?"

"Sir Ludlow's grandson, William Swift."

The reaction was immediate. Sir Horace's face darkened and he sputtered. Several of the others began speaking all at once, and all of them protesting. Lord Blackheath only waited for the torrent to subside.

Sir Horace rapped his knuckles on the table and the room fell silent. The ancient man stared at Lord Blackheath.

"We've discussed the boy before, Blackheath. Ludlow was always clear about him. William Swift could not perform the simplest coin pass or card trick if I showed it to him with my own two hands. He's got no interest in magic. To admit him simply because his family has a legacy with this club . . . that's the sort of thing you find at White's and Boodle's, but the Algernon Club simply does not work that way."

Lord Blackheath nodded. "I'm bloody well aware of that. But I believe we must take a closer look at William Swift. You must admit that now that Ludlow's dead, he bears watching."

Sir Horace sneered. "You think that boy is the new Protector? Ridiculous!"

Blackheath narrowed his gaze. "*Someone* prevented Balberith from rising several months back."

From a shadowed corner of the room came the sound of a man clearing his throat. Lord Blackheath knitted his brows and glanced at the figure in the corner.

"My lord Melbourne?" he said.

The directors of the Algernon Club had never formally admitted Melbourne as a member. Politically, it would have been unseemly for the prime minister to be associated with the club. And though he had an interest in the mystical, he had no skill with magic, neither stagecraft nor spellcraft. Thus, he was usually a silent observer.

Not so, this evening.

"We should not presume that the Protectorship passed to a member of the Swift family. Ludlow may not even have chosen a successor. If he did not, Albion might have chosen anyone. If it is a Swift, however, it seems more likely to be Ludlow's son, Henry, who has not been seen outside the walls of his home since his father's death. Word is that he is ill, but that may be merely obfuscation. From all that we have heard of William Swift, he hardly seems up to the task."

Lord Blackheath nodded slowly. Melbourne had pulled the center of power in the room away from him, and now he used silence to draw it back. One by one the directors gave him their full attention as they awaited his response, the pause lengthening and growing awkward.

At last, Blackheath glanced around the table once more and spoke. "There are many possibilities, but I am certain we can all agree that not enough effort has been expended attempting to discover the identity of the new Protector. Not knowing his identity could be dangerous for us all. I say that William Swift bears watching. Sir Horace pointed out that William has never shown any interest in magic. About that he is certainly correct.

"But it may be that magic has an interest in him."

Three

*D*amn William *for lacing me up so . . . emphatically.*

Tamara cursed her brother as she took baby steps toward a nearby love seat. In the midst of the Wintertons' dinner party, she had slipped away to steal a moment to herself in a sitting room beside the front parlor.

Dark spots drifted across her field of vision. She tried to take a deep breath but thanks to her corset, her chest could not expand, which meant that her lungs could only partially fill with air. Perhaps if she took only shallow breaths, she would be all right.

You should never have listened to Byron, she admonished herself. If she had worn a bodice without a plunging neckline, she would not have had to use the whalebone. It was the most unforgiving corset she owned, but it did give her décolletage a nice push heavenward. Looking down at her meticulously powdered chest, she sighed. Lightly. Oh, well, if she *had* to suffer for beauty, she supposed the effect was worth the trouble.

With a careful glance around the room to be absolutely certain she was alone, Tamara slid the bulk of her body onto the love seat. Since she *really* could not bend into a sitting position, thanks to the heavy saffron material of her dress, the effort was decidedly clumsy. She heaved a sigh, though, as she stretched her torso out so that her back took on a slight convex curve. *Blissful relief,* she mused.

Her peaceful respite was disrupted by the sound of a woman loudly clearing her throat. Startled, Tamara looked up to find Sophia Winchell standing at the threshold, her mouth twisted into a little moue of disapproval. It was, Tamara had discovered, the natural state of her countenance.

"You look as if you've swallowed something unpleasant, Sophia," she said, allowing a hint of exasperation to enter her voice. "Shall I call for someone to bring you a glass of water?"

Sophia sniffed superciliously and averted her eyes, as though unable to bear witness to Tamara's debasement. "It was William I sought. You'll pardon my interruption." She clutched her hands so tightly together that they were white.

"Yes, of course. As you can see, however, William is elsewhere. Might I be of any assistance?"

Sophia shook her head quickly, causing her tightly wound curls to jiggle like little insects. Tamara suppressed a snicker, knowing that if she at all exacerbated the tenuous situation, William would skin her alive.

"Right. Then, if you don't mind, I shall return to the task of breathing. This corset seems to require all my attention at the moment."

Sophia didn't respond, just rolled her eyes and turned on her heel. Tamara watched her retreating back.

Assured that she was gone, Tamara allowed herself to grin. So pleased was she with how well she had handled the encounter, and still suffering from oxygen deprivation, her grin quickly turned to a giggle. To her alarm, she found herself unable to stop.

"Oh, that does hurt . . ."

She and William had arrived at half past eight. Their lateness, while fashionable, had been Tamara's fault, not William's; he would do anything to avoid a public faux pas. But after her visit with "Father," it had taken her several minutes to clear her mind. By the time she was ready to leave the house, William was so red-faced it seemed as if he was caught in a fit of apoplexy.

Even then, she was mightily distracted by both the repugnant filth that had spewed from the demon's lips, and by the insinuation Oblis had made. The implication was that he might still communicate with other demons, other Vapors, and that he could observe the workings of the malign forces that hovered over Albion even from that locked room on the third floor of Ludlow House. The thought unnerved her.

You'll need me soon enough, he'd said. Tamara found the idea deeply unsettling. If they ever truly needed help from Oblis, surely they were already doomed.

His insinuations were usually merely a way for him to play with their minds, but Tamara knew they could not discount the possibility that the demon knew something. And if there was some new evil on the rise, well, she and William would have to look into it.

Those thoughts had been weighing heavily upon her throughout the night. Soon after they had arrived at No. 15 Half Moon Street and made their hellos to Marjorie Winterton, Tamara had taken leave of her brother and begun to wander alone through the beautiful Georgian town house. Her thoughts were too grim for her to be very sociable.

Unhappily for Marjorie, her husband's business these days lay in Virginia, and he was forced to travel frequently, leaving his young wife to her own devices for fortnights at a time. Indeed, Marjorie had put together this dinner party as a diversion. She had once told Tamara that parties were the only things that relieved the monotony of her lonely days.

The dinner bell began to chime. With a distinctly unladylike grunt she heaved herself away from the comfortable love seat, glad that dinner was forthcoming, but worried about where she would put the food, since her stomach seemed to be compressed to the size of a walnut. Perhaps she would ask Marjorie's maid to loosen her ties before dinner.

~

WILLIAM SAT STIFFLY in his chair and stared at Lord Delwood. They had been conferring about the old man's holdings in Barbados. Normally William would have been eager for the discussion. It was just the sort of business he had been attempting to nurture since he had taken the reins at Swift's of London, tapping into the enormous financial opportunities developing around the world. This evening, however, he was so preoccupied that all he could do was hope that he was nodding and mm-hmming in all the right places.

His memories of Sophia's afternoon visit to his office were driving him to distraction. Even now he found his thoughts returning to the way she had slid onto his desk, the nearness of her thigh to his hand, the taste of her lips—

Oh, that's quite enough!

"Young man? *Young man!*" Lord Delwood's face was a patchwork of angry, broken capillaries. "Are you *listening* to me, Mr. Swift?"

William snapped back into the moment and nodded mutely.

"Sir, Lord Delwood, of course—" he stammered, but it was too late. The old man wrinkled his nose in distaste.

"Just like you young fellows. Head in the clouds, heart in your mouth. Bah!" Lord Delwood exclaimed, spraying saliva in William's face. The old man's breath was abominable, like overcooked liver and onions. But William had regained his composure, so he simply smiled politely and nodded.

"Of course, Lord Delwood, you are absolutely correct in your estimation. The youth of today do nothing but laze about," William replied, hoping to confuse the man with this avowal. Delwood did appear to be taken off balance. He opened his pale, withered lips like a great codfish, then promptly closed them again, his jowls actually shaking with the aborted effort.

"Well, I say, I never—"

But William pressed his advantage.

"Yes, quite right, indeed, sir. Though I do hope that wasn't your estimation of *me,* my lord. On the contrary, I apologize that my thoughts were elsewhere, but certainly they were not far afield. I was merely contemplating how Swift's of London might best advise you upon an investment plan that would be both aggressive and secure—"

This blatant lie was interrupted by the dinner bell.

"I must say that it has been a very real pleasure, Lord Delwood, and if you ever have need of banking services, know that we at Swift's would be more than happy to oblige you."

William stood up and gave the old man a polite bow before escaping the confines of the study for the delicacies of the dining room. At an intersection of two corridors, away from the main flow of the guests, he saw Sophia waiting for him.

"I looked *everywhere* for you, darling," she began, but William quickly silenced her with a kiss. Their lips met for the briefest of moments, then Sophia pulled away from him, the darkness of the hallway hiding her expression from his curious stare. He was afraid he had gone too far.

"I am sorry. I shouldn't have—"

Then Sophia was in his arms again, kissing him with her soft, honeyed mouth, her corseted breasts pressed firmly against his chest. She drew her mouth away and peered about to make sure that they were alone. Then she leaned her head on his shoulder and sighed contentedly.

"Not tonight, my love, but soon," she cooed. "Very soon we will be together."

William blinked, and stared at her. What promise was this?

She took his hand and quietly led him toward the dining room.

Six other dinner guests were already settled at their places when Sophia guided him to their seats at the table. He was very glad of the gentle pressure of her fingers around his wrist. If she had not led him, he wasn't sure he would have been able to move forward of his own volition.

Tamara was one of the guests who had already found her place, and she fixed her gaze upon him the moment he entered. A knowing smile flickered across her face, replaced instantly by one of mock concern.

"William, you look ill at ease. Are you unwell?" she asked.

Tamara was seated across from Marjorie Winterton, at the far end of the large, square dining room table. Her blond head was the only fair one among a sea of dark coiffures.

"I am fine, thank you—"

Lord Delwood, his ornately carved bamboo cane thumping ahead of him with every step, came into the room, interrupting William.

"I am afraid the boy is of the sensitive type," the old man proclaimed loudly as he found his seat at the end of the table, beside Tamara and Marjorie.

"I beg your pardon, sir?" William spluttered.

Lord Delwood turned and smiled broadly at him. His crooked teeth were yellowed from years of tobacco addiction.

"As I was saying," he began, laying aside his bamboo cane so that it rested delicately against the dining room chair.

William assumed that the old man would lose his footing without the cane and collapse onto the thickly carpeted floor. But to his surprise the fellow actually straightened up to a height several inches taller than William himself. The hunched shape was revealed to be illusion, nothing more.

"I have found William Swift—" At this point, Lord Delwood produced a monogrammed handkerchief from his black frock coat and unfurled it with a dramatic snap of his wrist. Then he took the white cotton handkerchief and began to wipe the soft material across his cheek. "—to be a bit of a prude."

The old man's wheeze was now replaced with a smooth, rich tenor. "Sorry, Willy."

William spluttered again, and cursed inwardly for having done so. "Who in God's name—" he began.

But he was silenced by a gasp of shock that came from one of the other guests—a stocky, middle-aged woman called Mrs. Northrup— as the "old man" turned the handkerchief so that the assembled guests could see the greasepaint that covered it.

Sophia gave a cry of her own, her pale cheeks crimson with anger.

"John Haversham," she croaked out, "how dare you! How *dare* you! I shall have words with your mother!"

Marjorie Winterton gave a sharp giggle, then quickly covered a mischievous smile with her hand. William gaped openmouthed as "Lord Delwood" wiped away the rest of the greasepaint, revealing a handsome young visage. The now much younger Mr. Haversham turned away for a moment as he pulled something large and pliable from his mouth—a set of very realistic-looking teeth, which he dried with a napkin.

When he turned back, he spoke to Tamara.

"You will have to forgive my cousin Sophia. She, too, is of a delicate nature, I am afraid."

Sophia's eyes flared, but this time she held her tongue. Her anger was too raw to give polite voice, William supposed. Haversham paid no attention to her rage. Instead he continued to address Tamara, doing so with an impish grin.

"These were a gift from a dear American friend, who found that his invention of vulcanized rubber could be put to good use in the improvement of mankind."

"I can think of *nothing* of more import to mankind than the gift of rubber teeth," Tamara responded archly.

Haversham tossed her a wink before dropping the dentures into her hand. William watched with some amusement as a bright crimson blush came to his sister's throat.

"Yes, I had a feeling that these might be of keen interest to you especially, Miss Swift. I've heard tales of your grandfather, and about your curiosity concerning the art of stagecraft. These should enthrall you, no doubt."

Tamara nodded, smiling mischievously herself now. "Oh, indeed, sir. My curiosity is certainly piqued."

William just stared at his sister, all traces of amusement having evaporated. This man was a rogue, and Tamara was actually *flirting* with him.

Marjorie Winterton stood up abruptly and called for everyone's attention. "Thank you very much, John, for such an entertaining diversion. If only my Thomas were here to enjoy it, the evening would be perfect." She paused, giving Haversham a quick nod. "Please, everyone, take your seat, so that we may begin. I think you shall all thoroughly enjoy the treacle tart."

~

DINNER WAS SUMPTUOUS. It began with raw oysters and proceeded through a course of bouillon. There were fried smelts and then sweetbreads, neither of which Tamara fancied. But the main course— quail with truffles and rice coquettes—was the equal of any dish she had tasted in ages. By the time the fancy cakes and coffee were served, Tamara felt herself under the spell of John Haversham. During the elaborate meal she had quite enjoyed the attentions of the dramatic newcomer. He was an entertaining dinner companion: smart, witty, and very, very attractive. She liked the way he posed his slim, powerful body so casually in his chair, his hands lying on the tabletop, oblivious to etiquette.

As she sipped her coffee, she stole a glance at him. Haversham was talking animatedly to Marjorie's weak-chinned brother-in-law, Reginald. Tamara studied his face. She liked his strong jaw, and the way his brown hair was a bit ruffled at the top, as if he had just been out in the wind. His eyes were dark gray, and the lashes were long and thick like a woman's. There was still a bit of greasepaint on his chin, but she didn't mind the effect. Indeed, it added to his mystique.

Reginald must have noted her interest, for he gave her a knowing, gap-toothed smile. Thus caught, she quickly turned her attention back to her own plate.

Tamara had always found Reginald a bit unsavory. Sometimes, when he thought she wasn't looking, he gave her body a lingering stare that made Tamara shudder. Tonight, though, he seemed much more interested in John Haversham's company.

As if he had read her thoughts, Haversham extricated himself from Reginald's bossy baritone with a wry smile cast in Tamara's direction.

"Excuse me, Reginald, but it appears Miss Swift is in danger of drifting off into boredom, and I feel it's my duty to rescue her. The treacle tart does not seem to be keeping her as occupied as Marjorie had promised."

Before Reginald could protest, Tamara interjected. "Mr. Haversham, your selfless devotion to duty is an admirable trait."

He gave her another grateful wink—it seemed to be his trademark—and swiveled in his chair to face her. Reginald Winterton simply turned to find another unfortunate victim.

"Tamara Swift, where have you been hidden these seven-and-twenty years of mine?" Haversham's eyes sparkled with interest. She imagined that she could see herself reflected there, the candlelight suffusing her honey hair with a rich, warm glow. *What a silly thought,* she mused, but she continued to look.

"I've been at Ludlow House, waiting to be rescued from my boring existence," she said.

It was a lie, of course. Tamara could hardly call her life boring. But there was a kernel of truth in what she had said. It could be terribly dreary in Ludlow House, no matter how interesting things had become of late. The flutter in her heart when she sat so close to this intriguing stranger was a pointed reminder of precisely what had been missing from her life.

Yet how might he react if he knew what her life was truly like? If she were to tell him of her life as a magical Protector of Albion—instead of pretending to be the typical wilting English Rose—would he believe her? And if so, would he still find her as fascinating as he seemed to this evening, when she was simply a pretty young society woman? Or would the truth repel him?

"Boring? I find that difficult to believe, Miss Swift. You seem like a clever girl. I can't imagine you as being incapable of keeping both your mind and body . . . well, shall we say, *occupied*." As he spoke, his eyes flitted onto the swell of her breasts as they rose and fell with each breath. She felt herself starting to blush.

He quickly drew his eyes away and seemed to gaze upon the smooth hollow of her throat, then at last returned to her face. Was it her imagination, or were his eyes dark with desire?

She had only experienced the intimate attentions of a man once before, and that had been a very fleeting—though exciting—experience. After her grandfather's death, Tamara and William had enlisted the help of Ludlow Swift's old friend Nigel Townsend in battling the demon that had murdered the old man.

During that dark time, Tamara had found herself Nigel's quarry, despite the vast difference in their ages. His flirtations grew bold, and though Tamara was flattered by them, even aroused, she was not prepared to respond. The situation became such that William had been forced to intercede on behalf of her virtue . . . for Nigel was more than a family friend; he was also a vampire who had walked the Earth the better part of three centuries.

Not evil. No, not that. But he carried a hunger that could overwhelm him the way passion might take control of any man.

Now, as Tamara remembered the sensation of Nigel's lips on her own, she looked away from John Haversham, embarrassed that her own desire might show in her eyes.

Haversham cleared his throat and took a sip of red wine from the fine cut-crystal flute in front of him. He was a rogue, certainly, but at least enough of the gentleman remained for him to give her time to collect herself.

She stared at the glass of Bordeaux he held in his hand, thinking how much it looked like blood. And she shuddered at the thought.

"You've not caught a chill, have you, Miss Swift?" Reginald asked.

Tamara flinched as she glanced over at the repulsive man. She wondered how much of her exchange with John he had observed, and felt her cheeks flush crimson once more.

"May I fetch you one of Marjorie's shawls?" Reginald continued, smiling crookedly.

"No, thank you, Mr. Winterton. I'm grateful for your concern, but I'm quite comfortable, I assure you."

As she spoke, she noticed that dinner seemed to have reached its end. Thankfully, she could retire with the other women to the sitting room now, without offending Reginald too terribly. She took her leave of the men, following on the heels of Marjorie and Sophia, who seemed to be discussing the new art exhibit that had opened at the Egyptian Hall.

The hallway seemed darker to Tamara as she slowed her steps to look at the sketches that hung on the lime plaster walls. By the light of the oil lamps, she could make out few of the details in the artwork. They all seemed to be of the same subject, which was surprising to Tamara, as she had never noticed these particular sketches in her other visits to the house.

She stopped and peered at one of the drawings. At first, she could see only charcoal lines, but as her eyes adjusted to the half-light she saw that the sketches were actually quite beautifully rendered nudes. All of the same, buxom-bodied woman.

"Do you approve?"

She turned quickly at his words. John Haversham stood only inches from her, so close that she could feel his breath on the nape of her neck. His nearness caused a ripple of pleasure to travel through her, and her brain seemed to slow so that words might take hours to come to her lips.

"If I said yes, would you be appalled, then?" she asked.

He smiled, reaching out to tease a strand of hair that had come loose from her bun. "What if I were to reveal to you, Miss Swift, the identity of the artist responsible for these pieces," he began.

Tamara shook her head. "No, thank you, sir. I don't require that particular revelation."

This stopped him. He cocked his head, gazing at her curiously.

"You do not wish to know who created them?" He seemed utterly confused by Tamara's demurral. "I did not think *you* were as prudish as your brother. Perhaps I was mistaken."

With a bit of satisfaction she watched him floundering for something else to say, something that would ease them back onto level ground. Tamara knew he had expected her to flit about after him, hanging on his every word, to show that she was surely taken by him. But she was no hollow-headed waif. It was becoming clear that John Haversham was used to dominating his female conquests, and for Tamara to truly capture his attention, she had to place herself beyond his control, make herself seem less easily attainable.

"You complimented me earlier, Mr. Haversham, by calling me clever. Don't you think me clever enough, then, to examine the signature of the artist? You've an excellent eye for detail. Tell me the subject, though. Is she your lover?"

The word *lover* trilled from Tamara's lips. She felt wanton even voicing it.

John raised an eyebrow. "Would it matter if she were?" he countered, his words a whisper in the long expanse of hallway.

She didn't know how to respond. She knew she should say no, that this would impress him more than anything else she could say, but instead she found herself whispering back in return.

"Yes."

Tamara was shocked that she had confessed it, but it was the truth. The thought of this man wrapped in carnal embrace with another woman made her angry. No, not angry. *Jealous.*

They stared at each other for a moment, the silence heavy between them, then he took her hand and brought it to his lips.

"Come with me to the Egyptian Hall, tomorrow evening. If you are a connoisseur of art, even in the slightest, there is an exhibit there that I think you might find as fascinating as I find you."

Inside, she was shaking, but she managed to keep her voice steady. "That would be lovely. I accept. With great curiosity."

∼

HER FATHER'S STUDY had always been a friend to Helena Martin. As a small child, she had spent many an hour staring at all the curios her father had accumulated in his many years of travel.

In truth, those travels had kept him absent for much of her life. Most of what Helena knew of her busy father came from her time spent among his artifacts. She drew wide panoramas of his life and character based on what she saw there in his study. She often compared her fancies to the real man, and found reality lacking.

Her father had recently accepted a lectureship at Magdalene College at Oxford, and Helena's mother had joined him there, so now most of her parents' time was spent away from London. The traveling, which had always been so important to her father's work as an archaeologist, was placed on hold so that he could impart everything he had learned to the next generation. Except, of course, to Helena herself.

Helena knew she should not be jealous of other people spending time with her father, but she wished that *both* her parents had more time for her. When she was a tiny child, she had gone to Egypt and Mesopotamia with them, but the moment she had reached school age she was shipped back to England and a waiting tutor. Her half brother, Frederick, had endured the same familial disconnection, but where she found it painful, he actually reveled in the lack of supervision.

She had discovered her love of sketching when she was only nine and a half. Helena had been allowed to spend the summer on a dig with her parents in Lower Egypt, and had passed the months gazing in fascination as the old French priest, Father Louis, had painstakingly sketched every object her father unearthed. She had loved staring at his darting, birdlike hands as he dipped his pen in ink and transformed each blank piece of paper into a detailed picture.

She had begged for a sketchbook, and her mother had obliged. So Helena had spent the balance of the summer copying Father Louis's delicate example.

Now, it seemed, she could not exist without her charcoals and paper. She knew others found her habits odd, but she did not care. Her work was the only thing that kept her sane in a world she could not control.

This evening she had curled up in one of her father's large brown calfskin chairs, and was contemplating a strange new curio that had been sent to her father the week before by a family friend. She turned it this way and that, seeking the best angle for her next drawing.

Helena scratched her nose, smearing charcoal across the bridge, and sighed. The artifact was decidedly odd, and actually frightened her more than she cared to admit. But that was the very thing that had drawn her to it, and made her determined to capture its essence. When she stared at the artifact, it seemed to stare back. The figurine was toadlike in appearance, its bulk made up of jasper and lapis lazuli. It was a small creature, no more than four inches tall, but it had an alarmingly large presence, and seemed to draw the eye no matter where one stood in the room.

When it had first been delivered, she and Frederick had stood staring at it for what seemed the better part of an hour, in part repelled by the subject, yet admiring the detailed workmanship. Frederick actually touched it, but Helena could not bring herself to do so. She knew she was being silly, but something about the thing made her skin crawl.

Frederick had teased her, of course, but she didn't resent him for it. They were very close despite the difference in their ages. Frederick's mother had suffered from cholera until he was two years of age. Helena's mother, Rose, had nursed the dying woman, and when the ailing woman had finally succumbed, Rose had won the widower's heart.

Frederick had grown up almost believing that Rose was his own mother, and when Helena had been born, there was never any animosity or jealousy. The children had been treated as equals in the eyes of their parents, and had grown close in the face of their parents' frequent absences. Now adults, they still lived under the same roof, but it rarely bothered Helena. She and Frederick had never found much to quarrel about—until this past week.

She knew Frederick spent his days suffering in the employ of a bill discounting house, and lived for his evenings at play with the other so-called intellectuals he had studied with at Cambridge. Helena found them all rather trite, even boring, but she would never dare say as much. She knew that she would offend him deeply with her dismissal.

Yet the past few nights he had eschewed his usual pursuits and languished about the house—generally in his own rooms—seeming unusually pale and cantankerous. Helena had warned him that he was transforming into an ill-tempered lout, and rather than skewering her with some snide riposte, as was his wont, he had only glared. She had no idea what had him so aggrieved, and could only assume that his abhorrence of the financial world been exacerbated by some recent occurrence.

"Helena?"

She jumped at the sound of her name.

Frederick stood in the doorway, watching her. His thinning, light brown hair was rakishly disheveled, so that he looked a bit like a peacock. He was of middling height and carried his gut low on his hips, just like their father. She did not think him a handsome man, but there was a kindness to his face upon which her lady friends had often remarked.

Those same young women would not have been so quick to admire him this evening, though. For days he had not looked himself, and tonight there was a yellowish tint to his hazel eyes. His skin had darkened to an unhealthy gray that was disturbing to see.

"Yes, Frederick?" She smiled broadly as she spoke, hoping that her own conviviality would rub off on him. Her brother was ill, that much was clear, but she felt certain that his despondency was at the root of it.

He didn't smile in return.

"Helena, I must have words with you." His voice was more precise than usual, even clipped. And she did not understand what he meant. Was he upset with her about something she had done? She could think of nothing that would require that they exchange "words."

Determined not to add to his agitation, she simply waited as he crossed the room and came to perch on the side of her chair. The look he gave her as he scooted in close to her shoulder made her nervous. It wasn't the kind of look one gave a female, and especially one who was a blood relation.

"Frederick, you do not look at all well . . . and your eyes . . . have you been drinking?" She meant to continue, but he cut her off by running his hand across the side of her face. The touch made her feel sick to her stomach.

"You have such beautiful, smooth skin, sister."

Helena stiffened in her chair. The sketch she had begun slid to the floor. She moved to retrieve it, but Frederick moved more quickly. His hands closed around the sketchbook, and something about his actions carried a finality that filled her with dread. He put the book back in her lap, his hands purposely grazing across her waist.

Her mouth grew dry and she tasted copper—tasted blood—as she unconsciously bit too hard on her lower lip.

"I hardly think the state of my skin should be of interest to you," she said, her voice cracking.

Frederick smiled, then, a wide, teeth-baring grin that somehow didn't seem human. She realized with complete certainty that he was *enjoying* her discomfort. Enjoying it greatly.

Helena tried to stand so that she might place some distance between them, but Frederick grabbed her wrist. This time the sketchbook fell to the floor without interruption. She whimpered, heard herself telling him to let go of her, and struggled to no avail as he pulled her to him.

He stood up, and his gut pressed into the softness of her belly.

"Frederick, please . . ."

Her whimpers seemed somehow to inflame him, so that as her struggles grew more ferocious, his smile widened and his fingers dug into her. His grip became more powerful, and more painful.

He dragged her toward the love seat and, when she tried to stand her ground, hoisted her off the floor and carried her the rest of the way. He threw her onto it so hard that Helena's head struck the wooden frame with enough force to momentarily disorient her. But the moment passed, and she looked up to find him advancing upon her.

"Frederick, no!" she cried as he came at her. "Something's got hold of you! Please—"

"No, you're wrong, sister," he said, his eyes feasting upon her as he brought his weight to bear. "Something's got hold of *you*."

Helena screamed as he pulled at her nightgown, tearing her bodice and exposing her soft, white breasts to the lamplight. She tried to cover herself, but he grabbed her arms and held them above her head. His strength was uncanny.

As he undid his breeches, she closed her eyes, praying that this was all a nightmare, or an episode of insanity. Perhaps *she* was the one who was ill, and she would wake any moment, safe in her own bed.

With one hand he pinned her arms against the love seat, and with the other he raised her nightdress above her hips. He tore away the cotton undergarment that was his last obstruction, forced her legs apart, and thrust himself inside.

Something tore in her. Her mind shrieked in denial as she was violated.

Then Helena screamed, blackness billowing in her mind, swallowing her. As she slipped into unconsciousness, the reptilian eyes of the jasper-and-lapis figurine looked on, dolefully enjoying the show.

~

CHARLIE WATCHED AS the last remnants of purple faded from the sky, creating an inky backdrop that offset the pale glow of the moon. The night brought with it a chill wind that ruffled his hair and raised gooseflesh on the back of his neck.

The winter had been long, and he was used to the night coming early. Now the spring had arrived, and though the evenings were still chilly, daylight lingered longer. It was after six o'clock when he left the flower shop and started the long walk toward home.

Still, the night was coming on fast. He hadn't thought much of this at first, but as the wind and darkness grew, wariness crept into his mind.

The whole area by the river played host to many a criminal deviant. Before the home secretary, Robert Peel, had created the Metropolitan Police Force just a decade earlier, the criminal element in this part of London had made it almost uninhabitable. There were still areas down around the docks that were unlivable, though far too many *did* live there. Beggars, thieves, and harlots, mostly. Men wrapped in stinking, filthy rags, shrill women, and barefooted children with blackened eyes and bloodied cheeks.

Charlie had been one of them, once upon a time. But he had left the filth of Shadwell behind.

Not very far behind, of course. He still walked through those streets every morning and every night, getting to and from the shop. Conditions in the city had improved, but the danger of such lost, ignored districts remained. Even now, only the very stupid or the very wicked dared walk these streets alone. Knowing the peelers patrolled the city was cold comfort in Shadwell, where even the quiet echo of a footfall in an otherwise empty street would be cause for alarm.

Charlie put his hand in his pocket now, and felt the hilt of his dagger. There weren't many in this neighborhood brave enough to mess with Cold Metal Charlie's business. He wouldn't have categorized himself as the murderous sort, but there might be others, long since dead, who would decry that opinion. Still, Charlie picked up his pace as he passed the yawning mouth of a dark and fetid alleyway. There was risk in every moment of his life, but there was no sense in taking unnecessary chances.

Charlie's no fool.

The smell of the Thames was rich and meaty in his nostrils as he hurried down the cobblestoned street, avoiding eye contact with passersby. The stink of gutted fish and human waste at times made him want to gag, lending speed to his feet. As a young, towheaded boy, he had wandered the twisting streets near the docks, always looking to stay one step ahead of the law. His petty thieveries might well have consigned him to a long, dark stay in Newgate Prison.

Now that he was eighteen, and knew the ways of the world, he wasn't so terrified of being caught. He was smart, and knew how to wield a knife. He had only one weakness—women—of which he was well aware, and therefore stayed clear of the music halls and other immoral houses where prostitution was commonplace. Time spent with the ladies took his coin and left him no better off than he started.

But then, around the next corner, he saw a small, dark head and a petite body clothed in shimmering gold and red. The figure slipped out of a darkened alleyway up ahead, so that he found himself collected in her wake. He began to follow her as she made her way languidly down the street. Surely, this was no prostitute, Charlie mused hopefully. Indeed, he had no qualms about removing his trousers, as long as he didn't have to empty his pockets first. Fortunately for him, there were ladies as could be counted upon to be cooperative, if they took a fancy to him. And a handsome lad he was, or so he had been told.

The woman—more like a girl, really—must have realized that she was being followed, but she gave no sign that she cared. Charlie kept his distance at first, but as she turned in to another darkened alleyway, he picked up his pace so that he wouldn't lose sight of her in the maze of backstreets.

I'll just follow her to her destination, make sure she gets herself to where she's going, safe and sound, he thought. But he knew in his heart that he was hoping to at least get a closer look at this shimmering creature who so carelessly made her way through the festering boil that was Shadwell Street.

Through a window he heard the sounds of a fight, of men and women celebrating the violence, cries of pain and fury.

He hurried on after his quarry.

It might have been a trick of the half-light, or the lack of same, but Charlie found his eyes drawn to the swing of the girl's hips as she walked. It was as if she was purposely slowing her gait, to tease him with the nearness of her sex, to excite a lust inside him. He found his body responding, falling into rhythm with hers, riding her from fifteen feet behind.

She turned her head, and he caught a glimpse of honey skin and delicate bone structure; coal-black eyes bored into his own. She mouthed the words, *Come with me . . .*

Abruptly, she turned down a blind alley, disappearing into an inky darkness. Charlie could feel his loins tighten, all the blood in his body pooling there expectantly.

He made a mental note of how much money he had with him. He had no doubt now that she was a high-class prostitute who had been, for some unknown reason, forced into working the slums. She had been purposely leading him toward some anonymous darkened alleyway, where she would spread her legs and take his money. So with a smile on his pockmarked face, he moved toward the alleyway. In his mind, he could already feel the smoothness of her naked hips pressed up against his own.

When he arrived at the end of the alleyway, he stopped to allow his eyes to adjust. All that awaited him were three monstrous, contorted shadows. He looked around wildly, trying to locate his prize and an escape route at the same time.

The girl was nowhere to be seen.

Before he could turn and run, the three shadows emerged into the moonlight.

So Cold Metal Charlie, who had endured all the horror and ugliness, the cruelty and debasement that Shadwell Street had to offer, just screamed. Long white, saliva-flecked teeth gleamed against the darkness. Yellow eyes appraised him hungrily.

"No—" Charlie began, but no sooner was the word out of his mouth than the horrors descended upon him, ripping him to bloody shreds, savoring every piece of Charlie until there was nothing left of him but a pile of picked-over bones.

Four

Smoke clouded the gloomy interior of the Three Goats' Heads, a pub in Wandsworth Road where Horatio often met with J. W. Clark, a former cook and sometime layabout who had earned over the years a reputation as a friend to all, a trusted confidant, and an inveterate drinker.

He had other facets to recommend him as a companion, however. Though he hid it well, he was a man of deep conviction, and thus when it appeared that a bit of information might be useful in certain noble endeavors, J. W. Clark could be counted upon to discover that information.

His ability to do so seemed to know no bounds. In truth, whenever he and Horatio sat down for one of their regular chats, J. W. inevitably had stories to tell.

Tonight was no exception.

The laughter in the pub was loud and raucous. A barmaid cut across the floor through an ocean of wandering hands, bringing a tray of pints to a table just opposite the one Horatio and J. W. shared. She didn't so much as glance their way, which suited Horatio just fine. J. W. was in the midst of his latest account, and it was fascinating indeed.

"You're sure it was the earl of Claridge?" Horatio asked, knitting his brows.

J. W. ran a hand across the stubble on his chin and studied the table in front of them. There were two empty pints, as well as two others not entirely drained. The one in front of Horatio was half full yet, and J. W. eyed it thirstily.

"The earl, aye. That's the word. Went mad, he did. In the middle of a dinner party hosted by the bishop of Manchester. An august occasion if ever there was one, I'd say. That's the word. Claridge went a-bedlam, apparently. Got himself alone in the library with the bishop's niece. Her screams brought the rest at a run and they caught him, redhanded like, trousers down, trying to pluck her maiden flower, as it were."

"Or, at least, that's the—"

"—word, yes. So you've said," Horatio finished rather impatiently. He cleared his throat. He was no stranger to a woman's garden of delights, but had never approved of such cavalier talk. There was such a thing as propriety.

"Of course, it's all been hushed up, hasn't it?" J. W. continued.

"I wish I could be astonished," Horatio sighed. "Have you heard any further? What's to be done? I can't imagine the bishop would press the matter, given the black mark such idle talk would leave on his niece's virtue."

J. W. tapped a finger against the side of his head. "Right you are, Admiral. A clever sort, you are. Always said so. The earl's been put under lock and key. Sanatorium, they say, but not one where you'd ever find a commoner."

"Please don't call me that. I haven't been an admiral for quite some time."

The man nodded sagely. "Aye, well, none of us have been much of anything, have we? It's been far too long since I manned the stove aboard ship, sir. So you'll forgive me if I fall back on old habits, yeah?"

"Of course, J. W." Horatio nodded. "And you'll let me know if you hear anything further about this, won't you? It might be simple madness, but we know all too well that oftentimes such things are more complex than they appear."

As he spoke, he watched the barmaid cross the floor again. She ignored the fingers that grazed her bottom and thighs, but swatted away any hand that crept too near her breasts. Horatio thought it must make it difficult for her to navigate among the tables with her tray laden with ale and whiskey.

"Indeed we do, sir," J. W. said, his attention returning to the unfinished pint on the table before him. He ran his tongue out to wet his lips. "Say, how are the young ones coming along, the new Protectors?"

Horatio smiled. "Quite well, I think. It's no simple task, adjusting to having such responsibility thrust upon them—not to mention the magic. Can you imagine having that sort of power burning in you, more than any mystic master, and yet having only the skill and knowledge of a novice?"

"Think I'd be scared of me own shadow, if it was me," J. W. said.

"That's why they're remarkable," Horatio replied proudly. "They have so very much to learn about the supernatural and about how to wield their magic, but they both have natural skill and discipline that have kept them alive until now."

J. W. stared once more at the pint on the table. "It's good to hear you've so much faith in them. I only wish we could raise a glass and drink to their health."

The barmaid came toward them. Horatio smoothed his jacket and attempted to appear as though they had been discussing something more mundane. The woman didn't even glance at him as she cleared the glasses from the table. J. W. gazed longingly after the half-full pint as she set it on her tray, but he said nothing.

Balancing the tray precariously, she wiped the table down with a rag. A loose tendril of hair fell across her face and she blew at it, but kept at her task. Horatio watched the line of her jaw, the icy blue hue of her eyes, and the way her bosom heaved with the effort.

"You are lovely, my dear. Why do I have the feeling it's been far too long since anyone told you that?" he asked.

She reacted not at all, standing up to survey her work. Her eyes narrowed in consternation as she at last looked in Horatio's direction, and he felt a moment of triumph. Had his words touched her?

Then she leaned forward and ran her rag over the back of the chair, wiping it down, her hand and forearm passing entirely through Horatio's chest as though she were made of nothing but smoke and starlight.

But that wasn't the case, of course, and he knew it all too well, sitting there in the back of the Three Goats' Heads. For a few minutes' time, with all the talk and the laughter and the companionship, Horatio had allowed himself the illusion of life.

Though more than thirty years had passed, Admiral Lord Nelson didn't like to dwell on the lingering tragedy of his own death.

～

MORNING MIST MOVED in patches across the lawns of Ludlow House, yet the sky revealed scattered islands of blue. The sun had begun to combat the gray cover that attempted to throw its influence over the land, and William Swift was just optimistic enough to believe that it would succeed, at least for a time.

Two of the tall windows in the breakfast parlor were open, and he found that he was grateful for his frock coat. There were roses in a vase on the buffet, and their alluring scent whisked about the room, mingling with the smells of breakfast.

As a child, William had loved breakfast the most. He could recall with utter clarity the sort of grand event that each morning had brought, with his grandfather Ludlow and his mother and father gathering around the table, doing their level best to keep William and little Tamara from making a shambles of the entire proceedings. Mother, God rest her, had indulged her husband and father-in-law in equal portions to her children, so that every surface in the room was laden with food. The dumbwaiter would be arranged neatly with marmalade and jams, and there would be fresh cider, coffee, and tea atop the pier cabinet.

There would be oatmeal with sweet cream, cold veal pies, sardines with mustard sauce, grilled kidneys, bacon, and beef tongue with hot horseradish. An entire sideboard would be dedicated to half a dozen varieties of bread and rolls of differing grains, with butter and honey beside them, complementing the orange marmalade and assortment of jams on the dumbwaiter. William's favorite had been the cherry jam.

Father and grandfather had indulged in Spanish brandy, eschewing the French for reasons born more of politics than of taste.

Servants had hovered around them, one cadre to serve and another to remove the detritus.

He had loved the structure to the whole proceeding, the very orderliness of it all, the way all of the dishes had been arranged with such precision. And the food itself, of course . . . the multitude of textures and flavors. What he had loved best, however, had been the way that this breakfast tradition had brought the family together around the table. Young William had listened to the adults talking, and merely the sound of their voices in conversation had given him a sense of safety and security; the confidence his grandfather had always exuded had planted a seed of confidence within William himself.

Ah, how times had changed.

Mother had been gone so long that she was little more than bittersweet echo in William's heart, but in her memory the traditions of the house had continued. Until the previous year, of course. Until Ludlow had been murdered in his own bed by hideous beasts of unnatural origin, and Henry Swift had been taken by the evil that presently occupied his flesh. William did his best to continue tradition within the household, for Tamara's sake and for his own.

His efforts were undermined by the presence of the demon upstairs.

Oblis.

William didn't like to discuss his suspicions with Tamara. Not because she was of the fairer sex—he had never confused *fairer* with *weaker*, at least not where Tamara was involved—but because he was frightened that she might concur.

William thought his father was gone. He believed that the Vapor, the cruel demonic presence that lived within his father's flesh, had cored the man in order to take up residence. He feared that if they ever found a way to exorcise the demon, Oblis, all that would remain would be the brittle shell of a man who had once loved them.

But as long as he did not raise such fears with Tamara, she could not confirm them.

And so, as he did each morning before setting off to Threadneedle Street, William finished his own breakfast, then took a clean plate from the buffet. It was damnably hard to keep servants in his employ of late. The ghosts frightened them. Their current staff consisted of Farris, the butler and head of household, and Martha, who was Tamara's lady's maid. Martha oversaw three other maids, none of whose names William could remember. They rarely stayed long enough for him to bother.

There were a groundskeeper, two cooks, and a new stable boy. But there were no more servants attending to breakfast at Ludlow House. He and Tamara had decided it. Perhaps part of their decision was a reluctance to pretend to the happiness of a bygone era, though William preferred to attribute it to simple practicality.

He considered himself quite the pragmatist.

These days William rose much earlier than Tamara, and was generally out of the house before she deigned to descend for her own breakfast. This morning the breakfast buffet consisted of oatmeal, kippers, bacon, and bread. William did still enjoy his cherry jam, and there was always orange marmalade for his sister.

Upon the fresh plate, William placed a small portion of each item. He poured a small glass of cider, unwilling to bring a hot beverage upstairs, given what had happened the last time he had done so. The coffee stains still lingered in his gray twill trousers.

Rather than walk past the parlor out to the front entrance, so that he might use the grand staircase, William went through the kitchen and up the narrow servants' steps. The house was very quiet this morning, mercifully devoid even of the usual ravings of the demon. It ought to have been peaceful for him, but there were times that the quiet haunted William.

It should not have turned out this way. Even in the wake of their grandfather's death, even without Father being in control of his senses, there ought to have been more life here.

A spark of something. Of family.

William hoped that one day soon he, himself, might alter the state of things, with a wedding to Sophia Winchell. That there would be children, and that perhaps Tamara might find herself a suitable husband. Perhaps the house would be filled once again with the orderliness, the hope, and the confidence that it had once had. Despite the truth of their lives, their status as Protectors, and the evil that lingered in the very air around them, he held out this hope.

Despite his practicality, he still dreamed.

Nearly quiet as a ghost himself, William made his way up to the top of the house, to the corridor that led to the room where his father was imprisoned. Where his father *was* the prison, for the demon Oblis.

The mist had continued to burn away outside, and as he passed open doors he could see sunshine splashing into the rooms on that upper level. Yet the end of the hall remained in shadow, and at first glance Queen Bodicea seemed solid as any woman, fully fleshed. Her Majesty stood with her back to him, her spectral hand propped upon the door of the former nursery as though she was listening to something within.

For a moment, William allowed his gaze to linger upon the breathtaking curve of her backside and the languorously heavy weight of her breast as she leaned forward. This latter he caught only in side view, yet it was enough to bring a rush of blood to his cheeks.

He averted his gaze, never comfortable with her nudity. There was nothing brazen about it. Rather, it was an expression of her defiance to the dark forces arrayed against them all, a bold statement of her confidence. And it was also somehow a facet of her mourning. William had never had the audacity to inquire further.

"Bodicea?" William ventured, almost in a whisper.

The phantom queen glanced over her shoulder, wild hair tumbling in front of her face. Her eyes were alight with intelligence and curiosity. She extended one ghostly hand and beckoned him with a long finger. William balanced the plate in his hand and went to join her at the door.

Bodicea made room for him. Though he would have been able to pass right through her insubstantial form, neither of them would have been comfortable sharing space.

As he neared the door he heard a pair of voices engaged in energetic conversation, or some semblance of dialogue at least. Both of the voices were familiar.

One belonged to the demon, Oblis, and the other to William's father. But where Oblis most often spoke in Henry Swift's voice, rather than his own horrid tones, there was a difference. For when Oblis spoke, and the voice of Henry Swift answered . . .

"Father," William whispered.

". . . them alone, I beg you," Henry pleaded, his voice muffled by the door.

"I'll do with them as I please," the demon replied.

In his mind's eye, William could picture the two of them speaking with the same lips, facial expression changing with each shift of persona. He glanced at Bodicea, arching an eyebrow curiously, but she only nodded toward the door, indicating that he should continue to listen.

"I can see it in your mind. Do you think I am asleep, when you suffocate me here inside? I witness every bit of your filth. I suffer the torture of knowing how you conduct your depravity with my voice, using my hands."

A terrible sadness gripped William's heart. His father had rarely spoken with such strength of conviction, yet it offered no comfort. If this was real, and not merely Oblis toying with him, then he knew he ought to rejoice at the idea that his father still lived.

Yet to know what he was experiencing, every moment of this damnation . . . William could scarcely breathe.

"Of what importance is that to me?" Oblis mocked. *"There is nothing you can do. You always were a very small man. That's why there was so much room in here for me."*

"What are you hiding?" Henry demanded. "You listen to the voices in the ether. I know, because I hear them, too, though I cannot understand the languages they speak. Yet I have seen the way you flinch at their words, the way they trouble you."

"Of course you cannot understand, rodent. The tongues of devils are not for human ears. But to me . . . Your offspring might cage me, old fool, but I am not alone.

"The masters of the deepest pits speak my name, and I heed them. All

the merriment of Hell unfolds for my amusement. I am eternal, sir. And if I desire it, I shall occupy this tender, rotting husk of yours until it stumbles its last, and the rush and throb of blood subsides.

"*Darkness is patient, Henry Swift. Ever patient. Ever vigilant.*"

There was a pause that followed, long enough that William became concerned. He wanted to look upon his father's face, to see if he could locate the man behind those eyes, instead of the demon. But when he reached for the doorknob, Bodicea grabbed at his wrist.

Her fingers were cold upon his flesh and he looked up at her, startled. It required constant focus for a ghost to make contact with the physical world. Their yearning for the richness of life caused most ghosts to concentrate upon the senses, so that they could see and hear and smell. Taste was possible, but only briefly, as their ephemeral substance could not contain food or drink more than a moment, if at all. Touch was the most difficult. It required intense focus for a specter to make contact with the natural world.

The supernatural, however . . . that was different.

The Protectors of Albion were human, but they were suffused with the supernatural. It required far less concentration for a ghost to touch William or Tamara than an ordinary man or woman. The touch was fleeting, for maintaining that concentration was difficult, but it was possible. The knowledge was what caused William to be so unsettled that Tamara had allowed Byron such access to her boudoir.

Now, though, Bodicea's grip on his wrist was like cold iron.

And then her fingers passed through his flesh and bone, insubstantial again. But her message was clear. He should be silent and listen. There might be something to be learned, here.

When at last Henry spoke again, William was surprised to hear laughter in his voice.

"Do you mean to tell me that your masters—these things from the deepest pits, as you say—they know where you are?"

"*Of course. Nothing escapes their notice.*" Oblis snorted.

"And yet they do nothing to free you? Apparently you are even farther beneath their notice than I had thought. I'm both amused and disappointed. I'd hoped I warranted a more fearsome devil. Not some hellish court jester who—"

"Enough!" Oblis roared. "*You speak only at my sufferance, fool.*"

"And why is that?" Henry asked. "Why allow me my voice at all? Could it be that you know the truth? That you have been abandoned? You want to be quit of your prison just as much as I wish to be free of mine. Perhaps, if you agree to leave me, Tamara and William will permit your departure."

The demon laughed then. The sound was sickening, so that William felt bile burn up the back of his throat. He could barely hold on to the plate of breakfast he had brought for his father. For the demon, so that his father would survive.

Now he glanced at Bodicea. Her eyes had narrowed, and rage danced in them. If she had a voice in the decision, Oblis would not be allowed to leave. Not after what the demon had done to her daughters, those long centuries ago.

"*You are a fool, Henry Swift,*" Oblis sneered. "*Whatever you have seen in the depths of your own soul, you are mistaken. I enjoy the company of your children. I enjoy the pain in their eyes, every time they see me. In fact . . .* William, *it would be lovely if you would abandon your eavesdropping now, to bring me my breakfast before the kippers have gone entirely cold.*"

William froze. He held his breath. Oblis knew he was here. Perhaps he had smelled the bacon, or the kippers. Perhaps that meant the demon had known he was listening to the entire exchange. Which, in turn, called into question all that William had gleaned. How much of what had been said was for his benefit? Was it all an act? Did his father really still have a voice? A mind?

A soul?

"Damn you," William whispered as he balanced the cider glass carefully and turned the knob. He shoved the door open with the toe of his shoe and entered the room.

His father sat in his chair, as always. For just a moment, a sliver of an instant, really, he thought he saw the true Henry Swift in those eyes. Then the demon twisted Henry's lips up into a smile.

"I do so love breakfast," Oblis said in his father's voice. "Do you remember, William, those wonderful breakfasts we had when your mother was still alive? Each one a celebration of family."

It was as though Oblis could see right inside his mind, inside his heart.

"Damn you," William snarled again.

With a dark chuckle, Oblis lowered his chin so that he was staring up at William from beneath a heavy brow. "Something nasty in the air, young Master William. Something ugly. A plague of poisoned souls and twisting hatred. The darkness sings with it, and rejoices. Another strain of magic takes the stage and all the foot soldiers of Hell sit back and watch, waiting for the curtain to rise and the show to begin. Oh, you and Tamara are going to be very busy soon, William. There is going to be screaming, and blood. So very much blood."

William wanted to strike him and force him to be silent. Oblis often muttered about the voices of Hell, about the workings of devils that would threaten Albion soon. But there was something in his tone this morning, something out of the ordinary. Usually he intimated that he would be a part of the mayhem, but not this time. In his ravings this morning, he implied that some *other* force was at work.

A tremor of dread went through William.

"What do you know, demon? What is this plague you speak of?"

Oblis laughed. "I do like you, boy. You and Tamara both, though obviously for very different reasons. I could help you. Might be that I could be indispensable. But what pleasure would there be for me in that?

"Unless . . ." Oblis grinned obscenely with Henry Swift's mouth as he let the sibilance issue into the room.

"Unless what?" William glared at him.

"I have enjoyed the intoxicating scent of your Miss Winchell, whenever she visits. She is unique. I can tell that I should like to see her face, to *meet* her."

"Absolutely not!" William replied, fumbling with the breakfast plate so that a slice of bacon dropped to the ground.

"No?" Oblis asked playfully. "Ah, well. I can afford to be patient. Of course, so many will have died by then . . ."

William refused to allow the demon the satisfaction of a reaction. So he picked up a kipper and popped it into Oblis's mouth, preventing any further response. He fed his father's possessor as quickly as possible, but the conversation was over.

The very idea that he would expose Sophia to the horror of what his father had become, to the perverse tongue of Oblis, was madness.

And yet even when William at last left the room, numb and exhausted from his emotional sparring with the demon, Oblis's words echoed in his mind. What if some terrible darkness *was* afoot?

Could the demon actually be of use to them?

~

TAMARA AWOKE WITH an idea.

For weeks she had been scribbling away at a lurid tale of murder and damnation, a brand-new penny dreadful concerning a man, possessed by a demon, stalking women of ill repute and dragging them to a cavernous lair beneath the city. Into the shadowy recesses where the Fleet River—namesake of her nom de plume—traveled underground.

In the months since Ludlow's death and her inheritance of the power, she had written very little. This new tale, *Underneath,* was intriguing to her, yet it was a chore to write. She seemed to have difficulty finding the words.

How could she make thrilling fiction, portraying the darkest fears of humanity, knowing that the truth was darker still?

Yet this morning she fairly bounced from her bed and slid into her robe, tying it tightly around her. Through the window, she saw that the day had begun as gray as most Highgate dawns, but there seemed promise of sunshine, and the promise was ever and always enough for her.

The lace curtains danced in the breeze that slipped in through the narrowly open windows. It occurred to her that she didn't know the hour, that there must be breakfast awaiting her downstairs. But Tamara didn't have time for such concerns this morning.

Her muse had spoken.

Though she had plenty of space in her own chambers for a writing desk, Tamara had worked only in her late grandfather's rooms, ever since his death. She went out through her anteroom and opened the door to the hall, where she nearly collided with one of the maids. Melinda, she thought.

"Oh, miss, pardon me," the girl said quickly, backing away as though afraid Tamara might bite her. Melinda carried heavy, embroidered draperies in her arms.

"Not at all," Tamara said, smiling. "My fault entirely. Not looking where I was going."

Yet the idea seemed to panic the girl. "No, miss. I can be very clumsy. I'm sure you—"

"I tell you, it was my own clumsiness. Really. Don't give it another thought, Melinda."

In her uniform, with her straight brown hair and narrow features, the girl seemed plain. But when Tamara called her by her name, she positively glowed. The maid lowered her head in a sort of curtsy, accomplished in a way that wouldn't drag the drapes on the ground.

"So tell me, how are you finding Ludlow House?" Tamara asked. "Do you like it here?"

The girl's eyebrows shot up. "Miss?"

Tamara grinned. "A simple question, Melinda. Do you like it here?"

Once again the girl refused to look her mistress in the eye. "Very much so. It isn't . . . well, it isn't like any other house I've ever been in, is it? Never quite know what's around the next corner." The maid looked up now, clearly anxious to find if she had offended her employer.

"You're not frightened then?" Tamara asked. "So many of them are."

"Frightened?" the girl asked, as if she had forgotten her place. "Whatever the nature of those who come to stay at Ludlow House, miss, everyone's been quite kind to me. I've known what it means to be frightened in my life. This house is far more welcoming than my father's, I daresay."

The final words escaped her lips as though she wished to hold them back, but could not. Even before she finished speaking, her eyes widened with the fear that she had been too bold.

"I'm sorry, mum. I don't know what got into me."

Tamara uttered a tiny gasp, as if horrified. When she saw the alarm in Melinda's eyes, she laughed softly. "Don't worry, Melinda. It's not your outspokenness that caused me to react, but the fact that you called me *mum*. Dear Lord, don't *ever* do that again, I beg you. I'm hardly older than you are.

"As for your thoughts about Ludlow House, I'm pleased to hear them. And to have you here. Now you'd best get on with your work. Those drapes are for the rear guest room, I suspect. The room Mr. Townsend uses when he is here."

With a tender smile, the maid nodded. "Yes, miss. They've only just arrived this morning, but Mr. Farris has asked me to hang them straightaway."

"Off with you, then," Tamara said warmly.

She watched Melinda hurry away toward the rear stairs, and then turned in the other direction, following the corridor past the master bedroom that had once been occupied by her parents, and later by her father alone. Other rooms stood empty, ready to receive visitors. William's quarters were at the opposite end of the house, but that wasn't her destination.

Tamara reached the door to Ludlow's quarters and did not hesitate.

Inside, she crossed the outer room and paused at the interior door for only a moment before opening it. Dust motes danced in the brightening daylight. The room was precisely as they had left it subsequent to his murder. The servants had seen to it that the blood had been scoured from the place, the damaged furniture removed, and the broken glass replaced. Even so, the place resonated with the terror of those moments, just as it did with decades of love and laughter. Such things were now intrinsic to the memory of Ludlow Swift.

Tamara turned her back on the bedchamber and went to the writing desk that had belonged to her grandfather. All around her were the mementos of his career as a stage magician. The craft was only now beginning to earn respect. As a gentleman, Ludlow had risked public humiliation because of his passion for illusion and prestidigitation. For magic. But he loved the showmanship of it, and would have given up all of the lands and wealth he had inherited before he quit the stage.

There were items from all around the world in this room, from the smallest artifacts to the largest sculptures. There were tribal masks of North Africa and weapons from the Far East. Some of his tricks were there as well, black boxes that Tamara was still unable to make work.

Someday, she vowed, she would teach herself some of Grandfather's old tricks, if only to remember him better.

Tamara sat down at the desk. She pulled out a fresh piece of paper and dipped her pen in a bottle of ink, then smiled to herself. All the troubles she had faced trying to write *Underneath* dissipated as she considered her new mission.

She would come back to that story. But she had realized that the way to shatter the obstacles that had been built up in her mind was to stop attempting to ignore the dark truths she had learned over the past few months, and to embrace them instead.

What better way to do that than to write them down?

Ever since the previous day, when Oblis had intimated that some evil was rising, Tamara had been haunted by his words, and by his tone. Sinister, yes, but also curious, as though the demon actually wondered how it would all turn out. She had meant to mention it to William on their carriage ride to the Wintertons', but their disagreement regarding Sophia had caused her to put it off. She would have to tend to that today. It was probably nothing, but certainly it bore some investigation.

For the moment, however, she wanted to set pen to paper while the creative flame still burned. It had occurred to her that the way to dispel the mental obstruction that had interfered with her writing was, simply, to write from experience.

To the reading public, they would seem like nothing more than the latest outlandish tales from the pen of T. L. Fleet. No one would ever believe that they were true. She would write about the Protector of Albion, about the inheritance of great powers and great responsibilities, and all she need do was change the names, embellish the details.

After a moment's consideration, Tamara touched pen to parchment, whispered under her breath, and then took her hand away. She dictated, and the pen began to write, to transcribe her words:

There are things in this world that do not belong here—evil things.
Supernatural creatures that are neither myth nor legend. They are, in fact, quite real. These Enemies of Humanity would like to claim the world for themselves. Yet, in every corner of the globe, there

*are those who stand in their way—mystical guardians who protect
the primeval essence of the Earth.*

*The soul of England—its mystic spirit—is called Albion.
Throughout the centuries it has had many champions—brave men
and women who fought to maintain our freedom.*

*For many decades, one man kept Albion's enemies at bay. Using
magic and intelligence, Ludlow Swift protected England from the
encroaching darkness.*

But change is in the air—

With a deep satisfaction, Tamara sat back and regarded the paper.
She read the words again, then frowned at her own error. Quickly she
gestured and the pen dipped into the ink again and then flew to the
paper, where it scratched out her grandfather's name.

*Yes, wouldn't William simply love it if I told the tale of our legacy
with the family name intact?*

She contemplated what name might suffice to take the place of
Ludlow's. Not to mention her own, and William's.

As she considered the question, there came a knock. Tamara gestured to the pen and it lay down, even as she rose from her chair. She
opened the door to discover Farris standing there.

"Good morning, Farris."

"Good morning, Miss Tamara. I apologize for the intrusion, but
Miss Winchell has arrived, in search of Master William."

Tamara might have been concerned that some crisis had arisen,
but since the death of her own father the infuriating trollop had made
it her practice to visit Ludlow House whenever the urge took her, always with her lady's maid in tow.

"Hasn't William already departed for Threadneedle Street?"

Farris shook his head. "No, Miss Tamara. I'm to drive him shortly.
He has gone up to deliver breakfast to the elder Mr. Swift."

"Ah, I see," Tamara said. She pulled her robe more tightly around
her, perhaps due to the chill in the air that eddied through the house,
or perhaps due to the mention of her father.

Farris had done precisely the right thing in coming to fetch her.
Had he simply told Sophia where William was, she might have been

bold enough to seek him out. And though the Swifts had few secrets from Sophia Winchell, after the horror that led to her father's demise it would be ill advised for anyone to be in the presence of the demon Oblis unless it was absolutely necessary.

"Well done, Farris. I shall come down right away, and attend to my own breakfast at the same time. Let us see if we cannot distract her until William joins us."

Farris nodded, and turned to depart.

Tamara considered putting on a more appropriate housecoat, but decided against it. So she put away her scribblings, followed Farris to the stairs, and descended with him. Sophia would be inside already, no doubt, in the sitting room, with her chaperone standing by at the ready to testify to her virtue. And, sure enough, that was exactly where Tamara found her.

Sophia glanced up quickly at her approach, only to be crestfallen at the sight of her host.

"William is not at home then?" Sophia demanded.

"Good morning to you, as well, Sophia," Tamara said archly.

"Yes, good morning," the other woman said.

"My brother will be down shortly. He hasn't yet completed his morning regimen, I'm afraid."

Sophia raised an eyebrow. "Nor have you, it seems."

Tamara smiled, showing more teeth than necessary. "I have a more relaxed approach to such things. In fact, I was only now about to have my breakfast. Please join me, won't you? For a cup of tea, at least."

There was a moment's hesitation, a moment during which burning embers would have frozen in the frosty air between them. Then Sophia stood.

"I'd be delighted."

Delighted to leave your watchdog in the sitting room, Tamara thought, noting that Sophia made no attempt to bring her maid into the breakfast parlor. And the old woman offered no protest. Either she possessed little sense of propriety herself or she was paid well enough not to notice the liberties Sophia took.

The kippers were cold. Tamara was used to that, of course. She might have demanded a fresh batch be fried for her, but she never liked to trouble anyone about such trivial things. And, in fact, she had come to like them cold.

She sat at the mahogany table with a plate of bacon and kippers, ignoring the oatmeal that was coagulating in a tureen on the buffet, and sipped from a cup of coffee. Martha saw to it that there was warm coffee in the breakfast parlor for as long as it took Tamara to wander downstairs in the morning.

Sophia wanted tea and seemed entirely put out to have to fix her own. She chose the Indian blend, which Tamara had never liked. As she prepared her cup, she glanced over at the table.

"You really ought not to sully yourself with the company of John Haversham."

Tamara blinked twice, then turned to stare at her.

"Pardon me?"

"Please, Tamara, don't feign ignorance with me. My cousin John is as amiable a companion as one might find. He is an artist and a philosopher, and women find such things irresistible. Yet if he is enlightened, then he is an enlightened rogue. A true scoundrel, whose reputation is so unsavory that to appear in public with him might be enough to besmirch even *your* reputation."

The words were insulting enough, but it was the tone that almost pulled Tamara out of her chair and across the room with the urge to slap Sophia across the face. For several moments she breathed through her nostrils, not daring to open her mouth for fear of what rebuttal might issue from it.

"I thank you for your concern," Tamara finally said, wondering if her disdain was as evident in her manner as she hoped. "Nevertheless, I find your scandalous relation quite charming, and intend to accompany him to an art exhibit this evening. Provided I have the appropriate chaperone, I am certain a single excursion won't be enough to entirely dismantle my social standing."

Sophia sniffed. "Or so you hope. Well, I did warn you."

"And it was so thoughtful of you," Tamara cooed.

Sophia carried her teacup and saucer across the room and went to sit in the chair opposite her hostess. Tamara tapped her right foot twice and slipped her left hand beneath the table, contorting her fingers into a bizarre arrangement.

"*Caveo,*" she muttered.

The chair in which Sophia had intended to sit slid backward half a foot. Young Miss Winchell's slim derrière narrowly missed the edge of the seat, and she plopped onto the floor, spilling tea all over her cashmere shawl and spotting her bodice and wide skirts.

Tamara allowed herself a tiny smirk while Sophia was out of sight beneath the level of the tabletop. She heard the woman curse in a very unladylike fashion. Sophia's hands gripped the top of the table, and she hauled herself upward, her eyes ablaze with fury and humiliation.

"How *dare* you, Tamara Swift?" she demanded.

"How dare I? Why, I haven't moved from my chair, dear Sophia. Are you feeling all right? It isn't like you to be so ungainly."

The woman's face turned a deep shade of purple.

"I know exactly what you're capable of," Sophia whispered through gritted teeth.

Tamara met her gaze without blinking. "Darling, trust me, you have *no* idea. Perhaps you'll consider minding your own business in future."

Sophia sputtered. At any moment William would appear, and Tamara both dreaded and relished the idea of his arrival in the midst of this repartee. One day, perhaps, he would see Sophia as the bitter, belligerent cow that she was. Until then, however, he would continue to blame Tamara for any and all friction between the two. Tamara was resigned, yet seeing the expression on Sophia's face was worth any recrimination that might be forthcoming from William.

Before either of them could speak another word, Farris entered the breakfast parlor and cleared his throat. Sophia fumed, breathing heavily even as she snatched up a lace napkin and began to dab at the tea stains on her clothing.

Tamara daintily sipped her coffee and raised an eyebrow, looking toward the entrance.

"Yes, Farris?"

"Miss Tamara, you have another visitor. A gentleman caller. If you'll pardon my presumption, given his comportment I suspect he arrives with unpleasant news."

Unpleasant news. Tamara didn't like the sound of that. Given what her life had become, she had acquired a new definition of *unpleasant news.* It was with some trepidation that she went out to greet her mysterious guest.

Five

Troubled by the demon's words, William descended the stairs carrying a tray that bore the remains of his father's breakfast. Oblis's breakfast. It irked him terribly that the demon could so easily unsettle him. But the fiend's suggestion that he bring Sophia into that room—into the presence of such evil—festered in his mind, no doubt as Oblis had intended.

Yet what of his other ravings? What of that supposed conversation with William's father? And his intimations that some new breed of darkness was on the rise.

William decided to discuss his concerns with Tamara, and straightaway. The demon was, in all likelihood, only toying with him, but if there was any truth to what Oblis had said, it was their duty to seek out this nascent evil, and quash it before it could present a real threat to Albion.

In the beginning, he had tried to shirk the duty he and Tamara shared, and return to the normal life he had mapped out for himself. In time, though, he had come to realize that the responsibility could not be ignored. Evil was afoot in the world, and just as Maurice Swift had once chosen his nephew Ludlow, so had their grandfather chosen them to take up the fight. Now William looked on their commission with pride, and he knew that Tamara felt the same.

He sighed as his foot touched the last stair and he moved toward the kitchen. What a strange dichotomy their relationship had become. First he would discuss with Tamara his concerns about the things Oblis had said—the dread that had blossomed within him, even worse than the tremor that was always there in the demon's presence. Then he would plead with her to forgo the tryst she had set with John Haversham for this evening. Sparks would fly, but there could be only one outcome. She simply *had* to listen to reason.

In the back of his mind, there lingered a third conversation he knew he could not escape. But there was no easy way to broach the subject of his invitation to the Algernon Club tomorrow night . . . an invitation that had not been extended to her. An ordinary girl would understand that it was a gentlemen's club, and therefore off-limits to the fairer sex. But Tamara was no ordinary girl.

This girl loved a good fight.

"Excuse me, Master William—"

Farris had stepped through a door from one of the side rooms, and his large, callused hands were anxiously twisting together. Since William still held the breakfast dish in his hands, Farris took it immediately.

"I'll take this to the kitchen, sir."

Yet he made no move to proceed. Instead he cleared his throat and stared down at his feet.

"What is it, Farris?"

"It's something with the mistress, sir. She's had some bad news, I'm afraid. She's in a right state—"

The man was saved from having to explain further when the sitting room door swung violently open and Sophia emerged. Relief washed across her face when she saw him. William heard sobbing, and was momentarily confused, thinking it came from Sophia herself, that she might be unwell.

Then he realized his mistake, rushed to the door, and saw Tamara standing by the window. One hand covered her mouth, and her face was flushed with emotion.

"Tamara, what is it—" he began, rushing to her. She fell against him, and her whole body was shaking.

"It's Helena, Will, she's . . . she's taken her own life."

The words tumbled from Tamara's lips. William stiffened, then he looked up at Sophia, who nodded, her eyes large and wide.

"But . . . that's impossible," William stammered. Helena had been a friend of Tamara's from time immemorial.

"I'm afraid it is the truth. As much as I regret to give it credence."

The voice was soft and masculine, with a hint of grief floating underneath the calm surface. William had been so overwhelmed by his sister's agony that he hadn't even noticed the presence of another in the room. Now he turned and saw the man whom he knew must be the courier of this horrid news. Helena's half brother, Frederick Martin.

∾

THE ATMOSPHERE IN the sitting room did not feel real. Everything seemed transparent, as if shimmering in the morning light. Like a dream. Tamara put her hand to her own cheek. The feeling of soft skin under her fingertips wasn't enough to pull her back to reality. Even if she had pinched herself, she didn't think that it would have proved that this was the waking world.

When Frederick had first told her the news, she had refused to believe him. Her dear friend had absolutely no reason to take her own life, as far as Tamara knew. Helena lived in a world of her own creation, a place that was fueled with charcoal and paper and paint. What urgency could issue from that place, such that it would cause her to kill herself?

"I, myself, took dinner with her," Frederick recounted. "She seemed . . . how should I phrase this? Out of sorts, not herself." His words were low and melodious in her ear. It struck Tamara that his attitude was odd for someone who was dealing with so horrifying a discovery. Indeed, grief did strange things to people.

"It wasn't until this morning," Frederick continued, "that a passing charwoman found her body on the sidewalk below Father's study. She must have thrown herself from one of the windows during the night—"

The door to the sitting room opened, and Martha came in bearing a tea tray and some sandwiches. Thus interrupted, Frederick waited until the maid had finished her duties and departed before continuing.

Tamara had placed herself in one of the armchairs, so that she could be alone. It also had the added comfort of smelling faintly like the tobacco her grandfather had loved to smoke in the evenings.

Oh, how she wished that her grandfather were here now. He would know exactly what to say to make her feel better. Tears pricked the inside of her eyes, but she blinked, defying them.

She looked to where Sophia and William had taken up residence on the love seat. She noted how closely they sat together. *Hypocrite,* she thought. He went on and on about her lack of propriety, but he refused to see how improperly he behaved with Sophia. *And she encourages it.* Even as Tamara watched, Sophia's fingers snaked toward William's, between the seat cushions.

Tamara gnawed her lower lip. She didn't really care how her brother conducted himself, save that he held her to a different standard. It was more that she so disliked Sophia. And that this morning—just this morning—she so wished that she could have William to herself.

Helena was . . . she could scarcely credit it, but nor could she deny it . . . her dear friend was dead. Gone. Tamara wanted to sit with her brother and mourn. She didn't feel like competing with Sophia for her brother's attention.

Martha gave her a gentle nod, eyes full of concern. The pity that infused Martha's gaze made Tamara's heart hurt. She realized that Farris must have told their housekeeper the awful news.

When Martha had gone, Frederick once again took up his tale.

"I've sent a message to Father at Oxford. He and Mother will return as soon as it can be arranged, I expect."

Tamara watched him closely now, as he spoke. There was grief in his voice, but his eyes . . . his eyes said something else. He was upset that Helena was gone, that much seemed clear, but there was something strange in his gaze. Something *wrong.*

Granted, he and Helena weren't as close as she and William, but most likely that was because they hadn't spent as much time together. Still, she had sensed genuine affection between them.

What, then, was this?

Frederick stood to inherit everything upon his father's death. Helena had her dowry, but that wouldn't interfere with the bulk of the moneys.

Even so, suspicion lingered in her. There was an air about him that she could not dismiss. She was glad that her housecoat covered her arms so that Frederick could not see the goose bumps that rose instinctively in his presence.

Out of the corner of her eye, she saw that William's gaze was fixed on her. Did he sense it, as well? She turned and raised an eyebrow, as if to ask that very question, and William replied with the slightest of nods.

So he felt it, too. This made Tamara even more nervous. She felt horribly underdressed in her housecoat. She grabbed the robe's ties and pulled them taut around her middle.

Poor, sweet Helena. She did not deserve this death.

A shudder ran through her as she began to weep softly once more. Tamara wiped her tears away with the back of her hand, hoping no one would notice. Oddly, it was Sophia who offered her a handkerchief. She took the piece of dainty silk and dabbed at her eyes.

Something broke inside her then. She could barely see the room around her as tears clouded her vision into a muddled blur.

～

John haversham stood in his dressing gown, watching life pass by on Brook Street beneath his second-story window. He had decided that tea was best taken with a view. He had returned home fairly late the previous night, and wasn't quite awake as he watched an older gentleman in a double-breasted frock coat try to navigate his way against the flow of pedestrian traffic. He wondered where the old man was going in such a hurry.

His observations were interrupted by entrance of his valet, Colin Thompson. Colin was in his early thirties, but carried himself like a man of much greater maturity. He rarely spoke, but when he did,

John listened carefully. Colin was crafty and wise beyond his years, with a hint of Machiavelli in him. They met when he had come to John's aid once during a bar brawl in Bowmore, and ever since he had been John's man.

Colin was dressed in his signature black waistcoat. He eschewed color whenever possible, preferring the severity of black. Only if they were spending the evening by the docks would he stoop to put on clothing of dirty brown.

His light blond hair was shellacked to his egg-shaped head, and his blue eyes were rimmed with red, tired from the drunken evening they had shared the night before.

"I've made arrangements for a carriage to fetch Tamara Swift at her home this evening," Colin said. His voice was low and even.

John nodded, pleased that everything was as it should be.

"Thank you, Colin."

The valet bowed and left the room. John watched him go, then settled into the high-backed dressing table chair he had pulled over to the window and returned to his morning tea.

He had set up residence at Mivart's less than a year before, but already he felt more at home in these accommodations than he ever had at his childhood residence in Edinburgh. In Scotland, he had lived under the rule of his overbearing father, Weatherly Haversham—a self-made entrepreneur who owned a dozen whiskey distilleries. Even at the University of Edinburgh—where he had studied the classics—his father's notoriety had made it impossible for him to exist on his own terms.

Then, after university, just when he had thought himself free of his father's rule, he had foolishly allowed himself to be railroaded into running one of the man's floundering distilleries on Islay. Five years later, when the establishment was finally turning a profit, he had left Scotland, a husk of his former self, hungry for independence and the chance to write.

He had realized then that in all his life, he had never truly been himself. When he sought his fortune in London, it had opened his mind and soul, finally allowing him to be free. There was no one here to tell him what to do, and that suited him very well, indeed.

The rooms he kept weren't extensive, but they were quite comfortable, even for a man who had been raised as a child of privilege. He took such pleasure in maintaining his own lodgings that sometimes he found himself staying inside until late in the afternoon, using the hours to write extensively, then leaving only to dine at Hancock's on Rupert Street. Or, on special occasions, dressing down his appearance and his accent enough to pass as a working Scot at the Highland Mary.

There, he would take off his shirt and pull a few bloody noses, just for the love of sparring and the free whiskey his skill brought him.

Boxing was a love he had acquired at university, but it was only while in Bowmore that he realized what an asset he possessed. In the public houses of the small Scottish village at the head of the Loch Indaal, he had honed his skill, using his hands to butcher flesh with a beauty and grace that won him many an admirer—male *and* female.

John had found that, once they knew what he was capable of doing, the men who worked under him respected him, and did what he asked. He was able to win their allegiance in a way that his fortune could never have accomplished. This was a whole new world for him, far from the one in which he had been raised, and he found that he liked the coarseness of the working class, their drunken embellishments and homespun kindnesses, far more than the pretensions of the upper classes.

Tomorrow night, if all went as he intended, he would put on his rough clothes, and he and Colin would go out to the Isle of Dogs, looking to fight. It would be a reward he gave himself for all the hard work he had put into negotiating this evening's outing with Tamara Swift.

"Excuse me, sir?" Colin had returned, and his voice cut through his ruminations. John looked up to find the valet standing in the doorway, one eyebrow raised curiously.

"Yes, Colin?"

"A Mr. Llewellyn requests a moment of your time," Colin announced. He had an odd look on his face that piqued John's curiosity.

"Show him in, please."

Colin bowed and left the room, only to return moments later with a little old gentleman. It was the same fellow John had watched fighting the flow of pedestrian traffic on the street several minutes earlier.

"Good morning, Mr. Haversham," the man began. "Charles

Llewellyn, from the club. The director has sent me with a note," he continued, pulling a white envelope from his pocket. "This is for you."

The fellow's wizened face was small and ratlike, his eyes two black coals lodged in sunken sockets. John held out his hand, and wondered which gutter in Blackheath had produced this fellow. Llewellyn reached out and surrendered the envelope. It was light as a feather.

"Thank you," John said. The old man grinned, revealing rotten teeth, or what was left of them.

Colin reached into his waistcoat and pulled out a farthing, handing it to the old man, who nodded happily and made a grand bow to both host and servant. Then, with a snap of his fingers, he disappeared right in front of them.

"What the Hell—" John began, but then he stopped, realizing that this "Mr. Llewellyn" was more than a simple messenger.

"I suppose that's what we get for associating ourselves with magicians," he finished, offering a crooked smile. Colin nodded, but still he looked around the room to make sure the old man had really gone.

John tore open the envelope and pulled out a crisp sheet of starched paper. Colin crooked his neck to get a look at the note's contents.

"What's it say, then?"

John looked up, smiling broadly now. "It appears our excursion to the Isle of Dogs must wait. I've been summoned to the Algernon Club tomorrow at noon. I think our work has received some notice, Colin, my boy. Now let us pray that our evening at the Egyptian shall bear fruit."

Tonight, he would further endear himself to Tamara Swift, thus gaining a foothold in the famous Swift family. Thank God his cousin Sophia was so easily manipulated to do exactly what he required of her. She had facilitated his invitation to the Wintertons' the night before. Without her, certainly, he would still have found a way to encounter the Swifts, but her connections made his job that much easier.

His only real challenge came in the guise of Tamara's brother, William.

He and William had met only once before, though he doubted

that the easily agitated Mr. Swift would remember their first encounter. It had been a long time ago. *Well, better that he know me by reputation than experience,* John thought wisely.

He handed Colin the invitation, which the valet read hungrily.

"I think you're coming up finely, John. Finely indeed," Colin said, nodding at the invitation.

"I'll be exactly where we'd like in no time at all—*if* our luck continues to hold," John agreed.

"It's not luck, John," Colin countered. "It's magic."

～

$\mathbf{T}$HE MINISTER OF the choristers was looking for a pair of truant boys. He was sure they had slipped away from the others earlier in the afternoon, and he thought he knew exactly where to find them.

During the course of the year, it was typical to find a new chorister or two trying out the acoustics in the Whispering Gallery. He was sure that he would find the boys there, one on either side of the gallery. One would be speaking in low tones, the other listening intently. Even he, many years ago as a young chorister, had experimented with the seemingly arcane trick that carried the spoken word up and across the elliptical dome, clear as a bell.

As he walked past the choir stalls, the minister marveled at the beauty of St. Paul's. The old cathedral had been destroyed in the Great London Fire of 1666, and it had taken more than a decade before a design was approved by king and clergy, and rebuilding had begun in earnest. Now, almost two hundred years later, he could only give thanks that the architect, Christopher Wren, had seen fit to outfit the cathedral with its extended nave and spacious quire, elevating St. Paul's, in his humble opinion, above all other Anglican edifices.

He had always loved the quire best, probably because it had been the scene of many of his schoolboy triumphs. But there was still something to be said for the rich oak of the stalls and benches, the way his feet tapped out staccato beats as he walked on the cold stone floor.

Somewhere in the distance he heard raised voices, and a childish squeal. This wasn't play, though—it sounded like alarm. It made him pick up his pace, worry propelling him forward.

He knew there were others in the church who felt that he didn't discipline the boys harshly enough, but he was of the belief that in teaching one should spare the rod and spoil the child. He was known to be extremely lenient with his charges, and would punish them only if they showed genuine waywardness.

I hope this evening will be a case in point; that the Whispering Gallery will be my only stop, he thought.

Yet there was something in the air, something that made the hairs on his arms and the back of his neck stand at attention. Something that told him this night was going to be different.

The voices were coming from the southern edge of the Great Circle. He made a left and followed the sounds to where the southern transept connected to the nave.

"Boys . . . ?" he began, but stopped at the sound of hurried footsteps.

The two missing boys seemed to appear from out of nowhere, and ran directly at him. The minister of choristers stepped out of the way just in time to avoid being knocked over by the younger of the two, Benjamin Reynolds. The boy paused for an instant in midstride as he turned his wild-eyed gaze on the minister, then continued onward as fast as his feet could carry him.

"Boys!" he called out, angrily now, hoping to stop them in their flight. But they ignored him. He listened to the clattering of their feet, then heard the crash of doors as they found their way out through the west entrance.

The silence that followed was uncanny.

What in Heaven's name? the minister of choristers thought as he stood in the empty cathedral. Never in all his many years had he experienced someone else's terror so intimately. The very air around him seemed unnaturally cold.

A shudder went through him as he turned to gaze into the shadows from whence they'd come.

A young woman stood there, barely more than a girl. She was an exotic beauty, clad in red and gold, with skin like caramel and eyes that seemed to reflect myriad colors in the flickering lamplight. Behind her there were only shadows.

"What's this, then?" the minister asked. "What are you doing back there, miss?"

With a smile that stirred forbidden desires within him, she took a step backward and seemed to be swallowed by the shadows.

"See here, miss, you can't—" he began, but then stopped himself. He had the strangest feeling that she was not merely hidden in darkness, but no longer there at all—that he was talking to himself.

The minister frowned, thinking again of those terrified boys. Surely they had not been frightened by the sudden appearance of a beautiful woman. Boys were boys, after all.

Confused, he went to the narrow stairs and started down to the catacombs beneath the cathedral. He had never enjoyed going down here, had always found the place a bit morbid, in fact. But he did so now, and wondered where the woman had gone, and why the boys had chosen to wander among the crypts. As youngsters he and his friends had avoided the place, but then again, he had never been terribly adventurous.

If it had been chilly up above, it was colder down here than he liked. He had never been partial to London weather, but this was different. There was something *strange* about this coldness, as though all the warmth had been leached away. He felt chill bumps rise all over his body, and his chest ached as he drew in a frigid breath.

He smelled them before he saw them.

They were enormous things, with a reptilian aspect that conjured ancient, primal terror in his heart. Their skulls were swollen approximations of human heads, their skin varying shades of mottled brown and green, rough as though covered with scales. They plunged their long arms and thick, webbed hands into a tomb that had been forced open, stone fragments scattered in a tumble on the ground.

Others had been shattered, as well. The withered remains of the honored dead had been torn from their crypts, bones and rotting clothing strewn across the floor. Lord Nelson's beautiful black marble tomb was in ruins. Some had merely been staved in, but many were destroyed.

One of the monsters was gnawing on a jawbone. Some of the cadavers were fresh enough to have flesh and muscle still attached to the bone, but the creatures seemed more interested in the desecration of the tombs than in feasting on the dead.

This was sacrilege. An abomination.

He gasped with terror.

At the sound, three pairs of wide yellow eyes turned to regard him. He took a step back and slipped on something wet, then fell to the stone floor. With his free hand, he reached out and touched the substance, recoiling immediately from the trail of viscous filth the monsters had left in their passing.

The stench of the place—of the demons—filled his nostrils, and he retched. The minister scrabbled backward, trying to get his feet beneath him, to pick himself up and run away.

The trio of demons came for him, then, a grotesque rictus etched on their faces, exposing sharp, pointed teeth.

Only when they at last descended upon him, claws and teeth tearing his flesh, did it occur to him to scream. The sounds of his terror—of his murder—traveled up the stairs, all the way to the Whispering Gallery. Forever after, choristers would insist that they could hear the echoes up there, beneath the dome of the cathedral.

That morning, every stone trembled with the sound.

Six

The specter of death had invaded Ludlow House once again. The news of Helena Martin's suicide had cast a pall across the entire household, a heavy, gray blanket of grief that seemed even to dim the light that came through the windows, and made the air feel close and oppressive.

The death of her grandfather was still fresh in Tamara's memory, and here she was once again, enduring that uncontrollable part of mourning. Memories erupting into the mind without having been summoned, pictures of life and laughter, all so very bittersweet.

She took a deep, shuddery breath and forced away the mental picture of her dear friend. Helena was gone. Tamara had loved her, but her friend would be poorly served if grief was her only response. Something had to be done, and she wondered if the answers might begin with Frederick. There was something off-kilter there.

Frederick had suffered a terrible emotional blow with the death of his half sister. It made sense that he should seem somehow askew. *But it's more than shock, or grief,* Tamara thought. She wasn't certain how she knew this, but she was sure of it nevertheless.

There was something Frederick wasn't telling them.

Tamara stood by the tall windows in the sitting room, arms crossed in front of her, still dressed in her nightclothes and robe. The smell of flowers came to her on a breeze from the garden outside and calmed her somewhat. She had to put her thoughts in order.

"Frederick, please accept my condolences," William said gently. "We share your grief, old friend, and hope that you know that if there is anything we can do, any service we can provide, you have only to ask. Meanwhile, I'm afraid that my own duties require my presence at Threadneedle Street. You'll understand, of course—"

"Of course," Frederick replied without hesitation. "Say no more, Will. It was boorish of me to arrive at your doorstep unannounced."

Tamara raised an eyebrow at that, and turned from the window to regard the two men. William had stood to depart, and Sophia was perched like so much decoration upon the edge of a settee. Her expression of sympathy was so much like a mask that Tamara almost laughed at the garishness of it. She wondered if even Sophia could tell which of her emotions were genuine, and which counterfeit.

"Nonsense," William told Frederick, holding up a hand to forestall any argument. "It's only natural that you would come." He tugged at his sleeves, smoothing out his morning coat for his journey to the office. "You're welcome here anytime. And Tamara and I are pleased that you sought us out in this dark hour."

Tamara remained silent. Her focus was on Frederick Martin, for she noticed that his speech seemed oddly stilted. It was as though each word, each turn of phrase, was rehearsed, like dialogue from a play. Perhaps it was a result of his tragedy that he seemed so distant and disoriented. Yet there was something else.

Wasn't there?

Indeed.

Their visitor nodded. "That means a great deal to me." He glanced at Tamara, and a flicker of something in his gaze made her tighten her robe again. "I didn't want you to hear word of her death from anyone else. And to be honest, I think I wanted a few moments in the company of others who loved her."

He lowered his gaze, and for a long moment Tamara felt guilt beginning to creep into her heart.

This was Frederick. Had her experiences with demons and magic made her so thoroughly callous that everything and everyone became suspect, that she could not bring herself to lend comfort to or share her pain with a friend?

Frederick sighed heavily and shook his head. "I ought to be off, as well." But there was a question in the cadence of his voice, leading Tamara to respond.

"Not at all. Stay and talk, if you'd like," she said quickly, hoping that Frederick would take her bait.

He did, nodding as he offered a wan smile of gratitude, first to Tamara and then to her brother. William twitched, brows knitting as he turned to look at his sister.

"Tam, I've just said I'm due at Threadneedle Street. I'm afraid it would be inappropriate—"

"Inappropriate?" she said, challenging him with her gaze. "For me to offer a fresh cup of tea and some biscuits to a man I've known since he was a boy? When he's had the shock he's had today?"

She tried to communicate her intentions with her eyes. She needed her brother to understand. He had to let her continue her subtle observation of Frederick. There was something important to be gleaned from him about the tragedy. She was certain of it.

Then she laughed softly, and shook her head. She crossed the room and took Frederick by the hand. He had been standing, close to William, but now she led him to a high-backed chair by the window.

"If you cannot stand the thought of company just now, Frederick, by all means go along. I shall certainly understand. But otherwise, please do stay, and have another cup. We'll talk of Helena—"

Just saying her friend's name brought images into her mind again, but they were no longer pleasant. She had seen enough blood and death in recent months that she couldn't help but paint a mental picture of the gruesome death Frederick had described. The woman had fallen four stories to her death. Her skull must have been shattered on the stones of the street, and who knew how many bones. There would have been blood, but before that, tears and terrible anguish.

"I do wish she'd have come to me, if she was in distress. If only I could have spoken with her, perhaps—" Tamara whispered, and her own voice quavered such that when she looked at William again, she saw sorrow mirrored in his eyes.

Her brother nodded. "I'll speak to Farris. Martha is engaged at the moment, so I shall have Farris attend you in her stead."

William gnawed his lip for a moment, and then turned to Sophia. "Since your own chaperone has traveled with you this morning, Miss Winchell, would it be possible for your carriage to convey me to my office?"

Throughout the exchange she had remained silent, showing sound judgment for once. She had met Helena perhaps three times, and Frederick only once, so their contact was comprised entirely of social pleasantries. Now, though, she stood up as though tugged by marionette's strings.

"Indeed," Sophia agreed, as though her opinion mattered. "Under the circumstances, William, it's the only sensible thing."

Tamara almost laughed out loud at the absurdity of their charade. Then she realized the subtlety of what William was engineering. Martha was engaged in her household duties and certainly could have been brought to the sitting room. No, William wanted Farris there.

So you did *sense something wrong, something unpleasant,* Tamara thought. *And you're going to let me continue the investigation.*

Sophia, of course, only wanted the chance to be as alone with William as she could manage. Tamara saw through that, as well, and the thought turned her stomach.

Just give in, once and for all, dear brother, she thought. *Have a scandalous romance, and be done with it. Even marry and have a thousand babies. But put an end to this absurd charade!*

"That would be fine," she said aloud.

She glanced at Frederick again, and he replied with a pitiable smile. Once again she was troubled by guilt over her suspicion. But not so much as to make it disappear.

～

W HEN THE ARRANGEMENTS had been made and William had gone off in Sophia's carriage, Tamara stood in the foyer of Ludlow House and the loss began to sink in.

The news had hit her quite hard when Frederick had first arrived, but as she had tried to understand what had happened and to comfort him, she had pushed her own feelings away. Now that she had a moment to herself, the truth cut her deeply again. Her hand fluttered up to cover her mouth and she took several deep, shuddering breaths. Fresh tears sprang to her eyes and streaked her cheeks.

There was a hollow in her chest, an emptiness that broke her heart. Helena had been her friend, yes, but she had also been Tamara's contemporary. It was as though she, herself, had died, or a part of her.

"Oh, sweet Helena," she whispered.

Then, with a final, deeper breath, she gathered her wits and wiped away her tears. Her eyes were bound to be red, but she could do nothing about that. And it was a silly concern to begin with. Frederick would expect her to grieve. Her tears were the natural response, and nothing to be ashamed about. If she was worried about appearances, she would have retired to her rooms and changed her clothes.

"That's just what you ought to do," she told herself, comforted somewhat by the sound of her own voice. By its realness, the assurance that she, at least, was still alive. Foolish, yes, but necessary.

Farris was standing outside the sitting room when Tamara reached it. Despite her intentions, she hadn't yet dressed.

"Are you all right, miss?" he asked, and though he stood with his hands crossed in front of him, the true gentleman's gentleman, some of the reserve normally required for the job had slipped. There was concern in his eyes, and she appreciated it greatly. With her father inaccessible and her grandfather dead, there was no paternal figure in her life.

"Not by half, Farris," she confessed, patting him on the arm. "But I shall be."

When Tamara entered the sitting room, Frederick was no longer in the high-backed chair by the windows, where she had placed him. He had retreated, instead, to the settee recently vacated by Sophia. That corner of the room was swathed in gray shadows that seemed somehow appropriate for mourning, as though they fed upon the grief left in the wake of Helena's death.

Frederick looked up at her arrival, and in that instant something flickered across his face. A flaring of the nostrils and narrowing of the eyes that caused Tamara to utter a tiny gasp. Was there something else there, as well, a gleam in his eyes that—in those shadows—could not have been the glint of reflected sunlight?

She thought that there was.

For a moment she forgot to speak, forgot even her covert purpose. She had planned to announce that she would go upstairs and dress properly, but now all thoughts ran from her head.

"Is there anything you require, miss?" Farris asked. "I've ordered up a tray of tea and biscuits for Mr. Martin."

Tamara stared at Frederick for a moment longer, before turning to shake her head. "No, thank you, Farris. If I have another cup of tea this morning, I'm afraid I shall float away."

The comment was tossed off without a thought. Her mind was focused entirely on Frederick now. With one glimpse of him in those gray shadows, the conflict was over, and suspicion had won out over grief and guilt.

"Farris, give us a moment, would you?"

The butler arched one eyebrow, but did not question the propriety of her request. The Swift household had functioned, of late, quite differently from an ordinary English home. Certain things took precedence here over decorum.

"Certainly, miss." He excused himself with a nod and left the room.

When Tamara turned back to Frederick, she thought to catch that look upon his face again. But there was only pain there now. She felt the distant echo of it in her own heart, yet for the moment, her grief would have to wait.

"We have known each other a very long time, Frederick," Tamara began, crossing toward him, moving out of the sunlight and into the shadows near the settee.

"Since you and Helena were children."

Tamara crossed her arms. "Indeed. Then you'll forgive me, I hope, for being frank."

He blinked, and there was something odd about it. A hint of something behind his eyelids. Tamara stared at him for a moment, but he did not blink again, and it would have been far too awkward for her to simply gaze at him until he did.

"By all means," he said, gesturing for her to continue.

Still she hesitated. She realized now that something about his face wasn't quite right, but she couldn't determine what it was that was catching her attention. His skin looked dry and pale, and in the shadows there seemed to be a faint green hue, as though he was about to be sick.

"Are you all right?" Tamara asked. "Perhaps the tragedy has taken too great a toll."

Frederick smiled, then, and it was the smile that unsettled her the most. Sickly and far too wide, it lent a madness to his aspect that was more than grief. He seemed to her like a man who was on the verge of a scream.

"I'm as well as can be, pet."

Pet. When had Frederick Martin ever had the audacity to call her that? Never, of course.

Once again Tamara cinched her robe tight. Then she sat on the edge of a chair, only a few feet from the settee. Out of arm's reach, but close enough for her to see him clearly in the shadows, and watch his eyes. Her hair rustled in an unseen wind that did not come through the windows. Unexpectedly, there was the crackle of magic around her, and she let it surge up inside her. If he saw the way the dust motes in the air seemed to swirl in tiny storms around her fingers, sparking from time to time, so be it. Something was wrong here. Very wrong. And Tamara was determined to get to the bottom of it.

"Frederick, for some reason that I can't explain, I cannot help but feel that you haven't been completely honest with us. That there is some detail of Helena's . . . of her death that you've omitted. I can't imagine why. Perhaps you wish to save her"—*or yourself*—"some embarrassment or other. It occurs to me that there might also be some danger, and perhaps you hope to protect me from it."

There was that smile again, disappearing quickly, as though he had forced it away.

He shifted uncomfortably on the edge of the settee. He seemed on the verge of becoming agitated, as though it was difficult for him to remain seated. Frederick flinched several times in quick succession, and his chin flew up as though out of his control. He recovered, scratching the back of his head, but she felt sure this was an effort to make it appear as if his actions were voluntary. But she wasn't convinced.

Dear Lord, what is wrong with him?

Finally Frederick rested his hands on his knees, gripping them so the knuckles were white. He averted his eyes, as if he could no longer meet her gaze.

"Please," Tamara said. She reached out to lay her hand upon his. "Clearly, you are troubled by more than grief. I can see it. Speak to me, Frederick. What haunts you? Did you see her die, is that it? Was there something . . . unnatural about her end? How *did* Helena die?"

There it was. The question.

The shadows around Frederick's face deepened as he turned to face her, so that she could barely see his eyes in the pools of darkness. Then he leaned forward, and she saw the pain etched into his face, the weight of it, and her heart broke for him. This was what she had seen in him before. It had to be. The poor soul had witnessed some horror, something his imagination could not bear, and his mind was fraying at the edges.

His hand felt cold in hers. The skin papery. She ran her thumb over it and heard it rasp.

"No," he whispered.

Tamara felt her chest tighten, and a sick knot of realization twisted in her stomach. She glanced down and saw that her thumb was cracking his skin where she touched him. And there was something else.

Patterns.

There were scales on the back of Frederick Martin's hand.

She went to pull her hand away, but he grabbed it, held it, his strength uncanny.

Tamara looked up into his eyes and they were alight now, with a ghastly yellow gleam. She had not imagined it before. His face was no longer papery. A sheen of some sort covered it. He blinked at her and she saw again that second set of lids, the nictitating membranes that covered his eyes.

"Holy God," Tamara cried, and she forced herself to her feet, trying to yank her arm away.

Frederick gave a wet, throaty laugh, and tugged back. His strength was that of a madman. It was so great that he easily pulled her down onto his lap. The greenish tint to his flesh deepened as he grinned, face stretching, and he began to paw at her.

His hand closed upon her left breast and quickly found her nipple through the soft fabric, pinching her hard enough to make her whimper, pain shooting through her. Under normal circumstances Tamara could have destroyed him with a simple spell, but her focus was lost. And her mind was a tumult of conflict. This was Frederick Martin. Freddy, the half brother of her childhood friend. A boy she had teased, hiding her giggles behind a girlish hand.

For all her suspicion, when the reality became clear, her mind wasn't prepared to meet it. This simply could not be.

She gasped as he dropped his hand and grasped her leg. His touch on her bare flesh was moist and cold, almost sticky. He dragged his fingers up her inner thigh toward a more intimate destination.

Nausea roiled in her gut and she tried to force his hand away, kicking out, struggling to escape his grasp. In all her life she had never felt such crippling horror, the chill of the idea, of what those fingers might do.

But that wasn't what drove her over the edge.

It was his tongue.

Frederick shot out a thin tongue that must have been eleven or twelve inches long. Where he licked her face and her mouth, his tongue *stuck* for a moment, before retracting back into his throat. Pain throbbed where her breast had been bruised and twisted. She felt his fingers forcing her legs apart, but it was this sickening abomination that finally broke her.

Tamara opened her mouth then, and screamed. Her shriek echoed through the sitting room, and she was sure through the entire house, as well.

Heavy footfalls sounded, and Farris burst into the room. She felt a swell of love for the man as she saw his gentlemanly reserve shatter, and the fury that swept like a storm across his face. His big hands clenched into fists, and he ran across the room toward the settee.

Frederick laughed and threw her aside like a sack of rags. Tamara struck the chair in which she'd sat, then tumbled to the floor. She pulled herself up just in time to see Helena's brother—or whatever he was becoming—take two blows in the face without flinching. He only grinned and clouted the butler on the side of the head.

Farris crumpled to the ground, either stunned or unconscious.

Then the hideous man, whose features seemed less and less human with every passing moment, smiled a jagged smile and shot out that toad's tongue. That's what he seemed to her now. A reptile. A toad. The clammy, greenish flesh and those eyes, that tongue . . . this wasn't Frederick Martin anymore.

Tamara felt shame rise up inside her. She was a Protector of Albion, and had faced far more powerful evils than this. With William at her side, she had faced down one of the Lords of Hell. But Helena was dead, and Frederick was ruined somehow, and it was all too close to her. Tamara's heart had been vulnerable, and it had made her weak.

Even as it now made her strong.

An errant wind blew up around her, magic coursing through her body and her hair swirling around her. The gust was so powerful it whipped at her nightdress, but she ignored the salacious gaze of the monster that slinked before her.

Tamara threw both hands up into the air, fingers contorted as though she were conducting a mad symphony.

"*Malleus attonitum!*" she cried.

A rush of power swept around her and she hurled it across the room. The space that separated them seemed to waver with the force of the magic that went passing through it. The spell struck the twisted man like a cannonball, throwing him across the room and hammering him into the wall. Wooden beams cracked, Frederick's head struck hard, and then he fell to the ground, perhaps eight feet from where Farris lay groaning.

Even as she marched toward her attacker, she wondered what had happened. Had Frederick been possessed, like her father was? Had he killed Helena, or had whatever killed her now decided to torment him in this way? Too many questions. But Tamara Swift would have answers.

"Miss?" Farris rasped, drawing himself up to his knees. Blood trickled down the side of his head, but he seemed clear-eyed enough. He smoothed his gray hair and attempted to comport himself with dignity.

"You're all right?" she asked.

"Not by half, Miss Tamara," the butler said gravely. "But I shall be." Tamara smiled.

As she moved cautiously toward the unmoving form of Frederick Martin, she heard a familiar sound, like fingers run roughshod over the strings of a violin. She glanced over and saw the ceiling begin to shimmer. The ghost of Queen Bodicea dropped into the room as though she had leaped from the sky. She fell to the floor, crouching instantly into a battle stance, spear at the ready.

"*Tamara!* Where is the danger, girl?" the specter snarled.

Even in the sunshine, when she was little more than a glimmer of a presence, her appearance was fearsome. Her face and bare breasts and belly were streaked with the war paint of her people, and there was death in her eyes.

"It has passed, Majesty." Tamara gestured to her fallen attacker. "But many questions remain."

Even as she spoke, she heard Frederick stirring. She saw the alarm on Farris's face and the warning on Bodicea's lips even before the long-dead barbarian queen had shouted her name.

"Tamara!"

But the sorceress had already spun, even as the twisted creature that had been Frederick Martin lunged at her from the floor, that long tongue striking at her face as though he meant to suck the eyes from her skull.

Bodicea's phantom spear whistled past her ear, and Tamara watched it impale Frederick Martin, punching through his chest and slamming him back against the cracked wall. Despite all she had seen, she gasped aloud. The weapon itself was a ghost, and useful only against supernatural creatures.

The thing that had been Frederick screamed, shrieking incoherently as he tried to pull himself off the spear. And as he screamed, he *changed.* Within seconds, where a semblance of a man had once stood, only a beast remained. A monster.

The thing wasn't exactly a reptile, but it bore a resemblance to several. There was something of the lizard in its fingers and scaly, clammy flesh, and the rows of teeth in its mouth, but its bulbous, rheumy, jaundiced eyes and sagging features and that thrusting tongue all spoke of a frog or toad. Hideous.

The thing sprang away from the wall, refusing to be stopped, tearing itself off the end of that spear with such suddenness that Tamara staggered back. The demon toad dropped into a crouch and lunged in a mighty leap across the room, to land in front of the tall windows. Farris was shouting, and Bodicea darted in a spectral wisp toward it, even as it tensed to spring again.

"*Malleus attonitum!*" Tamara shouted again.

The spell erupted from her hands and struck the creature, knocking it backward with such force that it crashed out through the windows, showering broken glass onto the lawn. But even as it landed upon the grass it sprang up, turned, and fled across the grounds.

Queen Bodicea paused in front of the shattered windows. "Shall I give chase?"

Tamara almost consented, remembering the feel of those terrible hands upon her, and the way that tongue had stuck to her cheek and lips. The monster was wounded. How difficult would it be to run down?

Yet . . .

"No. There's no way to know where the thing might lead us. Or if it serves some greater master. We'll need to see William, first. He ought to know what's happened. Then we'll decide upon our next step." She glanced at the butler, who used a handkerchief to dab at the trail of blood that still ran down his cheek. "Farris, locate Lord Byron and inform him that I've asked him to stand watch over my fath . . . over Oblis, until Bodicea and I return."

With that, the distaff Protector of Albion marched out of the sitting room, with Bodicea close upon her heels. Tamara had stripped off her robe before she had reached the third stair.

"Do you really mean for me to believe that you haven't already decided upon your next step?" the queen inquired.

"There's safety in numbers. Should anything happen to me, I'll want William to know, so we go to him first. We'll translocate. He must be told what's happened here."

"Then, I think, Your Majesty, that no matter how deeply it grieves me, I must visit the scene of Helena's murder."

⁓

The carriage rumbled slowly south along High Street. Too slowly. The windows were curtained, and only a dim light filtered in. William sat stiffly on the cushioned seat, Sophia directly across from him. Her hazel eyes seemed alight with silent, giddy laughter, and the corners of her perfect bow lips were lifted in amusement.

William used one finger to draw the window curtain back. They were passing Cromwell House, and beyond its grand façade he saw that the sky had begun to darken with the promise of rain. This momentary distraction did nothing to slow his racing pulse.

He swallowed, his throat dry and constricted.

"Is it that difficult to look at me?" Sophia asked.

He did as she asked, and found those lips formed into a fetching pout, so that his breath hitched in his chest. Her dress and bodice were a deep gold with a hint of scarlet, and against such rich color the lace frill of her cuffs and the visible hem of her petticoat were a temptation all their own.

"Your lady's maid should be riding in the carriage with us, not up on the high seat with your driver," William chided her. He felt the heat in his face, and knew he was flushed, but couldn't decide if it was the awkwardness of having to admonish her, or the thrill of the intimacy of their situation.

Sophia shook her head. "William, darling." She reached up and pushed tendrils of her hair away from her face, those hazel eyes burning into him. "I've told you before that Elvira can be counted upon for her discretion. And my driver, Mr. Milford, has been with the family for twenty-seven years."

The mischievous gleam in her eyes quickened his pulse even further, and he licked his lips, not realizing he was doing it until it was too late.

As if it were the most natural thing in the world—as if she had only her comfort in mind—Sophia slid down a bit on the cushioned seat, and her skirts rode up toward her knees. Above the tops of her boots lay naked flesh, and William felt his eyes magnetically drawn toward the sight of that pale skin, the curve of her calves.

Sophia uncrossed her legs, moving her knees apart.

William could see nothing but shadow beneath her skirts, but his fertile imagination was enough. The lewdness of her action and the images in his mind ignited wild desire in him. He shifted upon his seat, his trousers suddenly far too confining.

Sophia noticed; she seemed to take great delight in the effect she was having upon him.

"I see we're beginning to understand each other."

His face was aflame now with the heat of embarrassment and yearning.

Sophia curled her fingers around the bottom of her skirts and quite deliberately drew them upward, a curtain all their own. She raised them halfway up her thighs.

William shuddered, his breath coming in short gasps, his erection almost painful. The carriage bumped over a stone in the road and jostled them both, and he thought perhaps it jostled some sense into him, for he forced himself to look away.

Purposefully, trying to get hold of himself, he looked out the window again. They had gained very little ground. He might have gone as fast had he chosen to walk into London, and felt certain that his darling had instructed her driver to maintain this snail's pace until otherwise advised. In the distance he could see Whittington College, and on the breeze he had the scent of London town, the filthy odors of her industry and her offal.

Silently he urged the coachman to snap the reins, to speed the horses on their way.

In the intimate closeness of the carriage's interior, Sophia Winchell sighed. "William Swift, you vex me so."

He let the curtain drop, but steeled himself before he could look at her again. His arousal was still painful, and far too obvious, but he made no effort to disguise it, knowing it would only be more conspicuous.

"I vex you?" he asked, perplexed. "What on Earth are you talking about, Sophia? It seems to me that it should be the other way around. Indeed, it's clear that you understand exactly what sort of effect you have upon me. But for propriety's sake, for your *own* sake—"

"Propriety be damned." Her breasts rose with the passion of her words, and her eyes narrowed. Her expression was eager, and she shook her head, fingers tracing the curves of her body. "I want your hands on me. That and so much more. Don't you want the same?"

"More than anything in the world, of course. But at the proper time, without a scandal that could sully your name, and your family's. We'll marry, Sophia, and then—"

She laughed. "Of course we'll marry. But don't you see, Will? A wedding is something we do for society, for appearances. We'll have a feast in our honor, music and dancing, and it will be precisely the way it ought to be. And to all outward appearance, I shall be pure when I walk down the aisle. Who's to say otherwise?"

Sophia glided across the carriage to slide onto the cushion beside him. Her hands went to his face, fingers in his hair, caressing his cheeks, tracing his lips. The passion in her eyes was like nothing he had ever seen. His chest ached with the love in his heart, and his lust pained him even more. When she whispered to him, close into his ear, her voice excited him further and he quivered with it. Her fingers slid down his chest, poking playfully between the buttons of his shirt.

"My parents are gone, William. The servants in the Winchell home answer to *me*, and they shall keep my secrets." She leaned in further, her hot breath upon his cheek. Her fingers danced downward, and he flinched as she began to trace small circles upon his belly.

"You worry so about propriety, and decorum, about appearances, about my virtue. The weight of society's expectation is heavy upon you," Sophia continued. "But *here* is what I do not understand."

She kissed him, and William could not help himself. He kissed her back with fervor, his hands reaching up to caress her face, to run down her back, to cup the shape of her breasts. Her tongue darted into his mouth and he stiffened, a spasm passing through him, but not the final one.

Sophia put her hands on either side of his face and held him there, staring into his eyes. Her hair had begun to fall loose across her face, and his heart fluttered at the sight.

"You know there is so much more to this world than appearances. Our society basks in the illusion of normalcy every day, and hides away from the truth each night. Horrors abound that most believe to be myths and legends, but you know as much as anyone this is merely a convenient self-deception. You wield magics that no ordinary man would believe, and yet you perpetuate the fiction that all is well. That there is nothing lurking in the shadows."

William swallowed. When he finally spoke, it was with a rasp. His hands continued to move over her body, as if they operated independently of his mind.

"Without that fiction, the illusion of normalcy as you call it, society would fall into chaos. It's necessary to—"

She hushed him with her hand. Then, deliberately, she took his own hand and moved it to her chest, tugging down the front of her bodice so that her breasts pushed up over the top. William gasped aloud at the sight of the pale aureoles and rose-petal-pink nipples. Sophia cupped a hand behind his head and drew him to her, bringing his face down to her breasts.

William kissed her there, soft, gentle brushes of his lips that he first bestowed upon pale, rounded flesh, then upon the soft skin at the undersides of her breasts, and at last upon the small, taut berries that tipped them.

"This," she said, voice hitching, "is no different. The fiction is necessary. But it is a fiction, my love. My heart. We are . . . not alone in this. What society does when the lights are out . . . oh . . . and the doors are closed, and what face it puts on . . . in the daylight are two . . . two different things. Don't you see?"

William was beyond seeing. Beyond thinking. Passion raged in him, though his actions belied everything he believed.

Sophia's right hand strayed farther southward and she ran her fingers over his swollen prick, then gripped it tightly through the fabric of his trousers, and began to stroke him.

In those few moments he would have done anything in the world for her.

As though it came from a different world he heard a muffled rap, a knocking. It took a moment for William to realize that it came from the front of the carriage, and that the coach itself was slowing. The clopping of the horses' hooves became more sparse.

"Milady?" came the voice of Elvira, Sophia's maid.

With a grin, the girl moved back across the carriage to her original seat and quickly arranged her bodice. William felt dull and stupid, as if his brain were soaked in gin, for his arousal had put him in a kind of fugue state. It was only when Sophia replied to Elvira's voice, and that good woman opened the small door in the carriage that allowed driver and passenger to communicate, that William straightened up in his seat.

The maid shot him a disapproving glance as he crossed his legs to hide his condition, then reached up to smooth his hair. He was certain that even in the dim interior of the coach his face must be flaming red.

"We are being hailed from the roadside, miss," the maid said, her lips pinched in their usual sour twist. The woman was stork-thin, her face almost cadaverous, yet she had the bearing of a ruddy schoolmaster.

Sophia might rely on Elvira's discretion, but that didn't mean she had the maid's approval.

"Well, tell Mr. Milford to drive on," Sophia said sharply. "We do not stop for strangers on a street corner."

Nevertheless, the carriage was stopping, despite the commands of its mistress. Even as William wondered what would cause Milford to halt, the driver answered the question for him.

"Ah, but it's no stranger, miss, but Mr. Swift's own sister," the driver said.

Elvira, up on the seat beside Mr. Milford, replied in a low voice William was sure he had not been meant to hear.

"How in the world did she arrive here before we did?"

～

ON THE ROADSIDE, out of earshot of the carriage, William stared at his sister. "Are we even certain it was Frederick? Could it have been some sort of doppelgänger?"

Tamara shook her head. "Perhaps, but I don't think so. I've known the man too long to be taken in by such a masquerade. There is clearly some darkness at work here, Will. Something monstrous. Helena did not take her own life, that much is certain."

William saw the way her face tightened with grief when she mentioned Helena, and heard the intensity in her voice. He glanced away, regretting his harsh response to her arrival. Of course there was trouble. Tamara would not have come to him this way otherwise.

"We'll need to speak about it straightaway. And somewhere more discreet," Tamara added, glancing around at the carriage, where the maid had climbed in with her mistress. Sophia was watching them intently, irritation plain on her face.

"Of course," he said, nodding.

William turned toward the carriage and strode to the window. He reached up to take Sophia's hand. Anger blazed in her eyes, and he thought perhaps there was embarrassment, as well, though she would never have admitted it.

"I'll find my own way from here, darling. I'll call upon you tomorrow afternoon, if you'll receive me."

Sophia hesitated, aware that Elvira was looking on. "I will," she agreed. "But . . . here, William? We're to leave you off here, so far from Swift's?"

"Indeed," he said. A smile spread across his face. "You might carry us both to Threadneedle Street, of course, if you're worried about appearances. Or we might simply rely upon kind Elvira and the good Mr. Milford not to engage in idle speculation."

Sophia seemed to consider both options, but a single unpleasant glance at Tamara made her decision obvious. As William had expected.

"You may rely upon them as you would me."

Brother and sister stood together on the cobbled walk in front of the inn, the soles of their shoes becoming tacky with spilled ale, and watched the carriage rattle on toward London at far greater speed than that with which it had begun the journey.

"You know," William said, arching an eyebrow, "she *really* doesn't like you."

"Oh, that's brilliant, that is. What was your first indication?"

They smiled at each other, and then all the humor left them.

William saw the pain in his sister's eyes. He looped an arm through hers.

"We'll walk, Tam, and you'll tell me all that's happened. Don't leave anything out. And then I have something to tell you, as well, about a conversation I had with Father . . . with Oblis, this morning."

"Oh . . . you, too?" Tamara said.

A chill went through William. The demon had been toying with them both. Of course he had. But to what end?

And what, if anything, did it have to do with the death of Helena Martin?

Seven

Having no corporeal form made life far simpler. There was no urge to fill the belly with food, no need to evacuate the bowels, or even to sleep. There was beauty in human existence, but Byron found it difficult to be poetic about the need to defecate.

Truth be told, he was glad that he no longer was constrained by form, yet there was one human feature he missed so terribly that he could feel the bitterness rise like bile in his throat whenever he thought of it: sexual congress.

Oh, how he missed the silky softness of a woman's inner thigh, slick with sweat and fluid, a taut nipple caught between his teeth, the feel of rock-hard buttocks against his abdomen as he strained and thrust, the heady perfume of carnal human musk thick in his nostrils. It had been a very long time since Byron had last touched real human flesh, but he desired it still with an eternal hunger.

Only by composing his poetry was he able to quell his lustful thoughts. Byron channeled his insatiable desire into his posthumous work, so that now his poems were almost always obscene. He had read a few of his wanton verses to Tamara, and even her staunch liberalism had been challenged by their lewdness. He had watched with interest the way the blood rushed into her cheeks as he read. It had made him wonder if the blood flow to other areas of her anatomy had also been increased.

Just the thought of the Swift siblings had the power to make Byron giddy. Tamara especially. His lustful thoughts toward William ranged more toward fantasy than reality. William was too priggish to ever be enticed into an affair, but Tamara, to the contrary, was an adventurous sort. He knew that had he been flesh and blood, it wouldn't have been long before he enticed her to come to his bed for her pleasure.

Tamara was a Protector of Albion. She and William were the mystical guardians of the soul of England, connected to the ancient heart of the land and infused with its magic. There were hundreds of such Protectors in the world, each burdened with the power and duty to defend their homeland from the forces of darkness.

They were touched by the supernatural. That meant, of course, that with focus Byron himself might be able to touch Tamara. But even if she would have allowed such a thing, it would have come to naught, for he would not have been able to maintain that focus for very long.

No, the pleasures of the flesh were only a memory to him now.

Lost in his musings, Byron was returned to the present by a loud belch that erupted from the corner of the room. He looked up to find the demon Oblis staring at him through Henry Swift's eyes, a long string of drool hanging disgustingly from his open mouth. The smile that spread across his features was sickening.

"What lovely, nasty thoughts you have, my lord Byron," Oblis spat, the words foul in the air as if they had substance, the texture of filth. His grin widened as Byron's upper lip curled in disgust. The presence of the demon tainted any pleasure his fantasies might have conjured.

He despised the task of looking after William and Tamara's possessed father. It was a job he took only under duress, mostly from fear of being lashed by Queen Bodicea's barbed tongue. The queen could be very persuasive when she wanted, and she had ever been immune to his influence.

Today, however, he had required less convincing—less bullying—than usual. Once he had seen Farris's bloodied face and the mess in the sitting room, and heard the tale of Helena Martin's death and her brother's hideous metamorphosis, he had simply thanked the man for passing on Tamara's message and come upstairs to begin his watch.

Now he and Oblis glared at each other across the room. The very substance of his spectral form shuddered in the presence of such iniquity. The malevolence that lurked inside Henry Swift's frail frame radiated throughout the room.

Yet despite the evil that festered in him, Oblis could accomplish little here at Ludlow House except offend and annoy those who looked after him. The Swift siblings had spent days devising just the right combination of spells to weave through the house, and particularly this room, to keep the demon prisoner.

"Did you hear me, *ghost*?" Oblis said, as if the word were an insult.

Byron sniffed. He shot Oblis a sour look.

"You should wipe your mouth, oh castoff of the devil, and then shut it," he muttered. There were those he loved, those he feared, and those who were beneath his notice. There were very few beings in the Lord's creation whom he hated, but he knew what Oblis had done to Bodicea's daughters, and here he sat with the physical evidence of the heart-wrenching grief the demon had caused the Swifts. Yes, he hated Oblis with every fiber of his soul.

Oblis smiled hideously.

"Shall I hurt you again, Oblis? Are you simply a glutton for punishment, or do you enjoy the pain? I wonder, for that has never been one of my proclivities. If so, however, I shall oblige," Byron said, his voice thick with warning.

Oblis only broadened his smile, until it was like a gash across poor Henry's withered face.

"Do your worst, *ghost*," hissed Oblis. He strained against his bonds, his body shaking with anticipation.

But Byron was no fool. The demon wished to draw him into a fight, hoping to shatter the magical bonds that restrained him. Byron recalled all too well how Nigel Townsend had been lured into battle with the demon, only to find himself unconscious on the floor, his captive having escaped.

"If you insist, Vapor. There is a bit of verse I have been composing for several weeks now. Shall I recite it for you, with all its dramatic inflection?"

"No!" Oblis shrieked. "No poems!"

Byron laughed softly, the spark of mischief in his heart. "Oh, this is no mere poem. This is an ode to love in rhyming couplets—"

Oblis covered his ears and shrieked as if his cries would protect him from the poetic onslaught. Byron hadn't even begun to recite his latest rhyme and already the demon was in agony. It made Byron giddy.

But just as he began to clear his throat, even though the need for that was a thing of the past, he was interrupted by a ripple in the ether.

Byron looked up to find the ghost of Lord Admiral Nelson floating beside him, as grim-faced in death as he had been in life. He was altogether too serious for Byron's tastes. But that made it easy to agitate him, which was a pleasure all its own.

"You've terrible timing, Horatio," Byron moaned. Oblis perked up, looking out through Henry's wretched eyes with curiosity now that he had been saved from Byron's poetic flogging.

"But I come bearing interesting news, my friend." Horatio spoke with a clipped, nasal cadence; years of commanding naval fleets resonated in his authoritative tone. "A tale that I know you will find very curious indeed. The earl of Claridge—"

Byron snorted, "That lecherous old windbag? The self-same syphilitic glock who pokes his prick into whatever poor chambermaid he can trap alone in a room?"

Horatio began to nod, but Byron cut him off.

"I detest him."

Horatio nodded again. "Yes, yes, I'm aware of his reputation. That is why this news bears such import."

Oblis sat up and watched the two ghosts, his ears taking in their every word.

"Has he died? Passed into the ghostly realm to torment our female peers? Bodicea shall make short work of him," Byron commented wryly.

"Nothing so fortuitous as that, I'm afraid. But far more colorful. It seems the earl has gone mad. Off to Bethlehem Hospital for him, for taking liberties with the bishop of Manchester's niece at a dinner party." Though he was a phantom, a pale, translucent shade, Lord Nelson's cheeks reddened at the word *liberties.*

"So they've taken this man to a sanatorium, have they?"

The two ghosts turned to look at Henry Swift, who stared at them with a man's face and a demon's eyes. He sat on the cold wooden floor with his back against the far wall.

"Do they know the curse that ails him?" Oblis asked, his voice perfectly conversational, as though they were all reasonable men. Then he grinned, and his voice dropped to an insidious whisper. "Could they still see the whites of his eyes, or had the change already begun?"

"The change?" Byron was on guard. Though it was rarely clear, Oblis never spoke without reason. He thrived on toying with their minds, and this new gambit might be some attempt to play them for fools.

"Ask the lovely Tamara if she saw the whites of his eyes," Oblis rasped cryptically. "Before he changed."

Horatio looked askance at Byron. The one thing Nelson abhorred was being left in the dark. Years spent with the Royal Navy had only encouraged his controlling nature.

"Has something happened in my absence? Tell me . . ."

Byron nodded, understanding now that Oblis had knowingly confirmed a connection between the lecherous behavior of the earl of Claridge and the encounter with Frederick Martin.

"It seems, Horatio, that a new shadow has fallen upon the land. Albion's defenders must unite once more."

❧

The building was small and squat, with no means of illumination except the candle stubs that its occupants brought with them to light their way in its depths. There were no windows, so that even at midday the interior was black as pitch.

It was inside this inauspicious building, not far from the stink of the Thames, that many foreign treasures lay hidden, wrapped tightly in linen and then ensconced in sturdy wooden crates between layers of brittle straw.

The crates did not stay in the building long, though, as the dampness that came from being so near the water could destroy their contents.

Two men kept watch over the place, though they both tried to stay well away from the interior, preferring to *observe* the building from the safety of a nearby public house. They paid one of the young street Arabs a few coins to keep an eye out, and report to them at the public house if there was trouble.

In the past six months, they had seen neither hide nor hair of the boy except when he came for his coin at the end of the day.

There were few other patrons in the Merry Lady this early in the morning. The two watchmen sat at their usual table, a tankard of ale each in front of them. They were both in their twenties, but the younger—who was more brawn than brain in the outfit—looked much older than his companion. He had stringy red hair and close-set eyes that shone dully with the blankness of apathy. His partner, a small, wiry man with dark hair and almond-shaped eyes, had a sly expression that was prominent in his eyes, and enhanced by his tiny cauliflower-shaped ears and pointy rat's nose.

They sat like this all day, staring at each other as they sipped their ale, until one or the other passed out face-first on the tabletop. After dark, the less inebriated of the two would carry his companion back to the flophouse where they spent their nights. When the next morning arrived, they started the whole process again.

Today was like any other. They sat silently sipping their drinks. The younger of the two watched the barmaid as she wiped down the wooden counter with a damp cloth. He liked the way her breasts jiggled in her bodice as she scrubbed. She was a thick-waisted girl with a pockmarked face and greasy blond hair that she kept pinned loosely at the nape of her neck. She paid no mind to the watchman's leering gaze. There was no shortage of lecherous drunks at the Merry Lady.

The barmaid jumped with fright at the sound of the front door being roughly thrown open by a scrawny, filthy boy with long hair and a dirty face. He must have been running, for his breath was ragged in his throat. Nevertheless, he galloped over to the two watchmen and began to speak in quick bursts.

"I were watchin' . . . as you liked . . . and then there were . . . this *sound*—"

The older watchman collared the urchin and yanked him bodily toward the table. The boy was wild-eyed and unfocused, and he struggled to control his breathing, until the man cuffed him roughly with the back of his hand.

The man's voice was low and hoarse as he spoke.

"Show me."

The street was almost deserted as the two watchmen opened the door to their place of employment and stepped inside. The older man fumbled around in the darkness before pulling two candle stubs from a niche in the wall. The meager light from the candles illuminated only the first few feet in front of them. The rest of the large front room was lost in darkness.

"Damn the boy!" the older watchman said through gritted teeth.

The child had refused to go into the darkened shanty. He had led the two men back to the building, but taken off toward the docks as soon as the older watchman loosened his grip. Now they had no idea what the boy had heard or seen. They were on their own in this unsettling blackness.

They moved forward, weaving their way through the unpacked crates. The candlelight barely illuminated their way, but the men could see in its flickering that a number of the crates had been ransacked.

On the floor lay the shattered remains of some antique marble busts. A pair of paintings, their canvases shredded, rested on top of the marble debris. When they reached the next doorway, the older man paused, holding up his hand for silence.

In the inky blackness of the next room, something was breathing.

There was a low chattering sound from deep in the darkness, and then a sound like knives being raked across stone. It filled the air. The two watchmen still couldn't see past the ring of candlelight, and their faces were twin mirrors of graven fear.

A shriek tore from within that darkened room.

The men turned as one and ran for the door, but the crates that littered the floor barred their way. The younger watchman tripped and sprawled across two large boxes, his limbs in a tangle, scrambling to right himself, flailing. Exposed and vulnerable.

The other watchman turned as his partner began to scream. Frozen in fear, he watched the scene that played out in the weak glow of his candle. The thing that leaped from the darkness was massive, its head nearly scraping the ceiling. Its eyes were green-yellow coals burning in the shadows, and they fixed on him with quiet intensity, even as their owner reached for his associate, hauling the younger man up by the leg.

The fellow thrashed in the air, caught in the grip of a thing that could only be the spawn of Hell.

"Help me, Dinsmore!" the younger watchman wailed.

But Dinsmore still could not move. He stared in horror as the thing grasped the fallen man's other leg and, in one swift motion, ripped him in two. The screaming turned into a bloody, burbling sound.

That broke the paralysis. Dinsmore spun, his own voice now rising in a scream of terror that came up from some deep, primal place within him. Breathless, he ran . . . and collided almost instantly with a second hulking monstrosity.

His heart seized up as his face struck cold, prickly, stubbled skin. The thing picked him up by the shoulders, causing him to drop his candle. It fell into a pile of dry straw that had spilled from one of the crates, and the straw began to catch fire. The creature stepped away from the flames, which had quickly begun to spread, even as it drew him up to its own height, his feet dangling beneath him.

Dinsmore's eyes were wide, and the scream continued to tear from his throat, though it was more like a throaty moan now. His nostrils caught the rotted-meat smell of the creature's breath, and he began to gag, interrupting the screaming.

The monster's jaws opened wide, as though unhinged, rows of needle fangs glistening inside. Then it shoved Dinsmore's face into its maw and snapped its jaws down, shearing his head off, teeth grinding through bone and muscle.

It swallowed his head whole, then threw the remains of the watchman's body into the flames, which had already begun to consume the rest of the building and the two halves of his partner's corpse.

As the flames took over more and more of the building, the monsters vanished into the smoke, leaving their victims to burn.

∼

THERE WERE MANY ghosts at Swift's of London. An institution of its age would acquire them simply through the passage of time. They tended to accumulate. But ghosts tended to be aimless, wandering things, haunting the world with their misery and loneliness until such time as they at last surrendered their passion and traveled beyond the shroud of life and into the realm of the spirit. Or simply drifted away to nothingness.

From time to time, employees would enter a vault or a darkened corridor and catch a glimpse of such a shade, and there would be whispers and perhaps a bit of hysteria. But these sightings were rare. Ordinary men and women rarely noticed the wandering souls, and the typical ghost wasn't even aware of human presence.

However, when a phantom of such extraordinary will and purpose as Queen Bodicea entered a room filled with living, breathing men and women . . . well, William Swift had no intention of discovering what sort of panic might ensue. Thus Bodicea remained unseen until the Swift siblings had entered William's office, and the door was closed and locked. Only then did she materialize, her spectral form dimmed by the daylight that was washing through the windows. Dust motes passed through her, eddying on unfelt drafts. She attended to the dialogue at hand, but her arms were crossed impatiently.

The spectral queen was ever enthusiastic when it came to warfare, to action, but rather less so when conversation was required.

"And then his eyes, Will," Tamara said, shuddering. She paced across his office, her footfalls echoing off the walls. "It was just horrid. Frederick *transformed*. There was something *wrong* with him. I think . . ."

William sat behind his desk, listening intently. All his frustrations had dissolved the moment he saw the ache in her eyes. First the death of one of her dearest friends, and now this fresh horror. When his sister faltered, he urged her on.

"I think . . . he *killed* Helena, Will."

William nodded. He had been thinking along the same lines, until his thoughts had been muddled by the distraction of Sophia's attentions in the carriage on the way to Threadneedle Street. It was odd how romantic notions could hold one completely in their sway.

"I don't know for certain, of course," she continued. "But I would like to take Bodicea and Farris, and pay the Martin household a visit."

William sucked in his breath.

"Lord Nelson, Horatio, sir, show yourself!" he called, keeping his voice low so that his assistant, Harold, would not overhear from the next room. And certainly one or more of his employees would be strolling by outside the door from time to time, attempting to eavesdrop.

A sharp noise rent the air, and Lord Admiral Nelson appeared before them.

"You called, William Swift?" Nelson said in his clipped, officious fashion. He drifted toward the desk, his one good eye focused on the male sibling.

"Horatio, have you heard Tamara's tale? The account of Helena Martin's death, and the strange metamorphosis undergone by her brother?"

The ghost nodded. "I have just received the horrendous details from Byron. A kind, good-hearted girl, Helena Martin, if ever there was one," Nelson whispered, floating toward Tamara as if his presence could ease her mind. He reached out with his one ghostly hand, letting it float directly above Tamara's shoulder.

"Horatio," William began, "we're going to require your services. Yours, as well as Bodicea's and Byron's, I think. Tamara and I will have to consider the best course of action, but to begin, please seek out all your spectral counterparts, those with whom you have contact in the city. Anything unusual must be brought to our attention, particularly if there are other instances of transformation."

"Already I may have news," Lord Nelson said, lifting his chin as though reporting to a superior officer. "The fiend, Oblis, was gracious enough to share certain information with Byron. Even though the demon must have some dastardly motivation for—"

"Oblis again," Tamara said. "He intimated to me only yesterday that he possessed some secret knowledge of a burgeoning evil, a new curse that was arising."

William turned in his chair. "And to me, only this morning."

"Do you think there's any truth in it, William? He said something about hearing voices in the darkness. Implying that he could listen to the conversations of other demons, even though he is imprisoned in Ludlow House."

William let out a long, tremulous breath. "I wouldn't like to credit it, since the implications are rather ominous, but it seems obvious that he must know something. Yet we must not forget the nature of the beast, the iniquity—"

"No," Bodicea said firmly, her voice cold. Her gaze burned into him. "We must not ever forget what Oblis is capable of."

There was a moment of silence among them as all the horrors perpetrated by the demon resurfaced in their memories. William nodded. He rarely allowed himself to consider it for long—to admit how much he loved his father, how much he longed for the quiet, muttering man to return to their lives, to their home.

"What has Father said, Horatio?" asked Tamara. "What did the *demon* say?"

"At a dinner party given by the bishop of Manchester, the earl of Claridge attacked a young woman, and has since been shut up in a sanatorium. That much I have confirmed. Oblis suggested that he was changed, as well. Like Frederick Martin."

Tamara pushed a loose strand of hair from behind one ear. Her eyes were lit with intensity, and she gazed about at the two ghosts, then focused once again on her brother.

"Perhaps there is a curse after all. We must begin our investigation immediately, Will. If these two men have been afflicted, I fear there may be others already, and no way to tell how many more to come."

William sighed, sinking down in his chair. "This isn't going to be pretty. We may have to ask awkward questions."

"For God's sake, William, this isn't the time to be worrying about how our efforts are going to be perceived by our *society* friends. We're the Protectors of Albion! Our duty is clear."

"Yes, of course," he agreed. "Whatever new horror has come to our shores, we must rise to meet it."

Tamara arched an eyebrow, and he was pleased to see a small smile on her face. "That's more like it," she said.

William smiled in return.

"As I was saying," Tamara went on, "I shall have Farris drive me to the Martins' residence, to see if I might find the truth concerning Helena's death, and any clue as to how Frederick has come to such a terrible end. Bodicea, if you'll accompany me, I would be greatly comforted."

"Of course, Tamara," the queen replied, nodding. The sun had stretched farther into the room, and by now she was merely a suggestion in the air, the outline of a woman.

"Excellent," William said. "Horatio, it's just as I said. Let's see what tales you can dredge from the ghostly world. I'm afraid I must stay and attend to at least the most pressing business here at the bank, but we shall meet at Ludlow House late this afternoon, and see what we have been able to learn. And then, Tamara, you will have to prepare for your assignation this evening with John Haversham."

"*What?*" Bodicea exclaimed.

Lord Nelson sputtered in disbelief. "You cannot be serious, William Swift!"

Even Tamara stared at him, her face crumbling. "Oh, Will, what must you think of me, to even entertain the notion that I could enjoy myself tonight, with Helena's . . . with Helena gone. And this new trouble. I could never—"

"But you must," William said.

She frowned, shaking her head. "I'm afraid I don't understand."

"You have no choice, Tam. I'm sorry, truly. I know the pain you must be in. But your Mr. Haversham is part of that social circle. He might have been at the bishop's party, in which case he would have seen what happened to the earl. You must see what you can learn from him.

"But have a care, sister. If this curse has touched more than one, it may have touched others. Watch Haversham carefully."

Tamara nodded slowly, her gaze distant.

"I shall."

~

GIVEN THE TIME it would take for a message to be carried to Oxford, and for Helena's parents to arrange for their return, Tamara did not expect them to be at home when she called. She would claim that she had come to offer her condolences, and then ask if she might write a note for them to be given upon their return. While she was there, she would indulge upon the Martins' butler, Geoffrey, whom she had known most of her life, to allow her a few moments to mourn in Helena's room.

It was a good plan, save that it chilled her to manipulate her grief in that way—her own, and that of others.

The butler met her at the door. He was an older gentleman with a hunched back and pale skin, but his smile had always been warm whenever Tamara came to call. Today, however, his face was bleached white with grief and his lips, pale and bloodless, could not form a smile.

He admitted Tamara into the foyer, and she was surprised to learn that Helena's mother had arrived from Oxford. Though the butler could not see Bodicea, he seemed to sense a *strangeness* at Tamara's side and took a step back. He had been in service long enough to recover himself quickly, but he seemed wary after that.

While she waited for him to take her card in to the family, Tamara took the time to examine the sitting room. She had spent many afternoons in this home with Helena and the other girls of their circle.

Geoffrey returned to the sitting room and announced that Mrs. Martin would see her. Tamara followed him into the study, where Rose Martin stood in front of a window, her fingertips lightly spread across the glass. Tamara cleared her throat and Rose turned, her gaze empty.

"I was already on my way home when the news reached me. Otherwise I don't think there would have been anyone here to receive . . . the condolences. Frederick has . . . *gone*. Somewhere. I don't know. We all deal with our grief in different ways. Father won't be able to return until the weekend. I don't know what I shall do in the interim. This house . . ."

She bit her knuckle, her fist as white as her face.

Tamara didn't know what to say. Everything that came into her head was useless. She wanted to reach out and take Helena's mother in her arms, protect her from the terrible grief that surrounded the house.

Instead she took Rose's hand and squeezed it.

"Oh, Tamara . . ." The words were no sooner away from her lips than her jaw began to tremble, and tears flowed down her cheeks. She released Tamara's hand to dab a handkerchief to her eyes, then swallowed back a sob and shuddered, her small frame shivering from head to toe.

As a child, Tamara had always thought Helena's mother cut a very imposing figure, but now she realized that Rose was no taller or broader than she was herself. *She is no giantess,* Tamara thought. *How the mind's eye plays tricks. Or is it memory that bedevils us so?*

"I am terribly sorry for your loss," she managed, hearing the mournful rasp of her own voice, the quaver in it. "Helena was a dear, dear friend, and I know the place she held in my heart shall be empty now, forever."

Rose nodded, once again dabbing at her cheeks.

"I know that she treasured your friendship, Tamara. Thank you."

Something caught Tamara's eye. She turned her head and instantly her stomach churned. Like one of the undead, she staggered toward the lapis-and-jasper creature that sat on a small pedestal by the bookshelves.

"What . . . is this?" Tamara sputtered.

Rose followed her to where the amphibian statue sat. Tamara reached out a hand and touched the cool stone. Its eyes, the cast of its features, reminded her with unsettling power of the creature Frederick had become.

"This . . ." Rose composed herself. "This was a gift from an archaeologist friend, David Carstairs. It's a ceremonial statue from India."

Tamara frowned. "India?" she repeated.

"Forgive me, Tamara, but I think I must go and lie down now. I cannot . . . I cannot . . ."

"Of course, Mrs. Martin."

"Please, feel free to stay as long as you'd like. Helena had a number of sketches in her rooms that you might like to have. Take what you will. I know that she would have given you anything, my dear. She thought the world of you.

"She'd have wanted you to . . ." Once again, Rose fought back tears. "I'm sorry. I cannot continue . . ."

And with that Helena's mother was gone.

Tamara watched her retreating back, then turned to Bodicea. "Does this figurine seem familiar to you?"

Bodicea nodded. "Too familiar." The ghostly queen reached out a shimmering, transparent hand and rested it on the little stone creature.

Tamara stared at the specter. "Bodicea? How is that possible?" She looked more closely. Her eyes did not deceive her. Bodicea's hand did not go through the statue, but rested like real flesh on its jasper-and-lapis head.

"The creature has magical properties, Tamara. Dangerously powerful magic. It is a representation of the goddess Bharati. The Hindu goddess of sacrifice."

Bodicea removed her hand from the creature's head and floated away from it. In the gloom of that room, she seemed almost solid, and that was a comfort to Tamara.

"I'm afraid something terrible has come to London. And that this will be only the beginning." Bodicea's words sent a chill down Tamara's spine.

"Let us go to Helena's room. Perhaps we shall find a clue there."

Tamara moved toward the door, but stopped at the threshold to take one final look at the figurine. At length she tore her gaze away, and Bodicea followed her upstairs.

Helena's rooms were decorated in pale ivories and lavenders. The bed was neatly made, as if it had never been slept in, but was merely an exhibit. The whole room felt devoid of any humanity.

With a glance into the hall to see that she was not observed,

Tamara closed the door and walked over to the small dresser. It did not contain toiletries, but instead was awash in delicate pen-and-ink and charcoal sketches.

Helena's sketches.

Tamara picked up a small portrait of Farris that Helena must have drawn the day before at Ludlow House. It was an excellent likeness, capturing the dignity and sincerity of the kindhearted man who was more friend than servant to the Swifts. She laid that sketch down on the bed and picked up another, a self-portrait Helena had drawn in pen and ink. Tamara touched the rough paper with a shaky hand. Her eyes began to burn with the threat of tears, and she gnawed on her lower lip.

"Oh, Bodicea, why? Why *Helena*?"

The spectral queen's eyes were sad, but she did not reply.

Tamara put the sketch down and walked over to Helena's bed. She picked up a small brown doll that sat primly against the pillow, and cradled it in her arms. Helena had loved this doll, which she had named Mrs. Scrumples, to everyone's amusement. But she put the doll down, and hardened herself with purpose.

"There has to be something here. Something to tell us what *really* happened," Tamara said. She began to pace the room, her blue eyes raking in its contents.

"There has to be something—"

Then the *something* caught her eye. Under the dresser was a piece of sketch paper. Tamara knelt and picked it up. It was an unfinished sketch of the little lapis-and-jasper creature in the study with:

FOR TAMARA

inked above it. Tamara held the paper out, faceup so that the warrior queen could see the subject matter.

"Strange, isn't it?" Tamara asked. "If this figurine was responsible for Frederick's transformation . . . Helena was exposed to it for a time as well, yet it did not affect her. Could it be that the curse it carried had no effect on women?"

"She has left the sketch unfinished . . ."

Tamara nodded. "Yes, unfinished. And Helena was compulsively thorough about her work. She would never have left this sketch undone, not without cause."

Bodicea rapped her spear on the carpet. "Unless something prevented her from completing it."

Tamara turned the sketch over and was surprised to find a short sentence scribbled on its back. She squinted to make out the words:

BEHIND THE DRESSER

With a breathless glance at Bodicea, Tamara went to the dresser and slid it forward on the carpet. A small, leather-bound book had been wedged behind it, which now fell onto the floor with a dry thump. Tamara picked it up and opened the cover.

"Her journal," she whispered, holding the little volume reverently in her hands. "Shall I?" she asked Bodicea.

The warrior queen nodded. "It can do her no harm in death." Her ghostly features had thinned, and Tamara could see the canopied bed through her face.

Thus encouraged, Tamara flipped the pages until she reached the final entry. There were large tearstains obscuring some of the letters. Tamara put her hand to her mouth as she silently read:

I have decided to end my life rather than allow the shame of Frederick's act to destroy my family. These words shall be my last. I only pray that my estimation of my dearest friend is accurate, and that it is you, Tamara, who has discovered this journal. I trust you and only you to be its keeper, and know you shall not let it fall into my family's hands.

They would be forever shamed by the knowledge of what has happened. My half brother, Frederick, forced himself upon me this very night. I cannot bear the shame of it, and worse yet, this strange certainty in my heart that something unnatural has overcome him, and perhaps laid its seed in me as well. Yet I could not leave this world without imparting the truth to someone.

Tamara, please understand that there was no option. Forgive me for my cowardice. I love you always, Helena.

The tears she had been fighting welled up in Tamara's eyes, obscuring her sight, and as she took a long, shuddering breath, they slid down her cheeks. Her lower lip quivered. Her chest ached and her stomach felt as though it were filled with ice. Only one thought echoed in her mind.

I will destroy you, Frederick Martin.

Eight

O n that ethereal plane where ghosts lingered between the corporeal world and the afterlife, there were countless wandering spirits. The very substance of the place was made up of those long-dead
phantoms, spirits who could not or would not tear themselves away
from the lives they had lived, and move on to their final rest.

Most of those who remained behind did so for selfish reasons, and
would tarry until they had reconciled with whatever they were hesi-
tant to leave behind. Others, however, had different pursuits. Many
remained behind to do mischief, or out of hatred or rage. Those could
be quite dangerous to anyone still among the living, manifesting as
poltergeists and other malicious apparitions. Often they were con-
scripted into the service of other, even darker forces.

There was a war going on. And Admiral Lord Horatio Nelson
never turned his back on a good war. All his life he had fought for a
cause, and his death had not persuaded him to surrender. In truth, he
was more fervent than ever. He was a soldier in service to Albion, to
the great battle waged by the Protectors and by his nation's other de-

fenders. There were forces for evil, both in this world and in the others. The forces wanted to corrupt Albion, to claim it for themselves.

The demon lord Balberith was one among many of these enemies. In this, the greatest war of all, Balberith represented the darkness, and Nelson fought on the side of the light. So long as he was capable of aiding in that struggle, he would remain upon the ethereal plane as a shade, a specter.

Truth be told, he relished it. What thrill, what pleasure, might be found in Heaven if the war against Hell was being fought on other shores . . . on other seas?

No, he would eschew Heaven for the nobility of this forever war. The admiral would stand upon the deck of a phantom ship whose prow nosed through a spectral ocean, until Armageddon came and the scales were balanced.

As his ghost moved through the ether, that was how he imagined it. The strength of his spirit seemed to bend the mists of the death-realm, binding them to his every whim, so that gray clouds rose in waves and he could almost see the masts and sails towering above him. The phantom vessel carried him across the churning ocean of souls. In the twilight of eternity, he imagined it would also carry him farther into the afterlife.

And what, then, he did not know.

For now, he rode the transient souls and the whispers of the restless dead and he kept his single eye vigilant for anything amiss. There were dark things at large in London, and even darker deeds afoot. Albion was tainted by some new manifestation of evil, and he and his comrades would aid the Swifts in discovering and eradicating its source.

Nelson knew he ought to return to Ludlow House but for the moment he had had enough of Byron's company, and though Bodicea was a stalwart ally, her presence always unnerved him. The poet had his own circle of friends and associates in the spectral realm—degenerates, each and every one—and Queen Bodicea had numerous wandering ghosts who bowed to Her Majesty.

But Horatio preferred oftentimes to make his own way, and so he had made many acquaintances in this strange, misty, endless place.

Where there was war, there were soldiers, and the spirits of a great many young men who had died before their time.

No, for now, until such time as Master William or Mistress Tamara should summon him, he would continue to seek any trace of—

Admiral . . .

In the swirling mists of that shadow realm, Lord Nelson paused, the sails of his ghostly ship flapping silently even as they dissolved around him. The spirit held himself still, allowing the soul stuff to churn like the surf.

"Who calls?" he said, his words merging with the fabric of that realm.

Horatio, come this way. We must speak.

Obeying a new master now, the mist seemed to separate, forming a path that stretched away in front of him. He might have suspected a trap, had he not now recognized the voice as belonging to a friend. With but the command of his mind, he sped through the ether, the soul mist rippling and rolling back at his passage.

Piercing the fog, he approached the world of the living. But from his vantage, it was as though the inhabitants of the world were the ghosts, and he was a creature of flesh and blood.

It was night in London, and horses clopped along the cobblestones. Firelight flickered in lanterns; laughter erupted from a passing carriage. A coachman shouted at his horses to pick up their pace. A policeman stood on a street corner, whistling tunelessly.

Horatio saw it all, and yet he hardly took notice. His attention was focused on the source of the voice, the elegant combination of late Renaissance and baroque design that was St. Paul's Cathedral in all its beauty.

It had been called the triumph of its architect, Sir Christopher Wren, and there was truth in that. The façade sported two tiers of Corinthian columns that intentionally echoed those of the Louvre in Paris, and towers inspired by the church of St. Agnes in Rome. Wren had borrowed the breathtaking dome from Bramante, and the curved porches from DaCortona.

The man's greatest achievement was nothing more than a collection of elements he'd nicked from other architects.

Arrogant fool, Horatio thought. But he had nurtured a certain bitterness toward Wren throughout his ghostly existence. First, because the man was a foppish buffoon. At least his ghost was. Second, and more specifically, because Nelson's remains had been laid to rest within St. Paul's. Though he knew it was irrational, Nelson somehow connected the thought of Wren to the acknowledgment of his own death.

He had lost an arm and an eye during his life, and suffered other wounds, as well. But still Admiral Lord Nelson had clung to his flesh and blood, and he missed the life he had led, missed it terribly.

So whenever he found himself in the vicinity of Wren's masterpiece, a certain melancholy descended upon him like a shroud. It was unsettling to know that what remained of his fleshly form, his bones and bits of dried skin and hair, still lay in that tomb, deep within the cathedral.

Yet he was a soldier, and if the battle took him into unpleasant territory, he would not shirk in his duty.

He drifted across the road, invisible to the gaze of those who still drew breath, and passed through the stone walls of the cathedral. A small smile touched the corners of his mouth. Wouldn't William Swift have been thrilled to learn that he had such a knowledge of architecture?

But to him, this was just a church. No, not even that. It was just another building.

The cathedral was as he remembered it. The Whispering Gallery shushed now not with the mutterings of playful children but with the susurrus of ghostly dialogue. There were many ghosts in St. Paul's. Nelson saw their flitting, translucent forms darting about as he entered, hiding themselves away so that they might observe his intentions without revealing themselves. But their whispers still lingered, and it was clear that they were agitated. He sensed their alarm, but it wasn't his arrival that had disturbed them.

It was the presence of monsters.

The creatures—demons—were gone now, he gathered that much immediately. But they had wound the cathedral's dead up into a frenzy.

Horatio ignored them all for the moment. Perhaps they might have told him something useful, but he was responding to the summons of a friend, and he refused to allow himself to be distracted. Ignoring the presence of the altar, and blurring past the nearly 150-year-old organ upon which Mendelssohn had once played, he went directly to the shadowed corner where his tomb had been laid. Columns rose high above, and there was his name engraved in the stone of the ridiculously elaborate tomb.

HORATIO VICS NELSON

A figure stood in front of the tomb, hands clasped behind his back, studying the plaque that adorned the stone. The ghost was also dressed in uniform, but where the admiral represented Her Majesty's Navy, his summoner was an infantryman.

Colonel Richard Dunstan had served under both Cornwallis and Wellesley during their governor generalships of the holdings of the East India Company. He was a good man. After his death, Colonel Dunstan had freely volunteered his services in the defense of Albion. He had never been a close confidant of Sir Ludlow Swift, but he had been an invaluable ally both as a scout and as a warrior.

"Colonel," Nelson said.

Dunstan turned to face him. His features were distinct in the shadows. He had been handsome in life, his skin a bronze hue thanks to his mixed parentage. Dunstan's father had been a wealthy English trader, his mother the beautiful daughter of a Bombay merchant of similar station. It would have been no simple thing for his Indian origins to go unnoticed at home, but abroad, he had been considered a vital asset to the governors general, able to immerse himself in both British and Indian cultures.

The colonel was generally an amiable sort. This evening, however, his expression was grim.

"Admiral," Colonel Dunstan said. He nodded once. They had never bothered with formal salutes or anything of the kind, but their titles remained. "I apologize for having brought you to this place. Since my death, I have never once visited the repository of my . . .

remains . . . and if the idea gives you a fraction of the trouble it does me, well, I can only beg your indulgence."

Nelson cleared his throat and raised his chin. Though he could have manifested himself to appear as he had at any point in his life, he always chose to be seen by other ghosts as he had been at the time of his death. One arm. One eye. He had lost their mates in service to the Crown, and that was a source of pride to him. So it was that he could look upon Dunstan with only one eye, but he did so now with utter gravity.

"And you have my indulgence, Colonel. Your aid is ever appreciated. However, I confess that it *is* a bit unnerving, even to an old sea dog such as myself, to be so close to . . . well, you've already said as much. So if you'll be kind enough to proceed, we can quit this place all the sooner."

Dunstan motioned as though to smooth his uniform. It seemed an unconscious motion, and though there was no cloth there to be smoothed, the ether responded appropriately. Indeed, he was smoothing the fabric of his spirit.

"Come with me," the colonel said.

Horatio followed, and they sifted themselves through stone and mortar and wood. Soon enough they were standing in a dark chamber, dank to all appearances, though they felt none of it. A black iron gate stood before them. Something had torn it apart, twisted the bars as though they were taffy, even cracked the metal in some places.

"They came through not far from here," Colonel Dunstan said, chin up, hands behind his back, feet spread apart. "A portal was opened, surely through some dark sorcery, and most likely not performed by the demons themselves."

Nelson nodded, examining the bars. "Do you have any idea what sort of demons we're dealing with here? And what their purpose might be?"

"I have my suspicions. Come this way," Dunstan said.

The colonel led him back the way they had come. Inside the main chamber of the cathedral, in sight of the High Altar, Dunstan showed him a stain on the stone floor. Candlelight threw shuddering shadows upon the walls, but there was no sight of any worshiper or minister.

Merely that dark stain, where blood had seeped into the porous stone. Some poor servant had likely already been set to the task of its removal, but Horatio was certain the stain would never truly come out. It was more than blood. Dark magic had tainted the floor of St. Paul's.

Only now, in the midst of that empty cathedral, did he feel the power of faith that vibrated in every stone. At last he realized what Dunstan was attempting to show him.

"Whatever did this . . . whoever is responsible . . . it wields powerful magic."

"Oh, yes. Quite," Dunstan agreed. He crouched and touched insubstantial fingers to the bloodstained floor. Where the blood lay, tainted by sorcery, his fingers actually came into contact with it. "Normally base, foul beasts such as Rakshasa would never be able to trammel upon sacred ground."

Rakshasa. Nelson had never heard the word.

"These Rakshasa are the demons you spoke of?"

"The legends are from India. Simply put, they are monsters. Some stories claim they have the ability to alter their appearance, but I have never seen proof of this. The few times I have encountered such horrific creatures, they have been hideous to behold."

Horatio ruminated on this news for a few moments, and then he recalled where he was. Perhaps St. Paul's *was* more than just a building. A ripple of distaste went through him, and he was seized with the urge to depart.

"You have my thanks, and that of the Protectors, Colonel Dunstan. I'm curious, however, about the Indian origin of these monsters. Another situation has arisen that seems to have ties to that colony, as well, and I'm forced to wonder if the two incidents might be related."

The dark glimmer in Dunstan's eyes was enough to quiet Nelson.

"Indeed, Admiral," the ghostly colonel said gravely. "This is merely the latest such appearance. In the areas near the docks where so many former employees of the East India Company live in squalor, there have been several strange events in recent weeks. Rakshasa have been sighted, and there has been a mysterious stranger, a woman unknown to anyone, who wanders the streets late at night. Perhaps the legends of the Rakshasa are true, and she is one of them. Or perhaps she is merely a woman. My mother's people are very superstitious.

"Yet there is still more." Colonel Dunstan passed his hand through the air, and an ethereal mist swirled into existence, as if from nowhere. It spread in tendrils of gray fog. "Come. Let me show you."

Nelson had seen much in his life, and far more since his death. Things that once would have been beyond his wildest imaginings. Towering demons that breathed the fires of Hell itself, insidious shades that possessed the minds and bodies of decent people, sorcery whose sole purpose was the twisting of human flesh, and worse. As a specter, at all times, he could sense the talons of true evil, disembodied things that made the minions of Hell seem like mere animals, scratching at the windows of the world, attempting to get in.

Albion itself had a living, breathing soul, like Aquitaine, Bavaria, and so many other regions of the world. This was the power of the natural world. But there were unnatural powers, as well, and their ultimate goal was to undo all that was right with the world, and remake it in their image.

So when Colonel Dunstan's words began to echo in him, and a ghostly shiver ran through him, he recognized the feeling for what it was.

Fear.

Something terrible was afoot. It came from a distance, and they had only just begun to recognize the scope of its influence.

The solid world faded into the mist, and the two ghosts slipped into the ether once more. Together they drifted. Direction and distance had little meaning. Destination had far more to do with intent than navigation.

After only a few moments in that gray, malleable place, the mist began to clear again, and Nelson could hear the sound of the river.

The Thames.

He did not have to breathe, of course. His senses still functioned, but only because he required them. The stench of the river would have bent him over with the urge to vomit if such an act were still possible. He might retch, but there was no stomach, nothing to regurgitate. It was one of the rare times Nelson was grateful to be dead.

"That's simply awful," he muttered.

All of the filth from London's industry fed into the river. The city's sewers fed the Thames, as well, and the surface of the river was clogged with human waste. Nelson surveyed the water, and what he saw there disgusted him. He was a man at home upon the sea, and it wrenched something within him to have to bear witness to this atrocity. The Thames ought to have been London's lifeblood, and instead it was the depository of her offal.

"Look there," Colonel Dunstan said, pointing.

Only then did Nelson spot the tiny figures on the near bank of the Thames. His brows knitted and he drifted closer. At first the small things that crouched on the riverbank appeared to be toads, but the closer he drew to them the more he realized that they were not like any living creatures he had ever seen.

Their eyes were red and bulbous, tinged with yellow, as though they were blisters full of blood and pus. And when something skittered by beneath a wooden mooring, surely a river rat, the toads raised their heads, then gave pursuit, leaping into the water or under the mooring, moving as a group.

"Good Lord," Horatio whispered.

Dunstan grunted. "Let us hope so."

The ghosts floated to the river's edge, though they kept well away from that rotting wooden mooring and whatever might have been going on beneath it. Supernatural creatures such as the things that had defiled the cathedral were quite capable of injuring a ghost, of wounding the substance of a specter. What was touched by sorcery might harm a spirit as easily as it could hurt a man. Even a minister.

There was something floating in the water, large and pale. At first Nelson thought it must be a corpse. There were enough river pirates, petty thieves, and other killers working the river and the wharves that it was not unusual to see a human body callously discarded in the Thames.

But then the thing moved, and dove beneath the surface, disgusting water churning above it. It came back to the surface a short distance away, its bulbous eyes shining in the faint moonlight. The putrid waste atop the river rolled with its deep passage and it swam away from them, upriver toward the London docks.

"What was—"

"The Rakshasa are not the only things to plague the Indian sections of London town," the colonel's ghost said, voice heavy with import. "There is disease, as well, of a sort no mortal physician is prepared to treat. Women who are infected are quickly swollen as if with child, ill with fever and covered in sores. In the end, they . . . give birth. Those toads you saw, Admiral. More than a dozen Indian women have borne such creatures, carried evil within their own flesh. They are tainted forever. The fortunate ones have died. There are easily that many more already infected, and who knows how many others will come?"

"And the men?" Horatio asked. "The men who are infected, what of them?"

The shadows of Colonel Dunstan's features seemed to darken, and Nelson saw fear there.

"First they go mad, and become violent in their search for a woman with whom to mate. Then they are *changed*," the ghost replied. "They undergo a terrible metamorphosis, their flesh contorted until they are no longer human. What you saw in the river a moment ago . . . that used to be a man."

Like Frederick Martin, Nelson thought. *Precisely like Frederick Martin.*

And what of the earl of Claridge? Could he have been infected as well? Certainly, he is not a man of the slums. Yet . . .

"The Protectors' experience with this has been limited. But if what you say is true, then this plague has begun to touch the nobility, as well. I am surprised these horrors did not come to our attention sooner."

The ghost of Colonel Dunstan, this soldier who had lived his life with an English name and an Indian face, raised an eyebrow. "And why should you be surprised, Horatio? Is it so odd that the aristocracy would fail to notice the spread of evil in the slums to which they have always turned a blind eye? Why would it warrant their attention, until it arrived upon their own doorsteps?"

Nelson scowled, stung by the accusation.

"Have a care, sir! Only our long association prevents me from demanding satisfaction for that remark. The Protectors defend all of Albion, not merely the upper classes!"

"Really?" Dunstan countered, his form almost solid black now, causing him to blend with the darkness. "But you said yourself it only came to their attention when some lord or lady was affected. Indeed, Admiral, though I was born in Bombay, the home of my mother, I was guilty of the same sins until my death. Until I had the time and inclination to think about where I was really from."

～

WILLIAM DIDN'T SIT so much as crouch in the back of his carriage as it clattered along the streets of London.

He perched on the edge of his seat, features set in grim lines, and held the curtain aside so that he might gaze out the window. There was little enough to see this night, however. The fog made sure of that. It wasn't the worst of its sort, not enough to leave a clammy filth upon every surface it caressed, but it was dense, and reeked of the choking exhalations of chimneys and charnel houses and the putrid excrescence of the distant marshes of Kent and Essex, far to the east. William breathed through his mouth as much as possible.

How Farris managed to navigate the streets—particularly the narrow, curving alleys that provided a more direct route to their destination—was beyond him. The man wasn't a coach driver by trade, but a gentleman's gentleman. Still, the Swift household had experienced a great deal of difficulty retaining the service of its staff just lately, so they'd had to make do with a curtailed household coterie. Farris had risen to the occasion.

He had performed so well as coachman, and was so unflummoxed by the terrors that regularly presented themselves in the company of his employers, that even were they able to find a reliable driver, William thought he and Tamara would be loath to use anyone else.

He was stout of heart and of body, and excellent in a scuffle. Good with his fists. William had come to think of him as not just a servant, but also a comrade in this war he and Tamara had undertaken.

From time to time William heard the muffled sound of Farris's voice as he coaxed the horses. In the distance, there came the tolling of church bells. The buildings they passed were gray shapes in the deeper darkness, looming up out of the fog. There were street lamps on the busier roads, but their illumination was broken into diffuse streamers of light that shot through the thick blanket of mist and accomplished little.

Without warning, he heard Farris call to the horses, and the rhythm of their clopping hooves began to slow, causing the carriage to roll to a stop. The coach shifted as Farris climbed down from his seat, and William saw him through the window. He waited while Farris lowered the step, then he swung the door open, descending from the elegant interior of that conveyance that had once belonged to his grandfather, and now was a part of his father's estate.

"Master William?" Farris prompted.

He had been staring into the fog, distracted by the diffuse light of a nearby lamp. Another carriage clattered by, this one a newer, sleeker coach with only one horse, and he wondered idly where its occupant was off to. Some party or other, he was certain. A life that ought to have been his, had other duties not taken precedence.

"I'm sorry, Farris. I seem to have been lost in my head for a moment." William took a long breath and then instantly regretted it, coughing out the stink of the London night. He tugged his coat more tightly around him, hating the damp, and nodded to his servant. "Well done."

"Not at all, sir," the man replied dutifully.

There were few others out on the street this evening. Other parts of the city might be busy, particularly the pubs and theaters, but thanks to the fog, there were no casual strollers here. It took William a moment to orient himself, gazing about at the façades around him.

They had stopped at the northwest corner of Red Lion Square, just in front of the last address on Orange Street. The windows would offer a view of the square, which likely explained why the building seemed in generally better repair than its neighbors.

William started toward the front door of No. 73 Orange Street.

"Sir, are you certain you wouldn't like me to accompany you?" Farris asked, keeping his voice low. Despite the precaution, though, the fog seemed to cause his question to echo loudly.

"Thank you, Farris, but no. I'm certain I can deal with whatever I might encounter. And Her Majesty has promised to remain close at hand."

"Very good, sir. Of course." But his expression remained stern.

William smiled. Much as he had grown used to the presence of specters, Farris was still unsettled by Bodicea. William thought it the combination of her nudity and her royalty, in almost equal measure, and sometimes he thought the latter brought Farris more discomfort than the former.

Bodicea had begun the journey with them, but shortly before they had arrived she excused herself and disappeared into the ether. Nevertheless, he was sure she would return.

William strode up to the door and raised his fist to knock. There was only one door, but at least three separate flats lay within. He had been told that David Carstairs retained rooms on the second floor, but it occurred to him that if Carstairs was somehow involved in whatever had transformed Frederick Martin, the last thing he ought to do was announce his arrival.

So William glanced about to see if he was observed—almost an impossibility in the fog—and then, though it pained him to perform even the slightest criminal act, he whispered a simple spell. He ran his fingers over the doorknob, and it swung inward several inches.

The hallway inside the door was so dark that it gave him pause. He drew a long breath, then stepped inside. When he closed the door behind him, he was swallowed by the blackness. A shudder went through him as he strained to hear the movement of anyone who might be about the premises.

Perhaps a bit more caution is in order, he thought.

Carstairs had given the Martins that strange Indian idol that had cursed Frederick. Twisted his soul, mind, and body. There was evil in him now, and there was no way to know if Carstairs's excursions to India had produced other such figurines, or if he had known from the start what it would do to Frederick.

William disliked situations that presented so many questions, yet so few answers.

Closing his eyes, he focused his thoughts there in the dark, and took a moment to search his memory. A smile touched the corners of his mouth. The spell was one of the very first he and Tamara had learned in the days after their grandfather had been murdered. As such, it came to him easily.

His fingers contorted and he swept them from side to side, drawing odd geometric shapes upon the air. He opened his eyes even as a blue glow shimmered to life around him, dusting him with sparks of magic like a light snowfall. It was a protective ward, used to defend against magical attack. There was no way to know if it would keep him from being tainted by whatever dark power Carstairs had brought back from India, but without deeper knowledge of the evil he was facing, it was the best protection he could conceive.

Emboldened now, he moved forward. In that dim light, he passed the door to the first-floor flat and went to the stairs at the end of the hall. As he ascended, treading lightly, he listened again for any sound that might indicate that someone was at home, but the entire building seemed quiet. There wasn't even the scratch of rats in the walls.

A tightness formed in William's chest. A touch of excitement, mingled with fear.

He tried to keep his breathing steady as he arrived upon the second-floor landing. The door to 73B was closed, but an orange light gleamed in the crack underneath. Once again, William chose expediency and caution over propriety. In fact, it disturbed him how accustomed he was becoming to eschewing manners. But not so much that it stopped him from doing what was needed.

With a simple caress of his fingers, the door sprang open a fraction of an inch. He steadied himself, then pushed it wide, stepping into the archaeologist's sitting room. William peered quickly about, noting the lamp that was burning on a desk in one corner and the documents that were scattered about the floor. A chair had been overturned. Alarmed at this sign of conflict, he raised his hands; the blue glow around him crackled as he channeled some of the energies into a form that could be used for offense.

He paused and waited.

After a few moments, he let out a long breath and frowned. Why had he not been challenged? With the lamp still burning, the flat was surely not empty, and his entrance couldn't have gone unnoticed.

Closing the door softly behind him, William ventured farther into the flat. He noted several other rooms, but the mess in the sitting room drew his immediate attention. As he moved toward the desk, however, the lamplight flickered, and he became aware of the many artifacts on shelves and side tables around the room. It reminded him of his grandfather's chambers, laden with souvenirs of his stage shows and his travels.

But the mementos in Carstairs's sitting room were not so playful. They were, in fact, gruesome. Or at least they seemed so to William. There were statues and carved idols representing the various deities from Hindu mysticism. Though William knew little about the colony in India, he was aware that the gods worshiped there often looked terrible, but in fact represented more benevolent concepts.

Gazing upon these artifacts now, though, there seemed only to be death and cruelty. A hideous woman with many arms and massive, swollen breasts wore a garland of flowers and held a cleaver in one hand. Another statue showed a similar goddess, adorned with a wreath of snakes and bones, seated upon a corpse. She was clad in purple and yellow, and had three eyes.

Three eyes that seemed to glare at him with savage accusation.

William took a deep breath and a step backward. There were many others. Other deities. Some seemed less cruel. There were tiny carved things, many of which seemed to represent lesser demons, though none like the toad-thing Frederick Martin had.

The blue glow of William's protective ward combined with the flickering lamplight as he bent over to retrieve some of the scattered papers.

William Swift was a businessman. He knew sales records when he saw them. There were references to Carstairs's travels to India, as well as items he had brought back with him. Yet as William began to sift through the papers, gathering them up while he did so, he found no documentation for the importation of the sorts of items that decorated the flat. Rather, there seemed only bills of lading for the importation of tea, coffee, and other common goods.

Yet Carstairs had sold artifacts, as a glance around the room easily confirmed. So where the records referred to simple foodstuffs, the truth was that the scoundrel was smuggling archaeological treasures from Calcutta to London.

There were other papers as well. Things unrelated to Carstairs's enterprises. Sketches done by a crude hand, of symbols, of gods and goddesses, of monsters, all of which appeared to be related to the archaeologist's research into the Hindu tantra, the magic of that faith. Some of the designs were beautiful; some of the sketches were frightening. One depicted a goddess holding a severed head, crouched upon a pile of skulls with her knees splayed, as though about to give birth.

A shiver crept spiderlike up William's spine.

A sound reached him, then, a wet sucking noise that came from behind him. Frowning deeply, almost afraid to turn his back on the effigies in the living room despite his protective ward, he tore himself away. There was a small dining area beyond one door, and a tiny kitchen adjacent to it. Both were wholly unremarkable. William glanced through the next door, which opened into the bath. He presumed the damp noise he had heard had originated there.

At least until he opened the final door, which led into the bedchamber.

Heavy curtains had been pulled across the windows. The stench of human waste befouled the air. Rows of candles had been set in odd patterns upon the floor, but most had burned down to nothing, and puddles of wax were cooling. A few had not completely melted, and their flames guttered and danced as the opening of the door disturbed the rank air.

David Carstairs lay naked on the bed, curled into a fetal position. He shuddered and wept softly, and clutched in his arms a broken statue not unlike the others in the sitting room, save that its face and body were both beautiful and elegant, its surface as black as night. The goddess's hair was disheveled, and she held a trident in one hand. The other had been snapped off by the man's clutching grip.

"Mr. Carstairs?" William ventured, voice low, as he stepped into the room. He raised his left arm and pressed his coat sleeve to his nose to block the stench. "David?"

The archaeologist flinched at the sound of his own name, and his face contorted as though he was in pain. Then he began to chant softly under his breath, and he rocked more forcefully.

"*Om Hrim Krim Kapalini Maha-kapala-priye-manase kapala-siddhim me dehi Hum Phat Svaha,*" he murmured once, then began again.

William took another step nearer. The blue glow of his protection spell cast a strange hue upon the man's flesh, or so William thought at first. Then he realized that it wasn't only his magic. Carstairs's flesh was tinted green.

He blinked, staring at the man. It took him a moment to understand what he was looking at. The wet, sucking sound he had heard from the other room had not come from the bath, but from David Carstairs's neck, where damp gill slits puckered and gasped at the air.

"Dear Lord," William rasped as he backed away a step.

At the mention of the Christian God, the archaeologist opened his eyes. There was a thin membrane over them that retracted after a moment, revealing black, gleaming orbs. His lips peeled back from teeth that seemed to sharpen even as William looked on, and his tongue split, thrusting out in a forked hiss.

The idol shattered in the archaeologist's hands, and now the fingers began to lengthen, claws curving into hooks. Connective tissue grew up between the fingers, pulling the flesh into amphibious webbing that had not been there only moments before.

Fragments of the Indian goddess showered onto the bare mattress, or onto the floor.

Oh, you idiot, William chided himself, for he now saw what he had interrupted. Carstairs had been clutching the goddess, chanting some kind of mantra, doing his best to hold off this transformation, this magical curse. And William himself had broken the man's concentration.

The man began to shudder violently on the bed, its frame squeaking, and in moments he was hardly a man at all anymore. So entranced was he by his own horror that William actually let out a small shout and took another step back when Carstairs abruptly sat up.

The movement was uncannily swift. His head twitched inhumanly and he turned those moist black eyes toward the intruder in his flat.

The creature hissed. That forked tongue thrust out again.

"I think not," William muttered.

In that very same moment, Carstairs leaped from the bare mattress. The frame thumped against the wall. William cursed loudly and raised his hands, his entire body shimmering with blue light. The amphibian rushed forward and crashed into him, clammy, webbed hands wrapping around his throat.

The impact knocked William back against the open door and his head collided with the thick wood. He was disoriented for a moment, but then the claws of the creature began to dig into his flesh, and he felt the scrape of its scales on his throat. The sensations cleared his head in an instant.

The thing that had once been David Carstairs hissed. Smoke rose from its hands where it gripped him. The protective ward William had cast upon himself was meant to dispel curses, not shield him from physical harm, but still it seemed to burn the demon-beast. It would not keep the creature from murdering him, but it did cause the thing to hesitate, to flinch back a moment, loosening its hold.

William twisted away, wresting his throat from the thing's moist grip, long enough to rasp out a spell. *"Claustrum luminarium."* Another day, he might have fumbled with the spell. The words were simple enough, but the skill it required was specific.

This day, however, his life depended upon it. Terror gave him strength and focus. The spell seemed to begin in his gut, twisting his viscera in knots, and pain cramped his stomach so that he let out an agonized gasp. The demon-beast found its grip again, one claw puncturing his throat so that a trickle of blood began flowing. It held him with one hand now, and drew back the other. He saw himself reflected in the mirror of its black, glistening eyes, and William knew it meant to disembowel him.

Then the spell erupted from him, channeled through his fingertips at first. He threw his head back and felt it surge up his gullet and spine, so that the magic erupted from his mouth and eyes simultaneously. Tears slid down his cheeks and his knees weakened.

He slid his back down the wall where the creature had pinned him, slumping to the floor. It took a moment for his vision to clear.

The hissing, spitting thing that had been David Carstairs was contained inside a sphere of crackling crimson energies, bands of light that had formed a cage around the beast.

"Ah" was all he could muster.

For long moments he only sat there, staring at the magical prison he had wrought and the horror that writhed within it. Then, as his strength slowly returned, he forced himself to his feet, and stumbled out into the sitting room. The accursed wretch would have to be dealt with, carefully examined, but it was likely too late for David Carstairs. There were others, however . . .

William slid into Carstairs's desk chair and began examining his documents again. What he wanted was the list of people who had bought artifacts from the man. There was no telling how many of them might be infected by this curse.

As he fanned through the pages, he discovered a small card among them. William held it before him and frowned as he read the words. It was an invitation to dinner at the Algernon Club the following evening, for the celebration of the birthday of Sir Darius Strong—the same event to which he, himself, had also been invited.

As he pondered this discovery, a familiar buzz filled the air, like discordant music. William glanced over and saw the ghost of Queen Bodicea materializing in the room, a golden glow emanating from her spectral form. Once he was certain it was indeed the queen, he averted his eyes.

"What have you learned, William?" Bodicea asked, her spear held tightly in one fist.

He showed her the invitation. "To begin with, it appears that Mr. Carstairs and I have both been invited to the same dinner at the Algernon Club tomorrow evening."

Bodicea frowned. "A coincidence?"

"Perhaps," William replied, unsure. "As to your question, Majesty, I have learned a great many things this evening. Not least of which is that in future, I shall await your arrival before venturing forth, regardless of how long you tarry."

"Trouble?" the ghost inquired.

William smiled. "Nothing I couldn't handle."

He could still feel the cold grasp of the monster, and warm blood still slid like a red teardrop down his throat. But he took silent pleasure in knowing that what he had told Bodicea was the truth.

Nine

Tamara had been to the Egyptian Hall once before. When she was a young girl, her grandfather Ludlow had taken her and William to see the magnificent landscapes by Turner while they were on exhibition there. Art was not the hall's main focus, however. It had been built in 1812 for William Bullock as a museum in which to display his vast collection of artifacts reflecting the natural history and art of ancient cultures. The focus had been Egyptology, of course, and the architecture of the place reflected that, its façade vaguely resembling an Egyptian temple. Seven years later, Bullock had sold both his collection and the building, and it had become an exhibition hall. Many of the exhibits that had been shown there in Tamara's lifetime had maintained the original intent, but there had also been entertainment productions and art exhibits, such as the Turner showing that had so impressed her as a girl.

She had been only five or six at the time, but she remembered distinctly the way the colors almost danced off the paper. To her, Turner was some sort of magician—the way he was able to capture light on paper and tame it to his will. So often, she wished that *she* were an artist; that she could bend words the way painters bent light. Sometimes she found herself so frustrated with her own writing that she rent the paper and threw it into the fire—

"Where has your mind wandered off to, Miss Swift?" John Haversham asked, peering at her curiously.

She blinked, not liking to be caught.

"I *am* sorry. It's just that the day has been so awful, you see. Horrid, if the truth be told. I would not have come, except that I thought I might go mad if I didn't have something to distract me from my thoughts tonight."

She had been trying desperately all evening to focus on the paintings that were so beautifully arranged around the hall. The subject was fascinating to her—hundreds of canvases depicting the savage Indian tribes of North America by an artist who had traveled and lived among them, the art richly textured and bright with color and life— but her mind had been drifting ever since she and John had arrived at the Egyptian Hall. Time and again she glanced over at Farris, who stood in a shadowed corner keeping watch over her excursion.

I should never have come, she thought. It felt inappropriate to her that, rather than being at home with her grief, she was passing an ostensibly pleasant evening with a man who fancied her.

Tamara had argued with William over his insistence that she keep her appointment. Their exchange had grown heated, but in the end she acquiesced, in part because she knew that William was right. Haversham *had* been at the bishop of Manchester's party. He knew Frederick Martin quite well. If he knew anything about the strange transformation that had befallen Frederick and the earl of Claridge, Tamara owed it to Helena to ferret out the truth.

So she had gone home to Ludlow House and put on a soft butter-yellow evening dress. She had wanted to climb into her bed, curl herself into a ball, and allow herself to cry, but instead she dutifully dressed her hair and applied a small amount of perfume to her neck. She realized afterward that the sweet-smelling jasmine would probably send John Haversham the wrong message, but it had been a present from her grandfather. She loved the scent, and the way it made her feel bold and attractive. It had helped even to wake her from the nightmare of the day, though she was certain nothing could fully shake her from the numbness that touched her heart.

A flutter of humor passed through her. Poor John had invited her out for the evening with no idea what he would get in the bargain. He was taking it rather well, though, this handsome young man who seemed far less a scoundrel this evening. In truth, he seemed quite the gentleman when he didn't have an audience to entertain. How shocked Sophia would be to discover that her cousin wasn't nearly the rogue he purported to be.

Tamara turned toward John, then, and found him staring at her, appearing slightly befuddled.

"Oh, I'm sorry, John. I must have been drifting again. Please forgive me. I probably shouldn't have come at all."

His expression softened, and the charm of his smile was undeniable. Only a few inches separated them, and Tamara was sure she could feel the heat coming from his body. Even in the midst of the Egyptian Hall, with Farris watching from across the room, there was a surprising intimacy to their closeness.

"No apology is necessary, Miss Swift. I'm pleased to offer any sort of distraction. I can barely begin to imagine what you must be going through.

"What a terrible blow, the loss of such a close friend. When you told me of Helena's fate, I was resigned to suffering without your company this evening. But now that you're here, perhaps art can dull the sharp edge of your pain. If that's the case, then I am grateful to the artist."

Tamara felt her face flush. She was attracted to the man, but her pleasure had more to do with his kindness than his other appealing attributes.

"It's not only the artist who provides the distraction I sought, John," she confessed.

He bowed with a dramatic flourish. "In that case, my wit and charm are entirely at your service."

Tamara smiled. She liked this man, liked his surprising sensitivity, the way he tried to distract her from the pain she knew must be etched on her face. Under normal circumstances, she would have thrilled at his attentions, but tonight she was simply grateful for the easy companionship.

"And what of the paintings, Miss Swift? Are they to your liking, as well?" John asked, studying her intently.

Tamara thought before answering, not sure how to put into words the emotion the images called forth, the gleam in the eyes of the Indians portrayed, the smoothness of their copper skin, the exotic quality of their clothing, and the customs on display in those paintings. She had never been to the Americas, but found the idea enticing.

Of course, she had never gone abroad at all except under the power of magic. In recent months, their battles to protect Albion had taken them to Italy and to northern Africa, but only briefly. Even before that, she and William had accidentally translocated to a French brothel, at the very beginning of their magical training. William had been appalled, and she had tried to act as though she had been disgusted, as well, by the things she had seen and heard.

But a part of her had been extremely curious as to what *really* happened behind closed doors between a man and a woman.

She had heard tales from her married friends but had, herself, never even been alone with a man, let alone a *naked* one. That brief glimpse of undulating flesh in the shadows of a French brothel had been her only firsthand experience with such things.

"Miss Swift?" John said. "The paintings?"

Tamara blushed, afraid that her expression might have given him an inkling of the nature of her thoughts. *How silly of me—there's no way he could know.* She would have been mortified if he even suspected, though.

"I like the paintings very much," Tamara replied. She moved to one of the nearby portraits and stood before it, studying its composition. "For instance, Catlin has achieved the essence of this man. He seems majestic, almost beautiful, and yet . . . he exudes such *strength.*"

"The Indian Gallery is impressive," he agreed, nodding. He took her arm and moved her closer to the portrait. When he spoke again, he lowered his voice to a whisper. "I must confess that I would like to go to America. But only in the company of someone special, someone who would appreciate the journey."

His words were soft, his lips only a few inches from her ear. A tremor went through her, a wave of prickling warmth. Tamara took a single, shallow breath and ran her tongue over her lips to wet them.

I can't allow this to continue, she thought, chiding herself harshly. *This isn't the time. It isn't proper.*

"I'm sorry, John, but I'm rather tired. Might we find a place to rest a moment?"

John smiled, showing his even white teeth to good effect.

"Of course, Miss Swift. Whatever you wish." His dark eyes bored into her own so intently that she had to glance away. Tamara was alarmed by this look, concerned that he might have misinterpreted her request. What if she had only convinced him that she was falling under his spell, that she wanted to be alone with him in some dark corner?

And what if he isn't mistaken at all? she wondered. She glanced over his shoulder and nodded to Farris. He followed after them, silent as a shadow.

They stopped at a small bench and Tamara sat down, her eyes suddenly heavy and burning with exhaustion. She felt strangely nauseous, a bitter taste forming at the back of her throat.

The hall was almost empty and the corner in which they sat completely deserted. Farris took up a position at the far end of the room. She knew she was close to placing herself in a compromising position with this stranger, something she wasn't emotionally prepared for, especially this day, but she was unable to change her course. She felt like the captain of a capsized ship, standing on the prow and watching the sea slowly pull her vessel into the depths.

John sat down beside her, and before Tamara knew what she was doing, her eyes were closed and she was leaning her head against his shoulder. The smooth cloth of his coat was cool against her burning forehead. She could feel the tears leaking from the corners of her eyes and she squeezed her eyelids tight, trying to assuage the sense of panic that was quickly consuming her.

"Tamara? May I call you that?"

She nodded, keeping her face pressed against his shoulder.

"Tamara, please don't cry. It is agony for me to watch."

She looked up, and much to her surprise she saw that John's own eyes were wet with tears. It somehow made her grief seem that much worse, seeing such tenderness in a man.

"Helena was my oldest . . . my dearest . . ." She faltered and began to sob openly, horrible, shuddering gulps of air that caught in her throat and choked her.

Farris started toward her, a look of concern etched into his face, but Tamara gave him a small wave to indicate that she was all right, and that he should remain where he was. Any other day he might have thought John the cause of her distress, but Farris knew as well as anyone how much she had been through today. He nodded, but he crossed his arms and kept a vigilant eye upon her.

John had wrapped a strong arm around Tamara's shoulder. She could feel his muscles taut against her, and felt oddly comforted, as though part of the weight of her grief had been lifted from her. That was all she had really wanted since the day had begun, and Frederick had brought her his terrible news.

Frederick.

"You knew her, as well," Tamara said, composing herself as best she could. "It isn't right, John, that such a wonderful girl, so full of light and life and talent, should be taken so violently from the world."

"I never knew her very well, but I had the pleasure of watching her sketch several times. She was quite an artist."

Tamara nodded, drawing slow breaths, and then she paused. She turned to face him. All the questions about Helena's death and Frederick's transformation mingled with her grief and became too much to contain. She needed to speak, to release some of the emotion within her.

"What is it?" John asked.

"It may be difficult for you to hear, but I believe that Frederick had something to do with his sister's death." Tamara gazed at him without wavering now. She had said it. Let the cards fall where they may, let him think her crazy, but at least she had said the words out loud, to someone other than William.

"I don't think—"

"He tried to . . . hurt me, this morning," Tamara began. She waited for him to stop her, but he didn't. Instead he just leaned forward, listening intently.

"Go on."

"He wasn't himself, John. Not at all. In fact, there was something profoundly wrong with him," she continued, watching his expression carefully. "I've even heard whispers of a dinner party where the earl of Claridge—"

John's face went pale as a ghost's, and he spoke up, interrupting her.

"Do you mean to say that Frederick tried to have his way with you? I was at the bishop's party. I, myself, had to pull the earl away from the young woman he was—" His voice trailed off.

Tamara shook her head.

"Frederick tried, but it did not go that far. I had . . . help to fend him off." She spoke quietly, remembering the mottled reptilian skin, the thick membrane that slid over Frederick's eyes before he attacked her.

"It was terrible," she said, her voice low.

John squeezed her tightly to him. She felt like a piece of Venetian glass, and hoped that he would not crack her. She could feel his heart beating against her, and at that moment it seemed as if the humanness of that heartbeat terrified her more than anything else had that day.

She pulled away, causing him to release her.

"I'm afraid I've been too familiar with you, Mr. Haversham. I have done us both a terrible disservice. I have . . . I . . ."

Tamara stood up abruptly. As she stood there, she was barely aware that she was swaying. Her heart raced, and she couldn't seem to catch her breath. Her grief had flooded her completely and seemed about to boil over, so that she couldn't construct a single coherent thought.

The darkness coalesced about her, and she fainted.

When she came to, she found herself in Farris's thickly muscled arms. He cradled her as if she were a wee babe in swaddling clothes. His wide, worried eyes stared down at her, and she felt guilty for frightening him so.

"You went right down on the floor, you did, miss," Farris said. He helped her to sit, but her head lolled back against his chest, too heavy for her to hold up herself.

John Haversham crouched on her other side, looking equally concerned.

"Are you feeling better, Tamara?" he asked, clasping one of her slender hands between both of his. His touch was warm and rough, his callused palms holding her gently.

She looked into his eyes—and for a moment she swore her heart stopped beating.

He was a handsome man, John Haversham. Yet there were tiny crinkled lines that curved in ellipses around his tired gray eyes. Laugh lines encircled his full mouth, and all of this made him that much more appealing to Tamara's eye. She wanted to reach out and touch him, make sure that he was real. Instead she looked away, letting time begin to flow again.

Letting her grief back in.

~

𝕿HE CELLAR WAS dark, but William still could make out stacks of coal lying neatly in their bins, waiting to be burned. He could smell and taste the sharp, acrid stink of burning coal coming from the topmost floors of the house, and knew that meant someone was upstairs, enjoying the light and heat.

Only moments earlier he had whispered the spell of translocation and been swept away, the whole of the tangible world disappearing from around him. The Protectors had powerful magic within them, and he and Tamara had mastered translocation soon after they had inherited the power their grandfather had wielded before them. Even so, he would never get used to the moment during the casting of that spell when he was between the point of origin and his destination. It was a single, wrenching instant in which he hurtled through a swirling maelstrom of shadows, much too quickly to make out more than glimpses of insubstantial shapes he presumed were the parts of the world he was traveling past.

Translocation always gave William a vertiginous feeling. The act itself was inherently dislocating, and attempting it without his sister's far steadier grasp on magic to anchor him only increased the vertigo. He had once likened the experience, in conversation with Nigel Townsend, to "paddling 'cross the English Channel in a teacup after having had far too large a breakfast."

William hadn't wanted to translocate at all tonight, but Bodicea had insisted that hailing a hansom cab would only waste precious time. He and the ghostly queen had agreed that it was best for her to remain behind to guard the thing that had once been David Carstairs. Then William had set off to begin tracking down the buyers who had purchased the artifacts that Carstairs had smuggled from India. The statuettes appeared to be a part of the bizarre curse that was transforming men into monstrosities, and the faster they gathered up those artifacts, the more lives they might save. The first name he had come across in Carstairs's records was that of Ernest P. Widly. Now he stood in the cellar of the building where Widly had his rooms and took several long breaths, trying to steady himself. Whispering the same protection spell he had used before, he steeled himself and moved with as much stealth as he was able toward the stairs and whatever awaited him above. He took another deep breath, fighting residual nausea, and threw himself upward, taking the stairs two at a time.

Blue flame curled and eddied around his fingers as he approached the door of the flat that was his destination, and he cast a quick spell, making short work of the iron bolt on the other side. He stepped through and into the kitchen, then slowly eased the door shut behind him. Remembering how stupidly he had blundered into Carstairs's rooms earlier in the evening, he was determined to keep the element of surprise with him now.

The kitchen was a mess, flour and rotten meat from the cupboard spread all over the floor and counters. It looked as though someone had ransacked the cupboard without finding anything to their liking. William's stomach gave another lurch, but he managed to swallow back the delicious pudding he had eaten earlier. He picked his way through the foul-smelling bits of a raw rack of lamb, and crossed the threshold into the living area.

With Carstairs's sales slips tucked safely in his pocket, William moved through the dining room, pausing outside a closed door. Inside, he could hear someone speaking in a harsh, guttural dialect. Part of him wanted to flee, but against all reason, he took a deep breath and opened the door.

The room was Widly's study. Four men in various states of dress were huddled around the fireplace, staring at the firelight. The coal hood had been upturned, and someone had tried to eat several pieces of coal before realizing that it made much better tinder than food.

As one, they turned and stared at him, their eyes bulging so enormously that they seemed about to burst from the sides of their skulls. Their skin was mottled and had the rough texture of scales. It gleamed in the firelight.

On the floor was the half-eaten corpse of an elderly woman. From what he could tell, she wore the uniform of a household servant.

William had seen death before, but the butchery with which this old woman had been dispatched made his blood run cold. Half the flesh on her face had been stripped away, baring bone and muscle. One of her arms was missing, presumably being digested by the same stomach that had enjoyed her face.

The creatures hadn't moved a muscle. They just crouched, staring at him.

He took a step backward, bumping into the door frame. His motion seemed their cue to act. The monster farthest into its transformation flopped toward him, long toadlike tongue hanging wet and flaccid almost to the floor. The twisted changeling tensed its hind legs, preparing to pounce, even as William fled into the corridor and toward the parlor. He needed room to fight.

The accursed creatures all burst into activity then, and scrambled after him, their odd croaking rasps unnerving William. He found a spot that placed his back safely to the wall and turned to face them. Crouching, they shambled from side to side as they moved in on him, but this time he was ready.

His command of magic was by no means complete, nor as acute as his sister's, but there existed an array of spells he had rehearsed over and over. Now he contorted his fingers into arcane symbols and muttered under his breath.

The things leaped at him.

The last words issued from William's mouth, and the reptile men froze in midleap, their malformed bodies hanging almost obscenely in the air. One by one, they dropped like stones and began to shrink until each was roughly the size of a hazelnut. William jogged to the sideboard in the nearby dining room and grabbed an empty bottle of wine and its stopper.

With the bottle in his hand, he reached down, picked up each of the twice-cursed miscreants, and dropped it through the mouth of the bottle. He forced the stopper back onto the bottle and chanted a simple yet powerful spell to seal it. The glass took on a subtle red glow, then slowly returned to its natural state.

"Well done, William," he whispered to himself. Someone had to appreciate his ingenuity, after all.

He put the wine bottle down on the large rectangular dining room table and went back to the study in search of the Indian statuary that had led these men to their abominable fates.

In the study, William snatched a throw rug from the back of a love seat that faced the fireplace and covered the corpse on the floor. With the woman's ravaged face out of view, he paused to admire the library her employer had amassed. The bookshelves had been lovingly carved from a rich, dark oak that glowed almost auburn in the firelight. They bore a beautiful design of intertwined grapevines. The small, pointed leaves looked so real that William had to resist the urge to reach out and pluck one of them.

From the many languages that graced the spines of the books, and the artifacts that sat in niches throughout, he discerned that Ernest P. Widly was a man of admirably eclectic tastes. William found himself hoping that he and Tamara could find a way to transform the man back to his normal state when this crisis was over. For now, though, he would have to remain content knowing Widly was secure at the bottom of a wine bottle.

Combing the shelves for any sign of an Indian artifact, William found that one of Widly's pieces was newly missing. It had sat in a small niche above the mantelpiece until very recently, for the mantel had a light covering of dust, save on the spot where the object had rested.

William stared at the empty space for a long moment, questions swirling in his mind. He took a breath, and then began again, thoroughly searching the flat in the hope of finding the missing piece. It made no sense. The only reason he could think of for the creatures to be there was that they also sought the accursed figurine, but he had arrived while they were still there. That meant it had been missing before they had paid their visit. It was possible, he supposed, that Widly had gotten rid of the artifact himself, but William thought it highly unlikely. What he had seen thus far of the influence the objects had on their owners made him believe Widly would not have had the moral strength to dispose of it.

Which meant someone else had removed it.

The idea troubled William deeply. If someone else was on the same trail as he was, he felt the odds were against the thief having some benevolent purpose. No, if someone had stolen the accursed thing, there must be some sinister purpose behind the theft.

William stood in the midst of the flat, trying not to feel as though he had botched the job. He shook his head, not letting the negative thoughts overtake him. There were many other names on Carstairs's list he had yet to visit, and there was not a second to spare. Not only did he need to stop the spread of this horror, but it seemed he now had competition for possession of the accursed artifacts.

Steeling himself, he muttered the words to the translocation spell and quickly vanished into the ether.

∽

SAVAGE AS SHE was in battle, Bodicea was not heartless. The spectral queen had empathy for those who had been mistreated in life, but she could summon not an ounce of compassion for the malformed creature that lay before her. David Carstairs was not some poor unfortunate soul. He was a criminal by trade—a liar, a thief, and a robber of other people's history and culture—and that was unforgivable. Others—even other ghosts—might have been appalled at remaining in the company of the accursed amphibian monstrosity, but Bodicea found his presence all the more distasteful because of what Carstairs *had been,* rather than what he had become.

"Water—" croaked the thing that had once been David Carstairs.

Bodicea scowled.

"I think not."

"Water, please . . . ," the thing croaked again. It was pathetic.

She stared at the creature, truly studying its deformities for the first time. Its head had grown too large for its spindly neck, its chin so weighted down that it almost touched its throat. It had bulging yellow eyes that protruded unevenly from the sides of its face, and its mouth was a gash of razor-sharp teeth.

"Water," it pleaded, in a thinner voice now.

Sick of its mewling, Bodicea laid aside her spear and approached it cautiously. The thing was bound, and lay on its side on the bed. As an ethereal being, it was easier for her to move the creature to the water than to bring water to the bed. It required focus and effort for a ghost to make physical contact with solid objects, and even more concentration for her to touch a human being, but she could easily grip the flesh of a supernatural. And as weakened as the scaly beast seemed now, she doubted it would put up any fight.

Bodicea picked up the thing, slinging it easily over her shoulder, then started toward the jug of water that stood on a table by the window.

She had taken only a few steps when the thing grabbed a fistful of her hair and yanked. The ghost howled in rage, dropping Carstairs onto the floor. William had cast his binding spell too quickly and inexpertly, and as the monstrosity thrashed against those magical bonds, they fell to ribbons of shimmering energy and then disappeared altogether.

Bodicea snarled and tensed for the attack, the pain in her scalp feeling all too physical, though she had been without flesh for centuries. Phantoms could inflict pain upon creatures of the supernatural, yes, but the converse was all too true, as well. She and William would have a talk about this.

The thing crouched, leering at her, then sprang with blinding speed. It collided with her, claws sinking into her spectral form, tearing at her spiritual essence and dragging her down to the floor.

"You bitch—" it snarled, dragging her across the floor.

Her ghostly essence sank partway into the floor. For a moment she slipped from its grasp and began to crawl away, but it caught her foot and pulled her back. Her naked body fell in and out of the wooden floor as she was dragged back toward the bed. The thing didn't seem to understand that Bodicea was a ghost. All she had to do was to dissolve this form and slip into the ethereal realm.

But her rage got the better of her. Bodicea reached out and grabbed her spear. Just as the thing pushed itself back on top of her and began rutting against her leg, she punched the tip of the spear through the creature's skull.

It let out a terrible scream, then abruptly ceased to move altogether, its body becoming deadweight.

She pushed its carcass away and spat on the thing that had been David Carstairs. Memories of the rape and murder of her daughters, and her own ill use at the hands of the demon Oblis, were fresh again in her mind, as though the crimes had taken place that very morning. Such was the reality of her daily existence. The constant presence of the demon in the home of the Swifts had wreaked havoc upon her emotions, and this creature had reignited all her grief and rage.

Queen Bodicea dropped to her knees, reached out a spectral hand, and ripped the monster's genitals from between its legs with a wet, tearing noise and a splash of brackish, stinking blood.

"No one takes liberties with me," she whispered. "Never again."

Bodicea let the fiend's manhood drop to the floor, where it lay limp and shriveled. Then, with no prisoner left to guard, she vanished into the ether.

Ten

The night air refreshed Tamara as she let Farris lead her out of the Egyptian Hall and onto the sidewalk.

Looking back at the building, she marveled at how anachronistic the hall's façade was compared with the rest of modern London. Large columns that stood like sentries guarding the front doors clashed with the honeyed brick and stone of its neighbors. She couldn't help wondering if Egypt really looked that way, or if she was only seeing an English bastardization of the genuine article.

"Miss, you're shivering," Farris said crossly. "We should wait inside, where it's a bit warmer." Even stocky Farris in his overcoat looked chilly in the London night, his breath wafting like dragon smoke around his mouth and nostrils.

Tamara shook her head, pulling her wrap more tightly around her shoulders. She would much rather weather the cold than go back inside where the atmosphere itself was stifling. The exhibit had been sparsely attended, but she was not in the proper frame of mind this evening. Its resemblance to a temple did not extend to the interior of the place, but still it had felt like a tomb to her. Mixed with the odor of paint and the dusty smell of ancient things, the air was entirely too oppressive.

Tamara found herself grateful for the crisp night air. The tension that had been knotted in her shoulders and neck seemed to evaporate as the cold raised gooseflesh on her skin.

"I feel better outside where I can see the stars, Farris," she said. "It's cold, indeed, but it's early spring in London town, and for once the wind is just right and the air is fresh."

Farris shook his head, tutting. "For a lass with such a keen mind, you've no common sense a'tall."

Tamara laughed, her thoughts clearer than they had been all day. She was grateful for Farris and his mothering, felt safer knowing he was looking after her. John must have thought it unorthodox to have her butler chaperoning their evening, as opposed to some widowed aunt or a proper maid, as was most common. But Tamara genuinely enjoyed contradicting society's conventions. Sophia was the sort of girl who wore one face in public, another in private. Tamara was only herself.

Truth be told, she was torn between despising Sophia for her duality and envying her the ability to adapt that way. Tamara possessed a great deal of passion, and it often caused her trouble. She spoke her mind far too often and too vociferously for most men's preference, and even then she preferred not to taint her family name overmuch.

It had occurred to her that writing penny dreadfuls under the pseudonym of T. L. Fleet placed her in the same sort of dichotomy as that Sophia practiced. Yet her own secret didn't feel nearly so duplicitous as the two faces worn by her brother's intended. This ought to have made her feel better, but somehow, the heiress's indiscretion left her somehow freer, and seemed more honest than any of Tamara's passionate declarations. For Tamara had never truly let go of her inhibitions. No matter how independent a girl she thought herself to be, she had never given her emotions free rein.

John appeared at her side. He had hired a cab for the evening, but the driver hadn't expected them to leave this soon, so John had been forced to search him out in one of the nearby free houses. The driver lit the lantern that hung on a hook at the front of the carriage, then climbed up onto the high seat at the front.

"Your chariot awaits, milady," John said with a smile that was halfway between rogue and fool, but entirely charming. Still, there was concern in his eyes.

Tamara smiled as he started to offer her his hand, but Farris beat him to it, helping Tamara into the carriage. Then he made his way to the front of the carriage, to climb up beside the driver. Tamara flashed John an apologetic smile. He just shrugged, taking the seat beside her and closing the door.

"I'm sorry for Farris," she offered. "He looks to me more as a daughter than as a charge."

"Then I'm grateful to him. You *should* be looked after, Tamara."

John's face was deep in shadows as the carriage began its journey back to Ludlow House. She wished that she could see him, that she could discern from his expression what he really meant by those words. In her mind, they were tantamount to a proposal of some sort, but without enough light to reveal his eyes, she couldn't tell for certain. And the lantern that rocked on its hook outside the window was not bright enough to dispel the darkness within.

"You're sweet," she said quietly. Her cheeks felt warm with her awareness of how close they were, of the fact that they were alone in the back of the carriage. They were out of the chilly wind now, but she did not try to tell herself the lie that this was the sole cause of the warmth she felt. The butterflies that she had hoped for earlier in the evening had finally made their appearance—*better late than never,* she supposed.

"Whether you like it or not, Tamara Swift, you are a very delicate creature." John turned with these words, facing her so that she could see his eyes now in the dimness, and his gray eyes were almost black in the darkness.

She suppressed the urge to laugh, to tell him that she was far—very far indeed—from the fragile English Rose he thought her to be. She opened her mouth to say as much, but John wasn't finished.

"When you fainted in my arms like that—"

Tamara felt her face flush with embarrassment, and she decided to hold her tongue. She was appalled at herself. Fainting like that . . . it was so entirely unlike her. And now she had given John reason to think she *was* just another demure female. A delicate girl, like a hundred others he had met and wooed.

"John, I—" she started, marshaling herself again, but he shushed her.

"Tamara, please." His smile, visible even in the gloom, made her catch her breath, and the heat from her cheeks spread quickly downward. "I know you're an outspoken girl, and I admire that, truly I do. But just for a moment, hush."

He took her hand in his, and she weakened at his touch. Tamara bit her lower lip to withhold the tiny cry that begged to be uttered, and cursed herself for entertaining the urge. This closeness, the warmth of his flesh, the glint of his eyes in the near dark, seemed to erase her hesitations about him, leaving only the powerful allure of the man himself. A fire licked across her belly, radiating downward. Like a flower turning to the sun, she felt herself yearning for him.

Tamara knew well enough how to ease the simplest aspects of the yearning, how to put her hand between her legs and move her fingers against the smooth wet flesh until her body jerked spasmodically against her bedclothes and she had to bite her pillow to keep from crying out. But she had never felt *lust* like this before, so that her entire body seemed afire, nor had she imagined what heat the touch of a man could elicit.

Caught in a cascade of conflicting emotions and influences, Tamara was at war with herself.

"I—" she began, but once again he silenced her, this time putting his finger softly to her lips.

Not only did she allow him to do so, but on impulse, Tamara took his finger into her mouth. He blinked in astonishment, then stared at her as the slick wetness of her tongue eased the friction so that his finger slipped back and forth against her lips, in and out of the warmth of her mouth. John let her continue for a moment, his eyes dark, with need, she assumed. She closed her eyes, enjoying the taste of his skin.

"What are you doing? Are you insane?" John rasped, his voice low. He pulled his hand away from her mouth and moved across the seat as far from her as possible.

"But . . . I thought . . . you wanted . . . ," she stammered.

Her eyes were wide, and they burned with embarrassment and with hot tears that slid down her cheeks and chin and down into the hollow of her throat.

Each tear was an accusation, a reprimand that came not from John, but from deep inside herself. She cursed herself for her stupidity, for thinking she could for a moment be free of restraints. Other women seemed able to throw off those bonds—Sophia managed it—but somehow Tamara had made a mess of it. For a moment her wantonness had felt wonderful and exciting, and now it was shameful.

William was right. I am a slatternly woman, she thought, biting her lip again to keep from sobbing aloud. She couldn't even bear to look at him, let alone speak to him again.

She had thought he was different, thought she had sensed a kindred soul buried inside the man who now rejected her. She realized now how terribly she must have misjudged him.

The cab came to a jarring halt, and against her will Tamara slid against John. She felt her breasts pressing against his chest, and her terror only increased. A moment ago his touch had been enough to stir her in ways unlike any she'd ever known. Now it horrified her.

She pushed herself away from him, her heart pounding.

She turned to open the carriage door, but John reached out and grabbed her hand.

"Tamara, wait! Please. I . . . I did not mean to use you so rudely. I was just . . . startled by your actions. Shocked, I should say."

She stared at him, desperately willing him to apologize, to help let her put the whole episode behind her. His flirtations had made his intentions clear.

Now that she replayed the scene in her mind, she was sure she had not imagined it. John had stoked that fire with great purpose, and then flinched away from it as though he had been burned. Could it be that he had actually *intended* to humiliate her, as he had humiliated William? Tamara couldn't find any other explanation for the way he had responded to her.

"I am sorry that I was hurtful to you, Miss Swift."

Tamara did not answer.

John sighed as the carriage began to move again. He glanced

away as though searching for something in the darkness of the carriage.

"Tamara, I know you think of me as a scoundrel. Some wild, feckless fellow who goes about tasting all of life's fruits, with not a care in the world. But that is not the truth of the matter. Indeed, I am the *antithesis* of that image, though I am sure Sophia would lead you to believe otherwise."

Tamara nodded, but remained silent.

"I find you truly admirable, Tamara Swift, but I am not looking for a wife. I'm not immune to your charms. You are . . . really quite exquisite. But when I hushed you, it was with humor, to cheer and calm you, and to take a moment to collect my own thoughts. Seduction was not my intention."

She was glad now that he could not see her face well in the darkness of the cab. How embarrassing it was to misunderstand him so horribly. Oh, how she wished that she could disappear.

This last thought gave her pause—she *could* translocate, if she were so inclined. The thought of doing so in the midst of his earnest entreaty cheered her, and she almost chuckled at the thought of how John would react. Then he continued.

"I *would* like to see you again, to spend time with you . . . as a friend," John said, his voice pulling her away from her imaginings. "I think that you and I have more in common than either of us might imagine."

Tamara swallowed, her throat aching with the aftermath of her tears. She wiped at her eyes and raised her chin proudly. "I am not certain that would be possible, Mr. Haversham. I find myself rather stifled in your company—"

John leaned down and kissed her gloved hand.

"Please do not be embarrassed. It was an honest mistake, one that I am sure I myself must have led you to. You are a very lovely woman, Miss Swift. I am sure you must have many suitors. It would only seem natural that I should be one, as well."

Lovely, thought Tamara miserably. *Now he assumes I am an egoist like his cousin.*

"This has been an . . . enlightening evening, John. I will consider your request."

She knew her words sounded cool, but she needed time to evaluate what had just occurred, and what John had said. Tamara wasn't sure what she would do if he called upon her again.

She guessed he would not, though; that all of this was just his gentlemanly way of attempting to leave her with some of her dignity intact. Oh, how she hated him, and was intrigued by him all at the same time.

"Thank you, Tamara. I appreciate your candor."

He released her hand, allowing her to slip out just as Farris opened the carriage door.

"And thank you for your kindness, Miss Swift. I hope your evening was not completely horrid. I really do look forward to enjoying your company again soon."

"Good evening, Mr. Haversham," she said, taking a step away from the carriage so that Farris could close the door, which he did much too abruptly.

Her shame and humiliation were beginning to diminish as she climbed the few steps to the door of Ludlow House, and now they were beginning to give way to something else entirely. The desire she had felt for the man was all too real, the memory of it all too fresh. Tamara had never felt its like before, and she could not deny that she *wanted* to feel that way again.

And she had seen in Haversham's eyes—heard it in the tenor of his voice—that he desired her, as well. Why, then, had he demurred? She did not know. But she wasn't going to be satisfied with his offer of friendship. If John Haversham wasn't seeking to court her, so be it, but when next they met she would do everything in her power to make him realize that the mistake was his. She would make him want her, make his body yearn for hers the same way she had burned for him back in the carriage.

I must be insane, she thought happily as she reached the front door and went inside.

It was only upon stepping into the foyer of Ludlow House that the day's events came back to her and she realized that, for a short time, John Haversham had made her forget her grief. Perhaps she ought to have been grateful to him.

Instead, by the time she had reached the privacy of her own room, she was deeply ashamed.

⁓

DESPITE THE GRAVITY of the day's events, by the time William returned home late that night he was feeling pleased with himself.

The ghosts entertained doubts about his capacity to serve as Protector. It was a duty unlike any other, to defend England from all the powers of darkness and evil, and it required courage and discipline. William had always had a great deal of the latter. It was the former that they weren't sure of. Oh, they tried their best not to show it, certainly, but he knew just the same. In his heart, he had shared those doubts.

After all, Tamara was the more instinctual of the two of them, and the more perceptive, as well. Those traits had allowed her to adapt far more easily to both the knowledge of the magical world, and the power they had inherited. Tamara had shown a far greater facility with magic. That meant William would have to work that much harder than she, simply to fulfill the duties they had both inherited.

But he was up to the task. William Swift was nothing if not a hard worker, dogged and filled with determination. And in moments when he wasn't wrestling with self-doubt, he thought he might actually have the edge over his sister in a situation that required quick decisions.

He had acquitted himself quite well at the Carstairs and Widly residences. Had, in fact, achieved great success thus far in pursuing their present line of inquiry. The documents he had taken from Carstairs had proven invaluable.

He was aware, however, that it had been a near thing at Widly's house and that going about on his own was perhaps unwise. So William had summoned Admiral Lord Nelson, pulling him away from his own inquiries, and the two of them had proceeded together. They had spent the remainder of the evening visiting the other buyers to whom Carstairs had sold artifacts.

Most of the gentlemen William found at home purported to be horrified to learn that they had purchased stolen objects, but William could not have said how many of them were honestly ignorant of the origins of their purchases.

Where they found the man of the house not at home, the wives seemed genuinely repentant. Husband or wife, none of them balked at handing over the objects in question, particularly once he informed them that Swift's of London would guarantee their return, or some form of compensation.

Far more important than their cooperation, however, was the fact that none of them seemed to have been tainted by the curse.

At a number of the places they visited, they found neither the master of the house nor his wife at home, and where there was anyone to be found, the servants remarked that they had been absent for an extended and unexplained length of time. In some places, even members of the staff had gone missing, and William was convinced that they had fallen victim to the same curse that had claimed their masters. He wondered, deeply disturbed by the question, where they had gone and if they had somehow been drawn to one another.

Troubled or not, though, William Swift was quite proud of himself . . . or he had been until Horatio had related to him the information that had been conveyed by the spirit of Colonel Dunstan.

"Did your associate say how long the Indian population of the East End has been affected by this curse?" William had asked.

"There are indications that the trouble began as long as two or three weeks ago, I'm afraid," Horatio replied.

That news caused William to pause, and debate with himself how best to proceed. Their logic thus far had been sound. The artifacts had certainly seemed responsible for the transformations of Frederick Martin, Carstairs, and Widly, and the connection to the smuggled goods seemed obvious. If the curse was affecting those responsible for the theft of the statuettes, and their export to England, he supposed it was possible there would be Indian men involved in that criminal enterprise, as well.

The hideous by-product of the curse, however—the impregnation of women in those slums—that development was unexpected, and it seemed to be affecting persons who had no discernible connection to Carstairs and his illegal endeavors. The darkest of magics, affecting those who were entirely innocent.

Still, the artifacts seemed the only tangible element that linked the transformations. At least for the moment.

He was troubled, however, by Dunstan's suggestion that he and Tamara did not care about the evil plaguing Albion so long as it affected only the poor. It was not true, certainly. Had they known of the plague any sooner, they would have acted. Yet he did wonder if they had been vigilant enough; if there was a tack they might have taken that would have brought word of those horrors to them sooner.

In the end, William and Horatio determined to follow through upon their present course, and then decide upon the next step—undoubtedly an investigation of the horrors in the East End—when this phase was completed.

Currently they stood in one of the attic rooms at the top of Ludlow House staring at their handiwork: an empty room.

Together, they had decided that a cloaking spell was the best way to protect anyone from accidentally stumbling upon the artifacts. That, coupled with a binding and protection spell, would keep everyone in the household safe from the effects of the curse. Similarly, they had decided to keep the imprisoned victims here, as well, still restrained in the wine bottle. Removing them for any reason seemed unwise. As an extra precaution, William had placed a protection spell around himself before he had started to weave the wards.

Thus, the seven idols and the wine bottle full of diminutive creatures were rendered completely invisible.

"I think that should hold them," William said proudly. "Well done, Horatio. Well done, William."

Nelson shook his semi-transparent head in wonder at William's strange proclivity to address himself in the third person.

"You know, Horatio, while I confess that I'm pleased we didn't encounter any more of those monsters, I'm also quite troubled by it. Presuming our absent buyers have been afflicted like Carstairs and the others, where do you suppose they've gone?"

"I'm sure I couldn't say, though it worries me as well," the ghost agreed, his voice low and thoughtful.

There was a knock at the attic door, and Tamara burst in. "Byron said that Horatio had received news from a comrade. Are we going to investigate the slums of London this evening?"

William frowned. "It's already quite late, and we've not had an opportunity to discuss a plan of action. I think it might be wise to wait until tomorrow. And when we do expand our investigation into those areas, I must insist that you not accompany me there, Tamara. To have a girl along would be inviting trouble."

Tamara pointedly ignored him and, instead, closed the attic door and came farther into the room.

"We are the Protectors of Albion, William. We're quite capable of dealing with a bit of trouble."

William crossed his arms and gazed at her coolly.

"Could we discuss this later? Horatio and I are right in the middle of casting an extremely tricky spell. We're using an invisibility enchantment to hide the idols, in case anyone—or anything—should come looking. You're disturbing the delicate nature of the—"

"Oh, surely we're through with that business, are we not, young Master William?" Horatio asked.

William arched an eyebrow and stared at him. It was no secret that Admiral Nelson had a paternal fondness for Tamara, and enjoyed stirring the pot in her favor. Bodicea had confided to William that Tamara reminded Nelson very much of his own daughter, Horatia, who had been born out of his affair with Lady Emma Hamilton. Afterward, Nelson had married Lady Hamilton, following her husband's death. But Horatia had still carried the stigma of being illegitimate, so the admiral had never really managed a relationship with her. Bodicea expressed the opinion that it still haunted him, even long after his death, contributing to the way he doted on Tamara.

Tamara sighed. A tremor of what he thought was suppressed emotion went through her. "This has been one of the worst days of my life, William. Yet I keep my head high, and I forge ahead, because we have a duty. Regrettably, I learned little of consequence this evening. Mr. Haversham did confirm, however, that he was at the bishop of Manchester's party, and that the earl of Claridge, in the midst of the filthy transformation we have seen ourselves, attacked a young girl there. John himself tore the monster off her."

"So it's John now, is it?" William asked.

Tamara rolled her eyes and sniffed dramatically. "You have no need to worry where Mr. Haversham is concerned. He has made it clear that he would like to be my *friend,* and that is all."

William narrowed his eyes suspiciously.

But he held his tongue. It was obvious that she had been rather roughly charged with this knowledge, her pride wounded in the process.

"I see. And you learned nothing more?" William inquired hopefully. He was sorry to have forced his sister into an unhappy situation, but he was glad that John Haversham had embraced reason. He was no match for Tamara. His courtship would have only brought her dishonor.

"I am sorry that I am not a better spy, William. I fear that I did not feel very well this evening, and my interrogative skills were much dulled. But I am entirely prepared to make up for my earlier shortcoming."

"I trust you did your best," William replied. "Now, look, back to this discussion of the East End—"

"Yes, back to that," Tamara said archly. "As Byron tells it, we've word of this curse having spread to the Indian population that lives there."

"Yes," Horatio confirmed. In that strangely empty room, the lamplight filtered through the ghost and made him somehow both more transparent and more substantial, all at the same time. "Though apparently they think of it more as a plague than a curse. Colonel Dunstan was a highly regarded soldier of both English and Indian descent. His ability as a translator made him invaluable in the Seven Years War. Though only a teenager at the time, he distinguished himself admirably, and later became one of Wellesley's most trusted men."

"He believes that the plague actually *originated* in the slums, Tamara," William said. "We cannot be certain, of course, which is why I must investigate as the Protector of Albion—"

"*Protector?*" Tamara countered, her voice rising. "As if there were only *one*? Do not allow yourself to think for one moment longer that you are going to investigate this curse alone."

William took a deep breath. "Actually, I hadn't thought I'd be alone. I'd have the ghosts for company."

Tamara glared at him. "Just because I haven't been myself of late, William Swift, doesn't mean I intend to shirk my duties," she said hotly.

"Now don't argue, my friends—" Nelson began, but he stopped as both Swift siblings turned and glared at him.

"I think I shall go and visit Byron, and Father—or Oblis—or *whoever* is in residence in Father's body at the moment," Tamara said. "At least there I am given *some* respect."

At that she turned on her heel and stalked out of the room.

William raised an eyebrow as Tamara slammed the door loudly behind her.

"Women," he said under his breath. "They truly are an enigma to me. I find them harder to fathom than calculus, and I had once believed *that* was going to be the bane of my existence."

Even as he spoke the words, he heard the familiar low trilling noise that so often accompanied the manifestation or departure of a ghostly presence. He frowned, thinking Horatio had abandoned him, but when he turned he saw that Nelson was still in the room and that they had been joined by Bodicea.

The spectral queen held her spear as though it were a walking staff, but there was an uncommon wariness in her aspect. Normally her manner was as brazen as her nakedness. At first William presumed that she had overheard and was offended by his words.

"Bodicea, I assure you that I meant nothing by—"

"I have failed you," Her Majesty declared. Her gaze was grim as she lifted her eyes to regard him. "I allowed myself to be baited by the man, Carstairs. Or by whatever he had become."

William hesitated a moment. It was Horatio who asked the question.

"Bodicea," the ghost said, "what have you done?"

"I killed him. Inadvertently."

William sighed. He'd entertained the idea that they might still learn something from Carstairs . . . that if they could determine the circumstances of his theft of those particular artifacts, they might find the ultimate source of the curse. Now that possibility, no matter how remote, had been erased.

"Inadvertently?"

"He forced my hand," said the queen.

~

TAMARA TOOK THE stairs two at a time, propelled by her fury. She had spent the entire day vacillating between grief, anger, and embarrassment, and now, finally, anger had won.

She opened the door to the room in which her father was kept and barreled inside, unmindful of the conversation that was already in progress between Byron and Oblis.

"The last time I put the old Nebuchadnezzar out to grass—" Oblis was saying. With a gleam in his eye he paused to glance up at Tamara. The face was her father's, but the malignance of the demon's mind shone through. He looked at her so hungrily that she paused and shuddered, feeling almost as filthy as she had when Frederick Martin had pawed her that morning.

"Excuse me," Tamara said curtly as she turned to leave.

"Tamara, wait," Byron said. The foppish poet gazed at her with a mixture of guilt and concern, and floated in pursuit. Their conversation had, no doubt, been more than vulgar, but Tamara thought Byron looked rather sheepish for one who was usually so open about his debauchery.

"Tamara, please, forgive me," said the ghost. "Boys will be boys, you know . . ." He looked at her hopefully, but she shook her head.

"This isn't something that can be accepted casually, Byron! You are not chatting with some stable boy or poet. He is a demon, not some drinking companion! A demon that has possessed the body of my father. Simply the fact that you sit here sharing an easy camaraderie with this fiend feels like betrayal to me, and I have had enough of disappointment for one day!

"And don't think that your tone escaped me. I'm quite familiar with your lascivious insinuations and obsession with all things sexual. Honestly, can you not think of anything else? Is there no *meaningful* conversation to be had with you that does not involve carnal lust? What next? Shall we speak of *my* sexual escapades?"

The ghost and demon both gave her a curious look.

Tamara blushed, but did not look away.

"There *are* none, you fiends! I am unwanted!" She coughed, and realized her throat was raw.

"Excuse me—"

She spun and started toward the door again, not wanting them to see how upset she really was. As she flung it open she was startled to find Byron's ghost already in the corridor. Tamara looked back into the room, where Oblis watched warily from behind her father's eyes.

"Tamara," the spirit said, reaching for her with insubstantial hands. His eyes were kind, though, and without guile or accusation. "Come and tell Byron what has happened to his dear girl."

It was his manner more than his words that drained the anger from her. She bit her lower lip and shook her head as she sagged back against the doorjamb.

"I . . . I was made a fool of this evening," she began in a rasping whisper, not wishing for Oblis to hear.

Byron tried to put a supportive arm around her shoulder, but it only passed through her.

"Oh, Byron," Tamara said. "I appreciate the sentiment." She sighed and pulled a handkerchief from her pocket, dabbing at her red-rimmed eyes.

"A man, John Haversham. He invited me to an art exhibit at the Egyptian Hall this evening. I did not want to attend, after the news of the morning, but William insisted that I go. It seems I was wasting my time with a man not at all enamored of me, while William was off trying to prove his worth as a Protector . . . as *the* Protector, to hear him tell it."

Byron issued a sigh that seemed to ripple through his spectral form.

"You know that isn't true, Tamara. Your brother is constantly comparing himself with you—how could he fail to, when the rest of us do the same? But he saw your rendezvous with Haversham as an opportunity to pursue a line of inquiry he could not, even as he pursued a different route. Doubly efficient."

Tamara knitted her brows and gazed at him. "You sound suspiciously like Horatio."

"He did inform me of the events of the day, a short time ago." Byron gave her his most intimate smile. "But don't damn me to the Hell of Horatio's precious propriety simply because we are all fighting in the same war."

She couldn't help smiling in return. "I wouldn't dream of it."

"Good. Now tell me all about this man."

Tamara was surprised to find that she had no more tears. Instead the heat of her embarrassment and disappointment had settled back into embers of anger. "I thought his interest lay in courting me, but now he has said that he seeks only my friendship, and I have done a terrible thing—"

"Yes?" Byron asked, without bothering to veil the prurience of his interest.

Tamara shook her head indulgently. "It was nothing. A trifle, really. The troubling bit is that I made *my* interest known to him, before I was made aware of his lack of intention."

She took a deep breath and let it out through her nose.

"Now I am humiliated."

Byron began to laugh, but stopped abruptly when Tamara glared at him. "My dear, we have *all* been spurned upon occasion. I, myself, have been made a fool of more times than I care to admit. I once even found myself called out over a misrepresentation of interest—"

The door was still open to the old nursery, where Oblis was kept prisoner. From the gloom that lay within, Oblis snorted. "The girl informed you that she did not require your services?" the demon asked.

Tamara started and turned to stare into the room. Candlelight flickered on the walls, casting the face of her father in dancing shadows. She ought to have known better than to forget, even for a moment, how keen the demon's senses were. How Oblis seemed to survive by picking at their lives like a carrion bird.

"Not precisely," Byron said, eyes twinkling as he glanced once at Oblis, and then back to Tamara. "You see, I was certain this particular young man was of a more *flexible* persuasion. Sadly, he was not."

"Byron!" Tamara said, raising a hand to her mouth in faux scandal. "You're *terrible*."

"Oh, yes. Certainly," Byron countered. "But I've made you smile, and that is worth a galaxy full of stars. Now I must take a moment to speak with Horatio, since you have so kindly consented to watch your father."

"I have?" Tamara said.

Byron nodded.

"Yes, you have." And with that, he disappeared into the ether.

Tamara hesitated outside the room, but then forced herself to enter again under the watchful gaze of the demon. She sat stiffly in a velvet chair that had been a favorite of her mother's. Her fingers tapped the soft gray fabric that covered the armrests. When she was a little girl, her mother had spent many an hour sitting in this chair quietly embroidering. She had rested at her mother's feet, fascinated by the quick movements of fingers on the cloth—

"What memory are you thinking on?" Oblis asked, shattering the vision she had conjured of her mother's long, beautiful fingers.

"Nothing," she replied quickly. "Nothing of import."

Oblis stared. "Tell me more of your evening, Tamara."

"Are you mad?" she said sternly.

"Share the tale with me, and I shall make it worth your while," Oblis hissed.

Tamara rolled her eyes. "Nothing you could offer would be worth that abasement," she replied tartly.

"You think not? I know many things, my little pet. I can see the future, and it is black, black, black. But pray, tell me more of this John Haversham."

"I told you I would not," Tamara answered. "And besides, my life is of no consequence to you."

Oblis smiled, showing blackened teeth. *Poor Father,* she thought miserably. He had always been such a *clean* man.

"I can offer you advice, Tamara Swift. I can help you in your quest to find the source of this curse. This *plague.*"

Tamara flinched and stared at him. But her interest had been piqued.

Oblis sat cross-legged on the floor, his hands clasped rapturously before him.

"What do you know of it?" Tamara said.

Oblis only smiled.

Her skin prickled with frustration and anger, but her curiosity got the better of her. If he had some knowledge of value, it would be irresponsible of her not to discover its nature.

"What would you like to know? What do I have to offer that you could possibly want, in exchange for information?"

"Tell me of your humiliation," Oblis said.

Tamara glared at him. "It was nothing. I told you—"

"Enough!" Oblis said in a terrifyingly loud voice. "I want to know what you did to humiliate yourself!"

She started to speak, but stopped herself. She took a breath and composed her words, before beginning again.

"I took his . . . finger . . . into my mouth . . ." Tamara's stomach turned as she spoke the words.

Oblis began to laugh gleefully.

"And then?"

She swallowed hard, but then braced herself, meeting his gaze with a steely glare of her own. "I suckled upon it."

Oblis clapped his hands together. "Yes! And did you enjoy it?"

She looked down at her hands before nodding. "Yes, I enjoyed it."

His laughter was giddy. "Of course you did, filthy girl. Of course you did!"

Tamara trembled with hatred for the demon, but she said nothing.

"Excellent. And what more?"

She frowned. "Nothing more. Isn't that horrible enough?"

"You're certain?"

"Completely," she said, shivering.

"All right, then. Now for your reward, as promised. A question. Why have you not sought the Protector of Bharath?"

"That is all my humiliation is worth?" Tamara said. "You promised answers, and instead offer a question."

Oblis nodded. "The question is its own answer. As to your humiliation, it was but a small thing, Tamara. You will experience far worse. Believe me when I tell you that."

Eleven

John Haversham rose far earlier than was his wont. He was scheduled to make an appearance later in the morning, at the Algernon Club, and the prospect had given him a fitful night's sleep.

Despite his exhaustion, however, he could not force himself to return to slumber, no matter how he tried. Nor did he wish to pass the hours within the confines of his home. So he roused his driver early, and set out for Covent Garden just after eight o'clock.

By the time he arrived, the frenzy of the vegetable market had faded entirely. Only once, several years earlier, had John visited the market early enough to witness the spectacle that took place there each morning. The sellers called to one another and to the throngs of people who arrived to buy their wares, and the customers wandered among literal walls of vegetation, piles of turnips, cauliflowers, and cabbages that towered a dozen feet from the ground, choosing what they wished for their shops and kitchens. The bustle of the crowds had been extraordinary, and John recalled with perfect clarity how magical it seemed, watching the towers of vegetables melt away, finally to vanish altogether. There had been fruit, as well, during that summer visit, and carts overflowing with flowers.

John had always intended to return, to witness that wild scene once more. But this time, his goal was quite different.

He stepped down out of the carriage and instructed his driver to retrieve him at half past one from his favorite pub in Piccadilly. He had far too much pent-up energy, and he needed to release it through a morning of brisk walking, to be followed by a quick bite at the pub. By then, he would know what, precisely, the director of the Algernon Club expected of him.

For now, though, he didn't want to think about the club. He had other things to occupy his thoughts.

As the carriage rattled away, he turned to survey the aftermath of that morning's market. The carts were gone, even the debris of cabbage leaves and rotten vegetables had been removed. This early in the year, there were far fewer flower girls on the street, but as John began his stroll through Covent Garden, moving briskly to burn off his anxiety, he spotted a petite Irish lass, her red hair shining even in sunlight. She looked freshly scrubbed, perhaps ten years old, and she had two large baskets of flowers, most of them arranged in pretty buttonhole bouquets.

Perched on the stairway of the church, she spotted him right away and stood, lifting a basket and tromping down to the foot of the stone steps.

"Flowers, sir?" she said.

John smiled as he strode toward her. There were others in the square, an elderly couple walking arm in arm, two costermongers with red faces who seemed engaged in a quiet argument, and any number of household cooks and other servants sent to purchase fruits and vegetables for their employers' larders. They were all moving in and out of the shops. Yet the girl had focused on him.

"Why, good morning, my dear. I must look like an easy mark," he said brightly, crouching in front of her to examine her basket.

"Violets from the South of France, sir! Brought over by steamship," the girl said, resplendent despite the plainness of her blue dress. She wore a matching bow in her hair. Her pale, freckled cheeks flushed red as candied apples with the chilly breeze, and he thought she might also be combating a natural shyness. "And the prettiest of roses from—"

"You're the prettiest of roses, young lady," John said, flashing her his most charming smile. He shook his head sadly, then. "If only you were a decade older, I might buy *you* such a lovely bouquet. But alas, I haven't a lady to whom I could present them at the moment."

She flushed even more furiously scarlet, but he could see that his flattery hadn't been enough to overcome her disappointment that he would not buy her flowers. So John reached into his jacket pocket and removed a small leather purse, from which he extracted two shillings.

"For the flower of Covent Garden," he said, shooting his cuffs and then taking her hand, placing the coins in her palm, and closing her fingers around them.

Her eyes were wide as saucers. "Thank . . . thank you, sir." The lovely little lass actually gave him a small curtsy. "Thank you so very much."

John returned the purse to his pocket and stood up, then tugged on his lapels, straightening his jacket. The stiff collar of his shirt was rough against his neck, and he twisted his head to try to give himself a bit more room to breathe.

"Entirely my pleasure to have made your acquaintance, miss," he replied. There was a young couple, newly married from the look of them, just wandering through from the other side of the square, and he gestured toward them. "Now get on with you. There's a lad who won't be able to resist a bouquet for his lady love. She won't let him, I daresay."

The girl giggled, ran back to the steps to get her other basket, then hurried toward the couple.

He wandered Covent Garden, at a more relaxed pace now, strolling into one after another of the small, enclosed squares on either side of the main avenue. His stomach growled to remind him that he had avoided breakfast, but that was, indeed, what had prompted him to have the driver leave him off here.

There were barrels of deep red American apples, winter pears from France, grapes from Hamburg, and boxes upon boxes of oranges. John sampled each, relishing the sweetness of the best fruit that could be had in all London. Soon his fingers and chin were sticky with their juices, no matter how meticulous he tried to be.

From one seller he procured a cup of water and a cloth that was only slightly soiled, and managed to clean himself up, laughing at the way the vendor rolled his eyes. *How vain I must look to this fellow,* he mused. To complete his breakfast, he bought a small bag of nuts, which he slipped into his pocket to eat as he walked.

When he emerged from the alley where he had procured the nuts, passing a small cluster of women shelling walnuts, John saw that the fruiterers and costermongers had begun to arrive for the sale that would begin at ten o'clock. Auctioneers had set up boxes on the street, from which they would hawk their wares. The prices for some of the fruit would be extravagant, and watching the bidding would have been entertaining, but he had planned a long walk before his meeting this morning and he wanted to enjoy himself, to take in the sights of the Strand and St. James Square at his leisure.

Clouds began to gather, and the sky became grayer, but still no rain fell. The wind was blowing toward the river, so rather than the stink of the Thames there was the odor of chimney smoke, which John had always been fond of, as long as it wasn't chokingly thick. A bit more sun would have been appreciated, but still the morning was altogether pleasant.

He walked southwest along the Strand, enjoying the leisurely pace that prevailed here. All across the city, pedestrians wore expressions of determination and purpose as they went rushing about their daily duties. Though it had a reputation that drew many visitors to its shops, the Strand was spectacularly unlovely. The architecture along the street was ordinary, and the wares hawked in the various storefronts were hardly worth the trouble. Nearly everything that could be found along the Strand could be found elsewhere in London. John knew that many people, particularly those in the upper classes, could not understand the lure of the street, but to him it was painfully obvious.

It was the walk itself. There was a bohemian air about the place, perhaps born of the presence of Booksellers' Row, or the many theaters that stood along the way. To wander down the street gazing in shop windows and admiring the marquees of the Adelphi and the Lyceum and the Gaiety, to take a moment to admire the church of St. Mary le Strand . . . it was peaceful, in its way. Relaxing. That was the problem. When the effete, snobbish nobility sniffed and turned up their noses at the Strand, it was simply that they were appalled by the relaxed environment of the place.

He loved it.

With carriages trundling past him, and men and women bustling by, he took his time walking all the way to St. James's Park. It was small in comparison with some of the great, sprawling, green spaces of London. Little more than an enclosed garden, really, but he enjoyed lingering there nonetheless. Admiring the ladies he saw strolling the Mall, he nearly stepped into a pile of dung left behind by the mounts of the Horse Guards. Their parade grounds were located in the park, and he had only just missed their morning outing.

There were few gardens blooming yet in the city, but he caught a sweet scent on the air. Turning, he spotted the line of stalls in front of Carlton House terrace, where vendors sold fresh gingerbread and sweetstuffs, and where fresh milk could be had, right from the cow. Several of the stalls had the beasts tethered there in front. It brought a smile to his face. After his visit to Covent Garden, he wasn't hungry at all, but the scent of gingerbread was tempting.

"Perhaps later," he muttered to himself, retrieving his pocket watch and opening it. He had only a handful of minutes before he was to appear at the Algernon Club.

Time to go, then.

The easiness of spirit he had so carefully cultivated all morning evaporated as he left the park and turned north onto St. James Street. John dropped into a demeanor that was now just as purposeful and businesslike as any of the society wretches he had been mentally condemning only minutes earlier, but there was nothing to be done for it. His stomach began to knot and his anxiety returned as he passed White's and made his way to the unassuming, featureless façade of the club.

With a glance around at the ordinary London street, he took a breath and rapped on the door. A moment passed, then it opened, revealing a gray-faced servant wearing black jacket and tie. He was broad-shouldered, and his nose looked as though it had been broken at least once. As an aficionado of pugilism, John would have thought the man a former boxer, but the way he stood ramrod-straight, almost at attention, bespoke instead a soldier.

"Yes, sir?"

John produced his card, which the man glanced at for a moment before nodding and stepping back. "Very good, Mr. Haversham. You are expected. Please do come in, and welcome back to the Algernon Club."

John smiled weakly in return, but the servant never noticed. Rather, he turned his back and started down a hall that led deeper into the building.

"This way, please," the former soldier said over his shoulder.

They passed several large drawing rooms where men of varying ages—though all of them were older than John himself—smoked and chatted and argued. There was a room where a small group was gathered around a lad no more than twenty, who seemed to be doing card tricks. The older gentlemen gazed on, obviously attempting to disguise their level of interest, acting unimpressed but putting on a poor show of it, John thought.

Soon, the fellow who had answered the door pulled back a velvet rope to allow John access to a quieter corridor that branched off, running, he thought, along the back of the house. Then came a narrow set of stairs, but John followed his guide to the second floor, and then up to the third, without incident.

They halted halfway down the third-floor hallway, at a thick wooden door with finishes carved in intricate detail, and the servant paused to knock.

"Come!" called a voice from within.

"He awaits you, sir," the servant said to John. The man nodded once, then turned on his heel and retreated the way they had come.

John found himself alone in a section of the Algernon Club he knew was reserved for its inner circle, perhaps only the board themselves. It was quiet here, uncannily so. His neck itched, and he slid a finger into his collar, trying again to give himself some air.

Part of him wanted to flee this place, but he knew it was best not to keep his host waiting.

John reached out and turned the knob. The heavy door swung open easily.

The room inside was cast in a strangely crimson gloom. There were red drapes at each window, tied back to allow the gray noon light into the chamber. A ray of sunlight briefly broke through, and dust motes swirled like mist in the air. Then it was gone. There was a fireplace, of course, but no fire had been laid. The chimney was cold and dark.

There were many shelves of books in the room, though he wouldn't have called it a library. A writing desk stood against one wall, and at the other there was a single low table with two high-backed leather chairs. In one of them sat an elegantly dressed gentleman with a graying beard. He clutched a pipe in one hand, a plume of richly redolent smoke rising from its bowl.

"Good morning, Lord Blackheath," John said.

"It is several minutes past noon, Mr. Haversham," the older man said, his words heavy with the weight of admonition. "The morning is gone."

"Yes." John nodded. "My apologies for not being more punctual. Good afternoon, then."

"Good afternoon."

The moment became awkward. John thought Lord Blackheath might want him to sit in the other chair, but the director offered no word or gesture, no indication whatsoever, so he stood and waited. Almost a full minute ticked by as the man puffed upon his pipe, so that when he spoke, John was startled by the sound of his voice.

"You spent a good deal of time with Tamara Swift last evening."

It wasn't a question.

"Yes," John admitted.

"And what is your opinion of the young lady?" Lord Blackheath asked.

A shiver went through him. John remembered the grief he had

seen in Tamara's eyes, but even more he recalled the heat of her body pressed against his, and the hunger in her when she had thought he was making advances. The memory of her lips and tongue upon his fingers, her mouth on him, ignited a fire in his gut that he knew must also have enflamed his cheeks. He hoped Lord Blackheath would not notice in the gloom.

"She is a charming young woman," he managed at last.

"Do you plan to court her?"

John frowned deeply. "Of course not. My life at present is occupied by other pursuits, as you well know."

"Indeed." The gentleman inclined his head. "But, you see, it would suit my needs—the needs of the Algernon Club—were you to see her again."

"I'm afraid I don't understand, sir."

Lord Blackheath's brows knitted in response. "You are not required to understand, Mr. Haversham. Only to perform the duties that are requested of you."

"Of course," John said quietly, lowering his gaze.

The older man took a long pull on his pipe, and then exhaled smoke through his nose. "I believe that William Swift has inherited the mantle of Protector of Albion."

John smiled. "William? You must be joking. Sir Ludlow wouldn't have chosen him. My cousin Sophia is quite taken with William, but he's far too stiff and unimaginative to be . . . well, he isn't the sort, is he?"

"Ah. And aside from having met Ludlow Swift a handful of times in passing and having seen him on the stage, what in your vast experience provides you with the insight to know who is and is not 'the sort' of man to become Protector?"

Lord Blackheath smiled, but there was nothing amiable in it. John pulled himself up, to stand straighter.

"Nothing, sir. I misspoke. Perhaps you're right."

The gentleman tapped the stem of the pipe against his chin.

"Perhaps. Yes, perhaps. I am not certain, as I said. William Swift will be making an appearance here at the club tonight. You've done well, thus far, insinuating yourself with the sister. But she may not even be aware of the truth about her grandfather, of the Protectorship. And I grow impatient. You'll join us this evening, and we shall determine whether or not William has inherited Sir Ludlow's position. That is your charge, then, Mr. Haversham. Their father hasn't been seen in months, you understand, and so it may be that Henry Swift is the Protector, and has gone into hiding for some reason.

"Or it may be that the power has passed out of the family entirely. I believe not. I believe it has fallen to William. But I want to know. And you will find out."

John's throat felt dry, and his heart beat too rapidly, but he sensed that he would be free to leave. The thought of getting out of there, and heading straight to the pub, gave him a mighty lift in spirits.

"Yes, sir. Of course, sir."

In her rooms at Woburn Abbey, the duchess of Bedford fussed over preparations for afternoon tea. She had sent invitations around to a good many of the wives of the members of Parliament, and the ladies were to arrive for tea at five o'clock precisely. There were hours to go, but already Anna Wickham was at her wit's end.

"What have you done to me, Petersham? What, indeed?"

Petersham was the handsome young man her husband, the duke of Bedford and marquis of Tavistock, had engaged only two weeks earlier, after the passing of their previous man. Now the butler dropped his gaze to the floor. His features were etched with remorse, and when he spoke, he seemed properly chastised.

"I beg your pardon, madam. I cannot fathom how such a thing might have occurred."

So despondent did he seem that the duchess was tempted to forgive him. But when she thought of the guests who were due to arrive in less than four hours, her ire was further stoked.

"My brother, the viscount Stanhope, is an aficionado of teas, Petersham. One might even call him an expert. His wife is going to be among the ladies in attendance this afternoon. Don't you think she will know if we promised her China tea, only to serve her India tea, or China for India? Perhaps I cannot tell the difference, even if the kitchen was to brew me a pot of each and I consumed them in their entirety. But that's not my concern, is it? How could you have allowed the two to become confused?"

Petersham hesitated, then ventured forth.

"I'm told the tea caddy is meant to keep them separate, but with my predecessor's . . . departure, no one can recall whether it was China on the right and India on the left, or India on the—"

The duchess threw up her hands. "Enough! Sort it out, Petersham. I don't care how you do it. I don't care if you have to send to Calcutta and Shanghai this very moment for more, so long as by five o'clock we are able to confidently tell our guests which varieties of tea they are being offered."

They stood on the landing of the second floor. The duchess knew that other servants would undoubtedly be listening, hungry for fuel that would feed their gossip and set their tongues wagging. But she did not care a whit.

"I shall attend to it, madam."

"See that you do. And will you *please* take the cook aside, and remind him that the crumpets should be slightly underdone. It's the only way to avoid having them burned. The man simply cannot—"

At that she stopped. She hadn't yet run out of vituperative energy, but she was distracted by voices from below.

Anna frowned and moved away from Petersham, descending several steps toward the first floor. She paused when two men came into view, one of them the duke's personal secretary, Richard Mills. The other was unknown to her, but by his attire she saw that he was a clergyman.

"I must see the duke immediately," rasped the man in rough, gravelly tones.

"Yes, Your Grace," said Richard. "Of course. But I am afraid he is resting at the moment. He's feeling poorly, and has instructed that no one disturb him."

The bishop's face reddened.

"*Damn* his instructions, sir. There is a crisis at hand. It can't be helped. He simply must be interrupted. Take me to him, Mr. Mills, or I think you shall find your services dismissed by nightfall."

This was enough to embolden the duchess. She did not take kindly to having others issue commands to her servants, or members of her husband's staff, clergy or not. Even as Richard kowtowed to the bishop, beginning to lead the man up the stairs, she continued downward and blocked their progress.

"Pardon me, Your Grace, but I could not help overhearing. I am Anna, the duchess of Bedford. As Richard has politely informed you, my husband has taken ill. I'm afraid I shall have to ask you to respect his wishes, regardless of the circumstances."

A look of disdain passed over the bishop's face, but he paused and gathered himself. He stood there on the stairs, peering up at her.

"The circumstances, as you call them, are beyond your conception, Duchess. Quite beyond, I'm afraid. I am the bishop of Manchester. Perhaps word has reached you, through your husband, of the horror that befell the earl of Claridge at my home several days past?"

Anna paled. She had indeed heard the tale, though she had found it impossible to believe entirely. "I . . . I thought it merely fancy, or an exaggeration. How could such a thing—"

"It happened, my dear," the bishop replied, more calmly now. There was even a spark of sympathy in his eyes. "And there was no exaggeration. I have never seen the like, and have prayed never to see it again. That prayer fell on deaf ears, I'm afraid, for it *has* happened again, this very morning. Sir Charles Ibbetson has been taken by this terrible malady, his mind driven to madness, his body twisted into a hideous parody of a man. Indeed, he has been given the face and form of a demon."

The clergyman reached out then, and took her hand. "Madam, the prime minister has summoned the members of Parliament. All are required to attend. But we must do this quietly. Secrecy is of the utmost importance, in order to avoid panic or scandal. I have been sent to retrieve the duke."

Her hands fluttered toward her face almost of their own volition. The duchess covered her mouth with her delicate fingers, and then nodded. "Yes. Yes, of course. Richard, please follow me. I shall ask you, Your Grace, to wait in the study while I rouse my husband. If you'd like anything, Petersham will remain here, at your service."

The bishop inclined his head in agreement, and the two of them hurried up the steps. Petersham had followed the entire exchange. Now he stepped quickly out of the way, waiting in silence in case he should be needed in this moment of urgency.

"Richard, come along," said the duchess.

She heard Petersham quietly offer to fetch the bishop a cup of tea. A mad, errant thought went through her mind as she wondered what would happen if the man stated a preference between China tea and India tea.

Such concerns seemed ridiculous at the moment. Some terrible infection had come to London, and if the bishop was correct, it was spreading. Her hands trembled, and she clasped them together, wringing them as she strode along the hall. The portraits upon the walls seemed to blur at the edges of her vision. Never since her husband had first become a member of the House of Lords had Parliament been summoned in such a clandestine fashion. It was entirely out of the ordinary, and that frightened her terribly.

At the door to the master bedroom, she paused. She glanced at Richard, who hesitated in an uncertain fashion.

"Would you like me to . . . ?" he began.

"No, no," she replied, managing a wan smile. How foolish it was to have hesitated. Her husband had demanded that he not be disturbed, but this was a summons from Parliament. There was a crisis at hand. It had already tainted two members of the House of Lords, and as such it had to be dealt with straightaway.

So Anna opened the door and went in, with Richard following behind her.

"Husband, Richard is with me," she began, crossing the darkened room to draw back the curtains. "The bishop of Manchester is here, and he demands to see you. I know that you are poorly, and am terribly sorry to wake you, but . . ."

Her voice trailed off, for her husband had not stirred. The duchess went to another window, nearer the bed, and pulled those curtains aside, as well. Before she could turn, she heard Richard gasp.

"Lord and savior."

Then there came a hiss from the bed. Trembling, her own breath ragged in her throat, she turned to see.

The duke lay on his side, the bedclothes in complete disarray, twisted around him as though he had been thrashing in his sleep.

His flesh was tinged green and yellow, and there were strange diamond patterns on that rough, scaly skin, like some exotic serpent. His hair had fallen out in clumps, and lay strewn across his pillow. His hands were oddly twisted, his face malformed . . . he looked nothing like himself.

The face and form of a demon, the bishop had said.

The duchess shook her head slowly, staggering back until she collided with the window frame and could retreat no farther. A loud rushing filled her ears, like the sound of a great waterfall. Richard was shouting something, but she could not tell what it was. Darkness seemed to float at the edges of her vision.

She could not breathe.

A long, forked tongue slid out from between the demon's lips.

Then the monstrous thing that had once been her husband opened gleaming, sickly yellow eyes, and it looked at her.

And Anna Wickham began to scream.

∾

WILLIAM AROSE FAR later than he had planned, for after the events of the previous day, he had found it difficult to get to sleep.

Whatever had really happened with Haversham, he felt the weight of the blame upon his own shoulders. His sister was grieving, yet he had convinced her to see Haversham simply to further the ends of their investigation. So as late as it was, he was determined to allow her to sleep to nearly noon.

Upon Tamara's waking, William learned of her odd exchange with Oblis. As slim as it was, it was still a lead in their investigation.

As she recounted the information the demon had provided, Tamara seemed ill at ease. William found it odd that Oblis would offer anything that might aid them, yet his sister seemed determined to pursue this line of inquiry. William could only take this to mean that Tamara had given Oblis something in return. Yet she offered no clue as to what it might have been.

The more he thought about it, the more the idea haunted him.

What had she sacrificed? What little piece of his sister might have been offered up to the monster?

William dared not ask her. There had been enough tension between them of late, and he felt guilty for that. She had chosen the high road this morning and behaved as though all was well between them. He had no desire to disrupt that peace.

And what vengeance could he take on Oblis, after all? He could not murder his own father, and even if he did, it would not destroy the demon, only free it to torture some other innocent, and seek new victims.

No, he decided instead to focus on the crisis that was developing in London. To that end, the Swift siblings retreated early in the afternoon to their grandfather's rooms to search Sir Ludlow's records and journals for references to the Protector of Bharath.

Queen Bodicea had returned with news that she had "inadvertently" killed David Carstairs . . . or at least the monster Carstairs had become. William had hoped Carstairs might still provide some further lead in their investigation, so he had been angry at first. But as the circumstances of Carstairs's death came to light, he could not find fault with what Bodicea had done.

Lord Nelson's inquiries in the spirit world had produced news that the curse was, in fact, spreading at an alarming rate among the poverty-stricken lower classes in Shadwell, and Wapping in the East End, near the Thames. Indian immigrants, lost in the secrecy of their shared culture and ignored by even the other residents of those dingy districts, had been among the first afflicted by these horrors. But because of the closed, secretive nature of the immigrant subculture, word had been slow to spread, and had in fact been suppressed by the few who were aware. The plague had been hidden even from the eyes of the ghosts.

The evil festering in London town had remained unknown until it touched the upper classes, until it reached a party at the bishop of Manchester's home and transformed the earl of Claridge. Even the Protectors of Albion had been in the dark until Frederick Martin's visit. How many had been twisted by this evil curse? For curse was what William felt certain it was. How many women had been split open by the darkness yearning to be born, by the iniquity bursting from their wombs? How many men had been robbed of their humanity, infected with malevolence, and turned into monsters?

"How many could we have saved?" William whispered under his breath.

He started as he realized he had spoken aloud. In the gray late-afternoon light that filtered in through the windows of their grandfather's room, he glanced around to find Tamara seated at the writing desk, the same desk at which she sat to put pen to paper for her lurid penny-dreadful tales. There were journals stacked to her left, and she had one open before her as she scratched notes on a separate sheet of paper.

At the sound of his voice, however, she turned, frowning, to look at him.

"William, are you quite all right?"

A hollow bravado filled him and he sat up straight in his chair. "Of course I am. I'm just . . ." With a sigh, he hung his head. "No. The truth is, I'm not all right at all. Too little sleep, I suppose."

He glanced at the papers strewn on the table in front of him. It wasn't a proper table, of course, but the Egyptian sarcophagus that Ludlow had so often used in his stage magic. The old man would have himself locked into the dreadful thing, and then when his assistant opened it, he would have disappeared. Audiences had loved the trick. How much more amazed would they have been to learn that it was real magic, translocation at work, and not some conjurer's game?

William shook his head and looked up at Tamara again. His back hurt from having spent more than two hours straight bent over the sarcophagus. The French mahogany chair he had dragged over beside it was elegant, but hardly comfortable for such a long stretch.

"What is it?" Tamara asked.

"I can't escape the feeling that Colonel Dunstan was correct, and we've been terribly remiss. It's *all* of Albion we're supposed to protect, not only the nobility. The aristocrats hardly need our help at all, in any case. It's those who cannot help themselves who need us the most, and they seem to have remained almost beneath our notice."

His sister set her pen down and turned in the chair to face him, smoothing her skirts. "That's a bit harsh, don't you think? Dunstan is a ghost, and has not the duties of the living. He has focused only on those who are his concern. After all, he might've come to us when he first learned that something was amiss there. And we hadn't heard of the trouble in Limehouse—"

"Not Limehouse. Wapping and Shadwell."

Tamara nodded. "All right. But the point is, we can't be expected to solve a problem that we don't know exists, to fight a threat that has snuck in under our noses."

"But it shouldn't have been possible, Tam, don't you see that?" William rapped his knuckles on the sarcophagus. "We're taking these artifacts from museums and private collectors . . . from cultural thieves, to be honest. Most of the things were smuggled out of India illegally. But from the sound of it, this curse has been spreading among the Indians who live in the filthiest areas, and it has been for as long as two weeks, yet we had no idea. Aren't we supposed to *sense* these things?

"We've got a small army of ghosts out there, acting as our eyes and ears, on the watch for supernatural threats, but either they did not know about the infestation, or they did not think it was the sort of threat they ought to bring to our attention. The impression Nelson got from Dunstan was that they thought we simply would not care."

Tamara stood, and strode toward the nearest window. She slid it open a few inches before turning to regard him thoughtfully. "I've no idea why they would think such a thing, unless, perhaps . . ."

"What, Tam? Unless what?"

"I shouldn't like to think it of him, but the only reason for the ghosts to presume we wouldn't care is if they'd come to expect it through experience."

William knitted his brow. "Experience with Grandfather, you mean? You're suggesting he might have ignored some evil prowling London if it confined itself to the slums?"

Tamara shivered. "Otherwise it means the ghosts have judged *us* as uncaring, Will, and I don't think we've given them any reason. How else are we to interpret this?"

"I prefer to think the wandering spirits were simply unaware of this new horror until now."

Tamara nodded. "As do I," she said, but her eyes were distant, her mind preoccupied now, likely with thoughts of their grandfather, and the duties they had inherited from him.

"Even so, I believe the responsibility lies with us, not with the ghosts," William said. "If we don't care enough—"

"We *would* have cared, William. We'll make that clear to them. We *do* care. I applaud your sentiment, I truly do. Frankly, I'm pleased to see you thinking so much about the poorer classes. But we would be trying to unravel this mystery regardless of who had been touched by this dark magic. The earl of Claridge is no more a human being than a beggar in the street, and no less. We are to protect Albion from evil, no matter where it strikes."

William felt a fist of ice clenching in his gut. "Then why didn't we know, Tam?"

"For Heaven's sake, we can't be everywhere," Tamara said, hands on her hips. "I feel as horrible as you that so many have suffered already. And we must get to the bottom of it as quickly as possible. But we cannot defend the whole of England at every instant."

"No," William agreed. "Only the places we bother to look."

A long silence descended upon the room. Tamara took a deep breath and reached up to push a stray lock of hair behind her ear. That sweet, lopsided smile appeared on her face, but there was a sadness to it, as well.

William pushed back the torturous French mahogany chair and stood up, both hands on his lower back as he stretched. His bones popped loudly, and some of the stiffness departed.

"Right, then," he said. "Have you found anything useful?"

Tamara began to pace the room. How often she had lingered here as a child, listening to their grandfather's wild stories and trying to learn his magic tricks. She hadn't had the dexterity for it, though. How ironic, William thought, that she had become so adept instead at the true magic they had inherited from the man.

"It is all connected," she said. "That much is obvious. The common thread is that each person possessed stolen artifacts from India. And those afflicted in the East End are almost exclusively Indian. The demons sighted are Rakshasa, also from Indian folklore. The one idol we've been able to identify represents the image of Kali. Or one of the goddess's facets. Even the mysterious girl mentioned by Colonel Dunstan appears to be Indian."

William threw up his hands. "Ye-yes—the more we gather these pieces of the puzzle, the more it's clear that they share an Indian origin. But we still can't seem to find the connection that linked the idols with the plague in the slums. We are wasting our time with these journals. We need to go to the East End, where all of this started. I believe that is where we'll find the connection we seek. It's also where this mysterious girl has been sighted. I've no idea what role she plays in all this, but I doubt her sudden appearance is coincidental. So we'll visit the East End and—"

"Yes," Tamara interrupted, pursing her lips and arching an eyebrow. "But not yet."

She strode back to the writing desk and picked up the paper she had been scribbling upon. "Bharath is, I've discovered, the soul of India, just as Albion is the soul of England. According to his journals, Grandfather came into contact with the Protector of Bharath several times. His name is Tipu Gupta."

Her skin flushed crimson and she glanced downward, unwilling to meet his eyes. "Whatever our feelings about Oblis, his clue seems to have been genuine, if maddeningly vague. Before we delve any farther into this horror, we'd be well advised to seek out the expertise of a man intimately familiar with the culture and magic of India." Tamara crossed her arms. "We must find the Protector of Bharath, and win him to our cause."

William nodded. He cast a quick glance at the books that lay upon the sarcophagus, glad to be shed of them and to be taking action at last. "Very well. Is there any hint as to where we ought to begin?"

Tamara smiled. "Nigel was still Grandfather's apprentice when last the Protectors of Albion and Bharath met. If anyone would know how to find Tipu Gupta, it would be our Mr. Townsend."

"Our . . . well, he's not *my* Mr. Townsend," William sniffed.

His sister didn't reply. Instead she just folded the paper upon which she had written her notes and slipped it inside her sleeve. Then she took William's hand.

"Shall we?"

He took a deep breath and nodded. Translocation always made his stomach hurt. Nevertheless, he clutched her fingers, and together they recited the spell that had become almost second nature to them.

"Under the same sky, under the same moon, like a fallen leaf, let the spirit wind carry me to my destination."

Twelve

Nigel Townsend was a private man who didn't appreciate it when company arrived upon his doorstep uninvited. He liked it even less when they simply appeared in his parlor.

Worse, when his guests happened to be the grandchildren of Ludlow Swift, he could be reasonably certain his life was going to be placed in peril. Not at the hands of William and Tamara themselves, of course, but as a result of whatever trouble they had managed to entangle themselves in as Protectors of Albion.

Nigel, himself, had once been chosen to inherit the mantle of Protector, but Ludlow had withdrawn that ordination. Nigel had never blamed his old friend, though. He seriously doubted the spiritual powers that be would have allowed a vampire to become Protector. Just as well.

It wasn't a job he wanted.

And yet somehow, he seemed to have taken on part of the job—the perilous part—without receiving any of the magical benefits. William and Tamara had turned to him for aid and instruction from the very moment they had inherited the power and duty of the Protectorship, and they always seemed to need him most when he was relaxing with a glass of fine whiskey and enjoying a Turkish cigarette.

He was doing precisely that, and reading the comedies of Aristophanes, when he heard the familiar trilling noise that announced translocation. The sound faded, to be replaced by the less musical one of brother and sister muttering indignantly at each other. The duo materialized.

"Hello, Nigel." Tamara smiled and tilted her head just so. Her eyes sparkled. "You look comfortable."

Ah, Tamara. He could never deny her.

"To what do I owe this unexpected pleasure, children?" Nigel asked, masking his irritation for her sake. He wore an Egyptian smoking jacket and black trousers, but his feet were bare.

Tamara's eyes sparkled as she took in the jacket and the Turkish cigarette, its smoke curled languidly toward the ceiling.

For his part, William only looked annoyed.

Nigel smiled, exposing his sharp white fangs. It gave him great pleasure to annoy the uptight William Swift. He had decided that it was his duty to loosen the boy up, however he could. He gathered that underneath all that stiffness lurked a berserker waiting to hear the call of battle, and Nigel Townsend hoped to witness the transformation when it finally did occur.

Being undead, he had to take his little pleasures wherever he could find them.

"There's a terrible scourge making its way through London, Nigel. A plague, of sorts, though rooted in dark magic. If you're willing, we're going to need your help," Tamara said.

Nigel saw William wince. The boy hated coming to him for aid.

"Go on, then. Let's have the tale." Nigel crossed his arms and drew sweet smoke from his cigarette.

Tamara regaled him then with a story of cursed idols and transmogrified men, of Indian people dying in the slums from a magical plague. He half listened to her words, while at the same time measuring the thrum of her heartbeat as it danced merrily beneath her breast.

When she finally ceased her tale, he looked up into her luminous blue eyes and shrugged.

"And you would have me do *what* about this . . . ?"

For the first time since their arrival, William spoke.

"How can you ask that?" His face was pinched into an angry scowl. "There is a threat to Albion! For some reason, our grandfather trusted you. You have an *obligation* to tell us what you know about this . . . this *Bharath*."

Nigel just shrugged, waiting patiently for William to finish. One corner of his mouth lifted into a smile.

"I still fail to see what I can do for you, William Swift. I know nothing of that strange Hindu culture. There are other Asian places of which I am fond, but that hellhole India is not one of them. I suggest that you speak to Byron for this sort of enlightenment. He traveled extensively in that region, if I remember correctly."

Tamara took a step toward Nigel.

"Nigel," she began, "what we need from you is your help in locating the Protector of Bharath. I found some reference to him in the journals you brought us, Grandfather's journals, and I think he might be connected with the danger we face."

She reached out and took Nigel's hand in her own. It was warm against the coolness of his skin.

"Please, it must be that if this man, Tipu Gupta, was a friend of Grandfather's, he was at least an *acquaintance* of yours."

He nodded. "I did have the occasion to meet him, once or twice, and he wasn't a bad sort as magicians go. I would suggest that you pay a visit to his home, in Alipore, a suburb of Calcutta. You can easily translocate from here," Nigel offered. He lifted Tamara's hand to his lips for a quick kiss, and a closer sniff of her blood.

William reached out and quickly yanked Tamara's hand away. "Thank you for your help, Nigel," he said, his voice pinched. "We shan't bother you again."

Tamara silenced her brother with a curt glance.

"Yes, thank you, Nigel," she said. "We will keep you abreast of what we discover. In the interim, if you think of anything that might be of help . . ."

Nigel's nostrils flared in amusement, and he arched an eyebrow. "It seems I remain your humble servant, despite my worst intentions."

～

$\mathcal{T}$AMARA AND WILLIAM translocated into the middle of a forest of well-tended ferns. He had been gaining confidence in his magical prowess of late and had insisted on directing the course of their translocation himself. But perhaps he'd been overconfident.

"Oh, well done, William." Tamara sighed. "Where've you sent us now? Some African jungle, perhaps?"

He shot her a dark look. "There's no need to be snide. Considering we've never been here before, you can't blame me if we're a bit off the mark."

His sister raised an eyebrow. "Can't I? I suppose that depends upon how far off the mark."

Once they got their bearings, they found a path through the ferns and shortly were making their way down the dirt roads of the southern Calcutta suburb of Alipore. On the road they met a small, bent old man who was, oddly, carrying three cricket stumps. Fortunately, he was acquainted with Tipu Gupta, and he gave them clear instructions that would lead them to the Protector's bungalow. It was all William could do not to ask the man about the stumps, for he was an avid player, but their mission had to take priority. As they continued, he cast a sideways glance at his sister.

"You gave me the most hideous glare back at Nigel's apartments, Tamara," William chided as he kicked up a cloud of dirt from the road. It gathered like a storm around them, and would not dissipate.

"You were rude. Rudeness does not pay, Will. Especially with Nigel," Tamara replied. "You *know* how he can be."

William didn't answer her, though. He was too busy shooing the bugs away from his uncovered face and neck.

The late afternoon was warm and pleasant. He found that he did not need the light jacket he had brought with him. In fact, he had taken it off; it hung casually over his right shoulder.

"Are you even listening to me?" Tamara demanded.

He gave her a blank look. "It's these damnable bugs, Tam. They seem hell-bent on eating me alive."

"Well, they're not bothering me at all," she answered, but she stared curiously at the swarming creatures.

William scowled, wondering if his sister was somehow getting the better of him, but he could not for his life figure out how.

"I think this is the place," Tamara said, stopping abruptly and pointing at an old bungalow with bits of greenery growing up its sides. It wasn't a small structure, but it wasn't a mansion, either. It sat back a distance from the road, so that the siblings had to traverse a winding dirt-and-stone path to get to the front entrance.

Upon reaching the bungalow's door, William positioned himself in front of his sister. He was reasonably certain Indian culture would look even less favorably upon Tamara's independent streak than did that of England. She tossed him an irritated look, but remained quiet as he knocked on the old wooden door.

"I think you'd best let me handle this, Tam," he said, but before he could continue, a tiny middle-aged woman opened the door. She wore the traditional Indian sari, and her graying hair was pulled back in a tight bun at the nape of her neck.

She stared at them, but offered no greeting, and her brown eyes were curious.

"We've come to see Mr. Gupta," William said in what he hoped was a respectful voice. The older woman cocked her head and blinked twice before breaking into a fast stream of agitated Hindi.

William didn't know what to do, and he looked back to his sister nervously. Given the expression on the old woman's face, he was sure she was calling him all sorts of horrible names. Tamara stepped forward.

"Let me try, Will."

Tamara closed her eyes and spoke quietly under her breath. "*Ostendo.*"

The woman's words crystallized into precise, accented English that both she and William could easily understand.

". . . and then supposed to arrive in Darjeeling, but the Protector was not to be found," the woman continued. Her words tumbled over themselves.

"You mean to say that he's missing?" Tamara asked, alarmed now.

The woman nodded. "I just said as much, didn't I?"

Thanks to the spell, she now understood Tamara's English as easily as if she had been speaking Hindi.

"We were having trouble with translation," William told her.

She raised both eyebrows, an expression of sudden comprehension on her face, and then shook her head as though amused. "I see. More magicians. I'm sorry, I shouldn't have presumed you spoke Hindi. I'm pleased you can understand me now."

Tamara smiled. "You seem rather relaxed about the idea of magic."

"I have served Tipu Gupta for twenty-three years. Very little surprises me after all that time."

"But Gupta is gone, you say?" William asked, pulling them back to their purpose.

"They are both gone, and cannot be found. It is not my place to keep watch over them. I am only a servant in this household, though I raised the child as my own from the very moment of her mother's death," the woman explained. She studied them carefully. "Why are you looking for him? Do you know anything that might help us discover where they've gone?"

"Our grandfather, Ludlow Swift, was a great friend of Tipu Gupta," Tamara said.

At the mention of Ludlow's name, the woman's eyes lit up, and her mouth curved into a smile, making it clear that she had known and been quite fond of their grandfather. But the effect was brief, and her expression darkened as she shook her head. "Why are you here? If the Protector of Bharath is in London, why are you *here*?"

"I'm sorry," William said, befuddled. "The Protector . . . you mean to say that Mr. Gupta's gone to London?"

The woman nodded vigorously. "Yes, of course. There is trouble there, he says. That must be where she has gone, too."

"It makes no sense," Tamara muttered, as though to herself. "If he knew what was happening there . . . if he went to help, why wouldn't he have contacted us? And who is this girl you mentioned?"

"His daughter, of course. They are both missing."

Tamara frowned. "And you know nothing else that would help us locate them? He said nothing that would provide a clue?"

The woman shook her head. "Nothing. You will find them, though, won't you? I worry for him. He is an old man, now."

William stood up a bit straighter. "Yes, madam. Of course we'll find him. Find them both."

"Thank you. I believe you will."

Abruptly the woman reached out and stroked the curve of William's jaw. He was so surprised by her action that he didn't stop her.

"So much like your grandfather. Ah, Ludlow . . . he knew how to treat a lady," the woman said. She winked at him, then, and closed the door, leaving them standing there staring in astonishment.

"Well, fancy that. Ludlow was a ladies' man," William said as he turned and grinned at his sister.

"Oh, William, do try to open your eyes once in a while," Tamara said airily. "I've known for ages that Ludlow was a notorious lothario. Haven't you paid the least bit of attention to Bodicea? The woman practically swoons every time someone says Grandfather's name."

"Oh," William said, feeling foolish in a way only Tamara seemed able to elicit.

"Back to London, shall we, Will?" Tamara said, taking his hand.

"Yes, and quickly," he said, frowning.

∼

𝕿HE ALLEY STANK of urine and human refuse. Tamara had to lend William her handkerchief, which she had perfumed that morning with lavender, so that he could cover his nose and mouth against the stench. "Thank you," William said, his voice muffled by the press of the cotton.

It was still afternoon, and the loud throng of voices and of cartwheels slapping against cobblestones filled the air around them, giving them a false sense of security. Here in Shadwell, no matter how many people passed by in the surrounding streets, Tamara and William would be considered fair game. Indeed, they were *too* fair, too cleanly scrubbed, and far too well dressed to be inconspicuous here. The accursed men, those twisted, reptilian monsters, would be less out of place in the winding streets and unwashed throngs.

"Come on, William," Tamara said, taking her brother's hand. "Let us go to meet Horatio and Colonel Dunstan. We cannot be far from the hospice Horatio described for us."

That was the magic of translocation. Even if you didn't know precisely how to reach your destination by foot, the spell would still manage to place you within walking distance. As long as you kept focus on what you desired, magic always knew. Their recent missteps had been prompted by William's inability to focus, the result of which was that they found themselves in the oddest places.

Fortunately, Tamara had taken the reins this time, and she knew enough about Shadwell to get them to the general neighborhood where they would meet with Nelson. She had spent time down here, among the sick and destitute, delivering food and old clothing. As much as William complained that they had been ignoring the plight of the poor, Tamara doubted he had ever set foot in these slums.

Blessed with good fortune and health, she had felt it her duty to assist others who were not so fortunate, making certain they had the basic necessities. She and several of her friends had donated their time, bringing supplies to the women and children who inhabited these streets. She and Helena, who had a particular fondness for sketching the street urchins, had come here together, accompanied by a few of the other women from the charitable society.

Sadly, recent events had caused her to discontinue her efforts.

"This way," Tamara said, leading William through the zigzagging alleyways. Turning a corner at a brisk pace, she uttered a small gasp and stopped abruptly in the middle of the narrow alley they had entered. William almost ran into her.

"What is it?" he asked, but he practically swallowed the last word as he saw what it was that had given her such pause.

A large green toad sat on a loose cobblestone, staring up at them. It made a loud croaking deep in its throat, and, as if summoned by the first, three others hopped from the shadows.

The toad*like* creatures—for upon closer inspection they seemed quite a contrast with any toads Tamara had ever seen—had small, glittering red eyes that fixed unblinkingly upon the siblings. Their bulbous, sludge-covered bodies shimmered darkly in the obscured light that streamed through the narrow gap between the roofs of the tenement buildings.

"What in the Lord's name—" William began, but his words died in his throat when he heard the clicking of something sharp against cobblestone.

"William," Tamara said, her voice a measured contralto. "Look."

A pair of long, dark shadows blotted out the light that came from a filthy lane running behind the tenements, intersecting the alley they occupied. The figures moved toward them, and their features became clear.

They were enormous, hunched demons with mouths full of gnashing, dagger teeth and skin like rough leather where it wasn't covered in filthy, matted fur. Their eyes were yellow, and crusted with a sickly glaze.

"Run, Tam!" William shouted, trying to pull his sister back.

"Are you *insane*, Will? You need my help!"

Tamara stood her ground, her head bent low, her eyes watchful as the creatures picked up speed and loped toward them. Their feet cracked cobblestones as they ran, muscles taut and shifting beneath the sheath of their skin. They opened their jaws in silent howls, further baring the rows of fangs that jutted like daggers in their angular mouths.

"*Ignate!*" William thundered, throwing his hands up in front of him.

A ball of red fire formed from the tips of his fingers, and he hurled it at the closest demon. Its eyes widened and it tried to escape the spell, its claws scoring the tenement wall as it lunged aside. But it was too late. The magical fire engulfed it, and it fell to the ground writhing in pain, its howl no longer silent.

Distracted by the stink of burning demon and the unearthly screech of its death throes, Tamara misjudged the speed of the other, and as it leaped at her she had no time to cast her own spell. She dropped to her knees and rolled out of the demon's path in a desperate move that slammed her shoulder into the tenement wall. She cried out at the impact but instantly climbed back onto her feet, her eyes wet with pain.

Her fingers were twisted into the sigil for a spell, but her attacker had been diverted by the screams of its companion and now rushed at her brother. William screamed as the monster raked its claws across his chest. He staggered backward and fell to the ground.

As the demon crouched to attack once again, William stared up into its tiny eyes, terror jamming his throat and paralyzing his body.

"*Ignate!*"

Tamara shouted the spell and the magic erupted from within her. The look on her face was almost one of ecstasy. With a thrust of her hand and a flick of her wrist, the arcane fire burned across the alley and struck the demon, spreading quickly along its shoulders and back. It turned on her, enraged and in pain, swiping wildly at her with its claws.

Still sprawled on the ground, William raised his hand, and the flame poured out of him as if he himself were ablaze with it. Already burning, dying, the monster could not escape. The fire engulfed it entirely now, burned away the matted hair on its body and then quickly set to work melting the flesh and muscle away until the thing was nothing but bone, and it collapsed into a heap on the cobblestones.

Tamara ran to her brother, helping him to stand. She fussed over him, looking at the scratches the thing had given him. Its claws had mostly torn his jacket and shirt, but there were thin gashes across his chest as well, and the blood was staining cloth.

"Are you all right?" she asked.

"I think I will be. Though I wonder if the claws of that creature could carry the infection . . . the curse."

Tamara frowned. "We've no reason to expect that. Even werewolves have to bite to pass along their curse. Still, a strong healing spell ought to close those wounds and protect you from infection, as well."

"We hope," William replied.

Tamara nodded. "We hope. How does it feel?"

He winced. "It stings quite a bit, but I'm mostly worried about wandering around with bloodstained clothes."

"Here?" Tamara asked wryly. "No one will notice."

With that the terror left her, and the excitement of the moment subsided. She smiled and began to laugh softly.

It must have been contagious, for William joined in.

"How did you manage that, anyway?" she asked. "I've never seen that spell work so intensely before. It consumed that creature until there was almost nothing left. Tremendous magicianship, Will."

William shook his head. "I don't know, Tam. I was afraid for you, and then it just *happened*. All in a day's work, I'm afraid."

But despite his casual words, he beamed at her compliment.

⁓

DEMONS WEREN'T NECESSARILY confined to darkness, but they did seem often to prefer the night. So Tamara and William had been surprised by the daylight attack in that filthy alley, and as they proceeded toward their destination they moved with a new wariness.

They sought the temporary hospital that Colonel Dunstan had reported, which the locals had set up. Twice Tamara pressured William to ask people for directions as they passed on the street, which he did, but they received no cooperation. In the end, they found the place largely by the stench of sickness and human waste, baking in the spring sunshine.

"Tamara!" a familiar voice called as they walked toward the building, from which issued the moans of the suffering.

She and William turned and saw a doorway lost in shadows; upon the doorstep were the gossamer images of a pair of ghosts, the specters of Admiral Nelson and Colonel Dunstan. The way they wavered with the interplay of sunshine and shadow, passersby would hardly have noticed a disturbance in the air. Tamara herself might not have been able to see them had she not heard Nelson's voice.

As surreptitiously as possible, William and Tamara pretended they were speaking only to each other. Horatio made his introductions, and Tamara related the tale of the attack that had just taken place. Colonel Dunstan frowned several times and stared at the stains on William's shirt as Tamara told the tale. Horatio was near apoplectic, particularly that the siblings had not summoned help.

"We were perfectly capable of defending ourselves, thank you," William sniffed.

Nelson's ghost stared at him with a dubious expression. "And what is that upon your breast, then, my young friend? Some sort of dye? It was reckless of you not to call upon me, knowing I was so close."

Tamara sighed. She would never get used to having to smooth the ruffled pride of men. "Honestly, Horatio, it was over almost before it had begun. Had it gone a moment longer, we would have realized our predicament and summoned you straightaway. I should think you'd be pleased that we acquitted ourselves so well."

The specter calmed at that. "Well, yes, of course, though I expect no less from the two of you. I daresay you've come a long way under the tutelage provided by Bodicea and myself."

William smiled. "Indeed. Thank you."

Nelson watched him to see if there was any sarcasm in William's tone, but after a moment he seemed to decide that the response had been genuine. Throughout the entire exchange, Colonel Dunstan only watched with interest, nodding gravely from time to time. Now he gazed at Tamara as he spoke.

"Very few have been the prey of Rakshasa, and lived to tell of it," Dunstan said. "You are fortunate."

He was a small figure, like Nelson, and there was a fierce intelligence burning in his translucent eyes. With his thick dark hair and olive skin, Tamara thought him handsome for an older man. Nelson seemed often to tremble with the need for action, but for his part Colonel Dunstan exuded a quiet strength. He was the sort who would examine every aspect of a situation before determining his course, she decided.

"What more can you tell us about them?" William asked. "If we're to encounter more, it would be helpful to know what it is that we face."

"Rakshasa," Dunstan said, "are the ghouls of the Hindu Pantheon. They usually hunt in pairs, though not packs, and their minds are small, easily harnessed with dark magic."

"They were horrid," Tamara said, remembering the yellow eyes, the crouched, feral stance, and the sight of those claws slashing at William. "Were it not for our magic, they would have had us for their dinner."

Suddenly the door to the makeshift hospital opened, and an elderly Indian woman stepped out. William and Tamara glanced at her, but the woman did not seem to even notice them—as if they were ghosts, as well. She turned to the right and started off along the narrow, twisting street, soon disappearing from sight. Then they were alone again.

Just as Tamara was about to speak up, there was a disturbance in the air a few feet away, at the entrance to an alley that ran between buildings, a place so narrow it could barely have been called an alley. The world seemed to flicker there, with a haze like the heat of a summer's day over dark brick or flagstone, and then the ghost of Queen Bodicea appeared. Like Nelson and Dunstan, she was remarkably transparent, merely a wisp of a phantom, an image upon the air, but she was there nevertheless, spear in hand, and looking as grim as Tamara had ever seen her.

William rushed to her, Tamara close behind him, and soon the two of them were crowding into that narrow gap. Nelson and Dunstan followed at a calmer pace.

"What's happened, Bodicea? Have you emasculated yet another of our enemies?" William asked archly.

The spectral queen lowered her chin and gazed at him through slitted eyes. Had Tamara not known better, she would have thought Bodicea about to run her brother through.

"I will not apologize. No one lays a hand on Bodicea and lives."

"Yes, of course," William replied quickly. "Too right. You went easy on the filthy tadpole, that's what I think."

Tamara would have rolled her eyes if she hadn't been concerned about offending Bodicea herself. Her brother was a strange man, courageous in the face of evil and yet intimidated by a strong-willed woman.

"After the frustration of my failure at Carstairs's residence last evening," the spirit continued, "it was a pleasure to have an enemy I was *supposed* to destroy.

"What do you make of them, my friends? Any connection between these creatures and the sort of hideous transformation Carstairs underwent?"

"There must be," Tamara said firmly.

Bodicea looked at William. "What of the Algernon Club? Can it truly be coincidence, William, that Carstairs had in his possession an invitation to the very same dinner to which the club has invited you for this evening?"

"The Algernon Club. William?" Tamara asked. "Why did you not tell me we had been invited to dine there?"

"Tam, you see, I, uhm . . ."

"It's about time we took a closer look at the place, all those magicians, and who knows how many of them knew Grandfather was the Protector. There may be other real magicians among them. I've been wondering how we might learn more, and here's the perfect opportunity!"

"Tam, please, listen to me for a moment—"

"I shall wear my burgundy gown. The one with the beading—"

"Tamara, there is no need to decide which gown you shall wear, since you were not invited," William said finally. His face was red with discomfort.

"Oh," Tamara said quietly. "I did not know. I supposed . . . well, that we would *both* be invited." She frowned deeply. "I suppose it only makes sense. It is a gentlemen's club, after all. Yes, that does seem to be the long and the short of it, doesn't it?" She spoke this last sentence almost to herself, as if she was justifying the slight in her own mind. "Though you'd think if any of them were aware that we shared the duties of Protector . . ."

"I'm sorry, Tam. I shan't go, if it would upset you," William said.

"No, you must go. One of us must make their acquaintance, find out what we can about the club and its members."

"There is more," Bodicea said. "Your friend, Tamara, this John Haversham. He has dealings with the club as well. I followed him there this morning."

"You what?" Tamara said. "Why on Earth would you do that?"

"That is why I was unavailable earlier today. I found his behavior last night quite curious. If his goal was not courtship, then I could not figure why he had gone to so much trouble to arrange for the evening at the Egyptian Hall."

Tamara shook her head, staring into the strange, ghost-filled shadows of that alley.

"Just a moment, Bodicea. Am I to understand that, in addition to following John this morning, you spied on *me* while I was in his company last night?"

The ghost gave Tamara the same darkly dangerous look she had given William moments ago, but Tamara wasn't so easily cowed. After a moment, Bodicea softened.

"You were grief-stricken over the death of Miss Martin, Tamara. I feared that you might not be entirely rational. My apologies for being surreptitious, but I was concerned for your welfare."

Tamara sneered. "Far too many people seem to think me incapable of looking after myself. I'll thank you all to mind your own business, from this point forward."

Nelson, Bodicea, and William all looked properly chastised. Colonel Dunstan seemed to fade somewhat. Tamara didn't blame him. None of this was his affair.

"In future," Bodicea replied calmly, "I shall make certain any such action is taken only with your consent. However, it seemed advisable at the time. And regardless of whether or not it was proper, it seems to me that Mr. Haversham must have some other reason to desire your company."

"Hold on," Tamara said, interrupting Bodicea and peering at her askance. "You were in the hansom cab last night?" Her voice cracked slightly.

But the ghost merely raised her eyebrows. "I am afraid that I spent the majority of the evening accompanying Farris. He seemed rather lonely, without his sprite at his shoulder to harass him."

"Thank God that flying pest has seen fit to go back to the forest," William said. He had found the little creature to be more than a trifle annoying.

"And of course, I had no desire to intrude upon the intimacy of your evening," Bodicea added.

Tamara felt herself turning a horrible shade of crimson. "There was nothing intimate about it, I assure you."

William stared at her, and Tamara returned the look, silently daring him to comment further about her night out with John Haversham.

Nelson cleared his throat, catching everyone's attention.

"My friends, Colonel Dunstan has much to show us. Perhaps we ought to postpone these discussions of drama and deception for another time."

∼

THE HOSPITAL TENT broke Tamara's heart. Misery lived there, sucking up what little bit of life was left to the poor, suffering, bedridden patients. She felt ill as they stepped over the threshold and began to walk among the afflicted. The same feeling was mirrored in William's features, which surprised her. Not that she thought her brother callous, but he could be dreadfully self-absorbed. Yet here, he was overwhelmed by the plight of the people around him.

"This is a terrible place," Tamara whispered to her brother. They stayed close together as they walked down the slim aisle that separated the cots. "I can feel death lurking in every shadow, Will."

He nodded, but seemed incapable of speech. He kept the handkerchief clutched to his face. A thin, gape-mouthed woman caught William's eye, and he knelt down beside her and took her hand.

"Hello," he said, his voice soft.

The woman turned and stared at him mutely. Tears pooled in the corner of her eye, and slid silently down her cheek.

"What're you doing?" demanded a hard voice behind him. They turned to find a small Indian man standing across the aisle, glaring at them. William stood up and turned to address the man.

"I . . . she is suffering. I just—" William began.

"I don't know what you want here. You have no right to be in this place!" The little man's voice was shrill, almost to the point of hysteria. He looked as if he hadn't slept in days; there was prickly stubble all over his jaw and upper lip.

"Please, we meant no harm," Tamara said, coming to her brother's defense. "We only came to offer our help."

The man spat on the floor between them. "No one wants your help!"

Tamara took a distressed step backward.

"How dare you behave so in the presence of a lady," William snapped.

"William, please," Tamara said. The little man looked as if he was going to cry, and she could not bear to add to his trouble. She grabbed William's arm and started to lead him away. The man, who seemed pleased to run them off, turned and walked back to the other end of the tent.

"It would do us no good to offend him further, Will," Tamara said quietly as they walked. "Just look at him. The wreckage of a man."

He shook his head, confusion and frustration showing on his face. "I cannot bear much more of this. I think I must step outside and take the air."

Tamara did not follow him. Instead she continued to walk the rows of cots, looking at the strange, round-bellied women and the men who were beginning to show the effects of the curse that had transformed so many others already. Their flesh was tinged with green and brown and yellow and had a rough, scaly texture that would only grow worse.

In the corner of the makeshift hospital tent, Tamara found an old man they had not noticed before, kneeling beside one of the afflicted women. She moved closer so that she might get a better look as he performed his ministrations. There was something strange about the man, and something familiar, too.

He was Indian, in his late middle life, but there was a youthful elasticity to his skin that was odd. She watched him as he spoke quietly to the woman. His words seemed to have some effect on her, because she smiled and lifted her hand.

Tamara smiled sadly, watching the interchange between the much younger woman and the old man. It stabbed at her heart, encouraging painful remembrances of her own father and grandfather. Things she would have rather forgotten.

Suddenly the woman screamed as the things in her belly began to writhe. She reached out, flailing at her distended midsection with both arms, pounding at whatever lay inside.

The old man did not hesitate; he pulled a small dagger from a sheath at his hip and slit the woman's throat.

Horrified, Tamara covered her mouth with her hand to keep from gagging. She looked around wildly for help, but no one else seemed to have noticed the murder.

Knowing what she must do, she took a step forward, and then another. The murderous old man looked up, sensing Tamara's presence. He bowed his head as she raced toward him, her hands aloft in front of her, lips just forming the words for a holding spell.

But it was for naught. Tamara never had a chance. He vanished right before her eyes.

Thirteen

Tamara stared, dumbfounded, at the dead woman who lay on the cot in front of her.

The man who had cut her throat had not simply disappeared. He had translocated. A magician, then.

The woman's blood was pouring onto the cot, dripping onto the floor beneath her. Already her bulging stomach had stopped twitching. The hideous things inside her were no longer moving, and in fact her belly seemed to be diminishing in size. Deflating.

Tamara's body began shuddering with revulsion and fury, with the need to pay someone back for this crime, this atrocity. She spun around, eyes searching the makeshift hospital for someone who might help or someone to blame.

The air shimmered off to her right, and she saw the terrible old man reappear, twenty paces down the aisle from where she stood. He stared directly at her and moved his head from side to side, as if to warn her away from following him. Then with an agility that seemed uncanny for one so old, he darted down the aisle.

Her skirts flapped around her legs as she took off in pursuit of the murderer.

The man was fleet for his age, she would give him that. Thinking back to John Haversham's attire at the Wintertons' dinner party, Tamara wondered if the man ahead of her had created some similar façade to trick her into thinking he was old when, in truth, he was nothing of the sort.

At the edge of the tent, the man broke into a gallop, leaving Tamara, who was hindered by her long clothing, far behind him. Escaping the last of the cots that up until now had acted in tandem with her skirts to impede her progress, Tamara picked up speed and raced down the road after the man.

"William! Bodicea!" she yelled as she ran, her voice loud and jarring in her ears, but quickly stolen away by the wind. She tried to listen for some sign that William and the ghosts had heard her entreaty, but she couldn't wait to be certain.

William, where in Hell are you?

The Indian man reached the street and continued to widen his lead on her. She could feel frustration wash over her in waves. She wanted to scream out a spell, stopping the murderer in his tracks, but if he was indeed a magician, he might have shielded himself, and her hesitation would certainly allow him to escape altogether.

Without warning, Tamara stepped on something large and spongy. Her ankle twisted at an angle, and she stumbled. Her forward motion continued, however, and she fell onto her knees, slamming her hands into the hard cobblestones of the roadway. The wind was knocked from her lungs, and she hissed out a pitiful cry, but immediately tried to stand.

It was impossible. Her right ankle gave way instantly, crumpling rudely underneath her weight.

"William . . . !" Tamara shouted, the physical hurt she felt only intensifying her anger and frustration.

"William?"

She looked up, peering down the alleyway to see how far ahead her quarry had gotten from her, but found that he had disappeared— most likely around a corner. She sat back so that her legs splayed in front of her and pulled at her skirts so that she could see her ankle. It had already begun to swell, but she did not think she had broken it.

Tamara glanced around to locate the thing that had caused her accident, and was surprised to find that it was one of the toad-creatures she and William had encountered earlier in the afternoon. She had squashed its head into a pulpy mess when she had stepped on it. The dead creature made her skin crawl with such revulsion that she dragged herself away from its remains.

"Let's see if this can be quickly repaired," she said, looking down at her injured appendage. She grasped her ankle between her hands and began to intone a simple healing spell to stop the swelling.

"Silence!" a sharp voice said behind her.

The magic she had begun slipped away from her, back into the ether. She twisted her head to find the old Indian man standing a few feet away. He seemed wary, every muscle tensed.

Caught off guard, she quickly covered her stocking-clad leg with her long skirts.

He had a long, hollow face that seemed old, and yet ageless at the same time. His dark eyes were full of pain. If she hadn't watched him murder the young woman with her own eyes, she would not have believed him capable of such a thing.

"No magic," he said tersely. She noted his clipped, anglicized pronunciation, realizing that he must have been schooled in England, for there was almost no trace of an accent in his speech.

"You will make us both sorry—" he continued in a softer voice, but his words were abruptly silenced by a horrible noise, like the hissing of a thousand snakes distilled into one terrible sound.

Dark shapes leaped out of every doorway and crevice and up from the sewer gratings. There were dozens of the toad-creatures of varying sizes, but all with those eyes, like massive, pustulent blisters.

Tamara found herself lost in a deluge of the hideous things. They filled the street and surrounded both her and the old man. A sickening thought entered her mind, and she shuddered. If all these things had burst from the wombs of the women who had been violated by the plague-stricken men . . . how many women had been touched by this horror?

How many?

She thought quickly, trying to figure out how to destroy them all at once, but to her surprise they did not attack her. Tamara wasn't sure if the creatures were here at the behest of the old man, or if they plagued him just as they did her. The little beasts stank of burning sulfur, and they continued that strange hissing and closed in around her.

"*Tamara?*"

William called from somewhere nearby, his voice echoing off the dilapidated tenement walls. Her heart lifted at the sound.

"William, I'm here! Hurry!" she shouted, her voice more high-pitched than she liked. She sat up straighter on the cobblestones.

William and Bodicea rounded the corner back the way she had come, but William came to an abrupt halt when they hit the wall of toad-creatures.

"Bloody Hell!" he exclaimed as he almost stepped on one of the beasts. He quickly jumped back as the bloated amphibians surged toward him. Disgust was plain on his face as he stared at the squirming wave of bodies.

Bodicea did not hesitate. She began to wade through the creatures. Tamara watched wide-eyed as the ghostly queen used the butt end of her spear to grind their tiny brains into the cobblestones.

Suddenly William yelped.

"What in the devil are these . . . things?" he said, taking another step backward. "And who the devil are you?"

He pointed an accusing finger at the old man. The murderer said nothing, trapped as he was like an island in the middle of a rippling sea of toad-creatures. Instead he stood with his eyes closed, muttering something quietly under his breath.

"What's he doing? Is he calling *more* of these things?" William shouted.

"He killed a young woman," Tamara called back. "One of the afflicted. I saw it."

"Then what are you doing sitting over there? Come away from him."

"You must move, girl!" Bodicea called to her.

But Tamara couldn't move at all. Though her ankle was throbbing, she could have overcome that. No, she realized with a sinking feeling, someone or something was impeding her ability to make her limbs do as she wished. She was quite literally stuck to the ground.

"I can't get up! Something's holding me here!"

William raised one hand to cast a spell against the toads, but the old man shouted at him.

"No magic!"

Hesitating only a moment, William kicked several of the toad-things away and contorted his fingers, obviously intending to ignore the killer. But Bodicea darted wraithlike across the space that separated them and stood before William.

"Hold," she said imperiously. He complied, and then she turned her glare upon the murderous old fellow.

"Explain."

"You must not use magic," the old man rasped. "It will only be turned and used against you. They"—he indicated the toads—"feed upon it. Also, it will alert other dark creatures to your presence."

"How do you know this?" Tamara said, swatting away a toad that had landed on her lap.

The old man stared at her with a look of disdain. "How do you not know it, foolish girl? The creatures are feeding from the magic that is your very nature. You *must* learn to control yourself. Your power seeps from your very skin, allowing the dark creatures to track your every step."

"I don't understand," Tamara said. His words had captured her attention.

"You must hide your power. Like he does." He pointed to William, who raised an eyebrow. "The creatures cannot use your power against you if you hide it."

Bodicea nodded at his words. "He speaks the truth, Tamara. I can feel the magic emanating from you, like mist upon the river. If they are leaching your own magic, then you must draw it back inside you."

This man had slit the throat of a woman before her very eyes. Tamara could not trust him. But if Bodicea thought there was a chance that he was correct . . .

She closed her eyes, imagining in her mind a beautiful crystal perfume bottle, and drawing into it all the magic that surrounded her. When the bottle had taken every last drop of the stuff, she conjured a stopper to keep the magic safe inside.

Unbelievably, she discovered that she was immediately able to stand. She did so, nursing her throbbing ankle. Though she could not cross to where William and Bodicea stood—the mass of bloated amphibians was too thick—at least she once again had control over her limbs.

As she considered her options, the hissing noise that had first signaled the arrival of the toad-creatures began again in earnest.

"We must leave this place—" the old man began, his voice reedy now with fear. Yet his words were no match for the horrible sound that filled the air and made William cover his ears with his hands.

A giant hole was rent in the air behind them, exposing a deep, penetrating blackness that seemed as if it meant to consume everything.

"What is it?" Tamara screamed.

A pair of Rakshasa stepped out of the hot wet blackness and into the cool London air. They turned their sickly yellow eyes toward her and crouched over, baring those needle fangs, thick drool sliding from their jaws. They moved toward her, and Tamara did not hesitate. After all, the old man was a murderer. His word could not be trusted. And even if she could trust him, what else was she to do? Without magic, she and William would be dead.

So she uncorked the bottle, and she screamed the spell at the top of her lungs, her voice cracking. She had never felt magic possess her so wholly before. The spell shot out of the tips of her fingers and slammed the two Rakshasa demons back against the brick wall of a tenement.

Behind her, she heard Bodicea give a whooping war cry, then the ghost launched herself at two more Rakshasa that had just stepped through the gaping hole in the ether.

Beneath Tamara's feet, the crowd of toadlike creatures began to disperse so that she could move freely on the cobblestones. She looked down to see where they were going, but they seemed to be vanishing into nothingness, as if they had been there only to herald the coming of the Rakshasa.

She had taken her eyes off the demons for no more than a moment, yet that was enough. Tamara screamed as she felt sharp claws rip into her shoulder in a blow that sent her reeling. Once again she fell to the ground.

Instantly she was swarmed by the toad-creatures. With the Rakshasa there, they no longer showed the hesitation that had held them back previously. The things crawled all over her, smothering her with a fervor, and Tamara screamed in disgust as they covered her entire body.

She could feel them now, silently sucking away at her magical energy.

Then there was a flash of heat that seared her exposed skin, and the creatures stopped squirming above her, some of them dropping away. William's strong hands gripped her beneath the arms, and he pulled her from underneath their charred corpses.

"Are you all right, Tam?" he asked, looking anxiously at her shoulder.

She nodded, but William was already turning away from her to continue the fight with the Rakshasa.

Tamara ripped a piece of fabric from the train of her dress and used it to stanch the free flow of blood that was coming from her wounds. Out of the corner of her eye, she caught sight of Bodicea valiantly battling three of the Rakshasa, plunging again and again with her spear, but the ghost was surrounded and could only defend herself, with no hope of really driving them off.

"Ho!" cried a voice to her right. "Come, filthy devils! Have at you!"

Nelson's ghost had appeared, with Colonel Dunstan by his side. The former sailor and former soldier both brandished spectral swords as they rushed at the monsters. Tamara didn't know if they had been delayed at the hospital, or if they had been searching elsewhere for her and only now had doubled back. Nor did she care. She was just pleased to see them.

A snarl off to her left made her snap around, and she saw that one of the demons was moving stealthily up behind William even as he cast a spell at another such creature, covering it in ice.

"William, behind you!" Tamara shouted as she raised her good hand. Whispering a spell, she struck the Rakshasa full force in the chest, shattering every bone in its body. It was a brutal, destructive spell that she had only read about, never performed. It required savagery and hatred, emotions that were not in her nature. Except when her brother's life was in peril.

The thing screamed and Tamara watched, satisfied, as it crumbled to the ground, flopping helplessly.

"Where's the old man?" she called to William, but he was in the midst of forging a massive sphere of magical fire, using both hands to do so, and he did not break his focus to answer.

She glanced around and found her quarry, battling two more of the Rakshasa with some sort of rendering spell that seemed to melt the monsters into balls of useless demon flesh. Her stomach lurched with nausea at the sight.

"We must close the portal," the old man called to Tamara. "I will need your help, child!"

She watched in horror as the demons continued to step in twos from the hole. The old man was right. The only way to end this was to repair that rip in the ether. She started to move toward the hole, but the Indian man was suddenly beside her, holding her back by her good arm.

"Wait. With haste comes error," the man said softly in her ear. He let Tamara go when she nodded that she understood.

"At least tell me who you are!" she demanded.

Yet even as she spoke those words, a cold suspicion formed in her. He had slaughtered the woman right in front of her, blinding Tamara with the violence of the act.

But what if there had been no way to save her? What if her belly had been about to burst, spewing forth more of these toad-creatures, such that killing could have been considered merciful?

"Tipu Gupta," she said, spinning to face him.

But she stood alone.

A moment later she caught sight of him again, and her heart lurched in fear. There was nothing she could do but watch as he bolted toward that portal and, with a blinding flash of light, threw himself into the rift.

The portal folded in upon itself, and almost instantly it was gone without a trace. Whatever spell he had cast, it sealed the breach behind him.

Bodicea, Nelson, Dunstan, and William made short work of the remaining Rakshasa, but Tamara did not help them. Instead she stared worriedly at the place where the hole had once been, where the old man—Tipu Gupta?—had passed out of the world.

She didn't know how long she stood there, staring at nothing, but she was so absorbed in her thoughts that she did not hear William call to her until he stepped in front of her, snapping her out of her reverie. Tamara had been focused on the magic around her, not merely her own but also that of William and of the old man. She felt as if she would have known if he had been killed.

But if he was still alive . . . where was he now?

~

Upon the siblings' return to Ludlow House, Byron was released from his post as Oblis's guardian. He was glad to give up the job, even though he had once again spent an enjoyable afternoon torturing the demon with some of his more flowery verse.

He tried to escape the orbit of the house, but before he could slip into the ghost world, William and Tamara intercepted him.

"You can't leave, Byron," Tamara implored. "Nigel said that you knew more about Indian mythology and history than any of us. He also told us that you had met grandfather's friend, the Protector of Bharath."

With her dirty dress—the hem ripped away to reveal a bit of virgin ankle—and her flushed face, the girl looked particularly appealing. So Byron was only too happy to answer to stay a bit longer.

"Of *course* Nigel referred you to me, darling. I am the most . . . well-traveled of us, am I not?" Byron said. "My adventures have taken me to Europe and Asia, and northern Africa, as well. You can't seduce a nation's people if you know nothing of its culture."

"That's not precisely what we need to know, Byron," William said tensely. "Just tell us what you know about this Tipu Gupta fellow."

"Well, you don't have to be rude about it."

"William," Tamara said, giving him a stern look before turning once more to gaze upon the poet's ghost. "Byron, please understand. Time is of the essence. We need to discover how to track Tipu Gupta, the Protector of Bharath. We believe we may have already encountered him once, and we need his help desperately."

"If that was him, it may be he needs our help more than we need his. But regardless, we must find him," William commented.

Byron cast his mind back to his last meeting with Tipu Gupta. It had been when Ludlow was at the height of his skill and activity as Protector of Albion.

"You'd need something that belongs to him, for a location spell, something to track him with. I seem to recall that he gave Ludlow a small token of friendship. Yes, I remember exactly! A brass figurine, a man seated on a coiled serpent, representing Lord Vishnu. If my recollection is correct, it's gathering dust on one of the upper shelves near the fireplace in Ludlow's study."

"Vishnu?" William asked. "What's a Vishnu?"

"The greatest deity of Indian worship," Byron explained. "And you really should learn to keep the disdain out of your voice, William Swift. Lord knows if you do find the Protector of Bharath, you should be a bit more respectful."

William didn't reply, so Byron continued.

"With this trinket, and a proper bit of magic, you should be able to find him wherever he may be, in the land of the living *or* the dead. The Egyptians believed they could track the spirits of their dead, and the demons that were their enemies. You've just got to find the right spell."

Tamara frowned. "I don't remember anything of the sort. Simple locator spells, yes, but all of them referred only to the world of the living."

Byron smiled. "Ah, those Egyptians. Always full of surprises. Of course, you already know someone with a predilection for all things Egyptian. It was something he shared with your grandfather. It's ironic that he sent you to me, but now I've got to send you back to him. Nigel ought to be able to help.

"Shall I go and fetch him for you?"

"Thank you, Byron, but no," Tamara replied. "Nigel may need some . . . prompting, and he's more likely to be intimidated by

Bodicea than by you. I'm afraid we'll need you to watch Oblis a while longer yet."

Byron sighed, resigned to his duty.

Yet he had to do something to fight the boredom. The challenge was to concoct love sonnets so absurdly sweet that they would cause the demon unending torment.

The ghost smiled. Perhaps the evening would be entertaining after all.

∼

I T HAD BEEN late afternoon when they had returned to Ludlow House, and now evening was arriving, stealing across the walls and floors, darkening the house until night had truly fallen.

Tamara and Nigel were to take on the task of locating Tipu Gupta while William attended dinner at the Algernon Club. Despite her disappointment, Tamara had insisted, in much the way he had insisted she keep her date with John Haversham. There were connections among the Algernon Club, David Carstairs, and John Haversham. That much was clear. And they had not issued William this unexpected invitation without reason. Tamara was right, as usual. It would be foolish of him not to at least determine what that reason was, and learn if there was more than coincidence in Bodicea's discoveries.

Yes, they all had a great deal to do this evening, but he was determined at least to wash up and change his torn and bloodstained clothing. He had been grateful, as well, when Tamara not only agreed, but suggested that they have something to eat. There was no telling when they would next have an opportunity to refresh themselves, she had said, and it made sense to take advantage of it so they would be at their best.

William's thought processes weren't nearly so logical. He was simply hungry.

The rest also allowed him to help Tamara with healing spells that closed the wounds on her shoulder and mended her ankle. The Rakshasa scratches that had been on his chest had been superficial. Hers had been much worse, and though the magic was sufficient to heal them, it would leave scars. She would bear those gashes on her shoulder for the rest of her life.

The thought troubled William. How would she explain them, one day, to the man she married?

As he hurried down the stairs, distracted by such thoughts, he walked right through Nelson's ghost, which had appeared before him quite suddenly.

"Horatio!" he said, taken aback. He hated touching the ghosts. It was like being thrust out into the snow stark naked. He shivered as he collected himself, and turned his attention to Nelson's worried expression.

"It's getting worse, I'm afraid. Not only in the East End, either. More of the upper class have been infected. Percy Highforth and Lord Charles Derby for certain, and one or two others have taken to their sickbeds, and may also have been cursed."

William was thunderstruck. The plague had made its way into the House of Lords. Before William could say another word, however, Farris appeared at the bottom of the stairs. As always, he took no more notice of Nelson than he would any other guest in the house.

"Sir, you have a visitor."

William frowned. "A visitor? Now is not the best time, Farris. As soon as Tamara has rested awhile, we're to go out to—"

His words were cut short by the arrival of Sophia Winchell at the foot of the stair. Though she had seen the ghosts before, Nelson took her presence as his cue to disappear. William believed it was because he knew she was uneasy around the supernatural, but he worried that it was actually because Horatio didn't enjoy her presence.

"William?" she called, a moment before she saw him there.

The relief that flooded her face filled him with a lightness he hadn't felt all day. He began to smile as she started up the stairs, her lady's maid trailing slightly behind her. Farris stood aside to let the women pass.

"Sophia, what are you doing here?" William asked, the very sight of her renewing his strength and resolve. "Had we made some arrangement that I've forgotten, for—"

When she glanced up at him, just two steps below, his words faltered. Her expression was etched in misery.

"What is it, my dear?" he asked quickly.

Sophia practically leaped into William's arms, pressing her face into the stiff material of his dark coat.

"Oh, William, I'm just so frightened. People are talking, saying horrible things. Word is spreading about a horrible illness. Some are calling it a plague. And there are rumors of other things."

She looked up at him, gaze heavy with meaning. "Darker things."

William nodded. "Yes. I'm afraid it's true. And I'm glad that you've come."

"Where else would I go? If evil is afoot, I can't imagine being anywhere but with you. In your arms. I cannot bear to be alone this night."

He stroked her dark hair and nodded.

"All right, darling, all right. You're here now. Safe in this house. No need to worry," William said. He looked over her shoulder at Farris, who still stood formally at the bottom of the stairs. "Farris, could you please arrange a place for Miss Winchell's maid to sleep this evening? I'll show the lady herself to one of the guest rooms."

Sophia's maid frowned deeply, not at all pleased with this plan. But William found himself too troubled by Sophia's fear, and too exhausted from exertions of the past couple of days, to pay much attention to propriety.

For his part, Farris didn't even flinch. He nodded at William's request, then gestured for Sophia's maid to follow him up the stairs.

"I'm sure Elvira must be thinking the worst," William said quietly.

"She's not a fool," Sophia replied. "She has seen enough to know that in sinister times, the one place we might be safe is among the only people in London who have a chance of understanding what is going on, of fighting back the darkness."

Sophia slipped her arms around him, and held on as though her life depended upon it.

～

I T WAS A damp night. The air was saturated with moisture, and the pale gray clouds that hung like fairy dust around the quarter-moon threatened to erupt with cold wet drops of rain.

The moderate warmth of the day had given way to a chilling coolness, so that the pedestrians who trod the strip of turf in front of the Drury Theatre on the Strand pulled their dinner jackets and wraps tighter around their elegant shoulders. Breath came in smoky wisps, making it seem as though the ladies and gentlemen—who had only recently left the theater's confines—had all taken up their cigars and pipes at once.

The man who slipped like a wraith through their midst didn't notice the chill in the air. He was wearing a thick woolen coat, and his hands were covered in black leather gloves. His thick-soled black crêpe shoes made no echo as he threaded his way through the shivering throng.

Leaving the crowd and turning off the Strand, he went quickly down the street, his heartbeat keeping time with his footfalls. He stayed close to the walls of the buildings that towered over him as he walked, keeping his head down and his eyes on the few paces of road that lay ahead.

He slowed, then came to a stop at a low brick wall. He crossed in one smooth leap, and made his way to the nearest side of the imposing two-story home that sat there like a sleeping giant.

With its graceful lines and decorative columns, the Palladian villa looked much better suited to the more temperate climes of Italy and the Mediterranean. The harsh English weather imposed an air of neglect and gloom upon the stately structure, obscuring its architectural beauty.

The man ignored the building's merits, instead finding more interest in its entrances and exits. Bypassing the front door, he moved stealthily toward one of the first-floor windows.

The appearance of the two peelers gave the man a shock. He hadn't been prepared to encounter policemen here. He threw himself quickly into the thick shadows and shrubbery that graced the side of the building, and held his breath as the men passed almost directly in front of him.

Then it must be true, he thought. *Lord Derby's been infected.*

Waiting for the two men to pass him and move to the back of the house, he knelt rigid as a statue underneath the safety of an overgrown shrub. When the two men were no longer in his view, the man whispered a quick spell under his breath. A protection spell. He hoped it would work.

Then he made his way to one of the windows at the rear of the house and did another quick spell. Small magic. The best he could do. The glass was gone, and he slipped inside without a sound.

He moved quickly through the house until he found the foyer, which housed the ornate spiral staircase that led to the next floor. He took the stairs slowly, trying to tread softly. At the top, he turned right and opened the first door he came to.

It was a library with a huge collection of books. In the darkness, he couldn't make out the titles on the hard leather spines, but he could guess at the contents: Shakespeare, Jonson, Keats, Marlowe, Shelley, Byron. Lord Derby was a noted collector of Elizabethan drama and British poetry. His library was the envy of many an English biblio-phile.

The man stalked over to a small glass case on a walnut stand that housed the item he truly sought. The little deformed idol sat like a skull, grinning under the glass. Its three eyes stared at the man as he lifted the glass and gingerly picked the stone creature up.

"I've got you," the man whispered under his breath as he pulled a small, dark, cloth bag from his pocket and slipped it over the statue. Holding the bag tightly in his fist, he moved to one of the library windows and began the spell that would grant him his freedom.

"Stop! Thief!" a voice erupted behind him. He turned to see one of the peelers standing in the library doorway, pointing a wooden club at him.

The peeler was tall and probably outweighed him by a good two stone. But did the uniformed fellow know how to fight? Only one way to find out.

Confident in his ability with his fists, he moved toward the brawny policeman, but stopped when he saw his opponent's partner standing quietly in the shadows of the darkened hallway, holding a dripping candle.

Damn, the man thought. There was no way he could take on the two of them.

In the moment of his indecision, the peeler who had discovered him lunged and tackled him around the waist. The bag containing the idol slipped from his grasp and fell to the floor. The two men landed in a heap on the cold wood.

The peeler made a grab for his head, but the man was too quick for him, slipping easily out of his grasp. He grabbed the peeler's head and slammed it hard into the floor, likely breaking his nose and knocking him unconscious.

He hurried to his feet even as the second peeler started for him, raising his wooden club as he attacked. This time the man didn't hesitate. He knocked the club away and drove his fist into the peeler's stomach.

The policeman staggered back, the wind knocked out of him. It took the thief only a moment to realize his mistake. The tallow candle had fallen from the second peeler's grasp and rolled over to one of the long velveteen drapes that encased the library window.

Fire licked along the drapes and quickly leaped toward the ceiling.

"Damn!" the thief snarled, looking around wildly to see if there was any way to stave off the fire. But there was nothing he could do, save let it burn. He grabbed the sack containing the idol and made his way through the smoke to the library doorway.

"Get out while you can!" he yelled back to the peelers over the roar of the flames. Then he disappeared into the darkness of the hall, flickering shadows nipping at his heels.

He nearly leaped down the stairs. It was only as he reached the ground floor that he realized his protection spell had dissipated. He was no real sorcerer, and didn't know how this had happened— possibly something to do with the fire, or the fighting. But he could feel the idol's magic working on his exposed flesh, slowly burrowing into his skin.

Immediately he tried to reconjure the protection spell, but knew instinctively that it was too late. He was as good as dead. He had been in close proximity to the dark idol, unprotected, and now, rather than being its savior, he was its latest victim.

Fourteen

William Swift's mind was racing as he led Sophia up the stairs to the second floor of Ludlow House. Several times he glanced down at her, to find her gazing at him with a weighty sense of expectation that was quite unlike her.

William raised the lantern he carried, dispelling the gloom at the top of the stairs, and reached back to take her by the hand. Sophia smiled wanly, eyes searching his. He turned away quickly, and wondered why he had done so. With her hand in his, he continued down the long second-floor corridor, and turned to the right into another hall that led into the eastern wing of Ludlow House. There was a library along this hall, as well as a music room that had gathered dust ever since his mother's death, so very long ago. And there were several guest rooms that in recent times had housed only the ghosts.

The feel of her hand in his brought a warmth to his heart, a spark of light in the shadow that had fallen over his mind of late. Despite her contentious relationship with Tamara, William saw in Sophia a strength and confidence that he admired greatly. She was intelligent and straightforward, beautiful and graceful. It bewildered him that the two women in his life could not see how much they had in common, and he hoped that one day that realization would make them, if not friends, at least allies.

Yet he also required certain things of Sophia. First among them was that she understand that while he would give her all of his heart, he could not abandon his other responsibilities simply to assuage her fears. He would comfort her as best he could, but she must have courage as well.

They had walked in contemplative silence, then he released her hand so that he could open the door to the bedchamber. He turned the knob and pushed the door inward. Holding the lamp high, he preceded her into the room.

"Oh," he said instantly, brow furrowing, "it's a bit musty in here, isn't it? Stuffy and warm."

He set the lamp down on the dresser, and went immediately to open a window, sliding it up several inches. A cool breeze swept in. "If you get too cold, you can always close it, but it'll do a world of good to get some fresh air into this room. You'll forgive me, I hope. We haven't been able to keep the house properly staffed since grandfather died. And we weren't expecting company."

As he said this last he turned to face Sophia and found her still standing just inside the room, hugging herself and studying him. The plea that had been in her eyes was gone, replaced by a quizzical expression.

"You don't want me here," she said. Her voice was flat.

William faltered. He felt the chilly air flow around him, and the vastness of the house seemed to represent a distance that separated him from his beloved.

"What do you mean?" He tried to sound reassuring, but it came out false, even to him. "That's ridiculous. I always want you with me. Had I my own way, you would never leave my side.

"It's only that—"

He took a deep breath, and found himself struggling to find the words to continue. How could he explain the things that weighed on him, without adding to her hurt? How best to make her understand?

"Oh, no, William," Sophia said, showing such sadness that it pressed upon his spirit.

"What *is* it, my darling?"

She hugged herself more tightly. "I can read your face, Mr. Swift. I know you. You are trying to find a way to be diplomatic, to hide from me your true feelings, or to soften them in some way that will make them seem less harsh."

He had nothing to say, for that was precisely what he had been doing.

Sophia waited a moment for his answer, then shuddered with a sigh. "If there is any hope for a future between us, you must dispense with such behaviors. There must be no secrets, no hidden agendas, no sweet lies that cause us to be dishonest with each other."

The lamplight flickered across the canopied bed, and the mirror above the dresser gleamed with its illumination. The shadows in the corners seemed to thirst for that light. Outside the open door, the corridor was dark, but the gloom did not trouble William. This had been his home for his entire life. He knew every creak and corner. They were safe here.

And suddenly he understood why Sophia did not want to be at her home. When she had heard the rumors of the spread of the plague, she had become frightened indeed, and she knew as well as William himself that there was true evil in the world. It was only logical that if something evil had come to London, she would want to be here, with the very people meant to protect all of England from that evil.

But there was more to it than that, William realized. Something more profound. At the Winchell estate, there were only servants. Sophia had no family at home. William was the closest thing to family that she had.

No secrets, she had said.

"Of course, my darling—"

"And," she interrupted, "I hope we never again stand alone in a bedchamber with such a gulf separating us."

A soft smile came to his lips, and he felt a kind of relief washing through him, as though a dam had broken. He nodded as he strode toward her.

"I share that hope with all my heart."

Sophia gnawed her lower lip in a way that was both charming and alluring, but also silently heartbreaking. She wasn't as strong as she liked the world to believe. When William reached for her hands, she threw her arms around him and embraced him with such vigor that all the breath was squeezed from his lungs.

Softly he touched her hair, and then bent to kiss her forehead.

"I am glad that you came. Even with your servants there, you are alone in your house. There is no family there, no one to hold you or tell you that all will be well."

He clasped her forearms and gently moved her back a pace, so that he could look directly into her eyes . . . so that she could see how serious he was.

"One day soon, I hope that you will join me here at Ludlow House, as my bride. And yet I confess that even that joy fills me with a certain trepidation. You know the duties Tamara and I have inherited. They place us—and all of those around us—in constant peril. Even within our own walls there are—"

"I can take care of myself, William. I am perfectly capable," she said crisply. The Sophia he knew and loved was coming again to the fore.

"Yes," he said, tightening his grip upon her wrists. "You *are* a formidable woman. But you must understand me. Though you may *feel* safer in this house, here in my presence, that may be only an illusion. Much of the world is illusion, Sophia, and willingly surrendering to such a pleasant mirage can be dangerous."

She pulled one hand loose and reached up to caress his face, running her fingers lightly across his cheek and touching his lips to silence him.

"You fear for me," Sophia said, her eyes crinkling now with affection. She paused a moment, and nodded as though to herself. "You worry that with all the troubles clamoring for your attention, both natural and supernatural, you will not be able to protect me."

William nodded.

Sophia let her hand drop to his shoulder, and pulled the other one free, then moved closer, pushing her body against his, cleaving to him, molding herself to him in a way that was unspeakably delicious. She gazed up at him, yet there was none of the playfulness that had accompanied earlier attempts to tease or seduce him.

She wore a mask of propriety in public, and beneath that William had seen a more playful persona, of the temptress. This was an entirely new face, and he felt as if it was the most truthful.

"You will do all that you can, William," she said, her voice low, a grave sincerity there and in her eyes. "As you have done thus far. My life has been in your hands before, and I have survived. From the time I discovered the life that you and your sister lead, I knew that there was danger involved—that I would find myself in the presence of evil. Something of that, I confess, is enticing. You and Tamara are involved in a grand conflict, and the nobility of it would have captured my heart, even if the boy who gave me my first dance had not already done so years ago."

William was taken aback by this confession. A smile came unbidden to him, and he even uttered a small chuckle.

"So long ago? Sophia, we barely knew each other then. It's only little more than a year since that party at the Hartwells', when we bumped into each other—"

She glanced down shyly. "Are you really that blind, sir? Well, I suppose men often are. Let me confess that our renewed acquaintance was hardly that casual. You might even say I arranged the entire thing, and had been wanting to do so ever since that first dance.

"I have acted the coquette, William, and invited the advances of other men who wished to court me. I have said cruel things to you, but it has all been to protect myself, to hide from you just how many of my hopes I have wagered on you. You have held my heart and my dreams in your hands for years, William Swift, though you never knew."

"We were just children," William said, amazed.

"Yes, but we're not children anymore."

Sophia reached up and undid the simple knot that kept her hair pinned. She let it cascade across her neck and shoulders. She shook it out, even as she touched William's face again.

"So, you see, I have only two choices. I can live a mundane life of shallow society parties, inventing new ways to spend my inheritance. Then, certainly, I would be safe. Or I can pursue the dream born of that little girl whose toes you once stepped on while trying to dance, and cherish every day of our courtship. Then become your bride, despite whatever dangers I may face at your side."

She laid her cheek upon his shoulder.

"I think I'll risk it," she murmured, "and thank God for the chance."

Sophia tilted her head back to meet his eyes again. "So now I have exposed myself to you fully, William. I have put my heart at your mercy."

He gazed down at her, and for a moment he could neither speak nor breathe. It wasn't the elegance of her features that so paralyzed him, however, but the openness and vulnerability of the light that shone in her eyes.

And it terrified him. William wanted Sophia beside him forever, wanted her to marry him and for them to fill Ludlow House with the laughter of family, of children, in a way it had not been for so very long. But now that she had revealed the depth of her love for him, he feared for her more than ever. Sophia had said this had always been her dream, and it was his as well. Yet it would not be a simple dream to fulfill.

"Your courage astounds me," he whispered.

Sophia smiled. "It is a reflection of your own. You give me faith."

William could not help himself. He pushed his fingers through her hair and stroked her face, and instead of stepping back from her for propriety's sake, he pressed himself against her.

If he had any hope of an ordinary life, it would require a woman of rare spirit. How had he had the fortune to discover such a woman as this, who loved him to distraction, just as he loved her?

"You are all I ever wished for," William rasped, voice thick with emotion.

Sophia slid her fingers behind his neck and drew him down to kiss her. William's chest ached as he surrendered. Their lips met tentatively at first, brushing gentle and moist. Then they kissed in earnest.

Her hands slid down his back. William cupped the back of her head with one hand and with the other he traced light lines upon her upper arm. Their tongues danced together playfully and for a moment they separated, foreheads pressed together, laughing softly. The smile on Sophia's face in that moment was a reminder of the little girl he had danced with so long ago, and he fell in love all over again.

He kissed her again, blood rushing through him, the heat of arousal turning into a blazing fire. Sophia took his right hand and placed it upon her breast. The hard material of her dress and the corset beneath were rough to the touch, but his thumb and first finger lay upon the soft and tender skin that was not covered by her clothing. In what little part of her breast was revealed he could feel her pulse, feel the warmth that flushed her.

Mustering all his strength, William stepped away.

"No," Sophia whispered, and she caught her breath as she reached out to take both his hands in hers.

"I . . . they'll be wondering what is taking me so long."

Sophia went to the door and closed it. "Let them wonder," she said, returning to him.

He shook his head. "If I stay, we both know what will happen."

Sophia smiled. "Yes. We do."

"And the desire rages in me like nothing I have ever felt. It is an ache so deep that it brings real pain. I wish this were our wedding night, Sophia, but it is not. It would be a disservice to you if I—"

She laughed, but there was only love in it. She pulled him close again, pressing herself against him.

"Quite the opposite, in fact."

This time, she was the one who stepped away. She reached behind her head and began to unbutton her dress.

"Now, you listen to me, William Swift. This may not be our wedding night, but one day soon I will be your wife. I care not a whit for the proper order of things."

The dress slid to the floor, crumpling around her ankles, and she stepped out of it.

William watched, entranced, his breath coming in shallow gasps. The lamplight flickered across Sophia's face and her pale skin as her loveliness was revealed to him in full for the first time. One by one her undergarments were shed until at last she stood before him, entirely nude.

The curve of her hip made his breath catch in his throat. The revelation of her. He felt a hunger like nothing he'd ever known.

"Now," she whispered, walking toward him. "I have burned for you all this time. And if I wait another day, another hour, I fear the fire will consume me."

"Oh, my God, Sophia," William said.

It was all he could manage. He took her in his arms, his hands exploring her, caressing every soft curve of her. She guided him, and he found her slick and warm. One finger slipped into her, and then Sophia's knees went weak. She collapsed against him.

William lifted her up and carried her to the bed. He laid her there and she watched, an angelic smile upon her face, there in the lamplight, as he removed his own clothes. There was no more hesitation in him now. Nothing he had done in his life had ever felt as purely true and right as this.

When he went to her she stopped him at the edge of the bed.

"I just want to look at you," she said.

But that was a lie, for her hands caressed his chest, her fingers running all over him. The chill breeze from the open window made him shiver, but her touch was warm. His arousal was so complete that it hurt him, and when she slid her hands over his prick it leaped at her touch. It seemed as if every nerve ending in his body had clustered there.

"Now come to me," Sophia said, and she gazed up at him as he slipped onto the bed.

At first he lay beside her. He kissed her deeply, stroking her face and hair and soft, pale breasts. His tongue made small circles around her dark nipples, hard and quivering, and again his fingers slid inside her, then caressed the slippery folds of her sex.

Their kisses grew more fevered, and Sophia lay back, her hair fallen around her, framing her face. The lamplight danced, and he shook his head in amazement as he gazed upon her beauty, as he looked into her eyes and saw there everything he had ever hoped to see. All other responsibilities, all other duties, were secondary in that moment.

Forgotten.

Once again her fingers wound about his pego, taking him in her grip. She guided him between her legs and as he thrust forward, pushing into her, she shuddered with pleasure and began to whimper, the edges of her mouth lifting in a smile of gratification, of fulfillment long delayed.

He took her in long, slow strokes and she drew her fingernails down his back and wrapped her legs around him, quivering anew with each thrust. William felt as though his entire being were focused at the point where their bodies met. The moist heat of her flesh gave way to him and now the twin fires that had so long been stoked within each of them were joined in a single exultant blaze.

∼

By THE LIGHT of oil lamps and the blaze of crackling flames in the fireplace, Tamara and Nigel Townsend sat in the library of Ludlow House poring through ancient texts her grandfather had collected throughout his life. Most of them had been stored among his personal possessions; others he had given over to Nigel for safekeeping, or stored in secret caches throughout the city. Since his death, they had gathered as much of his collection of Arcanum as possible into this room.

When Bodicea had delivered word that the Swifts needed his help, Nigel had come far more quickly than Tamara would have expected. In truth, it troubled her. For him to respond thus, he must have felt that the crisis they were facing was even more perilous than she had imagined.

Having summoned their ally, Bodicea had been restless, but there was no new task for her. It was difficult for ghosts to grasp physical objects, so even the turning of the pages of a book proved a significant effort. Thus, Tamara had asked the queen to relieve Byron at last of the job of standing guard over Oblis. This left her alone with Nigel. Once upon a time, that would have been unthinkable.

In the aftermath of their grandfather's death, Ludlow House had been overrun by supernatural creatures. Tamara and her brother had been in desperate need of a safe haven.

Nigel Townsend had at one time been an apprentice to Ludlow Swift, learning from their grandfather the trade of the magician. Tamara and William were aware, of course, that a rift of some sort had come between the two men. Indeed, Nigel had been largely missing from their lives for quite some time. But after Ludlow's death, Nigel had been one of the first people they'd considered going to. And the ghosts concurred.

Nigel had accepted the Swifts into his home, and had taught the fledgling sorcerers what magic he could. He had some small sorceries at his disposal, but he knew that the Protectors of Albion would most require guidance, and time to study. For their power was innate.

So Nigel had given them access to his occult library, had offered a place to sleep, and had fed them. And one night he had appeared in the shadows of the guest room he had provided for Tamara. At first he had attempted to seduce her, and then to taste her blood.

Nigel Townsend was, of course, a vampire.

The resultant horror and fury had led to a brief conflict, and the severing of their relationship with Nigel. The Swifts had even considered that Townsend might have been in league with the forces of darkness. But the truth was that Tamara had never believed that. Not for a moment.

Even during the time of their estrangement, her grandfather had spoken admiringly of his old friend. And Townsend had seemed genuinely forlorn when he had learned of Ludlow's death.

And that night when Nigel had visited her so secretly in her bedchamber . . . in her heart she knew that he ought not to bear the blame entirely. There had been a magnetism between them from the moment she had entered his home, and she had relished his attentions. Not that she had intended to take that attraction any farther. She was quite young, even naïve, and Nigel was far older even than she had known, and more than worldly.

She had not resisted when he went to kiss her. Not really.

But had she known he was a vampire . . . known that his supernatural bloodlust might drive him to do something terrible . . .

Nevertheless, while all of the others had been swearing vengeance against Townsend, Tamara had sought only to discover his true nature. For she believed that at heart he was the man her grandfather had called friend and ally; that he would be a defender of Albion, rather than one of its enemies. In the end, her instinct had proven correct. Nigel made amends, and a peace was struck in time for all of them to band together for the common good.

Nigel spent many a night at Ludlow House. He often helped to watch over the possessed Henry Swift. The vampire had proven himself their ally on several other occasions. But he and Tamara had never again spoken of that night in her bedchamber.

"Tamara," he said, that deep, honey-sweet voice snapping her from her reverie. "Are we keeping you from something?"

She blinked, cheeks flushing warmly, and smiled at him.

"Not at all. Sorry. I was a bit lost for a moment there. I'm afraid I'm not very used to fighting an enemy I cannot see. It's damnably frustrating, isn't it? To have had so much darkness spread through the city, almost under our noses, and to be no closer to solving the puzzle than we were at the start."

Nigel frowned, his face etched with the same dignity and nobility she had always admired. Beneath his roguish exterior, these qualities were what had allowed her to retain faith in him when others would not. He was handsome in his own way, his features bespeaking origins in northern Africa, perhaps Egypt, though he never spoke of such things. But it was the strength of character, the sincerity of his eyes, that led her to trust him.

"We are closer," he assured her. "Much closer. We know, at the least, what we are facing. Now we must discover who is responsible, and what they hope to achieve with all this horror, the spreading of this plague, the theft of Indian icons and the vandalism of the tombs in St. Paul's. Our enemy originates from India, of that much we can be reasonably certain. And the best way to find the answers we seek, to at last confront the evil directly, is to recruit the assistance of the Protector of Bharath."

Tamara nodded. "I believe he's already provided some assistance, and may be in need of it himself."

"Either way," Nigel replied. "Whatever he knows, we need to know. There are many pieces to this puzzle, and it seems as if we are missing the largest of them. Perhaps William will discover something useful at the Algernon Club. But I think our best chance is to . . ."

The vampire frowned. "Where is William? It's taking him an awfully long time to dress."

Tamara smiled mischievously. "Sophia arrived some time ago. Apparently the news of the plague has frightened her so much that she had to seek solace. I'm quite certain I don't know what's become of him since."

Nigel raised both eyebrows, and a twinkle appeared in his eyes. "I do so love to see the righteous brought low."

"Yes, indeed. He won't be chastening me for quite some time, I'll wager." Tamara laughed softly.

"All right, back to work, then. We've still got a great deal to do," Nigel reminded her.

A squat, powerful figure appeared in the open door of the library. Tamara twisted around, catching a glimpse of the figure in her peripheral vision, and saw that it was Farris, carrying a heavy iron pot in front of him. A vague, burned smell emanated from it.

"Yes, well," the butler sniffed, "p'raps if certain people would quit flappin' their gums, we'd make more progress."

Tamara's eyes went wide. "Farris!"

Nigel only smiled. "Ah, well, even a little garden snake has fangs. You don't like me much at all, do you, Mr. Farris?"

"Can't say I do, sir. Where I was raised, you get a leech attached to your skin, you've got to burn it off. Never believed in all the stories about your sort, but nothin' I've heard makes me want to trust a vampire."

With that Farris fell silent, and Nigel turned away. In his hands, he held the figure of Vishnu and the serpent that Tipu Gupta had once given Ludlow Swift, Protector of Bharath to Protector of Albion. He studied it now. By the light of tall white candles, he gazed at every facet of the arcane object, and for a moment it seemed as if he hadn't even noticed Farris's insult.

Tamara stared at her butler, this man who worked for her, but who had also become a friend to herself and her brother. She tried to put all her surprise and disapproval into her gaze, but Farris steadfastly refused to meet her eyes. Instead he stubbornly stared at Nigel, awaiting some response.

The silence in the room was palpable. This was the very library where she and William had spent long days and nights, poring over every volume of supernatural lore and occult instruction they could lay hands upon, trying to teach themselves mastery over the powers they had inherited.

Those had been terrifying times, and yet they had also been among the most exciting, the most tangibly real days of her life, for in that time Tamara had realized that in some horrifying way, a dream had come true for her. She had always believed herself destined for a life beyond the constraints of society. Something of consequence. She had received all she had desired, and learned to fear it, as well.

"Farris—" she began.

"You know, Tamara," Nigel interrupted, still examining the talisman. "I have endured the doubts and suspicions, even the animosity of your brother and your ghostly confidants, because despite outward appearances I do have a certain respect for them."

He picked up one of the white candles and angled it so that its dripping wax fell onto the bronze figure of Vishnu, cooling quickly and hardening in place.

"I will not, however, allow myself to be denigrated by the *help*." The vampire sneered, his eyes going crimson in the gloom, and his fangs glistening in the candlelight. "So you'd best rein in this yapping dog of a servant . . . that is, if you wish to continue to enjoy his services."

Farris's face grew ruddy with anger, and he took several more steps into the room with that cast-iron pot in his hands.

"Now, see here!" he began.

"That will be enough, Farris!" Tamara snapped, silencing the man immediately. He had the good sense to look chastened, but she could practically see steam rising from his ears.

Tamara pushed away the books she had been searching through and stood up from the study desk. Atop it stood a bronze lion William had once accidentally brought to life. Such amusing times were a distant memory at the moment, however. She picked up an apple that sat on the edge of the desk and opened and closed her fingers around it; then she crossed her arms and regarded them both.

"Why men run this world is a mystery for the ages," she said. A lock of hair had fallen across her eyes, and she blew it away with a puff of breath. "Nigel, you know well how staunch an ally Farris has proven since we first engaged him as our butler here at Ludlow House. He is as much a part of our crusade to defend Albion as any of us. He never shirks a fight, and has shown unmatched courage in the face of terrors that would have made lesser men soil their drawers and bawl like infants."

Farris stood a bit taller, lifting his chin proudly.

"And you, my friend," she continued, casting a harsh glance toward her butler. "Mr. Townsend combats an affliction, but he has acquitted himself admirably as our ally in the past. Regardless of what mutterings you might hear issuing from my brother's mouth, or your own superstitions, he would risk his life for yours simply because we are all allies in this struggle. Whatever prejudices you have, you must rise above them, or you are of no use to me."

Nigel raised an eyebrow and regarded her carefully for a long moment, then turned to Farris.

"Well, bring it here, then. We shall see if your household skills extend to the kitchen."

Farris hesitated only a moment. Clearly Nigel's jest did not sit well with him. Then the butler looked at Tamara, nodded once, and strode to the desk she had so recently vacated. He set the iron pot down upon the wood, paying little heed to whether it might scorch the surface.

"I did just as you asked," he informed them both, gesturing into the pot. "Several branches from a yew tree, a spool of white yarn, three red ribbons, and . . ." He looked a bit regretful, and shot another glance at Tamara. "A photograph of the late Sir Ludlow Swift."

Tamara peered into the pot. There was no trace of the ingredients Farris had just described. He had set them on fire inside that iron vessel and let it sit upon the stove as they burned. All that remained was a substantial amount of dark gray ash.

"All right," Nigel allowed. "Now, Tamara. The apple, please?"

She picked up a small, sharp knife from the desktop, and plunged it into the fruit. The smell of it was pungent and delicious as its juice slid down the skin, making her fingers sticky. Tamara glanced at Nigel, who was continuing to coat Gupta's Vishnu talisman, rolling the candle between his fingers and letting the melted wax drop onto the arcane artifact.

"Only one seed?" she asked. "Are you sure about that?"

"We seek one man. Therefore, only one seed," Nigel confirmed. "The talisman is linked eternally to Gupta by his previous possession, and the link between your grandfather and the Protector of Bharath was strong. We're simply going to follow it."

"So you've said," Tamara replied, "though it still seems difficult to visualize."

Nigel smiled. "Let's stop trying, then."

He set the candlestick down and held out his free hand to Tamara. She used the tip of the knife to pry a single seed from within the apple. Nigel glanced at Farris and the pot of ashes, then looked back at Tamara.

"You're the real magician here, Tamara. Prepare the map, please."

With a nod, she turned to Farris. "Would you mind spreading that on the floor?"

"On the . . . ?" The man looked stupefied.

"Yes, yes," Tamara said, hurrying him with a gesture. "There, where we've cleared a space. Right upon the wood. Don't worry about embers. I can put a fire out fairly quickly, if I have to. Just spread it out into a square or a rectangle, as large as you can without spreading it too thin."

As Farris did so, she set the sliced apple on the desktop, and began to reach for the book she had last held, only to pause as she realized how sticky her fingers still were from the fruit. Tamara glanced around for something to clean them and, seeing nothing, began to lick them.

A flash of memory went through her mind, of the way she had debased herself with John Haversham. In the same moment this memory brought an embarrassing flush to her cheeks and a rush of arousal. Glancing in his direction, she caught sight of Nigel watching her lick her fingers.

She dropped her hands quickly, wiping any remaining apple juice on her skirts. Nigel gave her a lopsided, playful grin and smiled. But it was innocent enough, and Tamara allowed herself a nervous, rueful chuckle, then shook her head.

Then she picked up the book.

As Farris finished spreading the ashes upon the floor, she opened the pages to the one she had marked. Nigel had found the appropriate spell for her, and she had practiced the old Celtic pronunciation. Now she took a deep breath and intoned the words. Her voice was soft, yet she spoke strongly, enunciating carefully.

Farris wore a grave expression as he stepped back to watch, and as Tamara repeated the words a third and then a fourth time, he gasped in amazement and stared down at the ashes on the floor.

At the map.

For that was what they had become. Every single ember, every grain of ash that had been in that pot, had shifted position slightly. And now what lay upon the wooden floor was a light covering that showed, in sharp detail, the entirety of the city of London. Every street, many structures, most of the major landmarks were there. There were no names, of course, but to any true resident of the city, they were unnecessary.

This was London.

Tamara smiled proudly and closed the book, then glanced at Nigel.

"Well?"

The vampire altered the position of the items in his hands. Now he held the candle beneath the wax-coated talisman, which still vaguely held its shape. The flame flickered up and began to melt the wax again. Nigel crouched over a small saucer he had placed on the floor. Upon it lay the single apple seed. He allowed the white wax to drip from Gupta's talisman onto the seed, coating it.

"If he has managed to return to this plane of existence, this spell will locate him. If he is dead, the wax will turn black. If he is still beyond this realm . . . the spell will tell us, though it will take a much stronger bit of magic to locate him then.

"We'll start simply."

Nigel set the candle and talisman aside, and waited for the wax to dry on the seed. It took only a moment.

Tamara watched in fascination as Nigel picked up the wax-coated seed, studied the ashen map upon the floor, and then set the seed down at a place on the map that roughly approximated their current location, at Ludlow House.

Then, of its own volition, the waxen seed began to glide across the floor, moving through the ashen streets of London in search of Tipu Gupta.

∽

THE FILTHY WATER of the Thames churned ever onward, but the wind had turned blessedly to the south, carrying the stink of the river away.

The old man was known only as Arun to those who worked the docks, and he wandered now among them. He passed slowly by the endless warehouses, leaning on a hand-carved stick that had been a gift from one of the women he had cured, whose sinister pregnancy he had terminated with a wave of his hand. The woman had been afflicted, but the demonic parasites had not fully taken root within her womb, and he was able to save her.

She had gotten sick, vomiting up the most hideous green and black bile imaginable, but her swollen belly had gone flat, and she had been spared the fate of so many other ragged women living in these poverty-stricken districts.

But it was little enough. He might alleviate the suffering of a handful, but they were merely symptoms. The plague was still spreading, a curse that transformed his own people, yet would have far greater consequences than to kill a handful of poor fools tainted by their yearning for the land of their birth.

No, he had to do more.

Dozens of men had been twisted and transformed by the curse, by the touch of Shiva, and he knew it was up to him to exterminate them all before the evil could spread even farther. He paused along the river and closed his eyes. Breathing deeply, he caught the scent he had been searching for. No wolf or hound could have tracked it, but he was attuned to it from a lifetime of tasting the arcane.

Eyes flickering open, the old man wavered a bit, and then pressed on. The London Docks lay ahead. Masts loomed almost spectrally in the night-black sky and the moist curtain of mist that always seemed to enshroud the river on these spring evenings, merging forever with the smoke that belched from towering chimneys.

He had visited London many times in his life, but he had never stayed very long. Duty had always called him home. How strange, then, that now—at the end of his life—duty would call him here one last time.

How many ships were docked here? Thirty? Fifty? A vast forest of masts loomed in the semi-darkness. And there were other docks than these. How many vessels floated in the waters of the Thames this night? He could only begin to imagine.

The old man continued onward, and soon found himself among the bustle of sailors preparing for departure. They spared him nary a glance as they shouted to one another. Mariners of all stripes, grizzled old men with the sea in their eyes and faces as weathered as the hull of an ancient ship, young boys with no other means of survival than to take to the sea. There were black faces and brown, including some of his own countrymen. He wondered if they missed the hot sun and golden sands of Calcutta. They hoisted pigs and horses on board, and crate after crate of stores for the journey.

The mates shouted to one another, the only form of communication they seemed to know, these sailors. They shouldered heavy casks with remarkable ease, and set about Herculean tasks as though there were nothing extraordinary at all about their stamina. For to them there was not. These were seafaring men, and their journey was more than just beginning, it was never-ending.

A Babel of languages swirled around the old man as he maneuvered among the crews of several vessels. Russians and Swedes and Danes and Americans, Spaniards and Frenchmen and Egyptians and Chinamen. This was a culture all its own, one they shared. He considered how much the world could learn from an hour spent in the confluence of the London Docks, among filthy laborers and wandering the mazes of Wapping and Shadwell.

But such was not to be, for men of consequence would be loath to sully themselves with such an excursion. And what would they see if they did make the effort? The value of the place, the richness of it would be lost on them. All they would find were the rotting boards and loose, slime-encrusted cables, and the despicable and suspicious characters who lurked about, feeding off of the industry of the place or picking the castoffs from the garbage and from the mudflats. Anything to scrape a few shillings together for a bit of drink or a roll with one of the slatternly women whose lives had led them to the numbing, purgatorial existence of the prostitute.

And yet . . .

And yet.

Foolish old man, he thought, and he went about his business. He could not save the people from themselves, but he hoped to be able to save them from a power beyond the natural world. From true evil.

He had barely escaped with his life earlier in the day, exhausting his body and soul and the reserves of magic that were left to him by opening a second portal in the very instant the first had closed behind him. The dark realm where the Rakshasa resided, a world that existed side by side with this one, had almost claimed him. The demons had clawed at him, tearing at his clothes, and he had just barely summoned a doorway out of their dimension and slipped back into the world of his birth, shutting the door behind him.

He had survived. He could no longer feel the magic in him, but he had made it out of that dark realm alive. Still, weakened or not, his people needed him, and he would fight for them.

Once again he inhaled deeply, but this time the wind had shifted, so he choked on the filth in the air and issued a rasping, wet, ragged cough. He shuddered, catching his breath, and then continued on. He knew now where he was going. If not the precise location, at least the general direction. He strode past the vast, two-story warehouses that stored much of the cargo brought in on vessels. There were customs agents in the shadows of those massive structures, but the old man waved a hand through the air and became invisible to their eyes. He had neither time nor inclination to bother with such men, nor offer any explanation for his presence.

So it was that no human eyes watched him as he went to the Shadwell Dock Stairs and began his descent. He could have taken Wapping Old Stairs, but some of those steps, so close above the river, were chipped and crumbling, and he was an old man, after all.

Only the toads observed him.

The toads had been watching him all along. They seemed not to realize or to care that he noticed them, but he could not have missed those bulbous, sickly yellow eyes with their unnatural radiance gleaming from the darkness in dirty alleys and the thresholds of closed-up shops, from the pylons around the docks and between crates of cargo. They watched.

In fact, even without the scent, he could have tracked his prey simply by following the toads.

Now, though, as he drew closer, he could *sense* them. He no longer needed even the scent of their iniquity; their very presence radiated an unease that made him queasy. Carefully he descended the stairs, the river roiling by, far too close now.

At a landing, he started off into the darkness of a ledge that ran along just above the river, to a door that he had been certain he would find. There were other ways into the vaults beneath the London Docks, but this was the oldest, a private door, constructed in a time before these vaults were used for their present purposes.

It was a heavy iron slab with only a ring to serve as both knocker and handle. Even had it not been locked—as he was certain it was— the old man's meager limbs could never have drawn it open. Instead he placed the flat of his hand upon the cold metal and whispered a prayer to his ancestors, and the iron door swung inward, scraping stone.

Torchlight burned within.

He entered and began to explore. Wine casks were piled on either side of the vast room. There were corridors upon corridors lined with casks and crates. He smelled spices and tea, tobacco and sugar, all of which were stored in massive quantities in that labyrinth. The vaults were like the catacombs beneath Paris or Rome, but instead of the dead, they stored the economic lifeblood of London.

There were acres and acres of tunnel vaults here. Torches burned in sconces on the walls and lanterns hung from hooks, throwing flickering shadows upon the casks. Puddles of bloodred wine had formed beneath taps. The sickly sweet smell of brandy clashed with the acrid odor of burgundy. But most remarkable of all the characteristics of this vast underground—in a city where there were so many secrets— was the fact that only a meager wall of earth and stone held back the power of the river's current, preventing it from flooding the vaults.

It was an old place, here, filled with mystery and reeking of commerce. Only a comparative few had access to these vaults. Tonight, though, they had been invaded by things that didn't belong, creatures that sucked the light out of the air and trailed shadows in their wake.

The old man was all too aware that he hadn't seen a single toad since he had entered the place. Yet he had no illusion that this might indicate the absence of his enemy. Rather, it was certain that those lowly, mindless creatures, the eyes of evil, dared not come so close to their master. No, the evil that threatened London had been here, and recently.

Exhausted and in pain from the ache in his hips and knees, the brittleness of bone and muscle, he walked on and on, around corners and through the valleys between tall stacks of crates and casks. But he moved quietly.

Quietly enough that when he at last rounded a turn and entered through an arched doorway into one of the smallest, oldest, and deepest vaults under the docks, the monsters did not hear him arrive. He caught his breath in his chest as he slitted his eyes, trying to pierce the gloom.

There were four, perhaps as many as six or seven, if the shifting shadows beyond them materialized into something more substantial. His hands trembled and his heart fluttered in his chest. All of them had once been men. Some were dressed in the garb of Hindustani men, long brown tunics over ragged trousers, waists girded with sashes of black or white. Others, however . . . it was clear they had once been men who worked in this place. Sailors and customs agents whose occupation had been to inspect the goods stored there.

They were not men any longer.

They hissed in the shadows, their brown and green scales gleaming in the dim torchlight. The old man had wondered what their presence here might mean, but he thought he understood now. The customs agents had been tainted by the smuggled icons, the little gods, as retribution for their part in the atrocious theft that had been conducted for so very long by London shipping companies. With them transformed, these vaults had become a natural lair for the accursed things.

A nest of vermin.

And he would exterminate them.

With a deep breath he intoned the words of a tantric incantation.

"*Om navah Shivayah. Om Shakti,*" he began. He was weakened, but not so much that he could not wield any magic at all. There was a moment when his body trembled, and then the power shuddered through him.

Once upon a time it had flowed through him, from the heart of the Earth itself, from Shiva, from the world and into his own hands. He could still touch the magic, but it was no longer inside him. Yet if he could grasp it, he could wield it. And he would. He recalled all the spells and rituals. His fingers could still weave.

Motes of golden light danced in the air around him, and he felt an unseen wind tousle his white hair. He let go of his walking stick; it clacked to the floor.

The creatures stiffened and then, as one, spun to face him. They hissed, forked tongues snaking from their mouths. Their sickly yellow eyes locked on the old man, and one by one they began to slither toward him.

"Yes," he said. "Come to me."

Those sparks of magic coalesced around his fingers, and once again he began to chant. He inhaled the breath of confidence, of righteousness. He had been charged with a holy mission, a sacred trust, and he would fulfill it.

A low snarl came from the archway behind him.

The old man turned, magic spilling from his hands, and blinking out as pain from the sudden movement—from the rigors of age—shot through him. He staggered without his stick, but even as he did so he saw them, two slavering demons lunging into the vault toward him. Their eyes gleamed red, and their claws slashed the air. Their snouts snuffled and they uttered low hyena laughter as they bared rows of jagged needle teeth.

Rakshasa.

They had been quieter by far than the old man.

He thought he had escaped them, but they had not allowed him to get very far. And now he was too weak to fight them. They descended upon him. He expected their claws to rend his flesh, but instead they only batted him like predators playing with a tiny rodent.

The old man fell to the ground beneath them. Their fetid breath brought bile up the back of his throat.

Then one of the Rakshasa picked him up and carried him farther underground. The old man tried to summon the strength to cast a spell, but the moment he muttered a word the other Rakshasa swatted at his head.

The darkness of unconsciousness claimed him, and all he knew was the motion of the demons running through the cavernous underground world beneath the docks.

He had failed in his sacred charge.

The curse would continue to spread. A plague upon London. A plague upon Albion.

Fifteen

William opened the door just a crack and peered out into the hall. There was no one in sight, so he slipped out, and then turned to gaze back into the guest room, loath to leave.

Sophia lay on her side, the pale curve of her hip causing him to flush at the sight. A smile played at the edges of her lips, and she drew a sheet up to cover her breasts. There ought not to have been any way she could be coy with him now, not after the way they had just lost themselves in each other, and yet there was something deliciously innocent about her expression.

Go, she mouthed, and waved at him to depart.

William smiled and nodded, yet still he allowed himself one final glance before pulling the door closed. Then he rushed along the hall to the junction with the main corridor.

He had to hurry now, or he would be dreadfully late for dinner at the Algernon Club. It was quite an honor, in his estimation, that they had invited him to the event they were hosting in honor of Sir Darius Strong. Ludlow had been a member of the club, and William wondered if he had inherited membership because of his grandfather. Or if perhaps there was another purpose to the invitation—so they might evaluate him.

Whatever their reason, he intended to make a good impression. With Farris unavailable, assisting Tamara in her research, he would have to prevail upon another member of the household staff—perhaps even the new stable boy—to drive the carriage. He could have driven it himself, of course, but that would undoubtedly be viewed as unseemly for a gentleman of his status.

All these things whirled in his mind as he hurried to his room. He ran a hand over his face, wondering if the bit of rough stubble there would require him to shave. A glance in the mirror would answer that question. He realized he would probably need to bring his original invitation with him in order to be admitted, and hoped he had not misplaced it.

"Well, well . . . who's a naughty boy?"

The words insinuated themselves into his mind, drifting from what seemed everywhere at once. But William knew that voice well, the melodious, amused, self-congratulatory tones of the enfant terrible, the poet laureate of the ghosts of Albion.

"Not another word, Byron," William whispered, glancing about to make sure none of the servants was within hearing distance. Then he peered into the shadows along the hall. "You truly are a wretched, reprehensible lech, do you know that?"

With a sound like a violin out of tune, and a flash of ethereal light, the spectral figure of Lord Byron appeared before him, just alongside his bedroom door.

"You say the sweetest things, William. Truly you do."

The ghost was close enough that his proximity seemed intimate, and to William that intimacy marred the pleasure he had just shared with Sophia. Determined to separate the two, he backed away several steps and crossed his arms in fury.

"My private affairs are none of your business, sir," he insisted. "You may have prevailed upon my sister to debase herself for your amusement, convinced her to believe that because you are merely haunting this place there is no shame in your seeing her unclothed, but her inappropriate behavior should not be construed as granting you license to—"

"You have the most adorable dimple on your left buttock," the ghost interrupted, stroking his chin and gazing at William in admiration. "I wondered if you were aware of it."

"Byron!" he snapped, sputtering. "How . . . how *dare* you?"

The poet appeared to lean against the wall, though part of his shoulder disappeared beneath the surface. He arched an eyebrow roguishly. "What else am I to do? Have pity, dear William. I am myself denied the pleasures of the flesh. When I hear the bestial grunting and the wet slap of moist skin, it is like a siren call to me. I cannot help but be summoned to bear witness.

"Your young lady is lovely, by the way."

William was speechless. He felt the rage and embarrassment rush to his face, felt the heat of the blood as it reddened his cheeks.

"Oh, come now, there are no secrets here. There have always been ghosts in this house, William, even when you could not see them. Now let's get you dressed for the Algernon Club . . . and not that ridiculous coat of your father's that you love so much. It's quite out of date, you know. While you're dressing, I'll do my best to provide helpful suggestions for your future assignations with Miss Winchell. You've really got to use your tongue more, William. And there are some fantastic positions I learned from a Tibetan mystic that—"

Unable to contain himself a moment longer, William exploded.

"Byron! Shut your bloody mouth, you filthy bastard! I have heard enough of such talk to last a lifetime." He shook his head, trying to get through to the specter. "Sophia is my . . . I love her, do you not understand that? Is there nothing in that cold, dead heart of yours that draws a line between the profligate pursuit of carnal delight and the true passion of the heart? For God's sake, man, have you no sense of decency at all?"

The ghost blinked and then, the picture of innocence, shrugged his phantom shoulders. "Well . . . no. None worth speaking of. And look, I was only trying to be helpful. You'd thank me, really, if you'd stop being so stubbornly proper and take a moment to—"

William threw his hands up in disgust and surrender. He pushed his hand right through the ethereal essence of Byron's body, and reached for the doorknob to enter his bedchamber.

Suddenly an unearthly howl filled the house.

It echoed down from the topmost floor, drifting in a long, shrill cry from eave to eave. The screaming, laughing voice of the demon Oblis.

The voice of his father.

"*Willllllllliam!*" the demon called. "*William!*"

There was a chilling, singsong lilt to it that made him cringe, and caused a bit of the boy he had once been to wither inside.

"*Willllllllliam! I can smell her, boy. I smellllllll her. The lovely stink of your sin is on everything. I can taste it in the air. I'll have her, one day, William! I'll have her in ways that would cause even the eyes of Hell to turn away.*"

Waves of revulsion passed through William and he glanced back the way he'd come, wondering if Sophia could hear the demon's filth from behind closed doors, hoping that perhaps she had fallen asleep. Anxious, he turned back to Byron. The apparition seemed less substantial now, so transparent that he was barely there at all. But the ghost rolled his eyes and smirked.

"*Pig,*" he said.

William did not smile. In truth, he had never been so chilled. It was all he could do to hide from Byron the way he shuddered, then, and the fear that scuttled across his skin like a thousand spiders. Once more he glanced back the way he'd come, waiting to see if Sophia would emerge. When she did not, he let out a breath of relief.

With a scowl at Byron he pushed through the ghost and into his bedroom.

He hesitated just a moment before closing the door, afraid in that moment to be alone. If he'd had the courage, he would have gone up to that small room on the third floor, the former nursery, and he would have driven a dagger through his father's heart, just to silence the voice of the demon.

But William Swift had never been quite that brave.

∿

NIGEL TOWNSEND CROUCHED over the map of ashes he and Tamara had magically created on the floor of the study. The wax-encased apple seed that was such a vital part of the spell moved swiftly across the ashen map of London. Farris muttered several times in amazement as the waxen seed floated a fraction of an inch above the floor, and made its way along streets and through squares on the map. The ashes were dark gray, almost black, but they shone with a glimmer that came not from the lamp and firelight in the room, but from the magic imbued in them.

Nigel silently admired Farris's loyalty to the Swifts, but he would have thought after all the man had seen that something so simple as this would fail to astound him.

When the seed paused, and seemed to hover near the River Thames, Tamara smiled that beatific smile of hers, pushed back the stray lock of hair that was forever her bane, and clapped her hands like the little girl she'd once been.

"Oh, well *done,*" she said. "I'd say Tipu Gupta is still in the land of the living after all. What a relief. At the London Docks, from the looks of it. If we get down there quickly enough, I'd wager we'll have no trouble locating him."

Nigel nodded, but with some hesitation. "Indeed. And perhaps we'll get some answers, as well. The docks are the threshold to Wapping and Shadwell."

Tamara frowned, standing up straight and twirling that lock of hair around one finger in nervous contemplation.

"Yes. I'd thought of that as well. A great many things have become clear to me just lately. The archaeologist, Carstairs, was transformed into one of these reptile men, just as so many others have been. In each case, it seems proximity to one of the statuettes that Carstairs smuggled into England from India is to blame. The statuettes themselves may be cursed, but there is a greater pattern to all of this.

"And what of the Indian men who have been plagued by this curse, then transformed? Surely they weren't wealthy enough to buy the statuettes from Carstairs. It's possible they may have been sailors for the East India Company, but living in those slums . . . it seems unlikely.

"Could it be that the accursed icons were *purposely* given into the possession of certain men, such as the earl of Claridge; that they were actually targeted by this plague? The magic and the demons involved are all of Indian origin. When we count in the defilement at

St. Paul's, it seems to suggest some sort of malicious intent, perhaps, due to the very act of smuggling sacred relics out of India through illegal means."

Nigel ran his tongue over his pointed teeth. His skin was cold. It was always cold, but this night it seemed a deeper chill had settled into his bones.

"Then the thefts from museums and such might be our enemy stealing back the smuggled relics," he suggested.

"Precisely."

Farris coughed into his fist. His eyes averted, he shrugged. "If you'll excuse me, miss?"

"Yes, Farris?"

"Well, it's only that, if it's some magical bloke from Calcutta or Bombay behind all this, why curse his own, like? From what we've seen, there are a lot more Hindu types turned into these scaly fellows than there have been Englishmen. And the women . . . well, the ones who've gone through the horror of all this, having been got at by the cursed ones and giving birth to . . . it'd be a terrible thing to curse yer own people with something like that, don't you think?"

Nigel saw something behind the girl's eyes, then. A shadow made of sorrow and dark knowledge. It pained him to see how much of her innocence was gone.

"You're right, Farris. It is a terrible thing. But it seems the only answer, at least for the moment. We are dealing not only with cruelty and hatred here, but with madness." Tamara set her lips in a grim line. "I cannot imagine how it must be to live in a conquered land, to see its riches despoiled, and to know its people must bow to the will of foreign rule. Perhaps madness and hatred are a natural response. But not evil. Not this."

Silence swallowed the room a moment before Nigel sundered it.

"It may be that our enemy has even grander plans. Dare I say it, but Farris is correct. Why curse your own people without reason? Whatever black sorcerer stands against us, he has done nothing without purpose thus far, and I can only imagine there is purpose to that aspect of the plague, as well. The toads are the eyes of our enemy, or so we've come to believe. The Rakshasa his servants. But the accursed ones certainly must serve his dark cause. Might it be simply a question of numbers? Could his plan require far more of the creatures than the curse of those relics can quickly create?"

Tamara nodded. "There's logic there. But to what end?"

"I'm afraid to hear the answer to that," Farris grunted.

"We'll have it soon enough," Tamara said, gesturing toward the ashen map once more, to the white waxed seed that trembled above the London Docks.

Nigel glanced down at the map, and a deep frown creased his brow.

"What's this, then?" He scowled.

The apple seed was moving again. Swiftly.

"Oh, my," Tamara said. "Magic propelled it before, but if it's tracing Gupta's movements now, he is moving awfully quickly for an old man."

"Too quickly to be on foot," Nigel observed, as the waxen seed raced away from the docks.

"Almost too quickly even to be in a carriage," Farris added.

"He must be in trouble. In the grasp of our sorcerer, I'll wager!" Tamara cried. With an air of command that came over her at such times, a confidence and courage worthy of the Protector of Albion, she threw wide her arms and lifted her chin. The candlelight cast lovely shadows upon her face.

"Lord Nelson, I need you now!" she called into the dark corners of the study, into the spectral world that existed side by side with that of the flesh. When formally summoned by the Protector, the ghosts of Albion would always hear, and appear.

A moment later, a phantom light shimmered in the corner of the room and the spirit of Horatio Nelson appeared, still clad in the uniform of the navy and with one sleeve pinned to his jacket where his arm had once been.

"You speak my name, and here I am," Horatio announced, chin raised. "Horatio Nelson reporting for duty, my dear."

"You must hurry, Horatio," Tamara began, and with a gesture and an intense gleam in her eyes, she gestured to the magical map on the floor and explained its function. "Here we have a map that shows the location of our quarry. You must go after Tipu Gupta. Follow him if you can. I'd translocate there myself this instant, but I don't think I'd be able to transport Nigel, as well, and I don't think it wise for me to go alone."

Nelson nodded gravely. "Yes, of course. I'll go straightaway. But what of young William? Why can he not accompany you?"

Tamara arched an eyebrow and glanced at Nigel before replying. "My brother is off to his affair at that *gentlemen's* club this evening. It's up to me to locate the Protector of Bharath, and I'm perfectly capable of accomplishing the task. At the moment, however, it looks as if Mr. Gupta may have run into trouble. Let's make certain he survives the night, shall we?"

Nigel smiled. She was headstrong, but he could not help admiring her. "Let's see we *all* survive the night, if you don't mind."

✑

A THICK YELLOW mist rolled along Shadwell Street, cloaking the crumbling buildings and hiding away a thousand nightly crimes. Nelson was as insubstantial as the mist itself as he appeared on a street corner. He had never entirely approved of Nigel's presence in the Swifts' inner circle, but he supposed the fiend had proven himself loyal enough. The two men had unpleasant history together. But the admiral would never have allowed his personal feelings to interfere with his sworn duty to Albion.

The ghost glanced quickly around to get his bearings. He was quite a distance from the river, here, though he could hear the tinkle of distant bells and thought, if he peered intently through the fog, that he could see a billowing white purer than the mist, a cloud that might well have been the sails of ships upon the Thames. And he was sure he could hear the flap of canvas, even from here. The sound brought a profound melancholy to his heart, for there was nothing Horatio missed more of life than the open sea, and the rush of wind in the sails.

There were plenty of sailors living in the hovels of Shadwell district, but this wasn't the sort of place Lord Nelson had frequented while still alive. He started east through the mist—the direction Gupta seemed to have been moving—and quickly passed through some of the iniquity that seemed drawn to such places, or bred there.

A pair of harlots, likely prostitutes, wailed as they clawed at each other, beating and scratching and then tumbling into the gutter where they rolled around, locked in bloody combat like wild animals. Dirty beggar children appeared out of the damp fog like ghosts themselves, sad-eyed creatures who watched the proceedings as though their hearts and minds had gone numb . . . which Nelson presumed they had indeed, long ago.

And the men . . . Nelson could barely stand to see the gin-soaked, grizzled shades of humanity dressed in rags and asleep in doorways. Their clothes and faces were layered in months of grime, and one in particular had open sores upon his face and a mouth left open and drooling.

Better to be dead, Horatio thought. *Far better.*

Sounds of another skirmish drifted from the mist ahead, and he rushed along the street, invisible to the eyes of the living. Harsh, dissonant music rose from the cellar of a small inn as he passed, but all his attention was focused on the noise ahead, for there was a horrid, bestial snuffling that mingled with the groaning of a man in pain.

As he passed a row of shuttered shops, the wind shifted and the mist parted just long enough for him to get a glimpse of his quarry. The very essence of Nelson's spirit shuddered at the sight of the malformed, reptilian creatures that had once been ordinary men. He thought of his feeling a moment earlier, that it would be better to be dead than to be one of the filthy lost souls in the alleys of Shadwell, and knew that even those wretches were better off than these, whose flesh—and perhaps even souls—had been so twisted by evil.

They shuffled along with that peculiar gait of theirs, something between a dart and a hop, and one of them bore a white-haired, copper-skinned figure over its shoulder. That could only have been Tipu Gupta. There was blood on the man's face and spattered in his hair.

The devils! Horatio thought.

But as he gave chase, the mist enveloped the creatures again. The ghost of Lord Nelson drew his spectral sword and raced after them, wishing that the fact of his death allowed him some special perception here in the world of the living. There were advantages to being dead, but that was not among them.

Only moments passed before the wind cleared the mist away

again, but his quarry had disappeared. The ghost paused, frustrated, and stared along the street ahead. Off to his right lay the entry to a narrow alley. Behind what appeared to be a rooming house stood a warehouse so vast that it disappeared into the darkness and the fog. As he peered in that direction, there came a creaking noise and a thump of wood upon wood, followed by a clanging as of metal chains.

"It must be," Nelson whispered to himself.

The air seemed to tremble around him, and even as another cloud of mist began to roll in he felt the presence of another ghost. Almost at the same moment, a voice reached him.

"Admiral," it said.

Horatio spun around in alarm, sword at the ready, but he lowered the blade when he found the ghost of Colonel Dunstan materializing just behind him. Dunstan wore a grim, disapproving look on his face. Though the mist passed right through him, along with the sickly yellow light from the lanterns of Shadwell Street, still the ghost's expression was clear.

"Two visits to the East End in one day. I'm pleased to see the so-called Protectors of Albion have finally taken an interest in what's happening in the less savory corners of London," Dunstan said.

Lord Nelson scoffed, and then added a scowl for good measure. When he spoke, it was a harsh whisper that came from him, though none of the living could have heard him unless he desired it.

"Now, see here, Colonel. I told you before that I do not appreciate your insinuations, and I'll have an end to them now, or I shall take it as a personal insult. It may be unfortunate that the sinister goings-on in this neighborhood came so late to the attentions of the Protectors, but that is no blemish upon their honor or the purity of their intentions. Now that they are aware of the situation, they are acting to remedy it with alacrity."

Dunstan hesitated. His handsome features were still cut into a frown, but after a moment he nodded. "I'll allow I may have rushed to judgment, Admiral. And if the Swifts are acting as you say, I shall give them the benefit of the doubt. But I'm afraid Kali's Children will not wait—"

"Kali's . . . I'm sorry, who are—"

"The transformed men. They bear a curse made in the name of the goddess. Their lives and souls are hers now. Whoever commands them in Kali's name, whatever master they serve, the monsters will slay the Protector of Bharath as soon as they have all gathered. And if that warehouse is their lair, the old bloke is as good as dead if we don't stop them now. We cannot wait for your Miss Swift, I'm afraid."

Nelson did not appreciate the colonel's tone. Though he maintained that he was no longer truly an admiral himself, merely another soldier in the eternal war between the light and the darkness, he would not be ordered about by a man he had outranked. Dunstan wasn't even a naval man!

Yet the logic was sound, and what truly mattered was the crisis at hand.

"You're right, of course," he said, turning the blade of his sword toward the narrow, dirty alley. "With me, then, Colonel. We must save Gupta, at all costs, for it seems certain our answers lie with him."

"Lead on, Admiral," Dunstan replied.

Their forms little more than mist within mist, they rushed across the street and down the alley.

The windows of the rooming house were open and shouting could be heard from an upper floor. Beneath that, the subtler, primal sounds of sexual congress came from a grime-encrusted basement window. They ignored all these signs of life, for it was death that concerned them now.

Horatio and Dunstan reached the warehouse and passed, insubstantial, through the outer wall.

Inside, the monsters were waiting.

◆

THE CARRIAGE CLATTERED along cobbled streets at dangerous speeds. As the horses galloped along Swain's Lane through Highgate Cemetery, Tamara sat forward, hands clutching the edge of her seat.

Nigel was beside her, and she could feel the darkness and the power radiating from him. He wasn't merely tense with anxiety and curiosity, but hungry in anticipation of violence. Nigel was darkly handsome, and his lusts for the pleasures of the flesh were eclipsed only by those of Byron himself. He had no trouble convincing the trollops in the pubs he frequented to let him suckle at their breasts or throats, and prick them with his teeth just enough to taste of their blood. He would not kill them, only take what was freely given.

And not always of trollops. Often enough, from what Tamara had heard and surmised, he was given such a gift from a lady or a maiden. Some of her own friends, upon meeting Nigel at Ludlow House, had spoken of their intense admiration for him, of the man's magnetism.

But this night, a different kind of lust was upon him. Not carnal lust, or bloodlust, but the hunger for battle. Once upon a time Nigel Townsend had been touched by evil, and it had tainted him ever since. It had been the temptation that led to the death of the only woman he had ever loved, and forever stained his friendship with Ludlow Swift. Nigel hated what he was, and though he posed as a reluctant fighter— even a coward at times—he relished any opportunity to turn his hatred outward.

Tamara knew him better than anyone, but she was keenly aware that even she knew very little of his life before he had come to London. He rarely even hinted at his own past, and she dared not ask. Someday, she would have the courage, she would find the moment.

But this was not the time.

"Can't the bloody horses go any faster?" Nigel called.

Farris was up on his seat at the front of the carriage, holding the reins. They could not see him, and he didn't bother to slide open the wooden panel that would allow him to address them directly. He did not respond at all, in fact.

"I'm sure he's driving them as fast as he dares," Tamara said.

"Perhaps he ought to be more daring, then," Nigel replied curtly.

She shot him a withering glare. "Farris is one of the bravest men I've ever encountered. And as he still must draw breath . . . as his heart must continue to beat for him to live . . . I'd say he has quite a bit more to lose than you do, Nigel. Caution should not be confused with stupidity."

The vampire seemed about to argue. He had the telltale gleam in his eyes. But then he only smiled, and reached out to pat her hand.

"Of course, Tamara."

"Don't patronize me!" she snapped.

Nigel scowled. "I wouldn't dare. I merely acquiesce to your greater wisdom."

She wasn't sure if he was mocking her, but before she could admonish him further, the horses whinnied loudly, and Farris shouted something she could not hear. The carriage swung to one side as they started to turn, and in that moment there came a melodious trill. A ghost began to coalesce in front of them.

Bodicea was meant to be guarding her father, so Tamara expected Horatio, or perhaps Byron. Instead it was the spirit of Colonel Dunstan who now manifested before her.

"Miss Swift," the ghost began. "I bring dark tidings. Admiral Nelson and I located the lair of Kali's Children . . . the cursed men who have been involved in such unpleasant deeds. But the creatures were waiting for us . . . not only they, but demons as well, Rakshasa summoned by the same master. I am . . ."

The ghost straightened up, as though reporting to a superior officer, but his expression was grim.

"I am sorry to report that in our effort to free the Protector of Bharath, Admiral Nelson has also been taken captive."

"What?" Nigel snapped, eyes narrowing. His upper lip pulled back, revealing his fangs. "But Nelson's a ghost! Those things could hardly keep hold of him for very long."

Dunstan's eyes darkened. "There are greater powers at work here, vampire, than you know. A ghost cannot die, but a soul can be ruined. Tainted. Destroyed."

The words were like needles in Tamara's heart. "Oh, no, Horatio," she whispered. And then it was her turn to shout to Farris—to speed the horses, and caution be damned.

Sixteen

He could still smell her musk on his fingers.

As he slipped from the carriage and stepped out onto the street, he let his mind linger on the image of Sophia's naked form pressed underneath him, the way her eyes widened in pleasure as he kissed her honeyed neck. He wished with all his heart that he were back in time, still being held in his love's warm embrace.

"Will that be all, sir?" the stable boy said, his disdain barely held in check.

"Ten. I will expect you back then," William replied curtly. He did not like the look of this fellow, and thought that when all the present insanity had passed, he would speak with Farris about it.

The boy shot William an annoyed glance—*as if he can read my mind,* William mused—then nodded and closed the carriage door before hopping back into the driver's seat. He hadn't wanted to put his boots back on after supper, and drive into London proper, but William had brooked no argument. They'd taken the open carriage, and the boy had sat for the whole of the trip in sullen silence.

Now William watched the carriage drive off, leaving him with no means of rapid departure, should the need arise. He just hoped the evening did not yield any surprises of that sort.

William pulled the bell at the front door to the Algernon Club, and waited. After only a moment, an old man in a black tie and short coat opened the door and stared at him, eyes narrowed.

"How may I help you, sir?"

"William Swift. I received an invitation to dinner."

The servant nodded, and stepped back away from the door so that William could enter.

"Thank you," he began, but the servant turned away from him and walked off. Not sure if he was meant to follow or not, William continued to stand in the hall, feeling stupid. The man paused and glanced back at him with an expression that suggested he thought William might be more than a little dim-witted.

"This way, sir," the servant said, his voice like aged parchment, coarse and reedy. He did not wait for William to reply, but continued on down the hall.

William followed, wishing that the place didn't make him so nervous. As he took in his surroundings, the rich brown paneled walls and the warm burgundy-leathered upholstery, he felt an undercurrent of power that belied the charm of the rooms. It was as though all the trappings of the place were a veneer that was meant to mask its true nature, but that the façade was made transparent by his new-found magical senses.

He decided to keep such thoughts to himself. He did not know these people—*supposed* friends of his grandfather—and did not want to offend them or, worse yet, place himself somehow in jeopardy.

The old servant made a left at the end of the entrance hall, and led William into a large, well-appointed library. There was a fire in the grate, and the gas lamps flickered like small fairies inside their glass sconces along the walls.

There must be real money among the members of this club, William thought. Gas lamps were a relative oddity in London. The rich had them, but the rest of society was still subsisting on coal fires to cook, heat their homes, and give them light.

"Wait here," the servant said, then turned and left William

stranded in the doorway. There were three other occupants of the room, older men whom he did not recognize, though they all looked as if they recognized him. He nodded politely to them and moved to an empty settee in the corner. The three men stared at him as if he were a curio in a cabinet, then whispered quietly together.

The room was very warm, and the settee so comfortable that William found himself becoming drowsy. The past two days had been extremely exhausting. He sat up abruptly, taking a deep breath and forcing himself to remain alert. When he glanced again at the three men, he found himself focusing on the man who sat closest to the fire. He was well into middle age, and his eyes shone with a curious light. He caught William looking at him and smiled.

I do know that man, William thought. *But from where?*

The answer hit him suddenly, and he felt foolish.

It was none other than his grandfather's friend John Dalton, the well-respected naturalist and chemist. William smiled back, acknowledging the connection and hoping Dalton had not been offended by his lack of recognition. The last time he had seen Dalton had been right before the Royal Society had awarded him the Gold Medal. Dalton had been in London on business, and dined at Ludlow House one evening before returning to Manchester.

William stood and was just about to offer his regards to the scientist when he felt a strong hand clap him on the shoulder.

"Excuse me," William said as he turned around to see who was touching him. "But I was just about to—"

"I had no idea I'd find you here," John Haversham said, a broad smile playing across his handsome face. "What a pleasant surprise."

"Yes, well, of course it's . . . well—" William said, a stiff smile hiding the nasty feeling in the pit of his stomach that told him the evening was just about to get *interesting.*

From another room came the tinkling of the dinner bell.

"Shall we go in for dinner, Willy boy?" Haversham said, clapping him hard on the back again.

"Well, I—" William began.

"Excellent."

Haversham put a friendly arm around William's shoulder and led him deeper into the belly of the club. As they walked, John continued to talk at William without even waiting for a reply, moving rapidly from one topic to the next. They passed another doorway, through which William could see more than twenty men—all at least five-and-thirty, most much older than that—standing around holding tumblers of cognac and brandishing spicy-smelling cigars as they conversed loudly. They seemed not to have heard the first call of the dinner bell, and it wasn't until it sounded again that they put away their pleasures and moved out into the hallway.

William lost his garrulous companion in the flood of other men from what he supposed was the drawing room. He did not know why he hadn't been invited to attend there with the others, but decided that it must be for members only, and since he was merely a *guest* . . .

He followed the other men down the hallway and into a massive room with two long tables. The men began to take their seats, and William realized that they must be assigned somehow. His stomach churned as he stood in the middle of the room, unsure where to sit.

"This way, Swift," a voice said. William looked over to see Haversham standing beside him once again. He gave William a devilish smile.

"You're sitting right next to me, old boy."

❧

THE DOCKYARD WAS dark as pitch when they arrived. Tamara could not even discern the shapes of the buildings through the windows of the carriage, because her eyes could see no farther than an arm's length in front of her.

"You are frightened." An unruffled voice, smooth as cream, sounded in her ear. Normally, Nigel's teeth being so close to her neck would have given her pause, but tonight she was so glad of his company that she did not even notice.

"Not frightened, Nigel. Worried."

She hoped her lie wasn't too transparent. Though she knew Nigel was concerned for her welfare, she preferred not to give anyone the satisfaction of seeing her emotionally unbound. Not even him. There had been enough of that in recent days.

Tamara felt as though she was fighting a constant battle to win the regard of the men in her life, and that she had lost ground of late. She was determined, however, to regain that respect. They had come to rely upon her—with good reason, she believed—and it pained her to think that her emotional outbursts might have led them to think their confidence had been misplaced.

It was a constant struggle to help them rise above the usual presumptions about women. Now that she had left them room to doubt her, she feared that the moment she lost control again, and let her weakness show, they would ignore her opinions and make their own plans.

"Of course, my dear. Nevertheless, I've heard it said that worry is cousin to fear."

Nigel's condescending tone irked her. "A cousin far removed. I promise you that," she replied curtly.

He smiled, and she could just see the white gleam of his incisors in the near darkness.

"Touché, my dear. Touché."

The carriage came to a halt in front of a row of abandoned warehouses that abutted the water. The air stank of rotten fish and human garbage, filling Tamara's nostrils with its putrescence and making her gag. She pulled a perfumed handkerchief from her pocket and placed the rose-infused fabric against her upper lip. The smell did not abate, but at least it was less overpowering.

"It smells like death," Nigel offered, his lips curled in distaste.

"Aye, that it does," Farris countered, slipping off the driver's seat and coming to stand beside his mistress. Tamara was glad that Farris was with her this night. He was a capable fighter and a true friend whom she had no doubt would defend her with his life.

The horse was restless, pawing the ground with her sturdy hooves and whinnying softly. Farris put a hand on her flank and the mare instantly calmed.

"Even the horse senses it," Nigel said, his eyebrow raised. He ignored the fact that the beast's wild looks were at times cast in his direction. "This is a tainted place. You should not have come."

"Nonsense. What choice do we have? This is where the Protector of Bharath has come, and now in pursuit of him, Horatio has some-how been captured. He may be beyond death, but there are still ago-nies that may be visited upon a ghost. He needs our help."

There was a wavering in the ether around them and then Nelson's comrade, Colonel Dunstan, appeared alongside them. He seemed calm, his brow unwrinkled by worry or fear. Tamara wished that she were a ghost so that she, too, could be impervious to the happenings around her. She had seen that same serene look on Bodicea's face many a time, right before she flung herself into battle.

"He is being held in there," the ghost said, pointing to one of the empty warehouses.

"Thank you, Colonel Dunstan," Tamara answered gratefully. Their spell to locate Gupta would have led them to these buildings, but Dunstan's guidance had shortened the time it would have taken to find the precise place where Horatio was also a captive.

When she glanced at Nigel, she saw that he was watching the ghost with an odd expression writ upon his face. "How was it that you es-caped unharmed, Colonel?"

Dunstan looked offended for a moment, then shrugged. "It was not me they were after, vampire."

Nigel hissed at the ghost, exposing his fangs.

"Please, Colonel, Mr. Townsend does not mean to be rude," Tamara said. "He was merely curious. We are all on edge, I'm afraid."

"No offense taken, milady," the colonel replied drily, but the wary look in his eye gave lie to his words.

Tamara wished that William were here with her now. Instead he was having a fine time at the Algernon Club, no doubt, probably smoking cigars and talking politics with the rich and influential. She wished, not for the first time in her life, that she had been born the man, and William the woman. Really, he was much more interested in things of the female persuasion—gossiping, clothing, society affairs—than she was.

"Mistress Tamara?" Farris said, interrupting her reverie.

She nodded, leaving those thoughts for another day. "It may be that we need every available hand here. Byron! Come to us now! You are needed!"

It took only a moment. The ether rippled around them, and then Byron materialized beside her with an insouciant toss of his head.

"You called, my precious pet?" Byron asked, giving her a wink. "Hello, faithful Farris, and to you, Nigel."

"Byron, please, now is not the time to be cavalier. Lord Nelson's been captured."

The spectral poet's entire countenance changed. All the lightness went out of him, and a grim cast came over his features. The twinkle that so often danced in his eyes became a cruel spark.

"Time for a rescue, then," he said grimly. "Shouldn't we have Bodicea along, though? She is the warrior among us, after all."

Tamara shook her head firmly. "She's watching over Oblis. If he were to escape, there's no telling what evil he might unleash. I won't risk it unless there's no other choice."

Byron nodded. "Right, then. What are we waiting for?"

"He's in there," she said, pointing to the dilapidated warehouse. "Colonel Dunstan was with him when it happened."

Byron turned to the other ghost, head cocked curiously.

"Dunstan? Have I not heard the name before?"

"Horatio has mentioned me, I'm sure," the ghost of the colonel replied.

"I suppose," Byron countered, but he studied the phantom soldier for a long moment before Tamara interrupted.

"You've been inside, Colonel Dunstan. What is our best approach?"

"I'm afraid the monsters will sense us the moment we enter, miss. As such, a frontal assault is as good a plan as any."

Nigel replied, "Yes, well, thank the gods for your unique military expertise."

∼

Bodicea chose not to go into the room.

She hated Oblis with a pure, black rage, and made it clear to the Swifts that she could not be responsible for what happened if she was left too long as his keeper. Truly, she did not trust herself in his presence. Bodicea would kill him with the least enticement, even though it meant the murder of Tamara and William's father, Henry, in the bargain.

So she stood guard outside his door instead, knowing he was much safer that way.

"Bodiceeeeea . . . Bodicea!" the thing within screeched, taunting her, willing her to enter its prison and indulge in her hatred. Oblis knew that such conflict could end only with his death or freedom, and was willing to take that risk. But the spectral queen was determined to keep Oblis in check, and stay out of his way at the same time. She knew it was possible—she had managed the feat many times before—but tonight she felt the old rage stirring even more violently than usual.

"Bodicea! I can still hear their cries. Your daughters begged for their lives . . ."

She wished for silence, trying to ignore his words. Oh, Ludlow, dear one, sweet magician, where are you now?

With grim purpose she let these thoughts linger in her mind, meditating upon bittersweet memories. She missed Ludlow, and though she cared deeply for his grandchildren, it was not the same. She wished with all her heart that he were here with her now. He would have made her suffering more endurable.

Instead she would have to satisfy herself with naught but his memory.

∾

COLONEL DUNSTAN LED the way into the warehouse, with Tamara, Nigel, and Farris following close behind. Tamara had misgivings about such an unsubtle attack, but agreed with Dunstan's assessment that the Rakshasa would likely sense them the moment they entered the building. Still, it seemed as if there must have been some more logical way to go about this, perhaps drawing them out, rather than going in after them. If it hadn't been that Horatio was a prisoner, and that they did not want to risk Tipu Gupta's life, she would have taken more time to consider their course.

Byron floated ahead of her, his form gossamer as spiderwebs in the dark. Nigel and Farris were behind, but she paused and gestured for them to wait.

"Hold a moment," Tamara whispered. "We'll need light if we're to accomplish anything inside this pit. And if we're not worried about the element of surprise—"

She muttered a few words under her breath, and a ball of pure golden light blazed to life in her palm. With a gentle flick of her wrist she released the magic, and the light floated a few feet above her head, staying there as if tethered to her by an unseen thread.

"All right, let's go."

The others waited for her to move, and when she did, they followed even more cautiously than before.

The inside of the warehouse stank terribly. Tamara pulled the handkerchief from her sleeve and once again placed it to her nose. She looked over at Farris, and saw that he was also holding a handkerchief to his face. He was a staunch ally, brave and strong, but only human in the end. Her supernatural companions did not seem bothered by the stench. Even Nigel remained stoic.

The light that Tamara had conjured made a small dent in the pervasive darkness. She supposed that Nigel could see better in the dark than either she or Farris, but even he squinted to peer into the blackness beyond her magical illumination.

"Colonel Dunstan, where exactly did you come into contact with the demons?" Tamara asked quietly, though even as her lips formed the question the stench began to grow stronger, and she knew that they were getting closer to their quarry.

"Just a bit farther," the colonel whispered. "Through that doorway and into the next room."

Tamara had a sudden image in her mind of their strange procession, and wondered what an ordinary person would think if they happened to be in the warehouse just then. How would a simple laborer react to the sight of their macabre parade?

Until very recently she, herself, had not believed there were monsters that lurked in the shadows and lonely byways of the world. She had thought tales of fairies and demons nothing but pure fantasy. Now that she knew the truth, there was still a part of her soul that longed not to believe. To bury her head in the mud and ignore the harsh reality the Protectorship of Albion had foisted upon her and William.

The smell changed as they neared the entrance to the next room. It had previously been merely foul, but now there lingered within it a sickly sweetness.

"Do you smell that?" Tamara whispered.

Farris nodded.

"Incense," Nigel said.

"The sort of thing one burns for rituals . . . often with an offering to one god or another," Byron added, his high, reedy whisper filled with dread. "It has been a good long while since I smelled this particular aroma, but I think it's sandalwood."

"Colonel?" Tamara began, but when she glanced over to where Dunstan had just been, she realized that he had disappeared.

"Where's he gone?" Farris grunted. "He was just there." The butler reached out with both hands to touch the air where the ghost had been floating a moment earlier.

"The coward has run off," Nigel snarled, voice full of loathing.

"Oh, I don't know if he's a coward," said Byron nonchalantly. "A traitor, though . . . that would be my guess."

"What?" Tamara asked. A cold feeling spread in the pit of her stomach.

Then a terrible noise rent the air around them, like the savage laughter of hyenas, and Tamara turned to see two Rakshasa demons emerging from the darkness of the warehouse, her magical light playing upon their hideous features as though it shrank away from their evil.

"What the Hell are those?" Nigel barked.

"Hungry, I think," Farris replied, his voice quavering.

As if on cue, the ghost of Colonel Dunstan returned, shimmering into existence in the dark, his features taking on an entirely different— and crueler—aspect.

"Hungry indeed," the turncoat sneered. "And you are to be their dinner."

"I think not, betrayer," Nigel roared as he lunged at the colonel, wrapping his fingers around the ghost's throat and throttling him, driving him to the ground.

Humans could not touch ghosts, nor could those specters lay a hand on a human being, but creatures of the supernatural were an altogether different story. Dunstan tried to flee, staggering back toward a wall. Most of him managed to slip through, but Nigel held the spirit in his clutches, and Dunstan was stuck.

The ghost drew his sword. Tamara shouted a warning to Nigel, but by then it was all she could do to defend herself.

Farris picked up a length of pipe from the ground and was swinging it viciously at one of the Rakshasa. Tamara wanted to aid him, but before she could do so, the other attacked. Her hands came up, a spell at her lips, but instantly it was upon her, driving her to the ground, claws puncturing the flesh of her upper arms.

"Tamara!" Farris shouted. He cracked the demon before him over the head, bending the pipe, and it flopped to the floor. The stout, thick-armed man leaped on the back of the one attacking Tamara and used the pipe to choke it, holding on tightly with his huge hands. The Rakshasa hissed and spat, sickly yellow eyes wide with fury and pain as it tried to reach back to tear him away.

"Let go, Farris!" Tamara screamed.

The man did as he was told, releasing his grip in the same moment the Rakshasa bucked with preternatural strength. Farris was thrown a dozen feet, to crash against a door frame. But at least he was clear.

Tamara weaved a sphere of fire between her palms and then hurled it at the creature, immolating the Rakshasa in seconds. It was burned down to the bones, which dropped to the floor as charred embers.

On the opposite side of the room, Byron and the second Rakshasa, which had recovered from Farris's assault, squared off.

"Come here, you drooling hunchback," the poet taunted. "You're ugly as a whipped dog, and smell even worse."

It did not seem to comprehend the words, but somehow it sensed that it was being insulted. It let out a terrible howl and leaped at the ghost. Byron vanished, immediately appearing on the other side of the creature, further inflaming its anger.

Tamara started over to check on Farris, but she was waylaid by the arrival of four more Rakshasa.

"Damn it!" she shouted. "Nigel, help me!"

But there was no response. She shot a quick glance toward Nigel and saw that the tables had turned. He was impaled upon Dunstan's phantom sword, crimson blood staining his clothes and dripping onto the floor. The pain etched in the vampire's features made Tamara herself ache in sympathy.

Colonel Dunstan twisted his blade with one hand, and with the other, he raked at Nigel's eyes.

Tamara feared for her companions. As she turned to face the approaching creatures, she said a silent prayer to God, and to the spirit of Albion itself.

∼

WHEN THEY HAD entered the dilapidated warehouse, Nelson had felt nothing amiss. It wasn't until he found himself alone, and surrounded by hungry Rakshasa, that he realized his mistake: there was a Judas in their midst.

Thinking back to Colonel Dunstan's betrayal, he felt the sting of sadness. He had known Dunstan for a very long time, and he would never have pegged the man as a traitor. Nelson wondered if Dunstan was somehow an unwilling servant to whatever devil was behind the demon plague.

He still could not believe his own stupidity. He had let himself fall into a trap, and now he was stuck in the hull of a half-rotted ship waiting for help that might never come.

Putting his ghostly hand to the wall of the moldy wooden vessel, he could feel a powerful magic humming within the timbers. Whoever was responsible for his incarceration was a strong magician. There was no hope of escape on his own. The magic that had bound him would keep him trapped forever, unless the Protectors found him.

There was a soft moan from the other side of the hold, giving hope that the man trapped down here with him would finally wake up. The man—really no more than a bag of bones wrapped in rags—had already been in the hold when Nelson got there. Though the man had not stirred, or even moaned, for the few hours they had occupied the same prison, Nelson had sensed all along that he was alive, if only barely.

He had seen the man before, of course, during the battle against the Rakshasa in an East End slum. Now, as the ghost floated toward him, the man forced himself up onto his knees, then seemed to collapse back into himself. But instead of ending up in a heap on a cold, wooden floor mined with rat droppings and assorted other bits of disgusting garbage, he fell into a yogic lotus position, his back pressed stiffly against the ship wall.

Amazing, Nelson thought. *He is not nearly as far gone as I supposed.*

The man did not look up at the ghost who floated only a few feet away from him. Instead he kept his head down so that his long, thin, white hair fell forward across his face, obscuring it.

"Tipu Gupta, I presume," Nelson said.

The man did not answer. He lowered his head even farther, so that his long hair swept the floor of the ship.

"I say, sir. Are you all right?" Nelson ventured again. He knew the man could hear him, because every time he spoke, the shaggy head moved almost imperceptibly in his direction.

The voice was soft and hoarse when it finally came. Nelson had to float closer to the man in order to hear what he was saying.

"I knew your master. He was a dear friend, and I mourn his passing still," rasped the Protector of Bharath. He lifted his head so that Nelson could finally see his face. There was caked blood where his nose had been broken—*probably when he was thrown down into the hold,* Nelson thought angrily—and his dark brown eyes were slits of pain and sorrow.

Astonishingly, the man smiled, and Nelson saw that he was missing one of his front teeth. It looked as if it had only recently been parted from its master, and that it must have hurt very much.

"Come now, sir," said the ghost of Admiral Nelson, "you cannot possibly find amusement in our predicament. London is in an uproar from end to end. Dark magic twists the flesh of men from the most repugnant alleys to the highest towers, and women grow heavy with the spawn of Hell itself! What could there possibly be to smile about?"

The man nodded, and his white hair fell across his face like a veil. Or a shroud.

"I was merely remembering the dangers I faced alongside Ludlow

Swift, the Protectors of Bharath and Albion united against the darkness. So it must be again, if we are to survive this . . . if Albion is to be saved from the evil that plagues it."

His smile disappeared, replaced now with a terrible sorrow. "And yet it is best that Ludlow did not live to see this day . . . to see my shame. I am to blame, you see. I have brought this plague to England . . . and before I die, I shall end it."

Seventeen

William leaned back in his chair and rested his hands upon his bloated belly.

He had eaten so much that he could hardly breathe. All he wanted was to close his eyes and sleep until the bulk of his dinner had been digested, though by his calculation that might take weeks. The treacle tart had been divine, just the right consistency, melting in his mouth before he could swallow it. He was going to have to get the recipe from the cook. It had all just been too good to pass up.

As an added benefit, the luscious dinner and the scrumptious dessert had proved so exquisite that William had found he did not even mind sitting beside John Haversham. At first he had been annoyed, but as course after course appeared before them, he and John had bonded, after a fashion. He would still not call Haversham a friend, but at least now he did not mind the man so much.

For the life of him, he couldn't understand why he had disliked Haversham so extraordinarily to begin with. Yes, he was loud, and almost absurdly jovial, with more than a bit of swagger in his manner.

But he was so convivial, so enthusiastic in his sense of fellowship that it was impossible to maintain a disdain for him.

He had hurt Tamara's feelings, of course, and William knew he ought to consider Haversham a villain for that reason alone. Yet how could he, when he was relieved to discover that the man showed no real interest in his sister? Enjoyable company he may have been, but he still had a scandalous reputation, and that hardly made him the ideal brother-in-law.

Still, how could anyone *not* like a man who extolled the merits of a good roast as heartily as John did?

"Are you feeling all right, Willy boy?"

Willy boy? Now that *I hate,* William thought as he looked up to find John Haversham staring at him. It was funny, but he had never noticed how much Haversham looked like a cow. He had such a long, protruding face, and those large, sad gray eyes.

"I do say, you look practically bovine, Haversham," William said. He clapped a hand over his mouth, horrified that he had spoken so. He had probably offended his dinner companion irretrievably. Yet he had been unable to stop himself. His lips felt swollen, and there seemed a fog around his very thoughts.

And had he slurred his words?

Incredibly, Haversham didn't seem in the least bit offended by William's faux pas. He laughed as if William had made a joke at someone else's expense, rather than his own.

"Bovine is fine. Yes, Willy boy, I must concur."

William blinked rapidly, trying to clear his head. The room seemed to be spinning, and he could not make it stop. How much wine had he enjoyed at dinner? Surely no more than two glasses. Not an amount sufficient to make him feel so disoriented.

"I feel . . . strange, Haversham. Does the room seem to be . . . spinning to you?" William asked hesitantly. *Maybe it is the room itself that is moving, and not my head,* he thought hopefully.

"Spinning, Willy boy? No, I think not," Haversham replied. William noticed for the first time how nicely Haversham's dress coat fit him. He particularly liked the shiny metal buttons, because he could see his reflection in each one. Without a second thought, he leaned forward and grasped one of the buttons.

"I like . . . your buttons," he said, a pronounced slur to his words. "I can see . . . myself."

He leaned nearer so that he could view his reflection more clearly, and was startled by his appearance.

"Bloody Hell, where did I get these horns?" William said, rather more loudly than he intended. He hadn't had horns this morning, he was positive of that. Would Sophia still love him, now that he was marked so? he wondered.

A middle-aged man with soft, dark hair and an aquiline nose came up behind Haversham. He gave William a confused look before turning to Haversham.

"Do we have a problem here?"

The man's voice was firm. William stood up abruptly, the room spinning dangerously around him.

"Soft," William said as he reached out and petted Sir Robert Peel's hair before fainting dead away.

⇆

"**N**IGEL?" TAMARA CRIED, peering off into the darkness.

She could hear the curses and grunts of the vampire's struggle with Dunstan's ghost, and she comforted herself with the knowledge that they proved Nigel Townsend had not been destroyed.

She had to go to him, to rid the world of the traitorous fiend of a ghost who had pretended to be their ally, and then betrayed them. When Tamara got the chance, she would shred Dunstan's very spirit.

But Nigel would have to fend for himself awhile longer.

Byron had disappeared deeper into the warehouse, scouting ahead for Horatio and Tipu Gupta. Tamara had sent him on that mission, hoping he would also ascertain how many of the fiends they faced, but now she wished she had not done so.

Farris was still on the floor of the warehouse, struggling to rise and clearly disoriented. When he'd crashed into the wall, he had struck his head, and now Tamara saw him reach up to the back of his skull and wince as he touched a tender spot. When he brought his hand down there was blood on his fingers, dark and glistening in the golden illumination of the magical light she had conjured.

The Rakshasa must have smelled the blood, for even as the four of them loped from the dark depths of the warehouse and into the glow of that conjured light, they all began to veer toward Farris. One of them hesitated, though, crouched a moment, then began to sprint toward Tamara instead, a second one following close behind.

Oh, I think not. I will not be eaten by a gaggle of small-brained demons. And neither will Farris.

Tamara screamed, raising her arms above her head as though in some macabre ballet, her fingers sizzling with bright blue flame. In one synchronized motion she thrust her arms out in different directions. Chilly gooseflesh rose on her left arm as the very air froze around her fingers, and a crackling sound filled the warehouse. The two Rakshasa lunging after her instantly went as rigid as statues, coated with blue ice, their momentum causing them to topple to the floor and shatter into hundreds of shards.

Simultaneously a second spell erupted from the fingers of her right hand and arced across the floor to envelop Farris in a sparkling cage of violet light, providing a ward against attack. It was one of the most powerful protection spells Tamara had mastered.

Never had she attempted two spells at once. Had anyone suggested it to her in calmer times, the mere idea would have left her skeptical. But these were desperate times, in the heat of battle, and she would tax her body, soul, and magic to the very limits to protect herself and her allies.

The two that had been about to attack Farris hesitated as they neared the cage of violet lightning surrounding him. One of them threw back its head and let loose a howl of frustration, but the other only growled, then emitted that high-pitched hyena laughter and turned away from Farris, eyes falling upon Tamara. Despite the scent of Farris's blood, they knew he was no longer viable prey.

But Tamara . . .

They started toward her. She held out her left hand again, the blue fire still burning bright in sharp contrast with her pale white fingers.

"Try me," she taunted the Rakshasa.

They moved toward her, their sharp claws making a clicking noise on the floor. Their fetid breath was staggering as they moved nearer, a miasmic cloud that was nearly enough to overpower her.

Then from the darkness behind the monsters came the ghostly

form of Lord Byron. The specter came darting from the shadows and attacked one of the demons. He wrapped phantom fingers around the filthy matted fur at the back of the Rakshasa's neck, and in one smooth motion plunged a fist through its skull. Though he was only spirit, pure ectoplasm, the penetration was devastating. The Rakshasa let out a high, keening wail unlike anything she had heard from the demons before, and crumbled to its knees, weakly batting at its head in an ill-fated attempt to reach for Byron, not realizing it had already been dealt a fatal blow.

"Good show, Byron!" Tamara cried.

"Tamara, look out!" the ghostly poet shouted.

The Protector of Albion spun, magic erupting from her fingers without as much as conscious thought, incinerating a pair of Rakshasa as they tried to attack her from behind.

"Well spotted!" she called, her hand still held aloft in front of her. The ghost, having disposed of a second demon himself, moved to join her.

∾

As tamara and Byron held off the Rakshasa, Nigel engaged Colonel Dunstan in a battle of wills.

Though the ghost had assumed an early advantage over the vampire, Nigel had kept the colonel at bay thus far. Dunstan was a ghost, but he was capable of destroying a vampire if he could do enough damage to the body. Yet Nigel Townsend had been in combat with ghosts before, and from the wild look of desperation in Dunstan's eyes, he thought perhaps the colonel had little experience with the undead.

Nigel gripped Dunstan's spectral arm with such strength that his fingers punctured ectoplasmic flesh. With his free hand he grabbed the back of the ghost's head and bared his fangs with a hiss. They were jutting from his mouth, elongated in the fury of battle, and his eyes gleamed a bright crimson. Nigel darted his jaws forward and tore a piece of Dunstan's ghostly essence away.

"Let go, leech!" Dunstan cried, and he thrust himself upward, flying toward the ceiling.

Nigel's grip slipped. That was the problem with ectoplasm: it ran like mercury through your hands if you weren't careful. He snarled in frustration and leaped upward himself, jaws gnashing in blind, berserker rage.

"Coward!" he screamed. "You flee like a girl child! Come, fight me like a man. Like the soldier you once were!"

"And let you tear me to ribbons? I think not!" Dunstan countered. High above Nigel, he raised his hand and manifested an ectoplasmic sword that seemed to grow from his palm and glowed with a pale, ugly green light.

Before Dunstan could launch another attack, however, the shadows around them exploded in shimmering blue fire, and a searing bolt of magic struck the ghost. The specter went rigid, letting out a cry of alarm that was cut short by the magical assault. The sword he had manifested dissipated, and the ghost simply hung there in the air like a fly trapped in amber.

Tamara appeared from the shadows, mystical blue energy still dancing around her fingers as though she had unleashed so much power this night that she could not stanch its flow. Even as she approached, the incapacitated Dunstan floated down within easy reach. Nigel grinned, baring his fangs.

"Well done, Tamara," he snarled, even as he took hold of the trapped ghost and drove his fangs into Dunstan's spectral throat, teeth pushing through ectoplasm as though the ghost's flesh were overripe fruit.

"Nigel, no!" Tamara screamed.

But the vampire paid her no mind. With fang and claw he began to shred Dunstan's spectral essence, and the ghost began to go flaccid, like a sail when the wind has suddenly died. Nigel might not be able to destroy the specter completely, but if the vampire tore him apart it would take time for Dunstan to reconstitute himself.

"Nigel, stop! We need him!" Tamara shouted again.

Staring at her right through the transparent, withering phantom held in his grip, Nigel continued to tear at the ghost. His brows knitted, and he tried to warn Tamara off with a simple glare.

With a flick of her hand, Tamara released Dunstan from her binding spell. Furious, Nigel pulled back from the ghost to upbraid her, and the wraith Dunstan had become slipped from his grasp. He disappeared into the ether, leaving only empty air.

"Bloody Hell, Tamara Swift! Do *not* interfere when you know nothing of the situation," Nigel said, his voice low and menacing.

"Do not think to correct me, Nigel! I told you we needed him, but you were set upon destroying—"

"I was incapacitating him. There is a difference, girl! I'm well aware that none of our allies trust me because of my nature, but I thought I had at least earned the benefit of the doubt from you. Now because of your impetuousness, we've lost him!"

As Nigel took an angry step toward Tamara, Byron materialized between them.

"She did not know, Townsend. Use your head, man. Obviously she wasn't aware what you were doing, and how could she have been? Their studies have touched only the surface," the ghost said hotly. He was uncommonly belligerent, hands up as though he might shove Nigel backward if he attempted to get any closer to Tamara.

"You want the same, *poet?*" Nigel rasped, spitting the last word as though it were a slur.

Byron held his ground. "As you wish," he said, keeping his gaze locked on Nigel's.

For a long moment neither of them gave way. At last, Nigel shook his head sadly and turned from them. "I am tired of being treated like an enemy," he said as he began to walk away, seeking the solace of shadows.

"Nigel, I'm sorry. I didn't understand. I still don't, really . . . ," Tamara called after him, but he ignored her, choosing to prowl the perimeter of the warehouse rather than respond.

"Don't let it bother you, my pet," Nigel heard Byron say. "Vampires are notoriously moody."

In the darkness, he sneered, but he did not rise to the bait. He needed time to let his anger go, to release the bloodlust and malice that had been nurtured by his fight with Dunstan's ghost.

"What was I to think?" Tamara said again, her voice low as though she spoke only to Byron, though Nigel knew she was aware that with his vampiric senses he could easily hear her. "Oh, Byron, there is so much I'm still learning, and I am afraid that one day the things I don't yet know about magic will be the death of me . . . or of those I love."

Byron muttered something soft and kind, and Nigel felt a black guilt settle over him. He ought to go to Tamara, and soothe her, to help her master the power of the Protectorship.

And he would. He just needed a moment to settle his nerves.

Even as these thoughts played across his mind, he heard a moan coming from an open doorway. He glanced up, thinking they had found Tipu Gupta, but it was Farris, emerging from the room with one hand clapped to the back of his head.

"Farris, are you all right?" Tamara asked.

"Thanks to you, miss. If you hadn't put that spell on me, I'd've been dinner for sure."

The butler winced and drew his hand away from the back of his head. He'd been injured, and the smell of his blood made Nigel's nostrils flare with hunger. He managed a smile.

"You fought admirably, my friend. You've a lion's heart."

The stout, barrel-chested Farris stood a bit taller, touched by this sentiment. "Thank you, sir. I do my best. Nothing special about old Farris, I'm afraid. No magic here, as you know. But I try to make up for that with my fists." He hesitated a moment before going on. "I hope you'll accept my apologies, sir. I was quite rude. Misjudged you, I did."

Nigel sighed. "You're far from the only one. It is in the past. Let's neither of us speak of it again."

Farris nodded gravely, and Nigel found himself pleased to have forged a new bond with that courageous man.

Tamara hurried over, Byron floating behind her, glaring balefully at Nigel. But all her attention was on the butler now. Nigel was pleased that Farris's arrival had drained away the tension between them.

"How badly are you hurt, Farris?" Tamara asked.

He gave her a weak smile and shook his head. "I'll have a knot on the back of my head for a few days to come, but I feel as hale as I was before those demons attacked."

Tamara raised an eyebrow and stared at him doubtfully. "Farris?"

The stalwart butler nodded. "Right, well, I could use another of those spells of yours, mistress. That might fix me up right good and proper."

Not for the first time, Tamara wondered at the healing properties of magic. She always felt stronger, better able to cope with intense situations after she had used a spell. Sometimes she pondered the idea that one could become quite addicted to the sensation. Or addict others to it. Nevertheless, she cast a minor spell, easing Farris's pain.

"All right, what's next?" she asked her friends. "We've got to assume that wherever Tipu Gupta is being held, Horatio is imprisoned, as well. Colonel Dunstan led us here to be slaughtered . . . a plan I'm pleased we thwarted. But I do not believe that our locator spell was incorrect. It worked perfectly, and it indicated Gupta's presence in this very spot, or near enough. Otherwise we would have suspected Dunstan's duplicity all the sooner. He must have brought us somewhere very near their actual location. We've got to search every alley, every building, in the area. And we've got to start now."

⁓

WILLIAM AWOKE IN near darkness, to find himself propped up in a stiff leather armchair. He drew in a deep breath and found that his chest hurt.

As his eyes adjusted to the firelight, shapes began to come into focus. The first thing he saw was a huge hearth with a roaring fire, blazing away. He was in a small study. A large teak desk took up a good portion of the room, and two looming curio cases stood as sentries on either side of it. A stuffed lion's head hung from the wall above the mantel, and at first William thought it was somehow attached to the robed figure that stood below it.

When he squinted, however, he saw that the lion and the man were indeed separate, but somehow that didn't make him feel any better. There was something sinister about the robed man, his face obscured from William's gaze. Something sinister about the room itself, and the Algernon Club in general, in fact. It wasn't entirely unexpected, but it was a disappointment.

He had so enjoyed dinner.

He tried to sit up but found that his body could not do what he asked of it. He was trapped here, probably trussed up like some sacrificial lamb for the slaughter. He knew now that he shouldn't have come, that all the good food they had served should have been suspect.

Now I shan't have a hope of getting the recipe for that treacle tart, he thought petulantly.

"What do you want?" William managed to ask. His tongue felt heavy in his mouth, and made the words hard to form. He was still slurring a bit, but it was better than before.

What exactly *had* happened? he wondered. He remembered dinner and John Haversham and . . .

Oh, no, William. You didn't really pet the hair of Sir Robert Peel, as though he were some lapdog! He felt his cheeks flush crimson. How horrible. He would never live the embarrassment down.

He vaguely remembered the look of shock on the parliamentarian's face. Here was the man who had brought about the formation of the Metropolitan Police—the *peelers,* for God's sake—and William had *petted* him.

On the other hand, his mortification was likely for naught. If things continued the way they had been going, he would never be in Sir Robert's company again. Perhaps there was a bright side to being murdered by a mysterious gang of occultists.

Then again, perhaps not.

"As you've no doubt surmised, Mr. Swift, your food was drugged. We required that your mind be dulled, to make it difficult for you to muster your magic, in the event this conversation goes . . . *awry.*"

That final word, so mundane, sounded so sinister now. William swallowed hard.

"It was the treacle tart, wasn't it?" He sighed. "Villains."

"Silence!" the robed man commanded.

"Right, fine. You said you wanted to have a conversation, but apparently what you meant to say was soliloquy. Go on, then. Have at it."

The robed man stood beneath the lion's head, ominous and still. William felt himself frozen, not merely by the drug in his blood, but by pure dread.

"The Algernon Club has existed in one form or another for centuries," the robed man said. "At first it was an enclave of magicians, a place where information was exchanged, truces made, and alliances forged. Dark sorcerers were not welcome, though they managed to infiltrate the group from time to time.

"Over the years we acquired a public face, that of the gentlemen's club, so popular in London in this new era. An interest in magic, and a certain position in society, were all that would be required to make an application, and soon enough the Algernon Club became known for its amusing eccentricity. We are well known now as a collection of sleight-of-hand artists and illusionists, tricksters, and stage mystics.

"Or so the world believes.

"Among the entertainers, however, there remains a core membership, including the directors of the club, who are true to its founders' wishes. There is real magic here, William, as I'm sure you know well.

"From its inception, the club was aware of the existence of the Protector of Albion. In the earliest days, the Protector was a sailor, a ship's mate named Harry Curtis. It was an unwanted anchor to him, curtailing his ability to pursue his love of the sea. His mother had been Protector before him, and had passed the mantle to Harry. He despised her for it. They were both commoners. Harry Curtis took his own life without naming an heir to the legacy, but the soul of Albion would not be denied, and soon a new Protector was chosen, and the legacy restored. In time—more than ninety years and three Protectors later—the legacy fell to Maurice Ludlow.

"In all the history of the Protectorship of Albion, Maurice was the first to accept an invitation to become a member of the Algernon Club. The directors of the club did as they had always done, attempting to share secrets and spells to better our fellowship of magicians, as well as safeguard the people of this great land. It was an honor to have the Protector among us.

"Upon his death, Maurice passed the duties and power of the Protector to his grandnephew, Ludlow Swift. Your grandfather, William. He was also a member of our club. Now, though, Sir Ludlow is dead, and we would like to know if the mantle has passed . . . to you."

The robed man stopped speaking and walked over to one of the curio cabinets. William held his breath as the man unlocked the case and pulled open the door.

Inside were three of the stolen Indian idols.

"Don't touch them. They are not safe—" William began, but he did not finish as the man lifted his hand and began a protection spell. A blue flash of light formed over the stone creatures, and William gasped.

"Your concern is understandable, but not necessary, William. The club became aware some days ago of the curse that had been laid upon these idols, and the plague of evil they were spreading. In the time since, we have had agents working ceaselessly to locate and re-cover as many of them as possible, doing our best to halt the spread of this horror. We have purchased them when possible, and stolen them when we had no other choice. Those in our possession have been made safe, counterspells cast upon them so that they are harmless, as long as they reside within our walls.

"In the time since your grandfather's death, we have been at-tempting to determine the identity of the new Protector. The disap-pearance of your father deepened the mystery. It would have been preferable for us to undertake this recent action with the Protector's approval, but under the circumstances we had no choice but to pro-ceed upon our own instincts. We hope, now, to remedy that situation, and to once again have the Protector of Albion counted among our number."

"Who *are* you?" William asked.

The man reached up and lowered the hood of his robe, revealing handsome, regal features and dark hair peppered with gray. "Lord Simon Blackheath. The director of the Algernon Club. At your ser-vice."

William stared. His head had begun to clear, the effects of the drug wearing off, and now he felt his pulse racing. He so wanted to believe Lord Blackheath. The idea that he and Tamara might have such allies to aid them in their cause was one that would make him rejoice . . . if it turned out to be true.

Of course they had been aware for some time now that there were other magicians in England, and that some of them belonged to vari-ous secret societies. According to Ludlow's journals, however, most of them were apparently black magicians, devoted to dark deeds and en-slaved to evil masters.

"There is no mention of the club in my grandfather's journals," William stated flatly, climbing to his feet and brushing off the seat of his trousers.

"Of course not. The true nature of the Algernon Club is cloaked in utter secrecy. Ludlow would never have betrayed our trust in that way."

Lord Blackheath respectfully lowered his head and waited for a response.

William studied the man. Blackheath could have killed him while he was unconscious, yet he had not. There was also the matter of the stolen idols, which explained many of the errant mysteries connected to the present crisis. It all seemed too good to be true. Which meant it probably was.

As he considered it, though, William decided that the only way to discover whether or not the man could be trusted was to see the conversation through to its natural conclusion. He could not find any reason not to confirm for Lord Blackheath what the man already seemed to know.

"You are offering me membership in the Algernon Club?"

Lord Blackheath smiled, his dark eyes ringed with tiny wrinkles. "Not only in the club, but on the council. The Protector has held a seat on the council for more than a century."

"All right, then. I accept." William grinned then, and raised an eyebrow. "But I should inform you, my lord, that you will need two empty chairs, not one."

Storm clouds passed across Lord Blackheath's eyes as he frowned at William. "I beg your pardon. Two?"

"I have inherited the Protectorship of Albion, just as you thought," William went on, straightening his jacket and feeling the magic of his inheritance surging up within him, sparkling just beneath his skin. "But I share that legacy. My grandfather chose two heirs, myself, and my sister, Tamara. I accept your invitation on her behalf, as well."

The older man's eyes went wide and he paled, his jaw working for several moments during which he seemed incapable of forming words.

"But . . . ," he said at last. "But, this is a *gentlemen's* club."

William crossed his arms and gazed at Lord Blackheath balefully. "Good," he said. "Then I can be confident that in my sister's presence, you will all behave like gentlemen. You desire to have the Protector of Albion among your ranks, my lord. So you shall have both of us."

❧

In the moldy, rotting hold of the creaking ship, Nelson watched Tipu Gupta quietly meditating, legs pulled beneath him. The man seemed to gather strength from the quiet chant he intoned under his breath. Finally, after what seemed an eternity, the Protector of Bharath looked up and gave the ghost another weak smile.

"I am sorry I have dragged you and your friends into my troubles," he said.

"Nonsense," said Nelson. "This plague affects us all. It is not your burden to shoulder alone. We must stand united against it."

Tipu Gupta shook his head sadly.

"Yet I am responsible, Lord Nelson. This evil has afflicted Albion because of me and my . . . poor choices."

Horatio raised a ghostly eyebrow. "Please explain."

The man nodded slowly, a pain deep as the heart etched on his face. "It was because of Ludlow Swift's passing that I was reminded of my own failing health," Tipu Gupta began. "I, too, had not chosen an heir, and I realized that, though I had a number of years still left on this Earth, I had much to teach my pupil. That the choosing had best be done soon, if I was to impart all the knowledge I possessed."

Horatio nodded.

"I was a fool. I chose unwisely—"

Suddenly a loud buzzing noise rent the air.

"What in the—" Horatio began as a blue light filled the hull of the ship, blinding Gupta and causing the ghost to retreat.

With a noise like meat frying in a pan and a flash of bright light, Tamara Swift translocated into the dank cargo hold. Her dress was torn and her hair unkempt, but her eyes were bright and gleaming with courage and determination. Even in his lifetime, Admiral Nelson had never been so happy to see the face of an ally.

"Tamara!" he cried.

"Horatio, oh, thank the Lord," she said, and rushed to him.

There was an awkward moment when, were he a man of flesh and bone, they would have embraced. Instead they only gazed fondly at each other for a moment before Tamara turned her attention to the old Indian man who still sat cross-legged upon the floor. She squatted down beside the man and stared at him.

"You *are* Tipu Gupta, are you not? The Protector of Bharath?"

The old man took a long, shuddering breath.

"I am."

The sadness on Tamara's face broke Nelson's heart. It was as though all her courage had failed her, and he knew she must have been thinking about Helena Martin, and perhaps all the others who had suffered so horribly in recent days, as well.

"Please, sir. Can't you explain this all to me? There has been so much horror. We fight against these demons, see women violated and men turned to monsters, so much death and cruelty, and we don't know why."

He gazed at her for long seconds. "Why?" he said, at last. "A single word, a simple question, but it never has a simple answer. Had you lived in India before the English came, or seen the way our people are treated in their own country, you might begin to understand. Had you spent time in this district, near the docks, in the filth with sailors from the East India Company who were carried here so far from home and then abandoned without any way to return to India, you might know. My country, my people, are trampled beneath the boot of the British Empire."

There was such bitterness in his voice that Nelson felt sympathy even as he bristled at the man's anger. As a naval man, he felt the call to defend the Crown, to defend England, but he said nothing. Gupta was a fellow prisoner and posed no threat.

Tamara's mouth gaped open. "You . . . you're responsible for all of this?"

The old man shook his head in despair. "Yes. But not in the way you think."

"I should hope not! For whoever's done this has cursed not only London, but slaughtered your own people, as well!" Nelson snapped.

Tamara shot him a withering glance. "Lord Nelson. Get hold of yourself." Then she turned her attention back to the Protector of Bharath. "Mr. Gupta, sir?"

He met her hard gaze with his own. "I trained my daughter, Priya, as the Heir of Bharath, the Protector-in-waiting. Upon my death she would look after our country and keep it safe from the encroaching evil. Just as your grandfather chose you and your brother."

He sighed and shook his head. "She was the wrong choice. The Protector is to combat supernatural threats. Evil and dark magic. War and diplomacy must be left to human society and its governments, for better or worse. It is not our place to interfere with civilization, only to protect it.

"I have no love for the British Empire. But my daughter has nurtured a hatred for the English in her heart her entire life, despising your control over our people and lands. Named as my heir and successor, she began to tap into the magic of the soul of Bharath, sapping my power from me before it was her due. When I had been sufficiently weakened, she attempted to kill me, so that she would receive what remained of my power . . . what she had not already stolen.

"I survived, but only barely. With most of my magic at her disposal, she fled India, bent upon vengeance against the British Crown."

"Your own daughter?" Tamara exclaimed. "I am so sorry."

Tipu Gupta nodded, his eyes sad and empty.

"Weakened as I am, I followed Priya here and tried to undo the evil she had perpetrated, tried to stop her. But I cannot. I do not know how to explain it. She must have been studying spellcraft for years, without my knowledge, abusing my trust, making supplication to the gods, courting demons . . . so that once she had even a fraction of my power, she was able to wield it with deadly skill.

"I am depleted. Most of what I was, I am no longer. But Priya only grows stronger. I think she believes she has allied herself with the goddess Kali, but the thing that whispers to her in the shadows of her mind is not Kali. It may be an aspect of the goddess, a dark, feverish, savage thing, but not the goddess herself. Still, it gives Priya more power even than she stole from me. The longer my daughter taps into that power, the more difficult it will be for me to stop her when we face each other for the final time."

Tamara took his shaking hand in her own and squeezed.

"Why did you not come to us? We would have helped you," she said.

The old man shook his head.

"I thought that your father was the heir, the Protector of Albion. And since I found him to be incapacitated, I chose to fight my daughter alone. And I was . . ."

He gazed up at her, jaw set grimly. "I was ashamed."

⟋

THE WIND WAS colder than the girl could have imagined. It whipped through the thin fabric of her sari and chilled her copper skin. Her long, black hair, her pride as a child, was held firmly in place beneath a piece of thin, white cloth. She had chosen white, the color of bone, the color of death, because it mirrored her mood, and because the goddess wished it.

Yes, the voice spoke in her mind, in the native tongue of her homeland. *White for death. White for vengeance. You have done well, daughter of Kali.*

Priya smiled to herself, no longer cold. The love of the goddess warmed her. She was here for vengeance. And it thrilled her to the very core to think how close she had come to fulfilling her aim. From the poor, suffering fools who had been cast aside in the slums of London like refuse, she had created a small army. Some of them had been traitors, serving their English masters, and others had been victims. Either way, they were better off now, transformed into the reptilian Children of Kali, serving both their country and the goddess. She had begun with them, and then proceeded to punish the guilty, using the Curse of Kali to destroy the thieves, one by one, and transform them, as well. They would serve the cause of vengeance for the very goddess they had defiled.

It was perfect. As Protector of Bharath, she had wrought monsters from the flesh of men, and she had them to do her bidding. With the help of the goddess, she had yoked the mighty Rakshasa to her command. And now the endgame had begun. One more night, and she would wrest control of the entire British Empire in the name of the goddess, and the accursed would destroy the city of London.

Never again would a foreign power look toward India with predatory eyes and imperialistic ambitions. Not after this.

Priya closed her eyes and placed her hands upon her abdomen, where she had tattooed the thirty-six *tattvas* in ink, etching the symbols with the tip of a blade and then staining the wounds black. All for the goddess.

Now, under her breath, she began to chant a mantra to soothe her mind.

"*Krim Om Kurukulle Sarva-Jana-Vasamanya Krim Kurukulle Hrim Svaha,*" she whispered, pausing only a moment before chanting the mantra a second, then a third and fourth time.

Yes, daughter, the goddess said, the voice in her mind warming her flesh and making her gasp, as a shudder of pleasure rippled through her, beginning at the tips of her fingers and ending deep within her *yoni.* The time had come at last. *Now you will be the true Protector of Bharath, safeguarding your people with the courage your spineless father could never muster. At last, a worthy Protector has risen.*

Priya opened her eyes and called into the frigid night. "Children, I call you! Come to me! Rise and destroy your enemies in Kali's name!"

~

THE NIGHT GREW colder, and freezing rain began to shower down upon the makeshift hospital in Shadwell district. Wind ripped at the coverings that protected the patients, and the rain slipped in through every crack.

The wind died suddenly, and there fell upon the place an unsettling silence. The doctor and the others who were caring for the suffering looked up from their tasks, sensing something in the air that filled them with dread.

A single shriek of agony ripped through the troubling silence and then was joined by another. Then another, one by one, until it was an unholy chorus. The women who lay upon the cots in that filthy hospice arched their bodies and gripped the rough blankets as their wombs began to tear. The curse that had afflicted them had followed a predictable course, days of discomfort and grief followed by excruciating labor and death while giving birth.

But now all the victims were engulfed. Regardless of how long since they had been infected with this plague, from women who had staggered into the courtyard this very evening to those who had been there for days, each and every one began to scream and thrash, their bloated bellies undulating . . . and from each there burst a stream of grotesque toad-creatures, erupting from the torn bodies to spill onto the floor.

The doctor could not bear the sight. He had seen too much. With a cry that matched their wails of pain, he struck his skull against the wall. Once, twice, a third time. Then, weeping and bleeding, he fell to his knees and vomited in the cold rain as the toad-creatures hopped off into the darkness.

It was only after those hideous things, with their bulbous yellow eyes, had all disappeared that the first of the accursed men, the twisted creatures that had defiled those very women, tore themselves free of their blankets and bindings and leaped from their cots. Their caretakers screamed and attempted to flee, but to no avail. They were caught and gutted with scaly fingers tipped with ragged claws. The accursed men ate their fill of the human flesh, steaming in the cold night air. The creatures were hungry after such a long time spent waiting for the call.

When they had finished, they lingered with the corpses of the women who had died giving birth to their spawn, waiting patiently until a pair of Rakshasa came and led them away to the waiting water of the Thames and the call of their mistress, the Protector of Bharath.

Eighteen

As impressed as William had been with the elegantly appointed interior of the Algernon Club, he had not been prepared for the room Lord Blackheath had called their inner sanctum.

Though all club members had been able to attend the dinner for Sir Darius Strong, along with invited guests, only elite members were ever allowed into the inner sanctum. Haversham imparted to him in a whisper that it was the cause of a great deal of bitterness among the general membership. To those who were never invited into that room—accessible via a long hall that led into an adjacent building— the selection process seemed arbitrary.

Yet it was anything but.

Only true magicians—those with some skill in spellcasting and genuine knowledge of the occult—were invited to the inner sanctum. Most of the well-to-do members of the club were used to wielding the influence that came of age and wealth. But though there was a brotherhood that existed among those who practiced the art of illusion, they had no gift for real spellcraft. Thus, there were doors barred even to them.

The inner sanctum was a huge room whose architecture and decoration were reminiscent of some of the more extraordinary ballrooms William had seen. The floors were marble, but inlaid with tile patterns that suggested a Moorish influence. The ceilings were easily twenty feet high, and all around were wide archways that led into an arcade that circumscribed the chamber. The columns supporting the arches boasted delicately carved woodwork, painted a startling white, as were the walls and the intricate friezes that went around the room above the archways. Oil lamps made of crystal and iron hung down from the ceilings on thick chains.

William was amazed by the place, not merely because of the ostentatious quality of its décor, but because the combination of styles and influences should not have worked at all. An architect by inclination and training, he had a sense for such things, and it surprised him to find the room immensely appealing.

It was shortly after he and Lord Blackheath emerged from the man's study that the party moved into the inner sanctum. The entirety of the situation was surreal. Men who had witnessed his succumbing to the embarrassing effects of the drug behaved as if nothing at all unusual had taken place.

All in all he was pleased. If they were keen to forget his embarrassment, he was all too willing to oblige, particularly now that he knew the reason for it all.

They meant him no harm—that much had become clear. Quite the contrary. In the space of hours he had been transformed from outsider to a true insider. Not merely a member of the club or its elite, but of its ruling council. More than once while he mingled with those influential men, sipping sherry, a smile came unbidden to his lips, while he thought what Tamara might say when she learned that she was about to become the first female member of the Algernon Club.

Her response would be something inappropriate. Of that he was certain.

He was also amazed, standing in that room and discussing politics and public affairs, by the number of members of the Algernon Club who *were* allowed into the sanctum. Granted, they had gathered from across the nation, but his experience with other magicians was limited, and to realize that there were so many . . . it was a bit daunting. Several times he caught gentlemen staring at him with looks that seemed to speak of disdain, and even anger. It unnerved him enough that he wanted to ask Haversham about it, and so he sought the man out.

William located him in a corner of the room, beneath one of those elegant archways. John was deep in conversation with a pair of men, one a seemingly ancient fellow with wispy white hair and a heavy cane, the other a broad-shouldered, ruddy-faced, fiftyish person who looked more like a dockworker or pugilist than a gentleman. Haversham gestured toward William as he spoke, and when he did, William caught his eye.

With a nod and a smile, Haversham said something to the two men, and all three began to work their way across the room. William met them halfway. The older man had skin like parchment and moved with the pain of age, but his eyes were alight with nimble intelligence that made his mind seem like a wild thing trapped in a cage of frailty.

"William, may I introduce you to Sir Horace Walpole and to the guest of honor tonight, Sir Darius Strong. Gentlemen, William Swift, Protector of Albion."

"Ah, yes," William said, turning first to Sir Darius. "I hadn't had the opportunity to make your acquaintance yet, sir. Please accept my best wishes on the occasion. A very happy birthday to you."

Sir Darius inclined his head in the slightest nod. "Thank you, Mr. Swift. It is an excellent birthday gift to learn that we will once again have the Protector as a member of the club."

"*Protectors*, Sir Darius," John Haversham reminded him.

The hulking man arched an eyebrow and lifted one corner of his mouth in the semblance of a smile. "Yes. That ought to be very interesting. Indeed, it will."

His companion, Sir Horace, grunted in outright derision. "*Interesting* is a wickedly sharp blade of a word, sir. It cuts friend and foe alike."

William flinched. "I'm afraid I don't take your meaning, sir."

Sir Horace sniffed. "Ah, but I'm certain you do. Your grandfather did us a grand disservice, splitting the Protectorship this way. Shameful. Though I suppose he performed his duties to Albion ably enough. We may only hope that you and your sibling are half as effective."

"Come now, Horace, don't be so hard on the boy," Sir Darius said jovially.

There was more to the conversation, but William began to drift. Despite his pique at the old man's insult, his attention was drawn elsewhere. Even as Sir Horace had been speaking to him, William had caught sight of someone moving in the shadows of an arch off to his left, back in the arcade that ran along beyond it. The figure was vague and insubstantial, yet still it took him a moment to realize that he was looking at a ghost.

Attempting to be inconspicuous, he took another look. There, little more than an outline, a flitting image in the gloom, framed within an arch, was the ghost of Lord Byron.

The specter of the poet beckoned to him with an upraised finger, then darted from sight into the shadows of the arcade, flowing across the air as though carried by a gust of otherworldly wind.

William frowned. Whatever Byron's purpose for showing himself there, it was obviously urgent.

"Gentlemen," he said, interrupting something Sir Darius had been saying, and not caring a whit. He straightened his jacket, back stiff, allowing his annoyance at Sir Horace's insinuations to show on his face. "If you'll excuse me, I've just seen an old acquaintance to whom I ought to say hello. It was a pleasure meeting you both." He nodded at Haversham. "John."

"Oh, yes, by all means," Sir Darius said.

But Sir Horace only scowled, and John Haversham eyed him curiously. William ignored them both and strode away, going directly to the arch where he had seen Byron. He passed beneath it and into the shadows of the arcade.

There were lights there, but they were dim, pitiful things that cast little illumination. The arcade ran along the entire length of the sanctum's outer wall. There were doors set into that wall at regular intervals, and within were rooms at whose purpose William did not take the time to wonder. He heard footsteps behind him, and the buzz of voices, and turned to see a man approaching as though to engage him in conversation. Beyond that, he saw Haversham talking animatedly with Lord Blackheath.

William ignored them all, turning again to search the shadows.

A spectral hand emerged suddenly through the carved wood of a closed door. Byron's face pushed from the wood, and he looked at William, beckoning once again, then putting a finger to his lips to hush him. Though already the man who was approaching seemed about to speak, William strode quickly through the arcade and opened the door. He stepped through, quickly closing it behind him and turning the lock.

"Well, I say, that was terribly rude," came a man's voice from the other side.

William felt sorry for having closed the door in the man's face like that, but only a very little. He might be a member of the club now, but these men had drugged him, after all. And he had been stung by Sir Horace's snide comments. If they regarded the Protectorship so highly, they were going to have to make him feel a bit more welcome.

The room he had entered was a small, private office with a pair of high windows protected by heavy drapes. It was dark, save for the glimmer of a street lamp through a slit in the curtains. What little light it offered was muted by the drapes, but it saved him from complete darkness.

"Byron?" William whispered.

His pulse raced, and his skin prickled with the feeling that he was an intruder in this room. When the ghost materialized beside him, flickering with an ethereal glow, he started.

"Do not sneak up on me like that!" he rasped.

Normally Byron would have been amused to have upset him, but tonight the poet only executed a half bow in apology. "I'm sorry to disturb you, William, but you're needed."

"What's happened? Is Tamara all right?"

"Quite. At least for the moment. This crisis seems to be building. We've located the Protector of Bharath. He is our ally, not our enemy. But trouble is brewing. Tamara has asked me to fetch you and return to the docks."

William sighed and glanced down at his formal attire. "Wonderful. I don't suppose I have time to change?"

Byron raised an eyebrow. "Shall I meet you outside, then?"

"Yes. I'll be along in a moment, as soon as I can make my apologies."

It was only after he'd left the room and was slipping through the arcade into the brightness of the inner sanctum that he realized the insouciant stable boy wasn't due to return with his carriage for at least another hour. He would need to translocate to the docks, of course, but it wouldn't have been acceptable for him to simply disappear from the midst of the party, and certainly not without bidding his host goodbye.

So he paused just inside the sanctum, glancing about. Several gentlemen stood in a group to his right, one holding a pipe whose smoke swirled and eddied above him. They nodded a greeting toward him, and William returned the gesture.

You're a member now. Grandfather was a member. They're here to help you, he thought.

Yet what did he really know about any of these men? To enter this room they had to have some degree of skill at casting spells, at manipulating the magical energy that existed as an undercurrent to the entire world. But that did not necessarily make them his allies. Even if the Algernon Club itself had been founded with benevolent purpose, might there not be less altruistic men among them? No, William doubted he would be willing to invest unreserved confidence in the Algernon Club without first getting Tamara's opinion of them. Her intuition was generally far better than his own.

Concerned for his sister's welfare, and worried that the action might begin without him, he moved in among the men, some of them jocular enough, but others grim-faced and leaden. The drone of conversation and the clink of glasses filled the room and echoed up to the high ceiling. He pushed through a cloud of cigar smoke and soon found himself within arm's reach of Haversham and Lord Blackheath.

"John," he said.

"William. There you are, good fellow. I was about to set the dogs after you. Where have you . . . I say, is everything quite all right?" Haversham peered at him curiously.

"Not entirely," he admitted, glancing at each of the men in turn. "I'm afraid I have to cut the evening short. I have a pressing engagement elsewhere."

Lord Blackheath's eyes narrowed. "Is there something brewing? We're at your service, you know. Might we send some of our spellcasters along to aid you, in any—"

"No, no, that's quite all right. It's a small thing, really. My sister has asked me to have a look at some documents she's found. Shouldn't be any trouble at all."

Haversham and Blackheath both looked dubious. William had never been a good liar. But he simply did not trust these men yet. He wanted to. It would be comforting to know they had such allies in the war against the darkness. But it would have been foolhardy to throw in with them without due consideration.

"All right," Lord Blackheath said, nodding. "But you know where we are, should there be anything at all we can do to help."

"Of course. And thank you, my lord," William said. Blackheath gave him a firm handshake.

William turned to Haversham. "John, it was an unexpected pleasure."

The man's face seemed to have grown a bit pale as the night wore on, and there were dark circles beneath his eyes. William wondered how little sleep John had been getting of late. When they shook hands, he found Haversham's skin cool, and a bit damp. It was entirely unpleasant.

William turned and made his way back into the main rooms of the Algernon Club, retrieved his coat from the same curmudgeonly servant at the door, and then at last was back out on the street again. He set off at a brisk pace; only when he was out of sight of the club did he step into the dark threshold of another building and call for Byron.

The ghost appeared instantly. "Shall we, then?" the poet inquired.

"Where, precisely?"

Byron propped his hand beneath his chin and described their destination. William had not spent much time around the docks, but that was the advantage of using magic. With that little description, he knew he could trust the translocation spell to get him within yards of the spot.

"The ship is called *Sea Witch*, appropriately enough," the ghost added.

William nodded, glanced around to be certain he was not observed, and raised his hands. "*Under the same sky, under the same moon—*" he began, intoning a spell that had become almost second nature to him by now, something the William of half a year ago would have been hard-pressed to imagine.

His entire body trembled with the magic that came up from within him, enveloping him in a strange glittering sheath of light. That discordant sound that accompanied powerful magic rang in his ears, rattling his teeth as though the noise were in his own head.

A flash of brilliance blinded him for a moment, and he felt the dislocation that always accompanied this spell, a moment in which he seemed to be floating and sensed around him nothing but unending, unyielding darkness. The ether. And out there in the ether, it felt as though he was not alone. In all the times he had translocated, William had never once tried to determine what else might be there with him, for he feared the answer.

It lasted only a moment, and he was glad.

He felt something solid beneath him, and staggered forward a step, shoes scuffing on wood. He blinked to clear his vision and found himself on the deck of a ship, presumably *Sea Witch*. The sway of the deck forced him to take a moment to adjust, but then he glanced around quickly.

There were other ships moored nearby, and he could hear the voices of sailors coming to him through the night. A light fog had begun to swirl up off the Thames, carrying with it a stink that churned his stomach. But there was no one else close around.

"Tamara?" he said, keeping his voice low.

William walked warily across the deck. In the fog he saw several figures lying there, unmoving, at the base of the main mast. When he drew closer, he realized they were Rakshasa, charred to little more than ragged flesh and bone, one of them decapitated. His mind ought to have been eased by this sight, but it only made him more nervous. The corpses did not steam in the chill night air, so they weren't exactly fresh. But there might have been others where these came from, and—

"In the hold, dear boy," came Byron's voice.

The ghost resolved out of the fog as though he were a part of it, spectral mist from river mist. William had grown quite used to the sight of the wandering spirits of the dead, and Byron himself was a jester and bon vivant . . . yet the poet's appearance sent a shudder through him.

There was a sound of footfalls to accompany the creaking of the old ship, and William turned to find Tamara emerging from the hold. A smile of relief washed across her face. In the fog he could not tell for sure, but he thought her clothes were torn. Her hair was a wild, unkempt mess.

"I thought I heard you up here. Come on, then, we've got work to do, and precious little time."

William grinned as he strode over to her, feeling absurdly happy to see her. "Haven't I heard that before? Seems to be a tradition for us."

There was movement behind her in the fog, and William saw a familiar face appear, the old Indian man who had aided them against the Rakshasa in the streets of Shadwell. Nigel was just behind him, the last to climb from the hold of the ship. When William glanced at Byron, he saw that the ghost of Lord Nelson had materialized in the mist, as well.

"Tipu Gupta, I presume?" William said, nodding toward the old man.

"Indeed," Tamara said. But her gaze was intense, leaving no room for niceties. "And he has provided all the missing pieces to this terrible puzzle."

William listened in growing horror, his stomach tightening anxiously as she revealed to him the sinister tale of madness and betrayal that had led to their current circumstances. Their enemy was a young woman no older than Tamara.

"But what is it all for? Creating all these monsters, rallying them to her, she must be building to something. If she truly believes she can destroy the Empire's hold on India, she must plan some hideous act of rebellion and—"

"Oh, she does," Nigel said, his voice dark and velvet like the night. He slipped up to William and Tamara in the fog, but then turned to look at Tipu Gupta.

The old man hung his head in shame. "Yes. My daughter's madness has reached grand proportions. This very night, I believe she will muster her forces and take the final step in her plan. Before midnight, she will assault Buckingham Palace."

William choked on the cold air and his own horror. "She means to kill the queen?"

"Not merely the queen," Tamara replied. "If Mr. Gupta is correct, Priya means to kill everyone at the palace, including the queen, her servants, and her entire family."

"Only together do we have a hope of stopping her," the old man rasped, leaning now on Nigel for support.

William stood straighter. "Right, then. If that's how it is."

The fog thickened and swirled around them, a cloak of stinking gray in the dark of the night. The air was heavy with the weight of the evil they faced, and the grim determination lodged in their hearts.

∼

𝔗AMARA AND HER brother sent the ghosts on ahead to survey the palace, and see if there was any sign that Priya Gupta's scheme was already unfolding. The Swifts could have translocated there as quickly as the ghosts traveled through the ether, but Nigel and Farris were incapable of journeying in that manner, so they retrieved the carriage. And though once it would have been a simple matter for the Protector of Bharath, too much of Tipu Gupta's innate magic had been leached from him.

Tamara was concerned for the old man, and wondered how well he would hold up in the battle to come. Gupta had been pale and unsteady getting into the carriage, so much so that William had had to give him a hand up. When the time came, she doubted they would be able to count on the old man.

Particularly if they had to kill his daughter.

They made their way west toward Buckingham Palace, and she watched him carefully. Though it was quite late, there were still a few people out and about on that cold, foggy night. Couples walked arm in arm, though most were likely illicit pairings. A pair of peelers argued with a well-dressed gentleman in front of the Temple Bar. They all seemed like wraiths in the mist.

As the carriage rattled along cobblestones, they saw fewer and fewer people. Long stretches were so solemn as to be almost funereal.

What had first seemed to be an ordinary mist coming off the river was proving to be far more. London fog was often thick and gray, choking off light and breath with equal devastation. Smoke from a thousand thousand chimneys had lingered all through the early evening in a heavy blanket over London until it was taken by winds that shifted direction from moment to moment, and swirled into a terrible stew with the stench of the marshlands of Kent and Essex and the rancid, strangling odor of human waste that floated off the river.

Tamara felt as if it were the stink of Hell itself. There was a hint of orange to the gray that only added to the effect.

At first the fog had crept along low to the ground, but by the time they reached the palace that had changed. That crawling mist had become heavy clouds that shrouded entire buildings, giving only brief glimpses of the dark, carved faces of the architecture they passed. It wrapped around lampposts as if hungry for the flames within, muffling and dimming the lights.

None of them spoke of the fog, even in jest. Yet Tamara was sure their thoughts must echo hers: this was no ordinary fog. In the silence of their journey, she contemplated asking William about his evening at the Algernon Club, but such questions seemed trivial at the moment, and Tamara felt that would be worse than no talk at all.

Almost on the heels of this thought, her brother spoke up, just loud enough to be heard over the rattle of the carriage.

"Do you think that in splitting the Protectorship between us, Ludlow did us a disservice?"

Tamara frowned, shifting uncomfortably on the seat of the carriage.

"What do you mean?"

William reached up and removed his tie, opening the collar of his shirt. One of the wheels hit a hole, and the carriage jounced. A moment went by before he continued.

"All due respect to Mr. Gupta, but his daughter's got most of the power of the Protector of Bharath now. Does that make her more powerful than you or me individually? Are we halves of a whole, or each whole unto ourselves?"

The questions troubled her, and she reached for her brother's hand, squeezing tightly.

"Don't turn to me on this. I've no idea. If there's some rule book concerning Protectors and their powers, I've never seen it, and I don't think Ludlow ever did, either."

The carriage seat creaked as Tipu Gupta leaned forward, his gaze taking in the both of them. "You protect the soul of Albion, my friends. I was charged with the protection of the soul of Bharath, and failed. There are Protectors in every region of the world. Though they may be part of a whole, part of an effort by the spirit and nature of this entire world to protect itself from evil, the attentions of the Protectors are nearly always turned inward. Where there is collected lore, I have found it is almost always about the legacy of the Protectorship of the region, not of the world."

It took Tamara a moment to digest what he had said. Then she frowned. "All of which is to say, you don't have an answer for me, either."

The old man smiled softly, copper skin crinkling around his eyes. "I do not. But I feel certain your grandfather would not have chosen both of you if he thought doing so might place you in danger."

"Well, that's a comfort," Nigel scoffed, trying to peer out the window into the fog, which had begun to seep into the carriage. "Looks like it's trial by fire once again. You'll have to find out the answers in the midst of battle."

Normally there would have been some muttered protest or attempt at humor from William, then, but the situation seemed to have drained him of any such temptations.

Tamara understood. The Crown was at stake. Blood would flow this night, and their only hope was to determine *whose* blood. She felt pity for those who had been victimized by the imperial aspirations of Britain, those who felt that they had been trammeled upon by the march of colonialism.

Yet no matter what offenses her own nation had committed, she could not stand by and allow the sort of retribution that Priya Gupta planned. The girl dreamed of slaughter and conquest, and whatever goddess she prayed to, whatever dark thing influenced her, Tamara felt certain it was no longer merely about vengeance. Inevitably, bloodlust became its own reason and reward.

"Here we are," Nigel rasped in that throaty growl that always filled his voice when there was blood to be shed.

They rattled to a stop. The fog muffled Farris's call to the horses, then the carriage tilted to one side as he climbed down from his seat. A moment later, the door opened and he stood aside to let them exit. Nigel did not bother to wait, but popped open the opposite door and leaped to the ground with a clack of leather soles on stone, landing like a cat. There was a spring in his step that made Tamara tremble, though whether from dread or anticipation she was unsure.

The city was like a dream now. A terrible dream. The orange-gray fog enshrouded everything, crawling along the street like the current of a lazy river, while an upper layer seemed not to move at all. Even when the wind picked up, the mass only danced and eddied, but did not drift away. To the west Buckingham Palace emerged, a mythical fortress floating in the clouds. That meant St. James's Park was just south, so close they must have been a stone's throw away, but Tamara could make out not a single tree. High windows in the palace gazed down upon them balefully, as though it had been waiting for them.

Foolish girl, Tamara thought, shaking herself. Here she was ascribing sinister intent to the palace itself, as though it had already been lost to the enemy. It may have stood sentinel above them, jutting from the fog, but ominous as it seemed, the palace was the stronghold of their allies, not their enemies.

For now.

"Farris, is there any sign of the creatures?" William asked, rubbing his hands together for warmth as he glanced around, trying to get his bearings. His face was wreathed in fog. "Rakshasa? Those reptile fellows?"

"Children of Kali," Nigel said, his deep voice riding the fog.

Tamara turned toward him, and saw only his eyes gleaming red in the mist. Then he stepped forward and without hesitation she reached for his hand and drew him closer. Watching her every move, Farris, William, and Tipu Gupta moved nearer, as well. It was better that way, she thought. There was no telling what lurked in the fog.

"They are not Kali's children," Gupta said, punctuating the words with a cough. "They bear her curse, but not her blessing."

"Call 'em what you like, sir, I saw neither hide nor hair. Nothing moving in the fog at all, in fact, the last half mile or so. Even with this dreadful soup, that's a surprise. Normally a fog like this'll bring out the thieves and scavengers. But not tonight."

"At least not this close to the palace," William said.

Tamara shivered. Stray locks of her hair had fallen into her face and were stuck there by the moisture from the air. "Horatio. Byron," she whispered into the fog.

William and Gupta looked up expectantly, but Nigel circled them all, prowling the edges of their little gathering, on guard for an attack from the tainted mist.

The ghosts appeared a moment later, shimmering into existence side by side, first Nelson and then Byron.

"Admiral Nelson reporting for duty," the spirit intoned with utmost gravity. "No sign of any disturbance 'round the palace. That's got me a bit worried, though. There's no one at all, you see. Not even guards at the gate."

Tamara gnawed her lower lip. "What do you suppose that means? Are we too late? Are the guards dead, the demons already within the palace walls?"

Nelson shook his head. "I think not. The gates are locked up tight. I spied not a single broken window. The doors beyond the outer walls are all closed, presumably locked as well."

"So where are the guards?" William asked.

"I haven't a clue," Nelson replied.

Byron glanced worriedly back toward the palace. "A mystery for another day, I should think. We've got work to do."

Their spectral forms seemed oddly substantial there in the fog, but it took Tamara a moment to understand why. This particular fog wasn't passing through them, as it should, but around them, as though they were beings of flesh and blood. William was the first to mention it.

"Yes. We had noticed," Byron told him, glancing down at his form. "If only I could muster such substance at other times. In any case, it's mostly illusion. We're no more solid than ever. Except where this fog is concerned."

None of them commented further. The supernatural origin of the fog had gone unremarked earlier because they were all certain of it. This confirmation was interesting, but utterly unsurprising.

"Right, then," Farris said, crossing his arms in defiance of the eerie mist and the air of malevolence that surrounded them. "What's the plan?"

As one, they looked to Tamara. She blinked in surprise as she surveyed their faces.

William.

The ghosts.

Farris.

Nigel.

Even the rightful Protector of Bharath. They all waited for her to determine their course of action.

She nodded solemnly, thinking a moment, and then pointed toward the palace. "Priya's behavior thus far has been full of arrogance. It would not astonish me at all if she strode right up to the gates. But we must try to cover as many approaches as possible. I shall take Nigel and Byron with me and go up Constitution Hill, moving around to the corner, in view of the gardens. William, keep Farris and Mr. Gupta with you. I suggest the southeast corner, just there, where you can keep a view of the gates, as well as the buildings to the south."

All their eyes were upon her, and she sensed their uncertainty. Tipu Gupta was still burdened by the weight of his guilt and shame.

"Do not hestitate," Tamara said. "The Rakshasa are nothing more than vermin. Wipe them out. As for the Children of Kali . . . they were men once, but no more. They have been altered irrevocably, and there is nothing human remaining. Slay them all, and send your prayers to Heaven for their families if you wish. But give no quarter."

"Well said," Nelson declared, drifting nearer to her. His good eye was narrowed with determination, the false one gleaming wetly in the mist. "But what of me, Tamara? Your battle plan has no role in it for me?"

"Indeed it does," she replied. "William was correct. We need reinforcements, but only those we know we can trust. My brother and I have only begun to access the community of ghosts who linger with this land, but Dunstan has made it obvious that not all of them are our allies. If we use the ability of the Protector to speak into the ethereal realm and summon them all, we may call up enemies as well as friends. I leave it to you, then, Horatio. Go into the shadows where only ghosts may walk, and sound the call. Send word along from spirit to spirit. The Protectors of Albion require the aid of any who are willing to fight for the soul of this land."

Horatio bowed. "Just so. What of Bodicea? Shall I fetch her as well?"

Tamara frowned. "Only as a last resort. It would mean leaving Sophia and the servants at Ludlow House with Oblis. The thought troubles me."

"All right," Horatio agreed. "I'm off and shall return with all due speed."

And he vanished.

The company remained together several moments longer, until William stepped nearer his sister and kissed her softly on the cheek. She saw something in his eyes, and thought he would speak, but instead he only gave her a reassuring smile and then turned to the others.

"Come, Farris, Mr. Gupta. While Nelson is marshaling our forces, we must see to it that Priya's monsters do not breach the palace walls."

"Pardon me a moment, sir," Farris replied. He went quickly to the carriage and reached under the seat, drawing out a large leather pouch. He lifted the flap on the pouch and withdrew, one after the other, a pair of guns that Tamara had never seen before. There were no flintlocks at all, and the barrels seemed immense.

"What on Earth have you got there?" she asked.

Farris smiled grimly. "A gift from my brother. They're revolvers, six shots each. Allen's pepperbox, they're called. Beauties, aren't they?"

Tamara only nodded as she watched Farris check both guns and slip them into the large pockets of his coat, then reach back under the seat. He withdrew a belt and scabbard, which he tied around his waist. The barrel-chested man did not draw the blade, only patted it where it hung at his hip.

"This, though, this was a gift from me dad. His own Pattern saber from his cavalry days."

"Excellent, Farris. Glad to have you at my back," William told him.

Then they moved off toward the palace, disappearing in the fog. Though Tipu Gupta still had his walking stick, Tamara thought the man leaned on it less than he had earlier. She imagined he was muster-

ing the reserves of his strength—physical, magical, and emotional—
for the confrontation with his daughter.

"All right, then," she said, turning to Nigel and Byron. "It's us. Stay
close."

As she darted into the fog, keeping an eye on the palace, Tamara
felt vulnerable. She envied the weight of the weapons that Farris had
brought, and wished for even a walking stick as solid as the one Gupta
carried to hold in her hands. But she knew that she was her own
weapon; she was connected to the very soul of Albion, and its magic
burned in her veins.

The knowledge propelled her faster. Byron kept pace, the fog caressing him as though it were urging him on, maintaining the illusion
of solidity though he rushed over the ground without once setting
foot upon it.

Nigel ran in a kind of crouch, almost loping, and when he glanced
at her she saw that his eyes were even more scarlet, and his teeth had
elongated to jagged fangs. Her heart staggered at the sight. He was a
frightening creature, no matter that he was her friend.

Tamara could barely see the palace gates as they moved in haste
toward Constitution Hill. They turned and kept pace along the northern wall, not slowing until they had reached the rear corner. The fog
churned around them, and she could feel it flowing by her ankles.

"Hold here," she said, catching her breath and peering into the
night, into the fog.

Nigel backtracked their steps half a dozen feet to see if they had
been followed, then rejoined them. His eyes were like embers in the
dark. Then he started toward the gardens to the west of their position.

"What are you doing?" Byron inquired, almost casually. "Get back
here."

The vampire turned and glared at him. "I can smell them. The
Rakshasa. I'd like to see if I can get a sense of how many there are out
there."

Tamara considered for a moment, glancing around again. There
seemed no trouble at the rear of the palace as best she could tell. And
she saw no one in the fog to the north, up Constitution Hill.

"All right," she said. "But go quickly, and do not attack. To the edge
of the gardens and no farther, then return."

Nigel grinned, baring his fangs. "I'm going to drink an entire barrel of whiskey after this." He slipped into the fog, and was gone.

Tamara had thought she would hear him moving out there, but ought to have known better. Vampires were stealthy creatures. She hugged herself, allowing a low hum to rise in her throat and a flicker of golden light to dance across the backs of her hands.

"I don't like this," Byron said, his voice barely a whisper.

The ghost started off the same way Nigel had gone, not bothering to pretend to walk. His dark, curly hair was like a puncture in the fog, his burgundy velvet waistcoat far paler than even his phantom nature would account for.

"Stay with me," Tamara said. "We cannot all separate."

"But—" Byron began.

The night was rent by loud hyena laughter. The voices of Rakshasa. It carried up toward the palace from the gardens, echoing within the fog.

Tamara stiffened, eyes searching the shrouded landscape for Nigel. Something shifted in the fog behind her, then, and she spun, those golden sparks blossoming into balls of lightning that seared the air, dispelling the mist around her.

The girl was beautiful, wrapped in white silk, her hair a cloak of raven black, her skin like smooth caramel. But the look in her eyes and the sneering lift of her upper lip made her ugly.

"For Kali," she said.

The magic that burst from her fingers in long, snaking ribbons was bloodred. They flowed, those crimson ribbons, and they were tipped with dagger points that whipped through the air and darted straight at Tamara.

"*Contego!*" Tamara snapped, and the balls of lightning in her hands exploded, that golden magic leaping upward to form a mystical shield in front of her.

Too late.

Most of those dagger-ribbons were deflected by her shield, evaporating the moment their malevolent power touched the pure light of Albion. But the protection spell took a moment to envelop her, and there wasn't time for it to be completed.

One of those dancing crimson ribbons sliced her left thigh. Another punctured her shoulder. The pain seared her and she cried out, but it was nothing compared with the third, the last of those to strike her before her spell of protection completely shielded her.

It impaled her, plunging through her abdomen, its tip emerging through her lower back.

Tamara's blood spattered Priya Gupta's beautiful white sari and her caramel skin, and the usurper, the madwoman, ran her tongue over her lips to taste it, grinning all the while.

"For Kali."

Nineteen

At the southeastern corner of the palace, William stood utterly still and listened for the sound of any approaching enemy.

The buildings across the street were cloaked in fog that clung to each brick and board and roiled in great clouds along the ground. There were occasional breaks in that filthy gray-orange wave, giving glimpses of a window or door or a stretch of empty street, but they were brief and only served to make the depth of the fog seem more unnerving. So William listened.

There were a great many sounds out in the fog. Though muffled, they told him what he wanted to know. Despite appearances to the contrary, he and his allies were not alone. There were snuffling, animal noises coming from the murk, and once a terrible screeching, like cats fighting . . . but these were not cats.

He heard a woman shout in surprise, then the slamming of a door, followed by a shattering of glass and then a more distant, more muffled shriek that he could have heard only because of the otherwise complete silence.

Poor woman, he thought. As tempting as it was to race off in search of her, he knew it would be utterly futile. She'd seen something she was never meant to see, and paid for it with her life.

"They're coming," he said to his companions.

Tipu Gupta, usurped Protector of Bharath, nodded gravely and pushed himself up on his walking stick. He could not have been considered hale, but there was a strength in his countenance and posture now that had not been there before. William thought he was getting a glimpse of what the man must have been like in his prime.

Though the young man had never quite considered it that way before, his grandfather was a hero to him. And Ludlow Swift had called Tipu Gupta friend and ally. They had stood side by side and fought the darkness, risking their lives and their souls. As William studied the old man, with his deep brown eyes and weathered skin, he realized that he was gazing upon a legend.

Something changed in William, then. He drew a long breath and stood a bit straighter himself. That was the sort of battle this was. There would never be history books written about it, no poems crafted or songs sung. But it would be spoken about in whispers, by ghosts and magicians and demons.

Beside him, Farris drew out both of his revolving pistols and held one in either hand. The gentleman's gentleman gave William a solemn glance, then peered out into the fog, weapons at the ready.

"Let 'em come, I say." Farris aimed his pistols into the gloom. "Let 'em come."

Moments later, as if in answer, the first of the Children of Kali darted out of the darkness. There were several off along the southern wall of the palace, shadows passing through the thick gray cloud so that they vanished and reappeared from moment to moment. The twisted, accursed men ran with a dangerous agility, knifing through the night, but it wasn't those few that concerned William.

Others had appeared almost immediately out of the mist-blanketed St. James's Park, and that band of monsters rushed toward the gates of Buckingham Palace as though the dinner bell had sounded.

And perhaps it had.

William started toward the gates, but Gupta snagged his arm.

"We must not separate," the old man rasped.

"Sorry to disappoint you, but we have little choice. The attack is on two fronts, and must be fought on both."

Farris gestured with a gun. "The vermin at the gates won't be turned away. They're on a mission, they are. But those others, well, might be you could make short work of them, drive them off with a nasty spell or two and then join us at the gates. After all, those 'round the side aren't going to be getting in from that direction. Unless they plan on climbin' the walls."

Gupta was correct. It would not do to separate. But Farris had a point. It might take him only a few moments to deal with the attackers heading for the southern wall.

"Go guard the gates!" William snapped. "I'll be right along."

With only a moment's hesitation, they did as he instructed. The old man used his stick to walk, but moved with surprising speed. Silver light swirled in circles around his legs, dispelling the fog there, and it became clear that he was propelling himself with magic. William had to wonder how much of his sudden vitality was magical . . . and how long it would last.

Then he turned west and started along the southern wall. More of those reptilian men, some dressed in the rags of the East End slums and others in the fine clothing bespeaking wealth, emerged from the alleys and side streets to his left, but he ignored them. Up ahead, those that had first shown themselves reached the wall. One did not bother to slow, leaping at the obstruction, scaly, webbed hands sticking to the stone, talons digging in. It began to climb.

Damn you, Farris, for being right, he thought.

There were too many of them for him to destroy quickly. He had to think of another way to keep them off the wall, to get them to focus their attack on the front, so that he and his allies could work together.

The Children of Kali began to hiss, some of them even to wail a kind of high, keening cry that made his stomach turn. Never had William been so aware of being on his own. He wished he and Tamara had not needed to split up. She was so much more clever when it came to magic, and so much more difficult to rattle.

William thought of Sophia, and images swept across his mind of the wedding they would have one day. He thought of the elegant interior of Swift's of London, and of the people who worked for him there, of the utter, wonderful ordinariness of it all. And a liquid fear raced through his veins. Not only fear of his own death, but fear, too, that no matter how much he struggled and fought to return his life to normal, every time one of these supernatural crises occurred, he would never really be able to do so. Never be able to rest.

"I hate you," he said in the dark, in the fog, and wasn't at all certain to whom he spoke.

Then a smile touched his lips. He had an idea.

Tamara would have come up with a way to stop them. But in that moment he had asked himself what Tamara would do, and suddenly he knew.

Something hissed in the murk over his left shoulder, but he ignored it, hoping he had the few seconds he needed. His eyelids fluttered, and the ice in his gut melted as he raised his hands. He felt the power of Albion deep inside him, thrumming in his bones, and he racked his brain for the words that would give his incantation form. The magic of the Protector of Albion was immense, part of his flesh. Part of his soul. But the skill to wield it, that had to be learned.

William had never had much luck with more complicated magic. Now he would see if that had changed.

His whole body ached as he summoned the energy, imagining the spell. He curled his fingers into claws, and slashed at the air in front of him, drawing symbols he did not even realize he recalled from his studies. The surge of power was like hammers pounding his arms and chest.

"*Mutatio cito lancea,*" he whispered.

Half a dozen of the reptile creatures had leaped up onto the wall by then, slithering upward, their scaly, mottled flesh gleaming wet from the moist air. At the last syllable of his spell, the wall wavered for a moment as though made of liquid instead of stone, and then in an eyeblink thousands of spikes *grew* from the wall, stone lances that thrust out and impaled the Children of Kali that were there, and several that stood close by at the bottom, preparing to climb.

They didn't even have time to scream.

He could practically feel the one that was rushing up behind him.

William spun and summoned a spell as he did so, and the monster was buffeted by magical fire that consumed it, leaving a tower of ash in the shape of a hideous man. With the next gust of wind it collapsed and eddied away into the fog.

"*Accendo!*" he cried, turning to the others.

A brilliant flash of light burst from his hands like a flare, reflecting off the fog so that it seemed a solid blanket of gray filth. But where there were breaks in the fog, he saw them. And they him. The Children of Kali hissed with hatred and hunger, and when William turned to race back around the front of the palace, they followed.

The fog grasped at him as he sprinted toward the gates, eyes narrowed in search of Gupta and Farris. There were figures in the mist, dark things outlined against the cloyingly moist gray fabric of the air. Some of them crept, but others barreled forward without hesitation or stealth. One of them was huge and crouched low, uttering a roar that came out like a laugh.

Rakshasa.

So there were demons among the accursed now.

He pushed past curtains of fog and came in sight of the palace gates. Tipu Gupta stood in front of them with his staff raised, guarding the royal palace, guarding the queen of England, not out of duty but of righteousness. Whatever spite he may have held in his heart for the way his people were ruled by the British Empire, this night the fight was not between nations, but between light and darkness. And Gupta had chosen his side ages past.

Silver light danced around his entire body, arcs of lightning that encircled him. Much of his power as Protector might have been drained away by his daughter, but he was still connected to the soul of Bharath, and had far more skill and experience in wielding that power than William could imagine.

Two Children of Kali rushed the gates, where Gupta held the staff in both hands and pointed its tip at them. Silver-blue energy flowed serpentlike from the simple walking stick and the twisted, damned men screamed as their hellish flesh melted from their bones. They collapsed together in a single wet heap.

A crack echoed across the sky, the sound ricocheting around in the fog. William flinched and tried to locate its source, and then he saw Farris, perhaps twenty feet beyond the old man, wielding those pepperbox revolvers. Another crack slapped the air, a gunshot, and this time William saw its effects. One of the Children of Kali, rushing toward the butler, wasn't merely halted, but staggered back as a bullet punched through its chest. It toppled to the ground, attempted to crawl toward him, then shuddered and died.

Farris started back toward Gupta, both guns raised, watching the fog for monsters. William ran up to the gates, falling in beside the old man even as Farris joined them from the north. The three formed a line of defense against the evil things that assaulted the palace. Farris fired again, this time taking a Rakshasa in the eye. The back of its skull exploded outward in a shower of gray matter and bone shards. The rightful Protector of Bharath let loose another searing arc of silver lightning that evaporated the fog it touched, and turned two of the Children of Kali to ash. By its clothes, William thought that one of them might have been his old friend Frederick Martin, and he felt the burden of that death upon his heart.

Yet it did not slow him. With a flick of his wrist and a bellowed incantation he froze one of the accursed reptilian creatures that had pursued him from the south. Another collided with it from behind, shattering it, and William cast a spell that immolated the newcomer and two others.

Still they came.

"You will fall" came a dark, insinuating voice that emanated from the swirling fog behind him.

He spun and found himself face-to-face with the ghost of Colonel Dunstan. The traitorous specter wore a hideous smile. William raised his hands, spheres of magic crackling around them, prepared to defend himself if Dunstan dared attack him.

"Come to watch the proceedings, betrayer?" he snapped.

"Too right," the phantom soldier replied. "Wouldn't miss it. I was loyal to the Crown, Mr. Swift. While I lived. In death, I saw the error of my life. And when the horror began in the East End, you proved me right. The British aristocracy looks upon my people as animals, house pets at best.

"So much for so-called nobility. Now you'll—"

"Please do shut up!" William said.

Before the ghost could react, he threw his arms wide and shouted a brief binding spell. Ethereal chains appeared in the air, wrapping quickly around Dunstan. If the ghost had been quicker, he could easily have vanished, slipping away into the ether. Perhaps Dunstan had assumed William not up to the task of capturing him. He was not the first to underestimate the grandson of Ludlow Swift. But William was becoming used to shattering such low expectations, and he liked the feeling.

The chains were as insubstantial as the ghost himself, but as they tightened the ghost was bound as though he were made of flesh and blood. Those spectral bonds shimmered with a pale blue light that spread over Dunstan's ectoplasmic substance, tainting him the same hue.

The sound of Farris's guns boomed once, twice, a third time. William heard the crackle of Gupta's magic. For the moment, though, he left the battle to them.

"What . . . what have you done? You cannot touch me!" the traitor cried.

"I haven't touched you, fool. But what kind of idiot must you be to think you could taunt me without fear of retribution? I am one of the bloody Protectors of Albion, Colonel. Capturing an errant ghost is one of the very first things I was taught when I inherited this power. Now, you wanted to watch; that's all right with me.

"Watch, and witness Albion's triumph!"

Suffused with magic and fury, he turned to rejoin the fray.

Only to find Sophia Winchell standing before him, gazing up at him in fear and need.

"So-Sophia?" he stammered.

She smiled. Her flesh seemed to *ripple*. Then it wasn't Sophia standing before him, but a beautiful Indian girl with hatred in her eyes. A glamour. He'd fallen for a simple glamour.

Priya Gupta struck him, clawing his face, and as William staggered back her fingers seemed to erupt with darting, jagged serpents of bloodred magic.

"Perhaps not," she purred.

～

IN THE GUEST bedroom where she had so recently lived out a delicious dream she had nurtured since her youth, Sophia Winchell slept fitfully. There was a chill in the night air, damp and cool as it slipped through the narrowly open windows. She shuddered beneath the heavy covers and burrowed deeper, but it wasn't truly the cold that disturbed her sleep.

Nor was it the barely audible screaming that came down from the topmost floor. What wrinkled her brow and drew her again and again almost to wakefulness was the vast emptiness of the house around her, the frightening loneliness that gripped her, even while unconscious.

She dreamed, there in that comfortable bed, of being alone.

And woke to the sound of her name being spoken with all the insistence of a rap on the door.

"*Sophia! Wake now, girl!*"

Flinching from the unpleasantness of her dreams and the hardness of that voice, she drew a long, abrupt breath as though her lungs had been stilled for a moment, then opened her eyes.

Above her there towered a naked woman whose face was painted for war, whose eyes were alight with a strange blue-white flame, and whose flesh was utterly translucent, shot through with shadows and the flickering light of the candles she had been too frightened to blow out before going to sleep.

"Good Lord," Sophia whispered, recoiling, drawing herself up toward the head of the bed, her legs pulled under her.

Sleep often erased memory and identity, and so it took her several seconds to realize that this was not some nocturnal shade there to haunt her. Ghosts terrified her, made her feel as though she might crawl out of her own skin, but they were not unknown to her.

Nor was this ghost, specifically, unfamiliar.

"Queen Bodicea," Sophia breathed, drawing the covers up to her throat in awkward counterpoint to the specter's brazen nudity. She could not help letting her eyes survey the warrior woman's transparent body just once, amazed at the firmness of her thighs and arms and the fullness of her breasts. The phantom's body was streaked with the same war paint as her face, though the colors were dull and the paint no less an apparition than the queen herself.

"Rise, girl," the ghost commanded, her form wavering slightly, floating there beside the bed. "Hurry. The Swifts have need of me, and I cannot leave you here."

Sophia threw back the covers and climbed out of bed, hugging herself against the chill in the room. She threw on her robe, but it was too thin to combat the cold.

"Where are we going?" she asked. "I must dress. I shall move as quickly as—"

"There isn't time. And you cannot leave the house. You are safe within these walls, from the crisis facing London this night. There are wards and defenses—"

"They've been breached before," Sophia countered.

"Only when someone was fool enough to leave the door open, or invite the enemy in. Heed my instructions and you shall be safe," the ghost declared.

As imperious as Bodicea's tone was, Sophia sensed a hesitation in her. Still, she did not argue further. If William was in danger, and Bodicea had been summoned, she would not hold the ghost back from going to aid him. She took a night coat that William had loaned her from Tamara's armoire, slipping it on even as the ghostly queen went to the door.

The air shimmered in front of Bodicea and suddenly she was holding the long war spear she often carried.

"Open it," said the specter.

Sophia tensed and drew open the door. Bodicea could have gone ahead of her but obviously did not want to leave her alone. The ghost flitted out into the corridor, and Sophia followed.

To her surprise, they were not alone. Martha, the maid who practically ran the Swift household, was there along with Sophia's own lady's maid, Elvira.

"See here," Elvira said, instinctively keeping her voice low. "What is this about?"

Bodicea shot her a dark look. "Follow me."

Her tone made it clear she would brook no argument, so when she floated toward the stairs, the women fell in behind her. Martha seemed grimly serious yet calm enough. Elvira, on the other hand . . . she had seen things she could not explain, but Sophia believed that this was the first time she had been so blatantly presented with the existence of ghosts as an inescapable truth. She had no idea what had been said to her maid before Bodicea had woken her, but Elvira's eyes were wide with shock, and she was entirely docile, a word that had likely never before been attached to the woman.

As they started down the stairs, following the specter, the silence of the house was broken by the howling of a madman. The screams of Henry Swift floated down to them. Beside Sophia, Elvira whimpered and grabbed hold of her employer's arm. Despite her own fear, Sophia found herself patting the woman's hands to soothe her, and escorting her as though Elvira were the mistress and she the maid.

Sophia had seen the cruel, slavering, vicious thing Henry Swift had become, had heard him speak with the voice of the demon, the glint of evil in his eyes. But she had never heard him shriek like this, as though he fully intended to scream until Henry's heart burst, or his throat became too raw to utter a sound.

"What is it, Bodicea? Please, tell me what's happening!"

The specter continued to descend the stairs. It was Martha who turned to Sophia after a moment's hesitation.

"We should be perfectly safe, miss. Nothing can come in after us, and . . . Oblis . . . himself making all that racket in the nursery . . . he's trapped there, just as if he were behind bars."

"Then . . . ," Sophia began, frowning as they reached the bottom of the steps. She looked after Bodicea, who paused at last, then at the two older servant women. "Why are we going wherever it is we are going?"

Bodicea floated back to her. The queen had been so tall in life that she had to gaze downward to look into Sophia's eyes. Her aspect was ominous.

"We have the utmost confidence in the spells that are binding the demon now. The Protectors have learned from their own past errors. But Oblis has not been without a guardian since his captivity began, and if I am to leave you here in the house with him, we must take precautions."

Sophia regarded her evenly, mustering courage she did not feel. "Precautions," she repeated.

"This way," Bodicea commanded.

She led them from the foyer deep into the back of the house, past parlor and drawing room, dining room and kitchen, and a small study that seemed to have been unused for some time. Sophia thought they passed the hall to the atrium, but was not sure. The house always seemed larger to her than she remembered.

There was a tall, imposingly thick ironwood door at the rear of the house that did not seem to match any of the other décor. Bodicea did not hesitate a moment, drifting through it.

Sophia hugged herself. The lunatic screams of the demon should have been inaudible all the way down here, but somehow she could still hear him, and her skin prickled with revulsion and dread.

She opened the door.

The spectral queen awaited within. The room was an arsenal, filled with swords and daggers, double-bladed battle-axes, longbows, and quivers full of arrows, crossbows, and armored gauntlets.

"Farris and William completed this sanctuary only recently. The door and walls are reinforced with iron. There are dried provisions on that shelf in the corner. If the demon were to get free, you would still be safe here. Oblis is a Vapor; he has no substance save the body he inhabits. Yes, he is remarkably strong, and indeed he may levitate. But he cannot translocate, and this room is built well enough that he will not be able to enter, as long as you do not open the door.

"So you will stay here, until the Swifts return. I do not abandon my post lightly. Lord Nelson came specifically to call me to my duty, and I will not ignore the call. But you will be safe, as long as you remain here."

Sophia stared at her. None of this felt right to her. How confident could William be of the spells binding Oblis into the nursery if he and Farris bothered to build this room? Certainly it would be helpful in other circumstances, as well, but they had to have had Oblis in mind while doing the work. Which meant they had allowed for the possibility of his escape.

And now she was going to be left here, locked in with two middle-aged women whose combat experience likely consisted of killing the odd rat or two in the kitchen.

The things she had said to William earlier came back to haunt her now. She had assured him that she wanted this life, that she would rather live with these dangers than without him.

It pleased her to discover that she had meant every word.

But that did not assuage her terror.

"Bodicea, I don't think that—"

"Lock the door," the ghost replied, and with those words her insubstantial image fluttered as though on a breeze, and she was gone.

Elvira stared at the place where she had been, mouth agape, and then took several steps toward the back of the room, shaking her head. Martha met Sophia's gaze with a firm nod. Sophia returned it, and strode quickly to the heavy door. With her hand on the bolt, she swung it shut.

Just before it bumped heavily into place, the sound of the shrieking came again, muffled but inescapable. It sounded joyful to her, as though Oblis knew they were alone down here, hiding from him behind locked doors, armed with medieval weapons. In fear of him, despite his bonds.

It sounded like a madman's glee.

Sophia drew a shuddering breath, bit her lower lip, and threw her weight against the door, sliding the bolt home.

And she could still hear him.

∽

CROUCHED IN THE lee of a thick stand of shrubbery, Nigel Townsend uttered a throaty laugh. It came up from deep within him, unbidden, and he bared his fangs.

The Rakshasa had been moving through the palace gardens, and he had intercepted their attack. There were more of them, out in the fog, or perhaps the other figures he had seen were the Children of Kali. But he was not concerned with the others, for the moment. Only these.

The filthy animals that had set after him in the garden, like wolves on the veldt.

What they did not understand was that he was a vampire, and vampires were not prey. Never prey. Even cornered, as he was, by three slavering demons with piss-yellow eyes and rows of ivory needles for teeth, he was the predator. There had been four of them, after all, but the corpse of the fourth lay a dozen yards away, its chest shattered and its heart torn out. Its blood stained Nigel's hands and clothes. The scent of it was maddening, and drew the laughter from him, brought his own monstrousness to the fore.

The vampire was risen.

The Rakshasa stood to their greatest height as if unfolding from the crouch they usually moved in. That was their stalking pose, Nigel thought, but this . . . this was the way they showed their animalistic dominance, before they attacked. The fog drifted languidly past them, moist air clinging to their patches of leathery skin and the filthy, matted hair that covered most of their bodies. Their long talons were like knives, and the three of them began to close in on him, raising their claws as if to promise evisceration.

Nigel brought his own hands up. The nails had elongated into claws of his own. "You're not the only ones with pretty blades, lads. Not at all."

They paused and threw back their heads, as if having taken offense. The howls that came out of their stinking maws began almost like those of ordinary animals, but then broke into a series of those unnerving, barking laughs. One by one the three demons lowered themselves again into their stalking pose and continued to move in slowly, pacing from side to side, keeping his back up against the shrubs that scratched against him.

Nigel only sneered.

"Fools. Have you never seen one of my kind before? You lot are demons. Evil, that's true. But you haven't the first clue about real cruelty. Only humans understand that. If you'd caught me with the others, with the Swifts or their phantom comrades at my side, you might've had a chance at me. I would've been fighting the monster in myself as much as I'd have been fighting you.

"But you caught me alone, with no one to see my true nature. That was your mistake."

Then the red hunger of the beast raged up inside him and his grin became a different sort of howl. A battle cry. He gnashed his jaws and darted toward the Rakshasa to his right. It flinched backward, attempting to dodge, but it had not been Nigel's target. As he lunged, one of the others reached for him, claws slashing down.

It was what he had expected. With the one on his right off balance, he sidestepped the other's attack, grabbed hold of its arm, and wrapped the arm around himself almost as though they were dancing. Spinning, he slammed himself against the demon, crashing into that filthy fur . . . too close to it for the other two to attack.

If the demon had had a moment to act, it might have crushed him to death then, shattering his chest and his cold, black heart. But its jaundiced eyes went wide with surprise, and Nigel reached up with one powerful hand and forced its head down toward him as though to kiss.

Ravenous with bloodlust and fury he opened his jaws impossibly wide, each of his teeth now extending to a sliver point. Then he tore out the Rakshasa's throat with a moist, ripping noise and the tug of muscle and tendon. Its black blood sprayed his face even as he shoved it away, turning to drop back into a crouch, facing the other two. He spat leathery flesh and sinew onto the ground.

Warriors—human or supernatural—would have been given pause. But the Rakshasa were not warriors at all. Just demons. Filthy vermin from some dark netherworld, doing the bidding of their mistress. Even so, they hesitated. Their chests rose and fell with fetid exhalations and then they began to move from side to side again, searching for an opening, for the perfect moment to attack.

Nigel did not intend to give them a chance.

The creature to his left looked younger and stronger, so he leaped at that one. It was quick, and it snatched him out of the air, claws gripping his throat, trying to choke him even as it brought its other arm around to plunge its long talons like knives into his chest. Pain seared him like fire blazing across his flesh and in the bones and organs of his upper torso. The demon was satisfied with its work and it let out another of those hyena laughs.

The vampire reached up then and grabbed its lower jaw, slicing off the tip of his left ring finger on its teeth as he tore that mandible from its roots with a pop of bone. The thing's screeching was pitiful as he ripped the remnants of skin that still connected it, and then the jawbone was in his hands.

The Rakshasa let him go, reeling away from him and staggering, dropping to its knees as black blood flowed over its chest.

"If you want to kill something like me, you'll have to do better than that," Nigel growled.

Something shimmered unearthly blue in the fog behind the screaming, suffering Rakshasa, and Nigel frowned when he saw that it was Byron. The specter rushed through the fog toward him with no trace of the pretty, clever words or fanciful pretense that were his hallmarks. Nigel knew instantly that something had gone horribly wrong. Yet even as Byron whipped toward him through the fog, he heard the shifting, leathery noise of the Rakshasa behind him making one final assault.

He spun and brought the stolen jawbone around in an arc, using it as a weapon. The rows of jagged fangs glistened in the damp air and he felt as though he were in a dream as he twisted through that gray-orange cloud of mist . . . and then he slashed the surviving Rakshasa across the face with its brother's own fangs, carving flesh and puncturing those eyes, which spurted yellow pus that sizzled on his skin like acid.

It shrieked, blinded, and he slipped around behind it and quickly snapped its neck, dropping the demon to the ground. The one with no lower jaw was still bleeding, still wailing, and it began to twitch. It would die soon, but Nigel would let it suffer.

There were other things afoot.

He ran through the fog to meet Byron, the ghost nearly passing through him in the thickness of that cloud.

"What is it?" Nigel demanded, all manner of terrible imaginings in his mind. "What's happened?"

The very fabric of the ghost, his spectral essence, seemed to roil with emotion. He brought his hands to his face, fingers bent as though he meant to tear at himself in grief. There was such horror in his eyes that the red beast living in Nigel's heart, that berserker soul in him, withdrew, and the part of him that was still human faltered. He had no need to breathe, yet still he held his breath.

"Tamara," Byron said, frantic. "The girl was there, Priya, and Tamara's been injured. Badly. You must come quickly." And then, the worst of it, the words that tumbled out of Byron with more anguish than Nigel had ever heard in a voice. "And I cannot help, cannot touch her, not even just to lend her comfort."

The ache that leaped into Nigel's heart astonished him. He was not in love with the girl, not that. But he loved her just the same. It felt, in that moment, almost as though he were alive again . . . alive enough to feel the acute emotion that made humanity an utter joy and total anguish.

"Come," he said simply, and then he raced through the fog. He could hear other things moving about the gardens, crashing through greenery and snapping tree branches as they moved toward the palace, but he no longer cared about the queen or about Albion. Not in that moment. The queen could bugger off.

Byron sailed through the air beside him, utterly transparent despite the bright shade of his velvet coat. How often had Nigel thought him a fool? And yet in their shared fear for Tamara, they were joined in a manner neither was accustomed to.

They left the gardens behind and raced for the corner of the palace in sight of Constitution Hill, the place where Nigel had left her—*and damn you for doing it, you fool*, he thought. For just a moment the fog cleared, and he saw her on the ground up ahead, slumped on her side with a pair of Kali's Children looming above her unmoving form. He thought he could hear their hiss, but it might merely have been the wind and the dark magic of that damnable fog.

Then the mist shrouded the palace again, and it was several long seconds during which he was sure they must be eviscerating her before he and Byron emerged again, a dozen feet from where Tamara lay.

The accursed monstrosities that stood above her were dead, turned to volcanic glass by sorcerous flames. Tamara's right hand was outstretched toward them, frozen in the act of casting that spell. It had been too much for her, though, and she had fallen unconscious from the effort.

Nigel rushed to her. Unthinkingly he lashed out, shattering the glass creatures in his frustration and fear. A shard of glass carved a gash in his arm, but he barely flinched at the pain as he dropped to his knees beside her, scooping her up.

Her blood soaked through his trousers, warm and sticky. The wound in her shoulder was small and could be easily patched, but the puncture in her abdomen was not so simple. The blood bubbled from it, drenching her dress and her jacket.

He was a vampire, cursed with the taint of Hell, of a horror to which God turned a blind eye. All of the gods, in fact. Nigel Townsend had not uttered a prayer to any deity in many years.

Tonight, he whispered a prayer to the heavens.

"Do something!" Byron cried. "You must! Look at the wound! She's going to die unless you can heal her."

"I . . . I've never studied healing magic. I can't—"

The poet could be shrill at times. Not now. He slid his fingers into Nigel's hair and yanked back his head. "You worthless bastard, with all that you owe these children and their grandfather's memory . . . you *do* something!"

The specter's touch was only a reminder that Nigel himself was not human. He glared at Byron until the ghost faltered and released him, glancing away shamefacedly.

"It's . . . Nigel, I'm sorry, but it's Tamara."

"Don't you think I know that? I can see her, Byron. I smell her blood! I . . ."

And an idea came to him. A very dark idea. The red beast inside him trembled with anticipation at the thought. Nigel narrowed his gaze and a low rumble came up from his throat as he stared at Tamara. There was a way to save her.

A way . . .

His nostrils flared with the scent of her, and he squeezed his eyes closed and twisted his head away, fresh sorrow and torment drowning him as he recalled the last time he had been faced with such a choice. Her name had been Louise, a young girl who worked onstage as part of Ludlow's magic act. She had discovered Nigel's true nature and fallen in love with him, and he with her. Yet the lure of what he was had tempted her. She saw romance and real magic in him, when he knew that it was only monstrousness and death. She had pleaded with him to make her like him and then, when he refused, she had slit her wrists. Louise had wanted to love him forever, but Nigel would not damn her to an eternity of bloodlust and darkness.

He had let her die.

There was no way he could allow the same thing to happen to Tamara, and yet once again he would not give in to the temptation to create another like him, to give her damnation instead of death.

"No," he said grimly.

There came more hissing from the fog, and the laughter of at least one more Rakshasa. The vampire turned and glared at Byron.

"Hold them off. Whatever it costs you, hold them off."

Black tree branches could be seen thrusting like skeletal fingers clawing from the fog, right through Byron's body. He was silhouetted in that fog. Insubstantial and yet with more presence than Nigel had ever given him credit for.

"They won't touch her," the poet vowed.

Then he was off, flitting through the fog.

Nigel turned to Tamara, her blood still soaking through the knees of his trousers, and he slapped her.

Unconscious, she flinched.

"Tamara! Wake up, damn your eyes!"

He slapped her a second time, then a third.

Her eyelids fluttered open, brows knitting in pain. "Nigel?"

"Wake up!" he snapped again. "Listen to me, girl. You will not surrender to this, do you understand me? You are the Protector of Albion and the granddaughter of Ludlow Swift. Your wounds are not beyond your power to heal. The magic flows through your veins, sweats from your very skin. Remember the way the Rakshasa could sense it before, because it was seeping from you? It's a part of you, girl. Seize it!"

Tamara shook her head, ever so slightly, eyes closing again. "I . . . I cannot, Nigel. I don't feel it now. I feel . . . nothing."

"Then by the gods I shall make you feel something!" he snarled, and he plunged a finger into the wound in her shoulder, twisting it around.

Tamara went rigid, eyes flying open wide, and she let out a scream that echoed through the fog and all the way up Constitution Hill. A stream of filthy invective the likes of which he had never heard from such a proper girl spilled from her mouth, and she snarled at him like an animal.

"You son of a whore!" she gasped as she completed her cursing of him.

Nigel smiled. "That's a story for another day, pet. Now you listen to me. You *will* heal your wounds. If not for yourself or for Albion, then for your brother. You are a far greater magician than William can ever hope to be. If Priya has made such short work of you, what will she do to him?"

He saw the fear appear in her eyes, but still there was no fire there. "It is more than the wound. Her magic has poisoned me, somehow. I can feel it burning in me, tainting me."

"Then flush it out!"

Her eyes went wide, but she was staring past him.

The Children of Kali had come. Byron was fighting them to the west, near the garden, but these came south from the hill. Nigel swore and leaped to his feet. He glanced around wildly as more and more of them emerged from the fog, closing in on him and Tamara. He counted no less than a dozen, probably more.

"Tamara," he warned. "I may have to leave you alone again."

But even as he spoke the words the air shimmered all around him, the fog shifting and shuddering as though battered by a hundred errant breezes. A sound like wind chimes filled the night, and then they were there.

The ghosts of Albion.

Like a wave they materialized, one after the other. Some he recognized but most he did not. Soldiers and playwrights, teachers and carpenters, men and women who had nothing in common during their lives, and yet shared one vital trait in death . . . they were all, now, soldiers in the war against the darkness.

"Take them broadside, my friends, and give no quarter!" cried a voice from above, a voice Nigel had never been happier to hear.

He glanced up and saw the fog shifting around the phantom form of Admiral Lord Horatio Nelson. The man could be a fool at times, with his priggishness and arrogance, but in war he commanded nothing less than awe. And he was not alone.

With a battle cry that made even the animal within Nigel cringe, Queen Bodicea appeared from the fog, her spear clutched in one hand and a small ax in the other. As always, her face and nude body were painted for war, and her scream curdled his blood. Nelson was courageous and brilliant, Bodicea cunning and savage, and the ghosts of Albion were their army tonight.

The Children of Kali began to die.

And then the sound of hoofbeats and the clatter of a carriage reached them, and a hansom cab rattled out of the fog. It had left the street and was coming across the grounds outside the palace, rushing at them, right into the midst of the fray. Only one man was inside, and the horses neighed as he reined them to a stop.

He leaped from the cab.

"Tamara!"

Nigel prepared to kill him. "Who the hell are you?"

But then he saw Tamara's face. There was confusion there, but also a tenderness that was surprising.

"John?" she said.

Nigel narrowed his eyes. "John? That Haversham bastard? I've heard about you. What are you doing here?"

"I've heard about you as well, Mr. Townsend. I'm here to help if I can. When William left the Algernon Club, we all suspected there was something amiss, but never imagined . . ."

He settled down beside Tamara in the very spot Nigel had just vacated, and gazed upon her kindly. "They sent me after him, Tamara. But I would've come anyway, if I could."

With the poison magic of Priya Gupta in her system and her wounds still bleeding, she barely had the strength to gaze at him, but she managed. "I . . . I don't understand. The . . . the club?"

"William hasn't told you?"

"Told us what?" Nigel demanded, though he glanced about as he said it, eager to rejoin the battle, listening to the sounds of monsters dying in the fog.

John was examining Tamara's wounds, and now he shot a dark look at Nigel.

"There isn't time." He looked back at Tamara. "What's important is that we know who and what you are. Both of you. And we've been trying to help. The idols that were stolen . . . we were trying to gather them up so no one else would be infected. I was the primary thief."

He bent lower then, holding Tamara's hand tightly, and though he whispered so low that no human ears could have heard him . . . Nigel was not human.

"They assigned me to you, do you understand? To discover the identity of the new Protector. That's why I reacted to your . . . enticement the way that I did. I hated the idea that you and I might have shared such intimacy under false pretenses."

He bent to kiss her forehead, and Tamara reached her hand up to caress his face, ever so weakly.

"It seems you're too late," she said.

"Nonsense," Haversham replied. "I can help you. The meager magic I have at my disposal is a pale shade of yours, but perhaps I can bolster—"

"No."

Nigel flinched. He heard Byron shouting something, but wasn't sure what it was. His attention was split between the war and Tamara's condition.

"I'm sorry, what was that?" the vampire asked, incredulous. "Don't let your pride destroy you, Tamara. Don't be a fool. Not with so much in the balance. If the man can help you—"

"I don't need help," she snarled.

Face etched with pain, she forced herself to her knees. Blood had soaked her dress in bizarre patterns. When she glanced up at Nigel and John, her eyes were alight with life; golden sparks flickered at their edges, danced around her fingers.

"I am the Protector of blessed Albion, gentlemen. The power and the duty are mine."

She set her jaw, her body swaying, and raised her arms.

That golden light began to flow from her, enveloping first her hands, then her arms, and finally sheathing her entire body. In the chaos of combat her hair had been coming unpinned. It was entirely unbound now and flew wildly around her in a wind Nigel could not feel, and waves of other colors went through the magic womb she had created for herself.

Her eyes were unfocused. She turned her palms upward and began to chant.

"*Vieo viscus cum animus,*" Tamara said, rocking with the words.

She chanted them again and again, and then, suddenly, she flinched as though she had been stabbed again. Gritting her teeth, she continued the chant. The agony was writ in her every movement and expression. In the midst of that incantation she let out a cry of pain that was like the roar of something wild. And perhaps it was.

She took up the words again, and as she did a kind of red mist began to ooze from her wounds. It wasn't blood, but something brighter, twisting in the air as though fighting her magic. Nigel knew this was the poison Priya's attack had left in her.

The mist rose from her wounds and began to evaporate, burning up in the shimmering light that surrounded Tamara.

"*Vieo viscus cum animus,*" she continued, but her voice had more power now, more strength, and she held her head higher as she invoked the magic of Albion.

The wound on her shoulder was hidden within the folds of her clothing, but the one in her abdomen was so large and the dress torn enough that he could see the flesh begin to knit itself together.

"Fantastic," John Haversham muttered, and Nigel was sure the young man wasn't aware he had spoken aloud.

Tamara stood up, her legs wavering a bit even though her gaze did not.

"Where is Priya Gupta?"

"There was more fighting 'round the front. I heard it as I came down the road," Haversham revealed.

Tamara nodded. "Of course. She thinks she's done with me. She's going to try to destroy her father and William now, then go right in through the gates."

Her smile both thrilled and unnerved Nigel.

"If that's where the real battle is taking place," she said, "then that is where we shall go."

Twenty

"**F**or Albion!"

Tamara let loose that rallying cry as she raced along the base of the northern wall of Buckingham Palace and rounded the corner that brought her to the front. Her hands churned with the golden light of her magic, spheres of power that rippled around her fists and made her skin prickle with pleasure and heat. Nigel was on her left and John Haversham on her right. The vampire seemed to have recovered entirely from his earlier encounter with Dunstan. The fog had thinned a bit, some of it burning off at contact with her magic, and with the arrival of the ghosts.

Above her, Bodicea and Horatio took up the cry. Regal and commanding, they led a charge of spirits too numerous to count. The specters flitted through the fog above, and others sped along the ground nearby, mere silhouettes in the night and the mist. Tamara heard the hissing of Kali's Children out there in the dark, but the ghosts made short work of them.

As she came around to the front of the palace, she nearly faltered.

There were misshapen, reptilian corpses littering the ground, with Rakshasa scattered among them. The mist rolled slowly over the bodies, filling every crevice, as though it truly were a death shroud.

But what almost brought her to a halt was the sheer number of horrors that still loped and staggered toward the palace gates. Even with the street and the park beyond draped in fog, she made out at least half a dozen Rakshasa and forty or fifty of the Children of Kali, and she was not yet close enough to see the gates through the veil of mist. Dark figures moved all through the gray, filthy blanket that lay over the city. Far, far more than Tamara had ever imagined.

"So many of them," she said as she began to run again.

"Do not worry," Nigel growled in the dark beside her. "Our allies are legion!"

Heartened by the strength of his voice, she nodded and ran on. Above her she heard Bodicea and Nelson shouting orders, and a moment later the ghosts who had dedicated themselves to Albion's cause darted ahead, rippling the fog as they descended upon the poor, accursed souls Priya Gupta had twisted to her own ends. The shouts of angry phantoms and the shrieking of hideous men filled the air.

"William!" Tamara shouted. "Farris!"

Yet there was no reply from within the fog. They were supposed to have been guarding the front of the palace, but thus far she had seen only monsters. Still they had not reached the gates. A tremor of dread passed through her.

A hiss filled the air and John Haversham grabbed her arm. Tamara let him pull her to a stop even as Nigel also halted. Just ahead, several of the Children of Kali were crawling *up* the outside of the palace wall, their talons dug into stone.

"Oh, I don't think so." Tamara grunted, and she raised both hands. She muttered a single word, burning two of the vermin off the wall with an arc of flame that erupted from her palms.

A new sound reached her, of something lumbering across the ground, and she turned just in time to see a pair of Rakshasa rushing toward her through the gloom. John began to work a spell, his fingers contorted, muttering in German as he weaved something out of the energy that already existed in the air. Being an ordinary spellcaster, he had no innate magic.

Nevertheless, a streak of silver light leaped from the ground right in front of him and speared the Rakshasa's chest, impaling the thing. It let out a roar of fury that disintegrated into that high, barking, hyena laugh. For a moment it was lifted off the ground on the spike of magic that had impaled it, and then it roared again and shook itself free, dropping to the ground in a crouch.

Its eyes gleamed that sickly, filthy yellow as it glared up at John and then lunged for him.

Tamara was about to intervene when Nigel leaped past her and threw himself directly at the demon, driving it back and onto the ground, where he began to scuffle with it. Ghosts swept down from the shroud of fog and began to tear at the other Rakshasa. Two of them grabbed hold of the powerful beast and a third slashed a spectral dagger across its eyes, blinding the demon. Then they began to tear it apart.

"Well done!" Tamara shouted, spinning to peer at the palace wall again, where several of the accursed men were still climbing. The tide had most certainly turned. The ghosts would swarm the demons and overwhelm them. But it would be up to her to make certain that none of the monsters got inside the palace before it was all over. It only required one for their mission to end in failure.

Even as she looked up, however, she saw a ghost sweep down out of the fog, laughing perversely. It was Byron, in that foppish velvet shirt of his. He seemed to be having a sadistically wonderful time as he grabbed hold of one of Kali's Children and tore the horror right off the wall, then began to fly higher. The spectral poet rose up and up and up, and then he simply dropped the monster. It fell like a stone, vanishing and reappearing in the roiling fog, until it struck the street with a wet crack and lay still.

"Right, then. Things are well in hand. Let's get to the gates and find William and Farris."

"Lead on," John replied.

Together they ran alongside the wall. They had gone no more than a dozen feet when the muffled boom of a gunshot filled the night. Tamara quickened her pace and saw several dark shapes resolving themselves in the billowing gray ahead. Her heart thundered in her chest and she held her breath as she forged on.

The wind gusted, parting curtains of fog ahead, and she saw the gates of the palace.

Farris stood before the gates, alone, one of those pepperbox guns clutched in his left hand and his saber in the other. Dark silhouettes emerged from the mist as Children of Kali. One of them wore the clothes of a nobleman; two others were dressed in rough, dirty fabric. Here there were no classes, no caste system. The very wealthy and the very poor had met the same horrid fate.

As Tamara ran toward Farris, summoning the magic that crackled around her fists, that courageous man raised his pepperbox and fired at the nearest creature, the bullet obliterating the monster's face and bursting out through the back of its skull. He swung the thick, revolving barrel toward the next and pulled the trigger, but it fell on an empty chamber.

Farris tossed the useless weapon aside and changed his stance, holding his saber at the ready and preparing for an onslaught.

"Take heart, my friend!" Tamara called to him. "You are not alone!"

She paused to steady herself, carved through the air with contorted fingers, and magic coursed through her body and burst from her fingertips. The ground rumbled beneath her feet and she could feel the connection between herself and the earth, then, through the spell she had cast. It felt as though the land were an extension of her being, her muscle and bone.

The street buckled and ruptured as enormous tree roots thrust from the soil of Albion and wrapped themselves around the accursed monstrosities that were lunging at Farris. The roots twined about their limbs and bodies, cracking bone and pulping flesh as the creatures were pulled down into the earth, dragged under the street. An arm was sheared off one of them before it disappeared into the ground, and then they were gone.

Farris turned and gaped at her, awe and perhaps a bit of fear there in his gaze. "Mistress Tamara, that was . . . it was simply . . ."

Then his eyes went wide.

"Watch yourself!" he cried as he ran toward her with his saber held high.

Tamara turned to see that she had nearly forgotten John Haversham, some yards back. And in that moment of her forgetfulness, something terrible had happened.

For John had fallen to his knees in the street and was staring at her with forlorn eyes that were growing darker by the moment. The fog swirled around him, but it was plain to see that his flesh had begun to take on a greenish-yellow hue, as though his entire body were bruised. His face was adopting the rough texture of scales.

"Oh, John, no!" she cried, and she raced back toward him.

Farris shouted at her to stop, to stay back, but she could not. This man had come to her and given her the gift of truth, had apologized for embarrassing her, had hinted at feelings far deeper than what he had previously allowed. He was an ally and a friend, and within her heart and the yearning center of her, she knew he might one day be something more. Or he might have been, for the memory of Frederick Martin's transformation was still fresh in her mind and she recalled the revulsion with which she had recoiled at his filthy touch.

"No," she whispered into the fog.

But she stopped a few feet away, knowing it would be foolish to get too close. The curse was taking him over. Soon he would be one of Priya's creatures, if he was not already.

"John, how?" she asked.

The grief in his eyes tore at her heart. "I . . . I was a clumsy thief," he stammered. "One of the idols . . . my protection . . . faltered and . . ."

He shuddered and groaned with the pain of transformation. Tamara racked her brain. *There must be some way to help him,* she thought. *Some way to stop the curse.* But she knew that once the transformation was complete, his humanity would be gone. *I need time to research, time to . . .*

There was only one way. She would have to somehow arrest the process, freeze John in the moment to buy the time that she needed.

Before she could act, however, her brother's voice cut through the fog, echoing all around her. He was calling her name.

Tamara spun, searching for William, but through the fog and the darkness she could not find him. There was chaos all around the front of the palace. Byron and other ghosts were plucking Kali's Children from the walls. With an unsettling savagery, Bodicea was hacking a Rakshasa to pieces in front of the palace gates with her spectral sword.

Tamara could hear Nelson somewhere above her, in the shrouded sky, shouting commands as though he were back on the deck of the *Agamemnon*. And Farris was running toward her, both guns discarded and his saber raised. He had seemed bent upon the murder of John Haversham a moment ago, but he had heard William's voice, as well, for now he slowed and began to search the night for her brother.

Once again, she heard William call her name. This time, though, it was more distinct. She peered to the east, where just the edge of St. James's Park was visible through the fog, and there among a group of Kali's Children, she saw him.

Priya Gupta was wrapped around William from behind, riding him like a child. Her legs twined around his waist, and her left arm was hooked over his shoulder. The upstart, the cruel witch, held a gleaming silver dagger against his throat. The streamers of pure crimson magic she had manifested earlier now seemed to stream from her sides, though the way she was pressed against William it was difficult to know for certain. They caressed him, those razor-sharp ribbons, and where they touched him he was cut. His clothes were dark, but blood streaked his white shirt, and Tamara thought she could smell the copper tang of it on the air.

"Oh, no," Farris said beside her in a low voice.

Tamara's nostrils flared and her jaw clenched. She took two steps toward the park.

"Leave him be, Priya. You've no choice here. We've already won, don't you see? The ghosts of Albion are here, and no matter how many of Kali's Children serve you, or how many Rakshasa you may summon, the ghosts will be here. And so will the Protectors. If there were only one of us, perhaps you might still be victorious. But if you slay my brother you shall still have me to reckon with. You have the advantage over him, but I swear on the souls of my ancestors and of Albion itself that you shall not be so fortunate with me. It ends here and now.

"His death will avail you nothing."

Her words resounded in the fog, and Tamara held her breath, praying that the madwoman would not see how it crushed her inside to see William so helpless. She set her chin high and tried to keep emotion from her eyes, to be cold.

The Indian girl's dark eyes were bright with mischief. She pricked William's throat with that ceremonial dagger and laughed.

"Kali whispers in my head, English whore! The goddess guides me and shows me the truth of your words. Your brother is worthless to me dead. I need his blood, you see. There is a ritual to be performed here tonight. My country has been trammeled upon by the boot of British imperial ambition for the last time. Your people have been the bane of India, a curse upon the land. Now that shall be reversed. Bharath will subsume Albion and by the will of the goddess, I shall rule the two nations as one.

"The blood of the Protector of Albion will be the ultimate sacrifice. The ritual requires the death of your queen and the blood of the Protector . . . but not his death. Make no mistake, however, I *will* kill him, unless you withdraw your forces, living and dead. If you comply, I shall still shed his blood, but I will spare his life.

"Choose."

Tamara could breathe only in shallow gasps. Her throat was dry and she shook her head as though she could not grasp the things that Priya had said. But she understood very well. The fog continued to swirl around her, rolling across the street that separated her from the sorceress and her brother. William's eyes were wide, but there was a grim determination to his features.

"Tam—" he began.

"Hush, now, William," Priya sneered, pricking his throat again with that blade. "It's in your sister's hands."

The battle continued around them; the monstrous sounds of the horrors that served the sorceress filled the night air. Yet their death cries were louder, as Nigel and the ghosts destroyed them one by one. Where was the rightful Protector of Bharath, she wanted to know. Where was Tipu Gupta? Had his daughter already murdered him?

And John . . . Lord, she had nearly forgotten John. She spared a quick glance over her left shoulder. The diamond pattern some of the others had shown, like the back of certain snakes, ran down the center of his forehead, but he was not entirely changed. Not yet. His eyes were wide and pleading even as they darkened further. If he made a move toward her, Farris would surely behead him.

"Help me," he rasped, fingers lengthening into claws as he tore at his clothes, sprawled there on his knees in the road.

Tamara could not look at him. She did not trust Priya to spare William's life even if she did as the girl asked. Yet even if she had . . . the queen? All of Albion sacrificed simply to save her brother?

She gazed at William now, studied his eyes as though somehow in their depths she could find the solution.

"Will?" she whispered.

Priya glared at her, raven hair blowing in the wind, mad eyes gleaming, and sneered.

"*Choose.*"

∼

TIPU GUPTA WRAPPED the fog around himself as though it were a cloak. It had been conjured to hide the horrors wrought by his daughter, so that the people of London and the soldiers in service to the queen would not realize what was happening until it was too late. Yet now he turned the fog to his own purpose.

The old man had been a master of the mystic arts long before he had been chosen as Protector of Bharath. The power of Bharath, the innate magic of his homeland, was an extraordinary weapon, but he was a skilled spellcaster even without it.

He held his staff in his right hand and used it to steady himself as he moved through the night and the fog, working his way from the gates of the palace and around behind Priya. The moment he had seen her attacking William, the old man had withdrawn from the chaotic battle. One malformed creature more or less would not end Priya's dark obsessions, her twisted ambitions. The dark goddess who whispered in her mind had too great a hold on her for a physical war to overcome.

There was only one way to end this. He had to take back what his daughter had stolen.

So even as Priya wrapped herself around William Swift and pressed that ceremonial dagger to his throat, Tipu moved through the fog as though he were invisible. His staff clacked on the street and he could not walk very quickly, but he passed unnoticed within inches of several Children of Kali, and only a few yards from a pair of Rakshasa.

The monsters ought to have been able to smell him, but he had erased himself from the world, hidden within that fog. It was magic he had learned forty-seven years earlier, and that sorcerous stealth had saved his life many times.

The spring night was cold, and yet there was a clammy warmth to the fog that sickened him. He shuddered at the way it slid over his skin. Tipu entered the park and began to work his way around behind his daughter. Images filled his mind of Priya as a child. Even as an infant her eyes were so dark and her skin so rich that she seemed somehow unreal, like a painting of a baby girl, idealized to perfection. As a toddler her laughter had been infectious, the thought of her enough to bring light to his heart even in the darkest of times. In the war against the darkness, there had been times when another man would have lost all hope, but he had held the image of her so close inside that Hell itself could not have wrung the last drop of hope from him.

And when, as a young girl, she had discovered his library and lost herself in the study of magic, trying so hard to make him proud of her, Tipu Gupta had known such contentment as human beings were rarely allowed.

How has it come to this? he thought, nearly faltering in both step and spell.

More than ever, he felt his age. His muscles were slack and his bones ached, joints popping and grinding against one another. The spirit of Bharath, the magic that was the gift of the Protector, had given him strength and filled all the empty places, summoned from within him a vitality unusual for a man of his years. Now that had been drained from him, along with so much of the magic of Bharath.

He was still the Protector—Priya had stolen power from him, but not his duty or the favor of his homeland. Yet he felt frail and alone.

A grimace touched his lips. *You do not feel frail and alone, Tipu. You simply are.*

A Rakshasa loomed out of the fog to his left. The thing paused a moment, seeming to sense him. Its filthy yellow eyes narrowed and it sniffed the air, growling low and ragged in its throat. The old man ignored it. The demon could not see him, even if it sensed the strange ripple in reality that was made by his passing.

Tipu focused on the street ahead. Through the churning fog he could make out parts of the palace wall and the upper portion of the gates. The ghosts were a remarkable sight, darting across the ground and through the air, translucent shades of muted color, spectral figures barely glimpsed until they paused to attack one of the Children of Kali or a Rakshasa.

And there, right in front of him, was his daughter.

The old man stood perhaps fifteen feet behind Priya. She still rode William Swift's back, and the image cut him deeply, so reminiscent of the way he had carried her on his own back when she was a small girl. But Priya was not playing with William. If anything remained of his daughter's mind, it was filled with malevolence. Tendrils of crimson magic stretched from her sides and whipped at the air, gently brushing against the young man, cutting his clothing and the skin beneath.

She would not kill him that way, though. No, Priya wanted him alive for her precious ritual.

"*Choose!*" she snapped at Tamara, who stood on the other side of the street with her man Farris. Another man sprawled beside her on the ground, in the midst of the transformation set upon him by Kali's Curse.

The memories of his Priya, his precious child, clamored to press themselves into his mind now, as if they had form and conscience and knew what he was about to do. He forced them away. Fate had chosen their path long ago, and there was no way to divert from it now.

"For Bharath," he whispered, even his words hidden in the fog-cloak he had drawn about himself.

Tipu Gupta had inherited the duty and power of the Protector of Bharath. The magic was his, connected to him just as surely as he was connected to the soul of his homeland, a circuit that could not be broken. Priya and whatever demonic sponsor influenced her had leached some of that power and used it to summon horrors from the darkest realms, to spread a plague of horrors . . . but if he could catch her unaware, he might still be able to take it back.

He took a step nearer. Clutching his staff in his right hand he raised the left and began to sketch circles in the air with his fingers.

The fog began to swirl and quickly took the shape of a tiny tornado, a spinning white funnel that extended from Tipu Gupta out toward his daughter. When his spell touched the magic that surrounded her, the old man flinched at the contact, a shock going through him. Pain clutched his chest, but he steadied his breathing and began to draw back the magic she had stolen from him.

So intent was she that she did not see what was happening. The air around Priya sparkled with red, as though a spray of blood drifted on the breeze. Those red flecks began to wink out, one by one, changing color from crimson to silver as they eddied in the air and were quickly drawn into the tube of fog he had created. The old man chanted silently to Shiva, keeping his pulse steady, shoring up the spell that kept him hidden.

He could hear her screaming at Tamara Swift, but had no idea what the two women were saying to each other. The hand holding the dagger to William's throat tensed, muscles in her arm tightening, and the old man hesitated.

The voice that came out of Priya's mouth did not belong to his daughter. It was a shrill, knife-edged sound, words uttered in his native tongue with an undertone like the distant shriek of the damned.

"What do you think you're doing, old fool?"

Tipu held his breath, but he did not break off his silent attack. The demon-goddess within Priya had sensed him, so he could not stop now. He grunted with the effort, and fresh pain spiked through his chest and along his arms as he siphoned the stolen magic from her.

When Priya cried out in pain, it was in her own voice. Her father thought himself the cause of her suffering, but then he heard the crack of bone, and a moist, tearing noise.

The ribbons of magical energy that she had manifested disappeared even as a second set of arms burst from her sides just inches below those she had been born with. They were dusky gray, the color of thunderclouds and the ash from a funeral pyre. Priya screamed and her voice was in harmony with another . . . a second voice from a second mouth, as the back of her skull warped and her head thrashed and her hair was tossed aside to reveal the source.

A face was emerging there, with blazing eyes and terrible fangs, blood streaming from the corners of that mouth.

"What in Heaven's name—" William Swift began to shout, whatever magic had kept him silent now broken.

Then he was thrown to the ground.

Priya leaped off him, dropping into a crouch, but did not turn to face her father. Instead her entire body inverted. Arms and legs reversed and her sari tore away to show the darkening of her flesh from copper to coal gray, that hideous shade of death. Her breasts were large and tipped with ebon black, and now in addition to that ritual dagger, she bore items in each of her hands, as if they had grown from her very flesh. A cleaver, a shield, and a bowl fashioned from a human skull and filled with fresh blood.

On her four arms were circlets fashioned from human bones. Her tongue lolled lasciviously from her mouth. As he watched in awe, her skin shifted from ash to indigo, the deep blue of evening, and a third eye opened in the center of her forehead.

Of his daughter, there was no sign. Only the goddess, this thing that had corrupted her.

"You are not Kali. The goddess is cruel, but not evil. What are you?" he demanded.

The demon brought her cleaver down and cut away his siphoning magic as if it were a limb. The funnel dissipated, and he felt a tug in his heart as though she had set a hook there.

"*Dakshina Kurukulla, two faces of the goddess in one . . . and soon greater than Kali herself!*" the thing hissed, black tongue spattering blood from her lips with every word. "*With the magic of the Protector in this body, this frail human girl flesh, I shall* become *Bharath's soul myself.*"

Tipu Gupta sneered now. Full of sorrow and rage and love, he raised his staff and summoned that same siphoning magic. Even as he did, he sent a tiny spell along the length of the wood—and its tip sharpened.

The old man stepped forward suddenly and ran the goddess through with his staff. Her expression became one of surprise, then pain. He shuddered where he stood, rocked by the power of the demon-goddess and by the return of his own energies. The magic of Bharath had been siphoned from him, and now he stole it back. It raced up the staff and poured into him, his muscles painfully rigid as it filled up those hollow places inside him once more.

"I am the Protector of Bharath, deceitful godling! Hear me, Kurukulla, the power is rightfully mine, and I shall—"

Suddenly he stopped, as he looked upon the creature that had been his daughter. Her red, rolling eyes cleared, and for just a moment it was Priya looking out at him from that monstrous face.

"Father?"

Once more he remembered the smile and grace of the little girl she had once been.

Then the four arms of the demon-goddess were in motion. The dagger punched through the side of his neck. Tendons split and veins burst, but it was merely to hold him in place while Kurukulla brought the cleaver down upon his skull.

∼

TAMARA SAW PRIYA release William and hope sparked within her. Then she saw him begin to rise, pushing himself up on his hands and knees. She called his name and he looked up. He was obviously weak, and had been injured, but he gave her a small wave to indicate that he would be all right. Relief flooded her, but then she forced herself to focus. William would live.

That knowledge left her free to see to John Haversham, whose fate seemed far less certain. He had already risen to his feet, and there was little trace of the human left in his face. His flesh was patterned with rough scales and tinted green and yellow, and his fingers had curved into wicked talons.

Yet he was resisting. She saw it in his eyes and the way he held back. His every motion was a struggle, a jerking, staggering progression as the human in him fought the Curse of Kali, laboring against the metamorphosis and the monstrousness of Priya's magic.

"If you cannot . . . help me . . . ," he said, gazing at her with eyes that seemed lost, as though he peered at her from a cage in Hell, "then you . . . must . . . kill me."

Farris was beside her, then, black bile and blood on his clothes from the creatures he had already slain. He raised his saber and started for John.

"Do as he says, miss! You've no choice. The evil's in him already. He'll have your heart out in a moment."

The stout, courageous man swung the blade in an arc and it whickered toward John's neck.

"No!" she cried, and already her hands were moving, her fingers twisting. There was no spell that she had studied that would accomplish her intent, but she was the Protector of Albion. She had magic in her veins, in her flesh, and now she collided several spells into one and felt the power rush up from the fiery core of her.

"*Claustrum articulus!*"

The fog around Farris and John evaporated, and the air grew still, trapping them both, frozen in that very moment. Frozen, until Tamara could figure out what to do with them.

Then she heard a terrible cry and Tipu Gupta began to shout. She spun and watched in horror as Priya's body bucked and her flesh shifted and the god pushed out from within her.

Tamara had no words.

~

H IS THROAT STUNG with tiny wounds and was warm with the trickle of his own blood, his body covered with long, searing cuts. William forced himself to stand.

His stomach roiled with nausea from the way Priya had violated him, binding him with magic, working him like some marionette, trying to force his sister to sacrifice the queen—Hell, all of Britain— just to spare his life.

"Fucking cow!" he screamed as he staggered toward her, tapping the magic within him again. He could feel the soul of Albion. A moment ago it had been dormant, but now it roared through him with such force that his entire body shook. His eyes burned and he could feel pressure coming from them, could see arcs of golden lightning sparking from them. His hands contorted and he began to summon all the destructive magic he could recall into one devastating spell.

So blinded was he with pain and rage and the surge of magic within him that he did not notice when Priya began to change. Now, as he turned to attack her, he saw what she had become, the hideous, blue-skinned demon-goddess. A belt of human skulls hung around her waist and her sari was in tatters, revealing naked flesh inscribed with whorls and sigils that might have been some ancient language.

Before he could utter a word of incantation, the goddess roared in pain and a wooden spear burst from her back, bright lights of crimson and silver dancing upon its tip. William hesitated. The fog coalesced around him and he took a step closer, trying to discover what was happening.

He saw Tipu Gupta, realized that the old man had run the demon-goddess through with his walking stick, and that he was draining magic from her, somehow. The Protector of Bharath seemed reinvigorated, as though he were growing younger before William's eyes. He shouted in triumph and sneered at the goddess, whom he called Kurukulla.

And then she killed him. Plunging the dagger into the side of his neck, she hacked his face in two with an enormous gore-stained cleaver. He fell to the ground, hands still clasped around his staff, which slid wetly from her wound.

William screamed in horror. This was not how it was supposed to end. Kurukulla turned, then, her deep blue face stained with Tipu Gupta's blood. Whatever was left of Priya Gupta, it was trapped inside the goddess, as twisted as Frederick Martin and all the others.

The magic had been building up in William, and now he roared words that erupted as little more than a guttural bellow, and thrust out his hands. The power that burst forth was twined gold and black—a black dark as pitch—and it shot toward the demon bitch goddess with such force that he intended it to tear her body to pieces.

Kurukulla raised her shield and William's magic struck home, shattering it. The fragments showered to the ground, some of them igniting with flames before they hit the buckled street. The hollow skull she carried as a bowl fell from her grasp and shattered, as well.

The goddess sneered, fresh blood sliding from the edges of her fanged mouth like the slaver of a dog, dripping from her chin. Her shield had protected her, left her untouched. Now with her two empty hands she reached for him. He tried to fight her but she batted his arms aside as though he were a child and grasped him by the shoulders, lifting him from the ground.

Her other two hands came up, ritual dagger in one and scarlet-stained cleaver in the other.

That was the moment when William Swift knew that he was going to die.

And then Tamara's voice echoed through the fog. "Nigel!" she screamed. "Now!"

William heard a rustle of clothing and a savage grunt from off to his right. He caught only a glimpse of the terrifying face of Nigel Townsend, no less gore-streaked than Kurukulla's own, as the vampire lunged out of the fog and threw himself at William. Nigel tore him from the goddess's grasp and continued moving, uncannily strong, carrying them both into the fog. Toward the palace, toward Tamara.

Nigel stumbled, and the two of them sprawled on the road, but William scrambled to his feet in time to find Tamara shouting in Latin, in time to see thick tree roots bursting up through the street and wrapping around the four-armed demon-goddess, who screamed, three eyes wide with fury, rolling and red. Blue-white magic leaped from Tamara's hands, and the air separating her from Kurukulla warped and crumpled. The spell struck her, buffeting the goddess. The air around her froze and ice formed on her flesh.

Kurukulla began to laugh.

"*What can you hope to do?*" the demon-goddess roared in thickly accented English. "Your empire is over and mine is about to begin. I claim vengeance for Bharath. I claim blood and fire and death! The might of Kali is in me! And now the soul of Bharath itself, the magic of Bharath, passes from that decrepit old . . ."

The demon took a halting step backward, clad in blood and rags, chest heaving with astonishment. Her empty hands grasped at the air as though she might capture what she had lost. She turned and glared down at the corpse of Tipu Gupta, then spun toward William, Tamara, and Nigel, her bloodred eyes flaring with a crimson storm.

"What have you done? The power . . . the magic of the Protector is meant to pass to me. The girl stole a taste of it, but she was his chosen successor, his heir. Now that he is dead it should all fall to this flesh, to this body."

Silver light shone around her, connected to the ravaged remains of Tipu Gupta. As they watched, that magic drifted away into the sky, slipping off into the night and the fog, returning to India.

To Bharath.

"Stupid tart," William snapped. "Did you really think old Tipu wouldn't have chosen a new successor after his daughter betrayed him? His first loyalty was to Bharath. The magic will never be yours."

Kurukulla almost seemed to shrink now. A ripple of crimson light flashed around all four of her hands, and she looked at them with hatred more pure than any emotion William had ever seen.

"Then whose? *Who is Protector of Bharath?*"

Tamara stepped up beside William, and once more that golden light roiled around her clenched fists. The street beneath her feet rumbled as though the Earth was yearning to answer her call again. William held his breath, awed by the natural force that churned inside her.

"We'll find out one day," Tamara said, her voice firm, yet almost gentle. "But not you, demon. Not you, *Priya*. You'll be dead."

"Priya?" William asked. "What do you—"

But Tamara wasn't listening. She raised her hands above her head and shouted into the already dispersing fog. "Bodicea! Horatio! Byron! Come to us, all you ghosts of Albion! Already she is diminished, but the night is not yet over! Come to us!"

And at her summons, they came. William and Nigel could only stand and watch as the ghosts swarmed them, darting through the air and across the shattered road, flitting across the top of the palace walls and out of the trees in the park. In seconds, hundreds of the specters had gathered around.

"Do you really believe they will be of any help to you?" Kurukulla snarled, starting forward, three eyes glaring. She brought up the ceremonial dagger with which she had planned to slit William's throat. *The blood of Albion will still run red this night!*"

Even as she spoke, the gathering of phantoms parted to allow a trio of translucent figures to the fore. Bodicea stood with her spear in one hand and sword in the other. Nelson was grim-faced and dignified, though his own sword had vanished. Even with one arm missing, the sleeve pinned back, he had an air of command that was undeniable.

And then there was Byron. All his humor had gone from him earlier, in the thick of the fight. Now he only rolled his eyes and crossed his arms, hovering slightly higher than the others.

"My friends, do you know what I hate about lunatics?" Byron sighed. "They never know when they've lost."

Tamara reached out for William's hand, and he clasped hers gladly. He felt the connection instantly, the magic that cycled through both of them. The Protectors of Albion stood side by side, hand in hand, and the entire street trembled. The few accursed men that had not been destroyed by the ghosts had been creeping toward that gathering, still determined to serve their mistress, but they paused now. Whatever remained of rationality in their savage minds was chilled by the sight of the Protectors.

The monstrous thing—the demon-goddess—let out a roar and charged at them.

"Destroy her," Nigel whispered, his voice velvety and dangerous. "You can't risk leaving her alive for another try at this."

William and Tamara exchanged a glance. He nodded.

"Bodicea. Horatio. Take her."

The spectral queen raised her spear and let out a war cry. Then she rushed at Kurukulla, first into the fray. The goddess's cleaver swung toward her but, warrior that she was, Bodicea dodged it easily. Without the magic she had stolen, the demon-goddess was weakening.

Bodicea ran her through with her spear and brought her sword down, shearing off one of Kurukulla's arms. "You might have had the power to stand against us before, demon!" she shouted. "But no longer!"

Then Nelson was there, and others joined him, moving so quickly that in seconds the demon-goddess was only barely visible among the semi-transparent forms of the ghosts, who tore and hacked at her, ripping apart that deep blue flesh, plucking out eyes and snapping bones.

A specter William did not recognize took up the ceremonial dagger with which Priya would have killed him, and drove it through the center of her head, into the hollow, bleeding socket of her third eye.

Despite all the demon-goddess had done, Tamara turned to William and buried her face in his shoulder, so as not to see. But only for a moment. Then she took a long breath and forced herself to look, to bear the horror of the war she was so much a part of.

At that moment, the scattered few of Kali's Children still alive let out a chorus of shrieks. They contorted in pain and began to wither, and in seconds they began to die. One by one they crumbled to the ground, leaving little more than ash and a few scattered scales.

All but John Haversham, who was frozen with Farris in some kind of magical stasis just a dozen feet away, trapped between human and monster.

Byron stayed out of the massacre of Kurukulla, and his expression was troubled. Just when it seemed he was about to call a halt to it, Nelson was the one who drew back from the remains of their enemy.

"Enough!" he cried. "She is dead. We are not barbarians."

Bodicea swung around, war paint still streaking her face and naked flesh, and glared at him.

"Well, not all of us, at least," Byron noted.

The ghosts began to disperse. All save Horatio, Bodicea, and Byron.

William began to walk toward the corpse of Kurukulla. Tamara fell into step beside him and Nigel followed along, his eyes dark and his nostrils flaring with either distaste or hunger, William was not sure which. Beyond the corpse was another, the broken, bleeding form of Tipu Gupta, the true Protector of Bharath. Nothing remained of his face that would allow them to recognize him, but William had seen him die. The old man was gone, and somewhere in India, another had risen to bear the burden and receive the gift of Protectorship.

All their enemies had been destroyed, so they were startled by the wet, shifting sound that arose from the remains of Kurukulla. Her followers were gone or dead, the fog dispersed. The ghosts had torn her apart. How could she have survived? William stared in shock at her corpse.

A low moan came from beneath the gore and shattered bone.

It shifted.

A hand worked its way up through ravaged flesh, and then a second. Long, slender hands.

Priya Gupta tore her way out of the remains of Kurukulla.

"Careful," Nigel warned.

Byron scoffed. "Careful, really? Look at her eyes."

370 ~ GHOSTS OF ALBION: ACCURSED

William did look, and he saw what Byron already had. The girl gazed around at the ghosts with wide eyes, lost and afraid. She did not know where she was, that much was clear.

"What's happened to her?" Nelson asked, his spectral essence shimmering in the night beside them.

"Something in her mind has snapped," William replied.

Tamara hugged herself and shivered as she stared at the girl. "I don't think so. I think her mind snapped a very long time ago. And I think she was more powerful than her father ever knew. I confess, I'm not sure there ever really was a goddess . . . except that Priya wanted there to be."

William gaped at her. "You don't think she did all this herself? The curse and the Children of Kali, summoning the Rakshasa to serve her . . . why, look what she became! The goddess transformed her from within, warped her flesh, and—"

"Did she? I wonder," Tamara said.

Then she strode away, back toward Farris and Haversham, arms still crossed, and shivering as though she was so cold she feared she might never be warm.

Nigel was beside William then, and he also watched Tamara go. Then the two turned to stare at Priya Gupta, who gazed around at the ghosts with wide and fearful eyes.

"If she's right—" Nigel began in a dark rumble.

He never completed the sentence.

A jangling discordant sound filled the night, and the space between Priya and her father's corpse wavered, then split open. There was only blackness beyond, a liquid dark that William had seen before.

"Tamara!" he shouted. "The Rakshasa!" For that tear in the fabric of reality was a portal to the realm of those vicious, bestial demons.

"Will, get back!" Tamara shouted as she ran to aid them.

Nigel shouted something to the ghosts. Bodicea and Nelson took to the air, floating above the Protectors. The vampire dropped into a crouch and bared his fangs, eyes gleaming red in the dark.

A pair of Rakshasa leaped from the breach with a sound like paper tearing. They did not so much as glance at William, Tamara, and their allies. With terrible speed they fell upon Priya Gupta. One grabbed her legs, claws puncturing her flesh, and the other took her by an arm and a fistful of her hair, and even as William and Tamara began to react, they hauled her back through that rippling black portal.

That jangling noise came again and the portal collapsed in upon itself, leaving only a small eddying breeze in its wake.

EPILOGUE

Colonel Dunstan bore witness to it all.

William Swift had bound his spirit to that spot in front of the gates of Buckingham Palace, and thus captured he could only watch as the Children of Kali were destroyed by the ghosts of Albion, could only stare in abject despair as Priya Gupta's grand plan unraveled.

He had lived his life as a faithful subject of the British Crown, largely ignoring his Indian heritage. After his death he had come to realize the injustice done to his mother's people, not merely as a minority in British society, but as a conquered nation under the rule of British generals.

His soul had seethed with the injustice, and when he had learned of Priya's dark deeds he had sworn allegiance to her cause. He had loved his father and he loved England, had served her in war . . . but he felt with all his heart that something had to be done to make the people see that British imperialism was unjust.

Instead he watched in astonishment as Priya Gupta was transformed, as something emerged from within her. The colonel understood that the thing was a representation of some facet of Kali, but not one he recognized. Yet how it had come about was a mystery to him. Priya had claimed to serve the goddess, but he had not given much thought to that.

Then, the moment the dark goddess killed the Protector of Bharath, it all came crashing to a halt.

The Children of Kali crumbled to dust. The last of the Rakshasa had been destroyed. The ghosts of Albion rallied around the Protectors and tore the goddess apart . . .

And so it ended, leaving Colonel Dunstan a prisoner of war, years after his own death.

Hours passed, the horizon began to lighten, and by then the Protectors had done their work all too well. The corpse of Tipu Gupta was removed, the ashen remains of the Children of Kali were scattered on the breeze, and the dead Rakshasa were burned with magical flame that reduced the monsters to little more than char upon the ground. Only the buckled street remained, as a mystery that would never be solved.

By the time the sun rose on a spectacular spring day, there was no trace of the war that had taken place overnight. No trace, save for the ghost held captive at the gates of Buckingham Palace.

For hours, Dunstan watched people come and go at the palace, saw couples strolling through St. James's Park, and watched carriages rattling by. But of course, they could not see him. Colonel Dunstan was a silent phantom, sentenced to the anguish of watching the very people he had betrayed, unaware that anything at all had happened, unaware that they were party to prejudice and oppression.

He was in Hell.

All that long day, he was left to suffer in defeat. It was just after dark when he sensed the presence of another ghost, and turned to find the specter of Admiral Nelson staring at him with his one good eye.

"Oh, let me guess," Dunstan's ghost said, each word filled with bitterness. "You're here to tell me that I'm a traitor to Albion and the queen, that I'm a disgrace, that as a military man you're appalled by my behavior, and if I weren't already dead—"

Nelson raised his chin, back straight. "Actually, no."

The colonel faltered. He felt the weight of the magic that bound him, and a strange tiredness that he knew must be of the soul, since he had flesh no longer. He stared at Nelson expectantly.

"Go on, then," he said finally.

"You are a disgrace to the uniform you wore in life," Nelson said, his tone matter-of-fact. "There's no doubt of that. And aside from all else, you betrayed me, Colonel. I'd thought us friends. Perhaps, though, it will surprise you to learn that I don't believe you were entirely wrong. It may be that our control of India is oppressive. And I'll allow that if the Protectors had been more vigilant they might have learned of the plague spreading through the East End sooner.

"But I have watched them, sir. They are learning, and meanwhile, they struggle to do their best. As for the empire . . . well, that is a war for others to fight now. For the living. I can only hope that those representing our interests abroad behave honorably. If they do not, they bring shame upon us all."

Dunstan had no reply to that. He was indeed surprised to hear a patriot like Nelson speak so, but he would not give the admiral the satisfaction of admitting it.

"And now?" he asked. "What's to become of me?"

Nelson floated toward him so that only a few inches separated the two ghosts. His expression was grave. "Now, Colonel, you will be given your fondest wish. You will no longer have to suffer the cruelties of Albion. In fact, you will no longer be welcome here at all. You were a son of Albion, Dunstan, and you spat in her face. There were other ways to accomplish your ends, and you chose the vilest path imaginable. A few minutes from now, William Swift shall be along to free you from your bonds, and to cast the appropriate spell to banish you from this place forever."

"Banished?" the colonel asked, his spectral essence recoiling at the word.

"From the only home you have ever known," Horatio confirmed. "Yes. Forever. I haven't the magic to do it myself, but I wanted to make sure that I delivered the news to you personally.

"Goodbye, Colonel. May your soul wander for eternity without rest."

Then the ghost of Admiral Nelson shimmered and was gone.

When a carriage arrived with the Swifts' man Farris on its high seat, and William stepped out onto the road, Colonel Dunstan did not say a word. He only glared at them until the spell had been cast, and then his essence was shunted into the spirit world and he felt himself dragged away . . . away from Albion . . . until he was deposited out in the ether somewhere, to find his own way.

~

SEVERAL NIGHTS LATER, Tamara Swift stood alone just outside the door of the observatory, looking out over the grounds of Ludlow House and listening to the breeze rustling through the gardens. The darkness was alive with the songs of night birds and redolent with the scents of the thousands of flowers that had bloomed in the past few weeks. Spring had brought rebirth, as it always did, the seasons turning around again.

It had been a chilly spring thus far but tonight, for the first time, it was warm. Even the breeze carried with it a comfortable warmth. And yet still she shuddered out there alone in the dark, cold on the inside.

The memory of the recent tragedies in London—the plague, the madness of Priya Gupta, and the murder of the girl's father—was too fresh in her mind for the warmth to reach her. From what she and William had been able to discover through gossip and through the spying of their ghosts, there was no trace of the plague remaining. Hundreds had died and were being mourned, but even the members of Parliament who had succumbed were said to have died of "sudden illness" or "accident."

Tamara was torn.

It was best, she agreed, not to panic the populace over a plague that no longer existed, that could no longer hurt them. And certainly she had no interest in attempting to convince them of the existence of the supernatural. Yet there were lessons to be taken from the horror that Priya had perpetrated, not the least of which came from the fact that had David Carstairs not smuggled stolen cultural artifacts into England, and had other men not knowingly purchased them, the curse would not have spread so quickly among the upper classes.

The events of the previous weeks ought to have inspired a great deal of thought. Instead they had been quickly erased.

"Pardon me, miss."

She turned to find Farris standing just inside the observatory, holding the door open. He had been quite pale when she had first released him from the temporal freeze in which she had trapped him with John Haversham.

Had the transformation been completed, there would have been no saving John. For once, however, fate had been kind.

Though she had already gone far too long without sleep, they had hurried back to Nigel's with him. Despite his own ordeal, Farris had even driven the carriage. And there, in the darkened flat of the vampire and after the extraordinary night they had just endured, they had spent most of the day attempting dozens of spells to reverse the curse upon the poor man's flesh.

Tamara was still exhausted. Though she'd had ample sleep in the days since, little of it had been restful. Her sleep was disturbed by unpleasant dreams. Often she would wake with a start, staring around in the darkness or at the windows, the tormented cries of the accursed echoing in her ears.

But now, at the sight of Farris, she smiled. It was genuine and lent her a warmth the spring night could not achieve.

"Farris. I presume dinner is ready?"

The butler inclined his head. "Indeed."

"You really ought to be joining us at the table this evening. You fought gallantly and well. It doesn't seem right—"

"Now, miss, we've been over this," Farris replied sternly. "It's my job, isn't it? Leave me a bit of dignity in my profession, won't you? It wouldn't do at all. Not at all."

Tamara was about to argue, but Farris stood straighter and cleared his throat.

"Now then, the first course is about to be served, and Mr. Haversham has asked me to announce him. He's just arrived."

Her smile faltered. John had been drained by the black magic that had tainted him. The curse had been lifted from him, but it had left him barely able to stand. Shortly after she and William had cast the spell to return him to normal, John's valet had been summoned to take him home, and as far as any of them knew that was where he had spent his time since.

Tamara had learned all of what had taken place at the Algernon Club, and though she did her best to hide it, she had been pleased to know that William had revised his estimation of the man.

For Tamara had also revised her own estimation of John Haversham. He had explained his behavior and had fought by her side. With his family and their society friends, he played the role of scoundrel so that none would ever suspect he was something else entirely. A novice magician, and an agent of the Algernon Club.

The memory of her own actions in the back of the carriage still caused her cheeks to burn with embarrassment, yet she was curious, as well. Now that she knew the truth of his identity, and the secret behind his motivations, how would John conduct himself in her presence?

She took a deep breath, relishing the fragrance of the gardens, and then strode to the door. Farris stood aside to allow her to pass, then closed the door behind her.

"Let's not keep the man waiting," she said firmly.

The butler followed her as she went through the observatory and along the corridor. John Haversham had not gone into the dining room with the others. He was waiting for her in the hall, and he studied her face when she approached, as though searching for a clue as to how he might be received. When he smiled, it was tentative, but full of promise.

"Mr. Haversham," she said. "We're pleased you could attend."

John bowed and kissed her hand. "Miss Swift, how could I refuse such an invitation? A celebratory dinner is certainly in order." He stood and regarded her. "Might I say that you are stunning?"

Tamara had taken a great deal of time in her boudoir, and had chosen a bone-white crinoline dress with pale green lace and ribbons. She had never been fond of ribbons and bows, but thought this particular dress to be understated enough. Apparently John agreed.

"You may," she replied.

He laughed softly.

"You're looking rather well yourself," Tamara told him. "Feeling better, I trust?"

"Back to normal entirely. Save an odd craving for flies."

Tamara astonished herself by uttering a girlish laugh that was just shy of a giggle, and she raised a hand to cover her mouth as though she might stifle it. When she had taken a deep breath and regained her composure, she regarded him steadily.

"I'm afraid I must ask, John. Are you here on the club's behalf, or your own?"

His expression grew serious, his gaze intense. "My own, I assure you. You and William are members of the ruling board of the Algernon Club now, a distinction I do not share. If there are things Lord Blackheath wishes to learn about the Swift family, he can certainly inquire for himself."

A mischievous light flickered in his eyes. "Though I must confess, I would love to be at the first meeting you attend. It will be quite entertaining to see how those rather rigid gentlemen respond to the presence of a woman in their inner sanctum."

He offered her his arm. After a moment, and with pleasure, Tamara took it. They entered the dining room together, to find an immaculate display of white linen, silver, flowers, and candlelight waiting for them.

It was a relatively small convocation. Nigel had been invited, but he stood in a far corner, deep in conversation with Byron. Nelson and Bodicea were there, as well, almost imperceptible in the flickering glow of candles from the sideboard beneath a portrait of Ludlow's great-uncle Maurice. There were only five places set at the table, however: the ghosts, of course, could not eat, and Farris had declined to join them. It would be Nigel, Tamara, John, William, and Sophia for dinner.

"Ah, Tamara, excellent," William said as she entered. "And you've found John on the way. Now we can begin. Why don't we all sit?"

Something was wrong. He was absurdly happy, almost giddy, in a way she had never seen him. If she hadn't known better, she would have thought him thoroughly inebriated. A terrible dread crept into Tamara's stomach, and curled up there.

Greetings were exchanged all around, as well as congratulations and compliments. Each time Farris entered the room, he was roundly praised for his efforts, though he seemed more embarrassed by the moment. The ghosts remained for the company, if not the meal, and an easy camaraderie was formed among the dinner companions. Even Sophia seemed at ease, and far more convivial than Tamara had ever seen her.

It was as two new servants—young men hired by Farris—began to bring trays into the dining room and to the sideboard that William stood and cleared his throat. He glanced down at Sophia and placed his hand upon her shoulder, and she gazed up at him so lovingly that Tamara could not bear to see it. She could barely breathe, for she understood, now, why William was so happy.

"My friends," her brother began, glancing around the table, "before we begin, I want to say how grateful I am to all of you, and how fortunate Tamara and I feel to have such staunch allies. We have endured dark days of late . . ."

William smiled at Tamara and she stared at him, wondering if he could really be so blind that he could not see how troubled she was. *Of course he cannot see it,* she chided herself. *He's in love. He sees nothing but love tonight.*

"But there are brighter days ahead," William went on. He squeezed Sophia's shoulder and gazed at her again. "Earlier this evening, I at last summoned the courage to propose marriage to Sophia. She has given me my heart's greatest wish by accepting that proposal."

Voices were raised in hearty congratulations. Toasts were made. Tamara found herself rising and walking around the table to embrace her brother and to grasp the hands of the woman who would be his wife. She kissed Sophia's cheek and smiled and said something about welcoming her to the family . . . and yet it was all a blur to her, like something in a dream, where she moved and spoke as though some divine puppeteer were guiding her.

Dinner was a happy affair. Even the dead were ecstatic to have something to celebrate. Tamara managed to make it through until dessert, after which she excused herself. Though they rarely stood on tradition in Ludlow House, it would not be long before she and Sophia were expected to retire together for the drawing room, albeit briefly, before the men joined them.

That, she could simply not abide.

Out in the hall, she found herself walking without truly realizing where she was going. Only when she was taking the last few steps to the third floor did she understand. After all, whom else did she have to speak to now? She did not know John well enough to confide in him, and the ghosts expected so much more of her. She could not face them with this.

The door to the old nursery was unguarded. The magical defenses had held the demon when no one had been there to watch over him, and so it had seemed safe to leave him untended during dinner.

Tamara opened the door and stepped inside.

Oblis's eyes gleamed in the dim glow of a single lamp, turned down low. He seemed to have been staring at her before she even entered the room. As though he had watched her approach through the door. It was impossible, of course. Yet now he gazed at her expectantly.

"Oh, this is rich," the demon whispered, one corner of her father's mouth lifting in a smile. "A portent of things to come, perhaps?"

She glared at him. "Let me speak with my father."

Oblis raised both eyebrows. "And what do I receive in return?"

Tamara felt her face flush, and her throat tightened with emotion. "What would you demand?"

"I do so enjoy your humiliation," the demon replied in a rasp that seemed a cruel parody of her father's voice. "Swear to tell me whatever I wish to know, and I will let dear Henry see through his own eyes, speak with his own voice, have control of his own flesh for one hour."

She hesitated, but only for a moment. "I will tell you nothing that could interfere with our duties as Protectors."

Oblis nodded slowly. "Agreed."

"Agreed."

The change was instantaneous. All cruelty and mischief vanished from his features. He blinked several times as though emerging from darkness into daylight, and then her father, Henry Swift, looked at her with such relief and happiness that she began to weep.

"Tamara? Oh, my dear girl. It is so wonderful to see you. Sometimes . . . sometimes he lets me hear things, but never what I would like to hear."

She gazed at him. "You . . . you truly do know what's happened to you, then?"

Henry sighed deeply. "I never should have doubted your grandfather. I was a fool."

"Oh, Father, no," she began, but he waved her away.

"We haven't time for such things. An hour is not nearly enough time. Just enough to break my poor heart again. But we shall have to make do. Now speak to me, darling girl."

She told him everything. About Ludlow's death and their duties as Protectors of Albion. About William courting Sophia, and the death of the girl's father. About their recent victory and the engagement just announced. It took far less time to tell than she imagined, less than forty minutes, during which he interrupted only to clarify certain details. He gazed at her with more love than she had ever felt from her father before. It seemed the predations of the demon had given him a new appreciation for life and for family.

Or perhaps, she thought, she was the one with a new appreciation for *him*.

"Is she really so terrible, this Sophia? Do you hate her that much?" her father asked. "That doesn't sound like you, daughter."

Tamara let her gaze fall. "I . . . no. I don't hate her. Sophia isn't very good at dealing with people, and she thinks far too much of herself. But I haven't made any effort to befriend her, either. It's only that I'm . . ."

Henry reached out and took her hand. "You're frightened, dear. I can see that. But I do not understand it. What is it you fear from this girl?"

She shook her head, biting her lip to keep from sobbing. Her tears had dried minutes after she had begun her tale, and she refused to let them return. The corners of her eyes burned with the temptation, but she would not cry again.

"Isn't it obvious?" she asked bitterly. "I barely remember my mother. Grandfather is dead. You are . . . a prisoner."

He squeezed her hand. Tamara gazed at him in sorrow.

"William is all the family I have left. Without him—"

Her father frowned. "No, Tamara, don't think that way. Your brother loves you. All your life he has been your greatest champion. Even in love, he will never abandon you. This Sophia may become his wife, but she will not replace you in his heart. He will always be your brother."

Tamara knew that this was the truth. Had always known it. But even now she could not quiet the voice of doubt that lingered in the back of her mind, telling her that Sophia was going to take William away, and that she would be alone.

"Come here," Henry said.

She let him take her in his arms, and she pressed herself against him just as she had done as a little girl. Her father held her tight. She let out a long, shuddering breath, and just for a moment she allowed herself to believe that one day, he would be free of the demon, and that William would never ignore her, married or not. In her father's embrace, she was able to believe just for a moment that everything would be all right.

∼

"Don't worry, my dear. Don't worry," the demon said, grinning, enjoying the feel of her pressed against him. He patted the back of her head, gently, thrilling at the smell of her. "Nothing to worry about at all. It will work out in the end.

"Trust me."

∼

In a drawing room in Buckingham Palace—thoroughly unremarkable in comparison with even the least of the other rooms that lay within those walls—three people sat together in private conference. The very ordinariness of the room was symbolic of what transpired therein. Other than the preservation of hierarchy, no protocol or convention was followed, and no thought was left un-uttered.

This was a room without diplomacy or secrecy . . . and yet it was entirely secret. Only a small handful of people in the world were even aware that it existed.

The table was round.

"They performed quite well, did they not?" Queen Victoria inquired.

The nineteen-year-old monarch studied the two men she had summoned to the table in that private room. The prime minister, Lord Melbourne, was four decades her senior and her closest adviser. Though publicly he was far more powerful than the queen herself, Victoria did not begrudge him that power. The Crown was far more involved with the affairs of the empire than the world knew. And she quite liked it that way.

"They did indeed," Lord Melbourne replied. "I had my doubts, I confess. Untried and unprepared . . . Ludlow might as well have thrown them to the wolves. Even now, having endured trial after trial, there is so much they do not know. As the situation with the Algernon Club has proven."

The young queen concurred. "But you agree they seem well suited for their duties?"

Lord Melbourne bowed his head. "I do."

"Excellent," Queen Victoria said. "And what of the guard?"

"Withdrawn the moment that infernal fog began to spread, as you instructed. Buckingham Palace suffered no casualties, Majesty."

The queen narrowed her gaze. "There were many deaths in London last night, Lord Melbourne. We look upon each of them as a casualty."

"Of course," the prime minister replied.

Victoria turned her attention upon the third person in the room. "Now, as to the Protectors. You will keep us apprised of their progress, we trust?"

"Of course, Majesty," said Lord Blackheath. "Though I had thought that after this episode, you might wish to meet them, so that you might evaluate them yourself."

Victoria mused on that a moment, then shook her head.

"I think not. The Protectors operate best in shadows. Most of their work involves enemies that attack from the sewers and sepulchers. We shall leave them to their own devices.

"For now."

GHOSTS OF ALBION ON THE WEB

In 1838, siblings William and Tamara Swift inherited a terrible legacy from their grandfather and became Protectors of Albion, the magical defenders of the soul of England. . . . In 2003, the BBC's cult website debuted *Legacy*, an animated serial drama by actress/writer/director Amber Benson—best known from her role as Tara on *Buffy the Vampire Slayer*—and novelist Christopher Golden—author of *Strangewood, Wildwood Road, Of Saints and Shadows,* and *The Boys Are Back in Town*. For seven weeks the first Ghosts of Albion story unfolded, and the serial averaged more than 100,000 hits per week and won a special commendation at the 2003 Prix Europa. *Legacy* detailed the return of the demon lord Balberith, the murder of Albion's protector, Ludlow Swift, and the efforts of his heirs—William and Tamara—to deal with the power and responsibility that had been left to them. Their allies, both ghosts and the vampire Nigel Townsend, rallied around them. Balberith was defeated.

Soon after, *Legacy* was followed by an original novella, *Astray,* and then a second hour of animation, *Embers,* which introduced new characters, including Sophia Winchell. To experience these early adventures of Tamara and William Swift, please visit www.bbc.co.uk/ghosts.

And don't forget the second full-length Ghosts of Albion novel, coming soon. . . .

ABOUT THE TYPE

This book was set in Minion, a 1990 Adobe Originals typeface by Robert Slimbach. Minion is inspired by the classical, old style typefaces of the late Renaissance, a period of elegant, beautiful, and highly readable type designs. Created primarily for text setting, Minion combines the aesthetic and functional qualities that make text type highly readable with the versatility of digital technology.